PE[...]

The Real Thing

'Her books are supremely readable, witty and moving in
equal measure and she has a brilliantly sharp ear for dialogue'
Daily Mail

'Possibly my favourite writer' Marian Keyes

'An addictive cocktail of wit, frivolity and madcap romance'
Time Out

'Sensitive, funny and wonderfully well written'
Wendy Holden, *Daily Express*

'Another charming tale of heartbreak from this wonderfully
warm and witty author' *Woman*

'A poignant but charming journey of self-discovery.
A bittersweet and captivating novel' *Closer*

'We defy you not to get caught up in Alliott's life-changing
tale' *Heat*

'A fun, fast-paced page-turner' *OK!*

ABOUT THE AUTHOR

Catherine Alliott is the author of twelve bestselling novels including *One Day in May, The Secret Life of Evie Hamilton* and *A Crowded Marriage*. She lives with her family in Hertfordshire.

The Real Thing

CATHERINE ALLIOTT

PENGUIN BOOKS

PENGUIN BOOKS

Published by the Penguin Group
Penguin Books Ltd, 80 Strand, London wc2r orl, England
Penguin Group (USA) Inc., 375 Hudson Street, New York, New York 10014, USA
Penguin Group (Canada), 90 Eglinton Avenue East, Suite 700, Toronto, Ontario,
Canada m4p 2y3 (a division of Pearson Penguin Canada Inc.)
Penguin Ireland, 25 St Stephen's Green, Dublin 2, Ireland (a division of Penguin Books Ltd)
Penguin Group (Australia), 250 Camberwell Road, Camberwell, Victoria 3124, Australia
(a division of Pearson Australia Group Pty Ltd)
Penguin Books India Pvt Ltd, 11 Community Centre,
Panchsheel Park, New Delhi – 110 017, India
Penguin Group (NZ), 67 Apollo Drive, Rosedale, Auckland 0632, New Zealand
(a division of Pearson New Zealand Ltd)
Penguin Books (South Africa) (Pty) Ltd, Block D, Rosebank Office Park,
181 Jan Smuts Avenue, Parktown North, Gauteng 2193, South Africa

Penguin Books Ltd, Registered Offices: 80 Strand, London wc2r orl, England

www.penguin.com

First published by Headline Publishing Group 1996
Published in Penguin Books 2012
001

Set in 12.5/14.75 pt Garamond MT
Typeset by Jouve (UK), Milton Keynes
Printed in England by Clays Ltd, St Ives plc

isbn: 978–0–241–95833–9

Export edition isbn: 978–0–241–96130–8

www.greenpenguin.co.uk

MIX
Paper from
responsible sources
FSC
www.fsc.org FSC™ C018179

Penguin Books is committed to a sustainable
future for our business, our readers and our planet.
This book is made from Forest Stewardship
Council™ certified paper.

ALWAYS LEARNING   PEARSON

For Fred, Emily and Sophie

Chapter One

I put the receiver down and felt panic rise. It shot through my body like a turbo-charged lift. My eyes glazed, my insides curdled.

'Jesus!' I breathed.

I glanced quickly at the kitchen clock. One o'clock. One o'clock! Only two hours to go.

'What? What's happened?' demanded Laura, bent at right-angles over my kitchen table, her icing bag poised precariously above the dinosaur's left eyeball.

'Spotty Lottie's got cystitis!' I yelped.

Laura's icing bag quivered nervously and she inadvertently gave Tyrannosaurus Rex a squint. 'Spotty Lottie?' she demanded. 'Who's that – a dog?'

'The entertainer, you fool,' I hissed, running my hands through my hair till it stood on end, and rising from the table like a sea monster coming up from the depths. 'For Clemmie's party! The female equivalent of Paul Daniels for four-year-olds has cancelled – says she can't possibly come, because she's welded to the loo seat. Oh God, Laura, what am I going to do?' My hands left my dark curls and began to wring desperately. 'In precisely two hours' time, seventeen four-year-olds will be thundering through that door,' I pointed a quivering finger, 'demanding white rabbits, puppet shows and hideously twisted balloons, and all I'll have to offer them are some Marmite sandwiches and a few bowls of Hula Hoops. I'll be lynched!'

'Oh, is that all?' My sister calmly flicked back her long blonde hair and resumed her icing. 'For a moment I thought something awful had happened. I mean, you don't *have* to have an entertainer, do you? Just play a few jolly games and give them a piece of soggy cake in a napkin like Mum used to. They're only four, for God's sake.'

'Jolly games? Soggy cake?' I gave a hollow laugh and sank back down on my chair again.

I regarded Laura in her casual yet immaculate navy-blue linen ensemble, which somehow reeked of taking the day off from one's PR agency to help at one's niece's party but not sinking to leggings, thank you very much. I shook my head grimly.

'Oh Laura, how little you know. Four-year-olds today are a different *breed*, they're nothing *like* we used to be at that age. For one thing they know their party rights, and those include –' I ticked them off on my fingers '– one large balloon filled with helium and not puff, one party bag containing at least five items – three of which must be edible and bad for teeth – and either one bouncy castle *or* an entertainer, preferably unseen at any other children's party in the neighbourhood within the last three months.'

Laura frowned. 'Sounds rather Draconian to me.'

'Of course it's Draconian!' I shrieked. 'They're monsters! They're manipulative little devils who know exactly how to – Oh, hello, darling!' I broke off breathlessly as Birthday Girl herself pranced into the kitchen dressed in her prohibitively expensive party frock. She gave us a twirl and we clapped dutifully.

'D'you like your cake?' I beamed. 'Isn't Laura doing it beautifully?'

Clemmie inspected it with an eagle eye. 'Very nice,' she concluded finally as she walked round the table, scrutinizing the dinosaur from all angles. 'I'm glad you're making it, Laura,' she said. 'Even Hugo couldn't eat the one Mummy made last year. Is Edward coming to my party too?'

Laura crouched down to Clemmie's level, beaming at this reference to her latest man. She smoothed her niece's smocked dress. 'No, poppet, he's at work. Why, would you like him to come?'

Clemmie wrinkled her nose. 'Not if he's still sad.'

Laura frowned. 'What d'you mean?'

'Mummy said he was a sad little man to Daddy last night. Didn't you, Mummy?' She turned to me.

'No, no, darling,' I said quickly, flushing horribly. 'That was a man Daddy works with, he's called Edward too.'

I turned to Laura who was looking decidedly hostile. 'Honestly, the things children remember. Mention someone they've never even heard of and they remember his blinking shoe size, say "bugger" once and they remember to say it every day, but try to get them to remember to say "thank you" and it completely slips their tiny minds! No, no, this Edward chappie's a barrister – in David's chambers. It's very sad, he lost his –'

'Leg?' offered my sister icily. 'Mind?'

'Er, no, wife. He's lost his wife.'

'How careless.'

'Quite. Now come on, Clemmie,' I hustled her out quickly, 'run and play in the garden, would you? I've got loads to do in here.'

3

Clemmie dragged her feet slowly to the back door. 'When will Spotty Lottie be here?'

'Soon, darling, soon,' I said weakly, watching as she scuffed her new shoes in the dirt on the way to the sand-pit.

I stood at the sink avoiding Laura's eye, and looked out instead across our side passage to the one next door, and beyond to the one next to that . . . So it went on, passage after passage, all leading to fifty-foot gardens behind our terrace of three-storeyed houses with four bedrooms – number four used either as a study for the childless or a nanny's room for the with-child – complete with knocked-through drawing room on top of knocked-through basement kitchen.

There were subtle differences, of course. Some kitchens had the sink at this end, which meant French doors onto the garden, and some had the sink at the other end (no French doors), and some had even knocked the kitchen wall down altogether and built a conservatory, thus eliminating the side passage entirely.

The occupants of these houses were startlingly similar too, chiefly in their respectability. The men tended to be doctors, barristers, accountants, solicitors, surveyors, bankers and Lloyd's brokers, and the women, the same again, but with more of a smattering of media, publishing and the art-world thrown in for good measure. In other words, all fully paid up members of London's professional classes, and all living cheek by jowl in tarted-up Victorian semis in the tarted-up boroughs of Putney, Fulham, Hammersmith, Wandsworth, Clapham, Balham and, at a pinch, Streatham.

And of course, I mused, as I picked a dried fruit gum off my jeans, there were the other women, too. Women like me who didn't work, whose lives revolved around children. Again, there were subtle differences. Like the way we filled our time when the little darlings were away from us at school, or ballet, or tinies' tennis, or yet another tea party. Some supplemented these gaps from child-rearing with charity work, or gardening, some with decorative art courses and some with the gym. I wiped the sticky mark on my jeans with a dishcloth and then dropped it back into the sink. I as yet hadn't decided what my particular supplement would be.

I gazed across the sunny, wisteria-clad walls, narrowing my eyes against the sun. None of this sameness bothered me; to be honest I found it rather comforting. Safety in numbers, so to speak. I'd even hazard a guess that some of my neighbours had sensitive, unmarried sisters like mine who lived in flats in smarter parts of town like Chelsea and South Ken and who put up a damn good front but secretly longed to acquire a husband and family and with a huge sigh of relief join their less glamorous sisters in these quieter, more restful, suburban parts of town.

I could sense Laura's eyes on my back now, could feel the offence I'd caused. I just knew how she was sitting, too, at my distressed pine table in my Shaker kitchen, one navy trouser leg crossed over the other, a Gucci shoe wagging nervously, one hand at her neck fingering a French scarf beginning with H (I never dared pronounce it for fear of showing my ignorance), her eyebrows raised, her lips pursed, waiting for me to explain, to dig myself out of yet another hole, to apologize.

I sighed. Suddenly I felt tired, old, and, more than anything, bored. Bored with having to placate, to bolster up, to calm down, to gently ease everyone back into position again. Bored with other people's lives. How come I never got soothed and eased myself? Who was it said: 'Never complain, never explain'? I took a deep breath, turned around and gave Laura a dazzling smile.

'Cystitis isn't that serious, is it, Laura?'

Laura blinked, wrong-footed. 'Er, well, I . . .'

'Doesn't it just mean you have to go to the loo all the time?'

'Well, yes, but –'

'Well, she can damn well sit on the loo and do her act there. How dare she cancel at the eleventh hour for something as piddling as bladder control? Good grief, Clemmie's bladder control is practically non-existent and I still send her to school! No, if she's that incontinent we'll have it in the upstairs bathroom. She can sit on the loo and wear one of my long Monsoon skirts draped over her knees – the children will never know. I'm sure we can squeeze seventeen in there, they're only little, after all. We could get at least four in the bath, one in the basin – Holly Bates can go in there, she's not much bigger than a bar of soap anyway, poor child – a couple on the windowsill, and I'll tie balloons and streamers to the loo chain and –'

'Oh, don't be ridiculous, Tess, you can't possibly have the party in the bathroom. Quite apart from anything else it's unhygienic,' snorted my sister. 'What an idea! Just call Clemmie back, sit her down and tell her gently but firmly exactly what the situation is and just why she can't have an entertainer at her party. She'll understand.'

I looked at my sister. For one so smart she'd been successfully deflected from the 'sad Edward' episode without me even trying. So I could soothe and ease with my eyes shut now, could I? How about that. Laura flicked her hair back confidently as if she were just about to walk into a meeting and advise a client on a slight change of strategy and possibly an increase in his budget.

'I'll talk to her if you like,' she said, giving me a bright smile.

I smiled pityingly and patted her hand kindly. 'No, darling, it's OK. It would take me ages to prise your eyeballs off her little fingers. You just be an angel and carry on icing the cake, and meanwhile I'll get on the phone and offer every magician in London double wages and as much booze as they can drink between three o'clock and five, OK?'

I seized the *Yellow Pages* and thumbed through to the Entertainment section.

Laura shook her head. 'You'll never get anyone at this late stage,' she said smugly.

'Watch me, everyone has their price,' I said grimly. 'If necessary, I'll throw in some casual sex. My body's pretty casual at the moment.'

'Ah yes, that's it – just mention the Caesarean scars, the stretch-marks, the varicose veins and the saggy boobs, and we'll have the house surrounded by the entire Magic Circle in no time at all.'

'Thank you, Laura,' I muttered, knowing full well she was letting me know she *hadn't* forgotten. 'Thank you for those kind words. Ah, here we are – Magicians. Let's see . . . Funky Frankie – no, can't have him, Clarissa Williams had him last week. What ab-ou-t ... Magic Malcolm? Oh goodness, no. I forgot, we can't have him either.'

'Why not?'

'Hugo had him for a Christmas party. We were down here with some other parents quaffing champagne when the ceiling started vibrating and plaster started coming off. We rushed upstairs and found this poor chap cowering in a corner surrounded by fifteen seven-year-olds stamping rhythmically and shouting, *"Magic Malcolm's got a tiny willy!"* He didn't work for months after that, and Sally Bateman tells me he's still in therapy. I feel frightfully guilty, but what can I do? Ah! Here's one I don't know – Perky Percy.' I picked up the book and ran to the phone in the hall.

Five minutes later I was back, flushed with success and smiling broadly. 'He's coming,' I announced, 'and guess what, with not just one, but *two* white rabbits!'

'I'm not surprised. With a name like Perky Percy he's probably got ferrets down his trousers, too. What did you offer him, if it's not too much of a personal question?'

'Oh, just a socking great wodge of money,' I said airily.

'You realise you've probably just wrecked some other poor child's birthday party, don't you? I dare say he's cancelling right now, complaining of the male equivalent of cystitis.'

'All's fair in the infant party world,' I said briskly, dropping the *Yellow Pages* on the table with a thud. 'Now shift yourself, Laura, I need that seat for Musical Chairs. Oh – and pop up and get a couple more from my bedroom, would you?'

'God, give us a chance – I'm still doing the cake. Anyway,

can't David help out? Where is he, anyway? Why isn't he participating in this joyous event?'

'He's in the garden pretending to prune the roses. Josie's stretched out on the lawn stark naked and he needs an excuse to ogle.'

'Not completely naked, Mummy,' said my son and heir, suddenly appearing at my left elbow. 'She's got something round her middle and up her bottom – look.'

I followed Hugo's ink-stained finger through the French windows – yes, we were lucky enough to have our sink at the *right* end of the kitchen – to where our buxom, bronzed, Australian au pair lay prone amongst the daisies.

'What is that thing anyway?' he asked, staring.

'That thing, my darling, is a thong.'

Hugo was delighted. 'The thing is a thong. A thing-thong! Laura – Josie's got a thing-thong up her bum!'

'Bottom,' corrected Laura. She found my ear. 'How can you let her lie out there like that?' she hissed, peering over my shoulder. 'Look at David, he's going absolutely *apoplectic* with desire. He's pruning that rose like a thing possessed – he'll dig it up in a minute!'

We watched as my usually calm, not to say languid husband, who normally wouldn't be seen dead in the garden unless it was to read Kierkegaard in a Panama hat under the apple tree, launched a frenzied attack on Madame Grégoire, at the same time keeping both eyes firmly on Josie's bronzed backside. Every so often he'd pause to flick a strand of blond, rather Heseltinian hair back from his high – and these days increasingly higher – forehead. He paused again, straightened up to his full six foot four,

9

flicked another strand of hair away, and this time, adjusted his trousers too.

'Adds a new dimension to the term "prune hard", doesn't it?' I murmured.

Laura giggled and frowned in Hugo's direction, but as we were constantly being reminded by his school reports, Hugo had a low boredom threshold and had already wandered off in search of something more stimulating like Power Ranger News.

'But don't you care?' she persisted. 'I mean, talk about putting temptation in his way! Why did you *hire* someone like that? There must be ugly nannies, surely?'

I sighed. 'I hired her because the agency sent her and I was too desperate to send her back.' I giggled. 'I must say, when I saw her staggeringly long legs – she had to practically limbo dance through the front door – it did occur to me we might have problems with David's blood pressure – not to mention the roses,' I added, watching him lop off yet another of my prize blooms. I banged on the window.

'Hey, David. Stop it!'

David swung round alarmed, immediately got the wrong end of the stick, averted his eyes from the luscious Josie and began attacking Madame Grégoire with renewed vigour. I groaned as he eventually hacked her off at her ankles.

'There goes another fifteen quid at the garden centre! God, sometimes I wish he'd just throw down his secateurs, whip off his trousers, stride over there and get on with it, just so long as he left my roses alone!'

'Tessa!'

'Well, why not? It would let me off the hook for a while, wouldn't it? Think of all that precious sleep I'd catch up on. I mean, that's what concubines were for, wasn't it? To let the poor, worn-out, child-encumbered wife have a lie-in on a Saturday morning . . . Jolly good idea, if you ask me.'

'Tess, you are joking, aren't you?' asked my younger, less child-worn sister anxiously. 'You'd be horrified if anything really did happen, wouldn't you?'

'Well I don't know, Laura,' I mused, shaking my head thoughtfully. 'Sarah Hooper's husband had a fling with the nanny and Sarah said it was wonderful. The poor man was absolutely dripping with guilt and kept the house permanently stuffed with fresh flowers – couldn't even buy petrol by all accounts without adding a cellophaned springtime-selection to the Access card – practically *fought* her to unload the dishwasher, and Sarah said she only had to mention Sainsbury's and he was in there, trolleying around like a lunatic. She said it was absolutely marvellous.'

'Tess, you can't be serious!'

I patted her shoulder and gave a wry smile. 'No, of course I'm not. But . . .' I hesitated. 'Just don't expect too much, that's all.'

'Of what?'

'Oh, you know, marriage, everything.'

I turned and looked back out of the window again. Josie, bored with the sun, had pulled on a T-shirt and was loping back up the garden, her long legs covering it in about three strides. Hopefully she'd make a few sand-wiches now, but since she wasn't actually on duty for another half an hour I didn't like to suggest it. She strode past us through the kitchen.

'Hi there,' she drawled to Laura in her relaxed Australian brogue.

'Oh, hello!' chirruped Laura, in her uptight English one.

I smiled. Back in the garden, it seemed to me David had almost heaved a sigh of relief. He dropped his secateurs, picked up his hat, staggered across to the other side of the garden and flopped down in a deckchair, his hand reaching down instinctively for his book, his comfort blanket. He put it on his lap, folded his hands on top of it and tipped the brim of his hat down over his eyes, visibly relaxed. I smiled. Even after seven years he was still quite an attractive sight. Tall, still lean, fair-haired – albeit veering towards grey – and with really rather noble features. He could be Lord Many-Acres sitting there contemplating his land, instead of an overworked barrister contemplating his garden fence. His eyes, pale blue, but flecked with brown like a gull's egg, slowly began to close, worn out by all that ogling, no doubt.

'I wasn't actually planning on marrying Edward,' said Laura, rather hesitantly. 'I mean, it's not that serious.'

I swung round. 'Really? Oh, excellent! That's terrific! I mean –' I quickly tried to temper my enthusiasm. 'Excellent that you're not thinking of marriage yet. Much too early. Plenty of time for all that.'

I turned back to the garden again. I heard Laura scrape her chair back from the table behind me as she came to join me at the window. David's mouth was open now. I couldn't hear him, but ten to one he was snoring.

'Tess, you'd never leave him, would you?' she asked tentatively.

I threw my head back and laughed out loud. 'Leave him? No, of *course* not!' I swung round to face her. 'I'm talking about *marriage*, Laura, not David. God, he's the same as any other husband – tired, jaded, stressed out, getting older, thinking ruefully of his far too guided youth and how he wished he'd misspent it a bit more when he had the chance . . . No, no, they're all the same. Why on earth would I want to leave him? And what would I swap him for – the same again? God, at least we get on. You should see some couples we know, like the Bartletts or the Frazers. Sniping away at each other at dinner parties, constantly at each other's throats . . . At least we like each other; at least we have a laugh. All I'm saying is –' I hesitated. 'Oh, forget it.'

'But do you ever think . . . Do you ever sort of wonder . . .'

'What?' I sighed. Laura, like most unmarried women, constantly wanted to talk about relationships, chew them over, discuss them. What she didn't realize was that most married women were exhausted enough living them, without constantly analysing them too.

'Do you ever wonder if you'd have married him if you hadn't been pregnant?' she blurted out.

Uh-oh. This old chestnut. 'Laura, you've asked me this a million times,' I said wearily. God, she did like to dredge everything up, didn't she? She was like a tabloid newspaper sometimes or, worse, *Titbits*.

'Yes,' I said patiently, 'I'm sure I would. I know I would.'

There was a pause. 'He is a lovely man, you know,' she said softly.

I screeched inwardly and contemplated reaching for the saucepan on the draining board to bash her over the head with. 'Yes, I *know* he's a lovely man, I wouldn't have married a jerk, would I? Some sad little git with a toupée or something?' Then, realising I'd said 'sad' again and that – oh damn it, Edward didn't have much hair either – I rushed on hurriedly: 'All I'm saying is you can't expect passion to continue on a grand scale for ever, that's all.'

Laura shook her head. 'I don't believe that,' she said firmly. 'I want someone who's going to light my fire every day till I'm ninety.'

I wiped the draining board down with the dishcloth and threw it back in the sink. 'Take my advice and settle for someone who turns your heater on twice a month,' I said drily. 'And if he'll take the children to the park on a Saturday morning too, you're laughing. Now if you'll excuse me, I've got some serious negotiating to do with my daughter on the subject of magicians.' I pushed past her, rolling up my sleeves. 'I tell you, I don't know why they don't just send a posse of mothers to the Bosnian talks, all we do is negotiate peace, I bet I could teach those politicians a thing or two.' And with that I marched off to hold a summit meeting in the sandpit.

Clemmie was busy burying one of Hugo's prized Action Men as deep as she possibly could and patting the sand down neatly so there was no sign of his grave. I made a mental note to retrieve it later. I sat down and began my spiel. Clemmie listened carefully to my terms, her dark, silky head on one side.

'Has he got a rabbit?'

'Two.'

'Funny balloons?'

'Hysterical.'

'Tricks up his sleeves?'

'Possibly even up his trousers.'

She thought for a second. 'OK, but I want a party bag too, all right? Not just the guests, and I want –' she thought wildly for a minute, then got realistic – 'seven things in it.'

I smiled and stuck out my hand. 'Done.'

We shook on it. No flies on Clemmie, I thought proudly as I heaved myself out of the sandpit, she'd be OK. She was no pushover. David, however, was less convinced. He lifted the brim of his hat.

'Perky Percy?' he murmured from his deckchair. 'Sounds a bit suspect to me.'

'David,' I said, exasperated, realizing he'd been feigning sleep for the last ten minutes to get out of party preparations, 'no one in their right mind is going to make a career out of entertaining four-year-olds unless they are indeed a bit suspect. Just keep your back to the wall and you'll be fine, OK?' I glanced at my watch. Two-thirty. Christ! 'And now that you've finished wrecking my roses, perhaps you'd be good enough to sort out the seats for Musical Chairs. There's a hell of a lot to do today, you know. We can't all sit around admiring the scenery!'

David looked surprised. 'All right, all right.' He put his book down and made to get up. 'You only have to ask.'

'Well, I shouldn't *have* to, should I? That's the whole point. It should be perfectly bleeding obvious, shouldn't it!'

I marched back into the kitchen ahead of him, slamming the door shut behind me. It shuddered in its frame. Laura jumped in alarm. I ignored her and pulled open the kitchen drawer, ransacking it for cake candles. Hugo popped his head round the door, saw my face and popped out again. I ground my teeth as paper napkins, cocktail sticks, etc. fell to the floor.

'Oh God! Why is it I can never *find* anything!' I stared down at the chaotic drawer. 'Well, there just aren't any, are there, so now I'll have to go to the shops. Great. Where's my purse? Where's my blinking *purse?*' I lurched around the kitchen, picking up bundles of newspapers, scattering children's drawings and piles of discarded clothes.

'Jesus!' I shrieked. 'Why is it that in order to get anything done in this house you have to split the bloody atom first?'

Laura slipped silently through the kitchen door to the garden. Through the window I saw her make a face to David. She jerked her head back in my direction and raised her eyes to heaven. David made a resigned face in response, shrugged his shoulders and slowly made his way up the garden path.

I picked my purse out of the fruit bowl on the dresser, wiped a bit of rotten pear off it, and sighed. At what stage in my career, I wondered, had I turned into this mini domestic tyrant? Last year? The year before? Five years ago? I hadn't always been like this, surely? I seemed to remember being a rather sweet, good-natured girl once. I shook my head and made for the back door, just as David was coming through it.

'I blame other people!' I snapped in his face.

Chapter Two

In the event, the party passed off smoothly enough. Perky Percy arrived complete with full make-up, ginger wig and manic smile and was instantly deemed too perky to be exposed to David. I hustled him into the playroom with a gin and tonic until his big moment. Then the first child arrived on the doorstep, accompanied by her rather perplexed mother.

'Um, the balloons on the door . . .' she faltered, flushing slightly.

'Yes, they're to show there's a party here,' I explained with a bright smile. 'It helps people find the right house.' I enunciated this slowly and carefully. Poor woman, too much day-time TV, clearly.

'Yes, it's just that – Well, look.'

I popped my head round and looked.

'HUGO!' I roared up the stairs. 'GET DOWN HERE IMMEDIATELY! I'm so sorry,' I murmured back to the mother. 'It's my son's idea of a joke.'

Hugo was duly cuffed and instructed to remove the pink phallic ensemble complete with two small round and one long pendulous, *now* please, and replace them with something more tasteful. Then the party went off without a hitch.

No one vomited after Musical Bumps, Josie managed

to keep her clothes on for five minutes and hand around the jellies, and Hugo gave us ten minutes of perfect peace as he invigilated Dead Lions, striding amongst eighteen supine, motionless four-year-old girls with a menacing look on his face and a plastic sword in his hand. It was only when one little girl started to go purple that we realized he'd told them no moving or *breathing* was allowed and we frantically lunged amongst them, shaking shoulders and shouting, 'BREATHE DAMN YOU, BREATHE!' not relishing the prospect of explaining to seventeen sets of parents that their children had passed away on the party floor. The rest of the games were then supervised by me, and it was only when two Sophies had a fist-fight over which Sophie was the true recipient of the final pass, that Pass the Parcel degenerated into Pass the Valium.

Finally, when all the children had been dispatched with bags and balloons and Josie had been sent upstairs to supervise the baths and bedding down of two hysterical, over-excited children, I ordered David to the off-licence.

'Wine – quickly – now!' I gasped, but he'd already gone, needing it even more badly than I did.

Laura and I collapsed on the sofa.

'Never again,' I groaned.

'You say that every year.'

'Ah, but this time I mean it. Next year it'll be a panto-mime and McDonald's with David at the helm.' I kicked my shoes off, swung my legs round and plonked them on her lap. I shut my eyes.

'God, I've never needed a break so badly,' I muttered. 'I can't *wait* for Scotland.'

Laura pulled a face. 'Hardly a break for you though, is

it? I mean, you still have the children and you still have to cook.'

'I know, but at least I've talked Josie into coming. I couldn't bear it without some help.'

Laura sat up. 'But Tess, she's appalling. She never *does* anything. All she did at the party was fanny around with a few jellies!'

'She's not paid to do any more than fanny around with jellies, Laura, she's a thirty-quid-a-week au pair, not a two-hundred-quid uniformed Norland nanny. Now please don't upset her, I couldn't contemplate life without her at the moment. Apart from anything else she keeps me from murdering the children. I'm much nicer to them when she's around *and* she keeps David permanently busy. It's amazing. Whatever room she's in, he's there too, on some spurious errand like cupboard-sorting-out or shelf-putting-up, and all so he can stare at her bum. He fixed every single appliance in the kitchen last week.' I shut my eyes again. 'And apart from anything else, Clemmie adores her.'

'Hugo doesn't.'

'Yes, but that's because he's at a boys' prep school now, they programme them to be misogynists from Day One. It's nothing personal.'

Laura sighed. 'Oh well, it's not my problem if she comes. I shall just lie by the river and ignore her.'

She clasped her hands behind her head and shut her eyes. I propped myself up a bit and looked at her. As sisters we presented quite a startling contrast. Her, small, sleekly blonde, blue-eyed and with fine petite features, and me, tall and long-limbed with dark curly hair, large grey eyes and a wide mouth. The only thing we had in common was our classic English pear shape, inherited from our mother – reasonably slim at a glance but on closer inspection, not much up top and quite a lot down the bottom, thank you very much, Mother. I pulled David's M&S jumper down over my jeans wondering how she always managed to camouflage it better than I did.

I watched as she yawned, quite prettily really, showing perfect white teeth. Laura definitely won the looks competition, always had done, which made it all the more surprising that I'd had such an easy time with men and she'd made such a hash of it. Half the problem, in my opinion, was that she went for such total nonentities. It was no wonder she got bored with them after five minutes. I sometimes wondered if she wasn't afraid of competing, afraid of going out with a chap as attractive and personable as herself in case he dumped her, so she stuck to safe, mousy little men who adored her and whom she ditched after a couple of months. This latest teacher chappie, Edward, was a classic example. He had 'Destined for Laura's Rubbish Heap' written all over him. Still, I thought, I really must try harder to like one or two of them.

She looked up and I gave her what I hoped was a conciliatory smile. 'Is Edward coming to the Tarn with you?' I asked.

She frowned. 'Not sure.'

'Why?'

'Well, it's all a bit *en famille*, isn't it? Mum, Dad, Penny and Piers and everyone, I don't want him to get the wrong idea. Don't want him to think he's meeting the in-laws.'

'Ah. So . . . it's not that serious, then?' I asked as innocently as possible.

'No, it's not that serious,' she snapped, 'and don't pretend you're disappointed. I think I might be going off him a bit actually.' She frowned and chewed the skin around her thumb. I kept quiet, knowing anything I said would be totally wrong.

'And also,' she went on, 'I'm a bit worried about Daddy. You know what he can be like, picking holes in people, making them look stupid. I'm not sure how Edward would fare under that sort of pressure.'

Pretty diabolically, I thought privately, but I tried to look non-committal. 'Well,' I hazarded, 'you never know, they might get on brilliantly. Daddy likes the strangest people.' God, why did I *say* that? Thankfully it didn't seem to have registered with Laura. She was looking at me and had a sly grin on her face. She sat up a bit, and suddenly I knew what was coming.

'Of course, you know who *is* going to be there, don't you?'

I sighed. 'Yes, Laura, Patrick Cameron. And if you really think you're the first person to bring me that piece of news, you're mistaken. Penny was on the phone a week ago, gleefully informing me of it, then Mummy rang yesterday to tell me exactly the same thing, and even David asked me the other day if I knew Patrick was going to be there. Then he watched my face really carefully to see my reaction. I couldn't believe it.'

'Really? Did he seem worried?'

'I don't know about worried but certainly apprehensive, and I just think it's such a huge overreaction on everyone's part. So what if he's going to be there?'

Laura raised her eyebrows and rolled her eyes

expressively. 'Well let's face it, Tess, you did have one hell of a fling with him and this is the first time you've seen him since, isn't it?'

'Yes, so what?'

'So it's only natural that David might feel a bit – well, as you say, apprehensive.'

'You mean in case Patrick gallops up to me at the river on his white charger and our eyes meet and some gigantic arrow pierces me in the heart and I drop my fishing rod and my cheese roll and stagger over to him in my wellies, heave myself up behind him in the saddle and disappear over the horizon with him?'

'I don't know about that, but –'

'Well, what then? I mean what d'you think I am, Laura? Some bored Putney housewife with seven-year-itch who's just ripe for bumping into her glamorous ex-boyfriend on holiday, ditching her nice, safe, comfortable husband and embarking on a steamy affair with him? And all in the name of *finding* myself, or something? Needing my own space? This isn't one of your Aga sagas, you know, this is me, Tessa Hamilton, happily married mother of two, and apart from anything else I went out with Patrick twelve years ago – bloody aeons ago! It's like hoicking someone out of your past and saying: "Ay ay, look who's here, it's that spotty boy from down the road who did wheelies on his bike to impress you, or – or Sandy from *Crossroads*, or –"'

'I *never* fancied Sandy from *Crossroads*!'

'Oooh, Laura! What a fib! You *know* you did, you were absolutely hot for him!'

'I was not!'

'You were, I distinctly remember it. You even wrote to

22

ask if you could join his fan club and you got a letter back – probably from Meg – saying Sandy didn't actually *have* a fan club as such, but would be delighted for you to be the founder member.'

'No!' Laura looked shocked.

'It's true. Let's face it, Laura, you've always gone for,' I hesitated, 'well – *sensitive* types, haven't you?'

'Unlike you,' she said nastily.

'David's sensitive,' I said defensively.

'Yes, all right, but Patrick's not, is he? He's completely wild, sex on legs.'

'And I'm not attracted to him,' I said patiently. 'I was once, but I'm not now – OK? In fact, the more I think about it, the more I realize he was never remotely my type.'

'So you've thought about it.'

I ground my teeth. 'Of course I've thought about it – and that's what I've thought, all right?'

We were silent for a moment. Remembering.

'He never married, you know,' said Laura after a while.

I sighed. 'You say that as if it's weird, it's not. He's still only thirty-something, not an OAP.'

'I know, but I just wonder if, well – if he couldn't. After you.'

'Oh Laura, you're so melodramatic! And if that's the case then I'm doing him a huge favour by going up there, aren't I? He'll take one look at me twelve years on and think – Christ, what a disappointment – and instantly be released from his chains. He'll be down at Invertarn register office with the first wee lassie he can lay his hands on.'

'His father died, you know,' she went on, not really listening to me.

'I *know*,' I said wearily.

'So he's coming back to claim his estate.'

'You're talking about him as if he was some returning Laird, swatched in tartan, surrounded by pipers, coming down the mountain to reclaim his kingdom.'

'And his queen,' she giggled.

'Oh, for heaven's –'

'Who's a queen?' asked David, barging through the door armed with clinking Threshers bags.

'No one – that Perky Percy probably,' I said, jumping up and taking them from him.

'Undoubtedly. Drink, Laura?'

She stood up. 'I won't, actually. I've got to get back and do my packing.' She kissed us both. 'And I'm seeing Edward later. I think. If I decide to ring him, that is.'

'Treating him mean, are we?' asked David with a smile.

'Not intentionally. It just seems to come naturally these days.' She shrugged. 'Not quite sure what to do about him actually.' She started to bite her thumb again. 'Anyway, I must go. See you up there. In Scotland, I mean.'

I let her out of the front door and watched her go down the path. She waved and I shut the door. Poor Laura. If only she was settled, if only she didn't *expect* so much. If only . . . oh, I don't know. I went back to the drawing room, twiddling a strand of hair.

David stretched out his hand from the sofa. I took it. He gave it a waggle.

'She'll be fine, stop worrying about her.'

'But I do, David, I can't help it.' I flopped down on the sofa next to him. 'She's so mixed up, highly strung, nervy – and everything has to be so damn perfect with her. She's just like Daddy really. I mean, earlier on I just vaguely mentioned that marriage wasn't all hearts and flowers and chocolates and that there was quite a lot of tedium involved, and she instantly asked me if I was thinking of leaving you! She's so unreal, everything's got to be either pitch black or snowy white with her.'

'She's got no stability, that's all. Once she's found the right bloke she'll be fine; she's just twitchy because she hasn't.' He put his arm round my neck. 'Anyway, come here. I'm sick of you worrying about your bloody sister and your mother and the children and God knows who else. Let's worry about you for a change.'

'Me?'

He kissed me firmly on the mouth. 'You.'

'David!' I drew back in surprise.

'What? Can't I kiss my wife?'

'Don't be ridiculous. You know very well there's no such thing as gratuitous kissing in this house. If we kiss it's sex and we can't possibly have sex because Josie's upstairs bathing the children!'

'She'll be ages yet, she's putting them to bed too, isn't she? And we could lock the door.'

I narrowed my eyes. 'You've been looking at that girl's bum too much, haven't you? It's made you all randy and – Oi, get off!' I giggled as he grabbed my hands and pinned them behind my head.

'I love it when you talk dirty,' he murmured, kissing me again.

'I did not!'

'You did – bum, randy – very dirty for you.' He bit my ear.

'David,' I hissed, 'any minute now Josie's going to be back through that door!'

He leaped up, and in two strides had slammed the door shut, locked it, lunged for the curtains and dragged them across the bay. 'There.' He leaped back onto the sofa again with a grin.

'Ow!' I shrieked. 'God, what's got into you? What's all this he-man stuff?'

'Don't know, must be all those jam sandwiches.' He thrust his head into my neck and nibbled my ear.

'Geddoff!' I laughed, pushing him away.

He sat up and narrowed his eyes quizzically at me. 'Am I to deduce, from your somewhat negative body language, that you're not on for this then?'

I stared up at him. He was serious! What – here, now? On the sofa? His eyes were unusually bright and very blue. For a moment he looked almost as young and attractive as when I'd first met him, but attractive or not, this was really most inconvenient. For one thing there was all that washing up to do in the kitchen and I hadn't even looked at the Sunday papers, and there was a new three-part Jane Austen thing on the telly I wanted to watch which started in about – I glanced quickly at my watch – about two minutes. I hesitated.

'Oh, all right, but for God's sake make it a quickie.'

David regarded me for a moment, then gave a wry smile and heaved himself off the sofa. 'Call me old fashioned, but that just about took all the romance out of it.'

I made a contrite face as he went to the windows and pulled the curtains back. 'Oh. Sorry.'

'Doesn't matter.' He found the Review section of the

paper on the floor and sauntered off with it into the kitchen.

I reached down, rather too quickly, for the remote control, snuggled back happily into the sofa and switched on the telly. Bliss.

Chapter Three

I first met Patrick Cameron when I was seventeen.

It was the usual family holiday at Kilmarnoch House, way up near Invertarn in the Scottish Highlands and we were the usual contingent. Two families of Fergussons: Aunt Rachel, Uncle Robert and my cousin Penny; and Mummy, Daddy, Laura and me. Kilmarnoch House stood on the banks of the river Tarn. Daddy and Uncle Robert had grown up there, and when Grandpa died, they'd somehow managed to avoid selling it and kept it as a holiday home. The theory was that we took it for the whole of August and rented it out the rest of the year, but in reality this was fraught with difficulties because Kilmarnoch was a thoroughly uncomfortable, unlovely house and my father spent the whole year literally pressganging friends, acquaintances and anyone he could trip up in the street into renting it and fretting about the loss of income in the months the house stood empty.

From the outside it looked like one vast slab of granite rising up out of the ground; flat, dour and grey, with no distinguishing features at all except for its cold glassy eyes and a network of black drainpipes that snaked frenetically about as if someone had scribbled all over its face. Inside it was huge, cold – even in summer – and dilapidated, and not in a gentrified, quarry-tiled and ancient

Persian rug sort of way, but in a lino-floored, moth-eaten fitted carpets and electric fires sort of way.

To us children though, it was heaven. It was a house to hide in, to run in, to charge through the empty attic rooms shrieking in, to play ping-pong in the cellar in . . . a house so tatty it could accommodate any number of buckets of seaweed and slime being accidentally tipped over it when searching for that crucial shell . . . a house that seemed to absorb sand and mud into its very substructure, leaving absolutely no trace.

Outside it had four acres of overgrown garden to explore, huge oaks to climb, streams to dam and woods to make camps in. At the bottom of the garden was the river. Here we fished, paddled or, in my case, just lazed around sucking blades of grass. I'd lie on my tummy with my nose over the edge, watching the clear water as it rippled over smooth pebbles, dreaming of being beautiful and fanciable and funny and exotic – Russian perhaps, or a Romany gypsy, or maybe even orphaned – anything, really, other than a vicar's daughter from Claygate.

When we were younger we started thinking about Kilmarnoch the moment Christmas was over, and were almost sick with excitement when instead of crossing off the weeks, we began to cross off the days. At seventeen, of course, one had to adopt a slightly more superior attitude to the family holiday, bored – contemptuous even, if possible – but I can still remember the secret rush of excitement as we crossed the border into Scotland, and the not-so-secret shout of, 'There it is!' from the back seat, as Kilmarnoch finally came into view across the valley.

Most of our days were spent standing on the banks sending flies skimming across the water. We'd watch the fly drift downstream, wait for a hint of movement, then with a flick of the wrist, cast again. After a couple of hours we'd throw a few rugs on the bank and stop to eat our piece, then we'd pack up, wander upstream to another pool and cast again. And so it went on. It has to be said that although fish *were* sometimes caught, it was a huge event, and more often than not, they weren't, and if three or four days had gone by without anyone catching a dicky-bird, we children began clamouring for a change of scene, which invariably meant the beach.

The day that I recalled now was a beach day. The sky was pure blue, without a whisker of a cloud, and the three of us, Penny, Laura and I, were stretched out in a row, motionless and silent in our bikinis, as if the stiller and quieter we lay, the browner we'd get. Penny and I were both desperate for tans. Desperate to go home with at least something to show for a holiday spent, not camping with friends in the Dordogne or backpacking round America, but fishing in Scotland with the parents. I was also aware that the cricket club dance was only three days after I got back, and if I was really going to wear that very skimpy yellow T-shirt pulled off the shoulder, I needed to at least get one of my shoulders brown. I lay there, feeling the sun scorching my eyelids, letting the fine dry sand drift through my fingers.

It was Penny who saw him first. I heard her bangles jangle as she sat up beside me.

'Wow! Look at that!' she hissed, digging me in the ribs. I knew from her hormonal tone that she'd found a man.

'Wow!' echoed Laura, who was fourteen.

'Not bad,' muttered Penny under her breath.

'Not bad at all,' agreed Laura, without the faintest idea what she was talking about.

I groaned, turned over and shut my eyes tight. Now I'm the first to admit that I was as obsessed with boys and sex as the next girl, but Penny at sixteen was just one huge walking talking gland. She was also a social barometer for all that was populist. Whichever blond Adonis was plastered on the cover of her teenage magazine was also plastered to her bedroom walls, but only for as long as he was in favour with her fellow glandettes, only for as long as he was *à la mode*. If he wavered in popularity for just an instant, he was ruthlessly ripped down and replaced by someone else. Penny followed the herd religiously, principally because when left to her own devices, her taste was execrable. She had no discernment of the male species whatsoever, which was why, when I finally deigned to take my nose out of the sand and turn my head to take a peek at what was riveting her – some airhead nutting a football, no doubt – I hated myself for being equally riveted.

He was sitting on the sand with his back against a rock, his brown legs crossed, wearing a pair of old white tennis shorts and a faded denim shirt rolled up to his elbows. His hair was dark – black, really – and quite long, curling well over his denim collar, and he was very brown, but somehow effortlessly so, as if it were merely an occupational hazard. His eyes were dark too, and they were flashing up and down, first down at his lap, then out to sea. Initially I couldn't work out why, then I realized he was drawing. A small pad rested on his bent knee and his hand was moving over it like quicksilver as his eyes captured a fishing boat gently bobbing out there in the water.

I turned my face away and feigned boredom. 'God, you're predictable, Penny,' I muttered. 'Tall, dark and I presume you think handsome, but I have to warn you, he won't be your usual beefcake type.'

'Why?' demanded Penny.

'Well, he's drawing, isn't he? He shows dangerous signs of having a brain, or at least some sensitivity. He may not even play rugby.'

'I don't *have* to go for the rugger-bugger type, you know,' she said huffily. 'Anyway, I'm going to take a look at his etchings.'

She stood up, giggled and adjusted the triangles of her bikini so a huge amount of her generous bosom protruded. Then she flicked back her mane of long blonde hair and sauntered off. I sat up in horror.

'Penny, you can't just —'

But with her figure she could and she knew it. Laura, in her navy-blue school costume went giggling in her wake, sticking out her non-existent chest and doing an exaggerated version of Penny's wiggle.

I smiled at Laura's bony, undulating bottom, then lay down on my side to watch as Penny sidled up, smiled and said something no doubt utterly puke-making.

The boy looked up in surprise and flushed, obviously startled as she bent to inspect his drawing. He recovered and allowed her to take the pad, gave a brief glance at her chest, which he could hardly miss since it was hanging in his face, then looked away embarrassed. She flicked through the pages slowly, giving him time to look again, but he didn't. When she handed back the pad, she held on to it for a moment, forcing him to look up at her. She gazed at him and her cherry lips parted in a coy smile. I cringed heavily. This was usually the moment for her to wind in her catch, to land him right there on the beach, but for some reason this boy didn't run true to form. He took the book back with a tight smile, nodded his acceptance of her gushing praise and carried on with his drawing. Penny knelt down next to him, bending forward so her blonde hair almost touched his paper, trying to make him talk while he worked, but he just gave the odd curt nod or muttered an occasional monosyllabic response. If he did smile, it was in Laura's direction. My sister was now doing an hysterical impersonation of Penny, wiggling furiously along the shore, hands cupped under imaginary bosoms which were clearly so heavy she was staggering under their weight.

Eventually Penny came huffily back, bangles and bosoms jiggling, face red, followed by a giggling Laura.

'He's too boring for words,' she announced sulkily, flopping down beside me again. 'Can't even string a sentence together, let alone manage a conversation. You were certainly wrong about him being intelligent, Tess. I think he's brain dead.'

'Or simply not succumbing to your charms perhaps?' I murmured, eyes shut.

'Don't be ridiculous,' she snapped. 'I wasn't flirting with him, if that's what you mean. I just wanted to look at his drawings.'

I turned my face away from her, back in his direction, watching through half-closed eyes as he carried on sketching, liking him even more for not admiring Penny. Of course, I reasoned, if he didn't fancy Penny who might be a little pneumatic for some people's tastes but was nonetheless a stunner, there was no chance he'd fancy me – unless of course he preferred the very pale and totally uninteresting look. I smiled at this. He smiled back. I froze for a second, then flushed and turned my head away. Christ! He must have thought I was smiling at *him*, being as obvious as Penny. After a while, however, I steeled myself to look back. He glanced over in Penny's direction, raised his eyebrows and grinned again, conspiratorially. This time I gave a huge, village-idiot beam in response.

I kept those smiles to myself all week, rewinding them, playing them back in my head a million times, hugging them to me. I imagined a quiet, sensitive boy, who'd sit by me on the riverbank talking of painting (his) and poetry (mine) – I secretly fancied myself as a bit of a poet. I saw us walking hand in hand having long philosophical discussions, arguments even, and then resolving our intellectual differences behind the gorse bushes in the moonlight, with a passion that knew no bounds.

Actually, it had to know no bounds because I hadn't the faintest idea what it was all about. As a vicar's daughter at an all-girls' school with one sister and one female cousin, where the devil was I expected to meet boys, let alone have sex? In fact my one and only sexual encounter to date had been with a very short boy called Nigel who, to my astonishment, had asked me to dance at some ghastly tennis club disco. Shocked but delighted I'd instantly dropped my hot dog into my friend Melanie's lap and shot onto the floor with him, thinking, Jesus, he may be short but at least I'm *dancing* – when suddenly, in the middle of *Lay Lady Lay*, and apropos of absolutely nothing, he stuck his tongue in my mouth. He circled it precisely twice, thrust his hand up my jumper, ferreted round to the front, boldly seized the middle of my bra and hoicked it up – and over. Now I'm sure the whole ghastly First Time business must be as horrific for boys as it is for girls, but excuse me, not even to *bother* to go round the back and attempt the bra strap struck me as not only cowardly but downright churlish. Round and round we went, me cut in half by M&S underwear, hideously uncomfortable, eyes boggling over his shoulder, and him, all sweaty and trembly, feverishly investigating whatever fall-out he'd managed to squeeze out of the bottom. When the Lady finally Lay across Bob's Big Brass Bed, Nigel walked me, dazed – and I think that went for both of us – back to my chair. He deposited me next to Melanie and my cold hot dog, and as I sat down, he bent to whisper in my ear.

'You were fantastic,' he muttered. Well, let's face it, my sex life could only get better.

Back at Kilmarnoch, eight days went slowly by until finally, my father walked out of the front door one morning, peered up at the cloudless blue sky and deemed the weather bright enough and the fishing poor enough for us to down rods and go to the beach again. Silently whooping with delight I quickly packed up the boot and urged the others to come *on* or the day would be wasted. We all piled in and I sat in the front, willing the car to go faster, willing the boy to be there. At last we arrived and made our habitual slow and motley progress across the dunes, a straggly procession struggling under the weight of too much beach equipment, me at the back gazing around hopefully, my father at the front, striding out and leading the way, bellowing, 'Come on, you lot!' over his shoulder.

My father has never been much of a style guru but in those days he took a hell of a lot of laughing off, particularly when dressed in his leader-of-the-pack beach ensemble. A vision in khaki – shorts to the knee, short-sleeved shirt buttoned to the neck, socks, sandals, and an Australian bush hat – he put his head down and belted along at breakneck speed, carrying an assortment of pots and pans, a kettle, a primus stove, bags of sausages, bread rolls, kitchen utensils, collapsible chairs – anything, in fact, that one would normally find in the kitchen, because yes, we were that family. The one that cooks on the beach.

Now as anyone who has ever attempted a fry-up in a force eight gale on a Scottish beach will testify, one or two windbreaks are crucial. One or two, not seven, as we invariably had. My father was obsessed by windbreaks; he fussed about them all holiday, constantly fretting he wouldn't have enough, and was never really happy until he was totally surrounded by the bloody things and couldn't actually see the sea, the mountains or even the sky, just acres and acres of red and white ticking with all of us huddled in the middle like something out of Custer's last stand. He'd bang the final post in and bawl, 'There! Now can anyone spot a gap?' All heads would shake vehemently. 'No, no gaps, Daddy!' Because of course it fell to us children to carry the bloody things.

'Don't dawdle, Tessa!' he yelled back to me as I brought up the rear, balancing a couple of the wretched things on my head. I ignored him, and stopped at the top of a dune, gazing around, hoping he'd be there. He wasn't. The beach was empty apart from a couple of families with young children over by the rocks and a man walking his dog along the shore. Damn it, just my bloody luck. I swallowed miserably and walked on slowly, looking all around and just praying that any minute now I'd see his dark head peeping up from behind those rocks where it was more sheltered, or maybe over there where –

'Hey! Look out – bugger!'

Suddenly I was flat on my face, nose down in the sand with a windbreak on my head and papers flying all around me. I looked up into his furious dark eyes.

'You stupid bloody – oh!' He stared. 'It's you.'

I sat up. 'Sorry,' I gasped. 'I didn't see you there – oh, I've ruined your drawings!'

I scrambled around after them, covered with sand and embarrassment, vainly snatching at sheets of cartridge paper as they whipped around us in the wind.

He grabbed them from me. 'Leave them. It doesn't matter, they were crap anyway.'

He retrieved a few more then screwed the whole lot up in a big ball and tossed it over his shoulder with a grin. The wind picked the ball up and bounced it along the sand, whipping it further and further away. We watched as it sailed off into the gorse bushes behind and stuck fast.

'That's not bio-degradable, you know,' I said prissily and instantly wished I hadn't.

'If it's crap it is, isn't it?' he countered, raising his eyebrows.

'Actually, it looked rather good to me,' I said timidly, desperately trying to claw my way back in.

'Shows how much you know about art then, doesn't it?' he said, but he grinned.

We stood, staring at each other. Out of the corner of my eye I could see that down on the beach, Camp Fergusson had paused during windbreak erection and all eyes were focused on me. Even from this distance I was aware that Penny's mouth was wide with fury.

'Off to frazzle another layer of skin off your body then, are you?' he said.

I drew a circle in the sand with my toe. 'Well, there's not much else to do. The water's freezing and I'm too old for sandpies.'

'I'm going for a walk,' he said suddenly. 'It's too windy to draw. D'you want to come?'

I jumped. 'Um – er, well I'll have to –'

'Ask Mummy?'

I flushed. 'No, put these windbreaks over there with the others, actually.'

'Well, I wasn't suggesting we took them with us. Go on then, hurry up.'

I fled obediently and dumped the windbreaks. My heart was pounding.

'Just going for a walk,' I muttered to my boggling family, surreptitiously taking a rather juvenile ponytail out of my hair.

'With whom?' demanded my father.

'Um, that boy over there. We were just . . . chatting.'

My father peered over my head, frowning. 'But who is he? Do you know him?'

'Well, sort of. I met him with Penny.' I looked desperately at Penny for corroboration, but she was still speechless.

'Oh Ian, she'll be fine,' soothed my darling mother, putting her hand on his arm. 'Stop fussing. Go on Tess, off you go.'

I flashed her a grateful smile and took off back over the sand, just as my father was saying, 'Well, I do think she might at least introduce us. That's typical of Tess. Why does she have to dash off like that without even –' But whatever else he thought was lost in the wind, and I'd gone, skimming across the sand, back to the dunes, back to Patrick.

He grinned. 'I see you're built for speed, unlike your buxom cousin.'

'How d'you know she's my cousin?' I panted.

'Checked up on you,' he said as he marched off. 'You're Ian Fergusson's daughter, aren't you? He's going to be thrilled when he discovers you've been taking cliff walks with me. He loathes my parents.'

'Daddy? Really?' I scrambled over the dunes after him. 'Who are your parents?'

'The Camerons. We live at Gilduncan. Hasn't he ever mentioned them?'

I shook my head, still panting a bit from my run. 'Don't think so.'

'Oh well, I loathe them too, my father anyway, so I don't really blame him.'

'You loathe your father?' This was a new one on me. I found my father oppressive, domineering, hypercritical and impossible to please, but I'd have trouble forming the word 'loathe' about him. 'Why?'

'Because he's a shit,' he said simply. He turned and grinned. 'Shits do have children, you know, and just because they're our parents we don't have to be blind to their shittiness. We don't have to like them.'

I stopped and stared at his back for a moment as he strode on. Somehow this wasn't quite the shy, sensitive artistic boy I'd had in mind; this boy was foul-mouthed and angry. I clambered up the cliff after him again, silenced.

He stopped ahead of me and turned back. 'You're off on Saturday, I take it?'

'How d'you know that too?'

We'd reached the top of the cliff. He sat down and lit a cigarette. He offered me one. I glanced quickly down at the beach below. They were a long way away but I could still see my father. I shook my head.

'Because you've been here nearly three weeks. You don't have to be Einstein to figure out you'll be heading back to the comfort of the home counties soon, back to your tennis lessons and your pony and discos at the cricket club, getting on down to Shawaddywaddy on a Saturday night.'

I flushed. 'You're deliberately making it sound tame and suburban.'

'Well, it is tame and suburban compared to this, isn't it?' He swept his hand around at the majestic blue heather mountains behind us, the huge stretch of beach below and the sea that ran out for miles and miles ahead of us.

'Yes, of course,' I said crossly, 'but we can't all live in the Highlands, can we, and if we did it wouldn't look like this, you know. It'd be overrun with leisure centres on those hills and municipal swimming pools in the valleys, you wouldn't be able to see the beach for badminton nets, so from your point of view it's probably just as well we're not all up here admiring the heather.'

'Thank God I am,' he muttered, pulling at the rough grass and staring out to sea. 'It's about all that keeps me sane.'

There was a silence. I didn't like to break it and apart from anything else I didn't know what to say. He seemed so strange and – well, haunted almost.

After a while he turned to me and grinned. 'Well that's promising. It's not often you meet a girl who doesn't feel she has to fill the air space.'

'God, you're patronizing!' But I couldn't help feeling pleased. 'What did you ask me up here for anyway if you don't want to talk – or did you just want to get up my father's nose?'

'No, I just thought you looked all right. Sort of approachable and normal.'

I grinned. 'And I've spent the last seventeen years trying to be extraordinary and mysterious.'

He made a face. 'Mystery's very overrated. Nine times out of ten it's just a front for something very banal and boring.'

'Oh really?' I sucked at a blade of grass. 'You're pretty mysterious, aren't you? All this pent-up aggression and dark brooding looks out to sea and allusions to your sanity – it's all a bit Heathcliff, isn't it? I mean, what's it all about?' He opened his mouth to speak but I interrupted. 'No, no – don't tell me, let me guess. A broken home, terrorized childhood, misunderstood adolescence . . . am I close?'

He stared at me with narrowed eyes, and for a moment I really thought he was going to hit me. Then suddenly his face broke into a grin. 'Not far off, but you forgot to mention under-exposure to suburbia. I'm a seriously deprived child in that respect.'

Suddenly he stood up, seized my wrists and hauled me to my feet. He looked into my eyes. 'And let me amend my last, rather muted compliment, to approachable, normal and really rather extraordinarily smart. Better?'

I grinned. 'For the minute. We'll get on to my finer points later.'

He held my eyes. 'Fine by me.' We stood looking at each other, and for a moment I really thought I was in grave danger of fainting and toppling over the edge of the cliff.

'There's a film I want to see in Brookenhead tonight,' he said abruptly. 'D'you want to come?'

'A – a film?'

'Yes. We have cinemas here as well as heather, you know.'

'I – I'm not sure. It's just that I'm with my family and –'

'OK, fine. Don't.'

He turned and set off back down the cliff path at a cracking pace. I ran after him.

'Hey, hang on a minute. All I meant was I'd have to ask my parents, or is that just too incredibly mundane for you? Would you rather I knotted my sheets together and shimmied out of my bedroom window without telling them where I was going?'

He turned back and laughed. 'You're not afraid to take the piss out of me, are you?'

'Why should I be?'

'No reason. I'll pick you up at seven then, OK?'

'OK.'

Chapter Four

What he didn't know was that it would have been far easier to shin out of that house on knotted sheets. Although part of the blame for my sheltered existence lay with my female-oriented life, it has to be said that the lion's share lay with my father, the Reverend Ian Fergusson. To say he kept an eye on his daughters was like saying the Gestapo kept an eye on the Resistance. Sometimes I felt I couldn't fart without clearing it with him first.

Back at the house at teatime I steeled myself to break the news. Daddy had been holding forth for twenty solid minutes, berating poor Aunt Rachel about the ignominies of the Church of England, telling her precisely why he was still a rector when lesser men had accelerated past him to become bishops. I looked at the clock. Five-thirty, only an hour and a half and he'd be here, and if I wanted to have a bath and iron my shirt . . . I cleared my throat.

'Daddy?'

He didn't even pause for breath. 'You see, what they *really* want, Rachel,' he went on, banging his tea cup down in its saucer and making her jump, 'is some poncy git with a beard and a guitar who's going to *question* the Scriptures, who's going to *doubt* the Virgin Birth and the parting of the Red Sea, or any of the other miracles come to that, entirely missing the point that that's what they bleeding well are! Miracles!'

My mother, sitting over in the window seat, raised her eyebrows and smiled sympathetically at me over her newspaper. It suddenly occurred to me that she'd guessed I had a lot of ground to break here and had positioned herself quietly in the wings to help me chip away at him. I was always glad of her support. My father ranted on.

'We won again yesterday,' she murmured across him.

'What?' I looked round. She was reading the football results. 'Oh, good.'

My mother was an ardent Chelsea supporter. She followed every match they played and much to my father's horror even went to watch them sometimes. No one quite knew why she supported them with such zeal, but I secretly suspected it had a lot to do with the fact that it wasn't considered a particularly fitting hobby for a vicar's wife. It was my mother's way of rebelling. It amused her to hold sherry parties at the vicarage and discuss the latest new player's transfer fee instead of the verger's rose garden.

She sighed and closed the paper. 'We're away to Liverpool next week, though – that won't be quite so easy.' She nodded over in Daddy's direction. 'Try again, darling.'

I licked my lips. 'Daddy, please can I just ask you –'

'– I mean, Christ, even the bloody *Creed's* under suspicion now,' he stormed. 'I believe in God, the Father Almighty, Maker of heaven and earth – who says so, eh?' He glared at Rachel, who blinked nervously. 'Who says He made heaven and earth? Oh yes, that's what the powers-that-be want to hear, Rachel. They want a bit of lively discussion, because in their ignorance, they think that shows intelligence! And of course what they don't want is faith. Oh no, that's a really dirty word. Faith's not fashionable at all, faith's right out of the window. They don't want any namby pamby *believers* in their churches, they want doubting bloody Thomases!' He paused for breath and to slurp his tea. Alf Garnett in a dog collar. 'And d'you know what else they want – eh?'

Rachel shot me a glance. 'No, Ian, but I think Tess wants to –'

'D'you know what else those bloody bishops want – do you? Just a minute, Tessa, I'm talking. D'you know what else they want, Rachel?'

Rachel sighed. 'No, Ian. Tell me.'

'They want pederasts.'

'Oh Ian, please –'

'Oh yes, yes they do.' He nodded vigorously. 'They want fashionable little pederasts, and it's no good you sighing, Daphne, you know very well it's true. It's not enough these days to be a red-blooded heterosexual family man. What the church wants is a groovy gay vicar – Larry – who introduces his partner – Brian – to the congregation at the church door every Sunday, and if Larry's been done for a spot of indecent exposure in the local park and it's made it into the Sunday papers – well, so much the better! Oh yes, halle-bleeding-lujah, that's wonderful, because then we can all forgive and forget and it'll all be so cuddly and lovely and we'll all pray for Larry and Brian and have happy clappy and join hands with our neighbours and give them a good old snog – kissing's more or less mandatory in churches now, Rachel – and Larry will play his guitar and Brian will sit in the front pew and sway a bit and think how heavenly Larry looks in that long white dress and – yes, Tessa, WHAT IS IT! For heaven's sake stop mumbling and spit it OUT!'

'Daddy, that boy I met today,' I blurted out. 'He's asked me to go to the cinema tonight. Please can I go?'

My father stared at me as if I had two heads. 'Boy? What boy?'

'On the beach, you saw him.'

'To the cinema? When?'

'Tonight.'

'Of course you can, darling,' said my mother smoothly. 'You go and get ready.'

'What's his name?' barked my father as my bottom rose from my seat.

'Patrick Cameron.'

My father's tea cup froze midway to his mouth. He put it down slowly. His eyes were like stone. 'It's out of the question.'

'Daddy, please I –'

'Don't argue, young lady, you're not going. That boy is Marcus Cameron's son. He's a reprobate, a layabout, a dropout and most probably a drug addict to boot.'

'Who?' enquired my mother mildly. 'The father, or son?'

'Both probably!' exploded my father. 'Like father like son! Willie tells me that boy was thrown out of Marlborough and Harrow and then sent down from Oxford. All he does now is arse around at the fisheries pretending to work and then drip around drawing wild flowers on his days off!'

'That's not fair,' I protested. 'He's a very talented artist – I've seen his pictures.'

46

'And that's all you're going to see of him, my girl,' he barked.

I stood up, shaking with rage. 'Oh this is wonderful, this is marvellous, you've been checking up on him haven't you? You've been talking to the gillie about him already and all because I spoke to him on the beach today! And how come Willie knows so much about him?'

'Tessa, the Camerons live at Gilduncan,' he said with studied patience.

'So?'

'So everyone knows their business. The locals always know what goes on at the big house, half of them work there for God's sake, and no one in their right mind would let their daughter touch that boy with a bargepole!'

'I'm not going to touch him, I'm just going to see a film with him,' I shrieked. 'You're behaving like a bloody Victorian! I'm seventeen years old and —'

'Don't you swear at me, young lady!'

'Tessa, go upstairs.' My mother put her hand on my quivering arm. 'I want to speak to your father in private.'

I turned and fled, tears streaming down my face. Out in the hall Penny and Laura were sitting on the stairs, mouths open, eyes huge, listening intently to the action. I ran past them up the stairs.

Ten minutes later my mother came up. 'Dry your eyes, darling, and get ready.'

I looked up from the wet pillow. 'Are you serious? Am I going?'

'Of course.'

What she said to him I'll never know. No one ever knew how my mother got round him, but once in a while, when

47

the chips were really down, she did, and an hour or so later I was leaping down Kilmarnoch's front steps as the lights from Patrick's red Spitfire lit up the drive.

We didn't go to the cinema in the end, we went to the beach and watched the sun go down. We talked a lot, laughed even more, and at eleven o'clock precisely Patrick drove me back to Kilmarnoch. He bade my father – who was waiting, silhouetted in the open front doorway – a polite good night, and left. The following day the Ian Fergussons piled into the car, waved goodbye to the Robert Fergussons and drove the 600 miles or so back to Kent, and that was the end of that. Or so my parents thought.

What they didn't know was that within minutes of sitting on that cold, windy beach I'd felt that pang. That sharp one that makes your heart stop for a moment and then dance around like mad as you realize this is different, this is real, this is *it*. All the short Nigels, shy Malcolms and reasonably attractive librarians I'd ever vaguely considered in my short and limited career sank into obscurity as my toes curled with excitement in the cold sand. I hugged my knees and pressed my chin into them thinking, this is it, Tessa. This is *it*! Quiet and sensitive he certainly wasn't, but clever, irreverent, original and hilarious he was, and not in a cynical way that made you give a twisted smile and think, Gosh, how clever – but in a throw back your head and laugh out loud sort of way.

It was quite clear he'd had one hell of a childhood, with parents who rowed constantly – and sometimes violently – and a father who far eclipsed mine in ghastliness. Marcus Cameron was a cold, starchy, sneering Dickensian figure who dined in a dinner jacket every night and then proceeded to get as drunk as a Lord and pour scorn on his only son and heir for being such a huge disappointment to him. Mr Cameron's disappointment stemmed chiefly from Patrick's not wanting to either row for Oxford, join the Army, or become a Conservative MP, but to do what came naturally – to paint. What must have been irritating in the extreme for Marcus was that Patrick could have done all these things, and more, but chose not to. He wasn't a chinless wonder living off his trust fund: he'd got a scholarship to Oxford, even though he'd been thrown out of one school and been 'this close' to being thrown out of another – not, incidentally, as my father had snidely suggested, for 'doing drugs', but for what Patrick laughingly referred to as 'kicking against the pricks'.

For someone like me this was still awesome talk. The model daughter, the diligent student who always did her homework and her violin practice, I'd never so much as nudged let alone kicked the pricks he was referring to – teachers, tutors, dons – people in positions of authority, positions that to my mind were not up for debate. But Patrick debated everything and everyone, questioning things I considered unquestionable, like the validity of having a piece of paper with 'first-class Honours degree, Oxford' written on it.

'What's the point?' he demanded, narrowing his dark eyes at me in the moonlight and dragging on his cigarette, 'when I know I want to paint? What's the point in a degree in history, for God's sake?'

I gazed at him in astonishment, longing as I did with all my heart to go to university, to get away from home. But Patrick was not so easily fobbed off.

'I'm buggered if I'm going somewhere I don't want to go just to get away from somewhere else, and no one, particularly my bloody father, is going to make me.'

I came away from that beach reeling. Not only had he affected my heart but my head, too. For the first time he'd made me think independently of the people who took it upon themselves to guide my cerebral processes. I was still reeling in Kent a week later and when I got back to boarding school two weeks after that. But gradually, as I sat doodling at my desk, or lay staring at the cracked magnolia ceiling in my dorm, the euphoria wore off and grim reality sank in. Here was I, at a girls' boarding school in Dorset, and there was he, working at a salmon farm in Scotland. I had a whole year to get through until I could conceivably see him again, if indeed he even wanted to see me. Would he write, for instance? Every night I said three Hail Marys – I'm not even Catholic – tapped my headboard three times, kissed the Bible twice, crossed myself, turned three small circles, touched the floor for luck, got into bed, and prayed to God that he would.

He did. I went through the whole rigmarole nightly, and amazingly, the following Friday another letter appeared, and then another, and another, until it began to look increasingly likely that whatever it was that had made us sit together on that cold windy beach stood more than a cat's chance in hell of lasting until the following August.

I for one went to crazy, adolescent lengths to make sure it did. Never had a set of A-level exercise books been so elaborately graffitied with hearts, initials and true love arrows. Never had I been so obsessed with art galleries and all things Scottish – the tartans at the local drapery store were fingered lovingly, Campbell's Mulligatawny soup, which I loathed, was supped in gallons. I even, in very lovesick moments, took to lingering in the fishmonger's, gazing fondly into the cold grey eyes of the salmon stretched out on the slab.

All very juvenile, but all crucial for keeping true teenage love alive. And it worked. When I returned to Scotland the following year, I didn't have to worry about rekindling my fire; my embers were still piping hot. Of Patrick, I wasn't so sure. He was older, had certainly had more experience and must have had many more distractions than me in the past twelve months. He might well have gone right off the boil. It was therefore with a certain amount of trepidation that I prepared to keep our first clandestine meeting at midnight – timed to thwart my father – on the very first night.

I lay in bed, watching the illuminated hands of my alarm clock move slowly round to the twelve. When they'd both almost made it, I pushed back the duvet, pulled on a pair of jeans and a jumper and crept stealthily out of the bedroom I shared with Laura. Shaking with nerves I tiptoed downstairs in the dark, lingering for a moment on the bottom step to make sure no bedroom doors were opening above me. My heart was pounding. No one seemed to be stirring so I crept quietly through the hall, unbolted the huge front door, wincing at every creak and groan the archaic bolts gave, and swung it back. I shut it softly behind me, tiptoed out into the night, and ran down the hill towards the river.

As I crashed through the brambles at the bottom of the garden I came to the clearing where we'd arranged to meet. My heart was galloping around in my throat now; I could hardly breathe for nerves. It was pitch black and I couldn't see him, and for one ghastly moment I wondered if he'd got cold feet, decided not to come. Then suddenly, softly, he called my name.

'Tess!'

I swung around. He was sitting on a low stone wall with his back to the river smoking a cigarette. He was wearing an old blue fisherman's jumper, a pair of jeans and that fatal, devilish, lock-up-your-daughters grin. As he stubbed his cigarette out on the wall, sparks flew everywhere. He jumped down and came towards me and as he got close, he reached out and took my hands.

'Hello.'

'Hello!' I gasped.

I'd envisaged this meeting for a whole year, planned it, rehearsed it, and my God I was going to be so cool and sophisticated and now here I was – damn it – hardly even able to speak.

He smiled, eyeing me closely. 'Well, well. I really wondered if you'd make it.'

'You mean you doubted it?' And there was me doubting him.

'I wasn't sure how your courage had come on in a year, but since you're here I think we can safely say leaps and bounds. Sneaking out at midnight to meet your undesirable boyfriend, eh? Whatever next?'

Boyfriend. He'd said boyfriend. 'Oh, I think I have a pretty shrewd suspicion,' I gulped brazenly, meeting his eye.

For a moment I think this even took the wind out of

his billowing sails, then his face broke into a delighted grin. He swooped forward and collected me up in his arms.

'Good heavens, Tess, you want to watch it. You'll lose that nice shiny halo if you're not careful.'

'The sooner the better,' I murmured, burying my face in his jumper. He gave me a squeeze then set me down, gazing at me, exploring my face with his eyes. Then he bent his head and kissed me, beautifully, slowly, deliciously, the second kiss I'd ever experienced and so terribly different from the first.

That night, of course, I lost more than my halo. We walked, talked and made love down by the river, as we did for virtually the next thirty-two nights. And every morning at four a.m. I'd sneak back into the house and go to sleep with a smile on my face. No one could understand why I couldn't wake up until about midday and why, when I did eventually drag myself out of bed, I just lay by the river, smiling, dreaming, watching dragonflies, not even bothering to fish much. My whole family were exasperated by me, but still no one knew, or even suspected. Only Daddy, over lunch on the bank one day, came vaguely close, asking me abruptly, but *sotto voce*, if I'd heard from that damned fellow Patrick. I said no, I hadn't, adding slightly miserably that I thought he'd probably forgotten all about me.

'Well, of course he has,' he barked, not bothering to hide his relief. 'He's probably got a string of women spread all over Scotland!'

No, just the one, I thought quietly, nibbling my cheese roll.

'Probably forgot you the moment you got out of his swanky little car,' he added gleefully.

And my father thought he knew so much about faith. *Oh ye of little* . . .

And so the holiday went on, the days – and nights – going by all too quickly, until around came the one I'd been dreading. The last. Or so I thought. Patrick, it transpired, had other ideas.

'Come to Italy with me,' he said, as we lay on the bank together, staring up at the stars.

I turned my head. 'To Italy?'

'I'm going to go and paint there.'

I sat up. 'You never said!'

'I only decided yesterday. I've got to get away from here for a while. I'm twenty-one next week so I come into a bit of money. Whether my father likes it or not, I can do what the hell I want.'

'Really? You mean you're suddenly going to be loaded or something?'

He grinned. 'Do I detect a sudden spark of interest? No, not loaded exactly, the trustees are pretty mean with their dosh, but certainly I'll have enough to cover our air fares and the rent on a flat somewhere, Florence perhaps, or Siena. Then I'll get a job.'

'As what?'

He shrugged impatiently. 'Oh, I don't know, Tess. Maybe teaching English or working in a bar or something. Perhaps you could waitress at the same place, then we could be together.'

I boggled. 'Blimey. Daddy would have a fit!'

'Of course he would. He'd have a fit if you so much as

mentioned my name. You wouldn't be able to *tell* him, you'd just have to get on a plane and come.'

I gulped. My courage may have come on in leaps and bounds but this called for out-and-out rebellion. Patrick had been a rebel all his life and was just doing what came naturally. For me it was different. I was a law-abiding daughter, fond of my parents.

'So what d'you think?' he demanded.

I pulled at some grass on the bank. 'I don't know, Patrick, I mean it's all so sudden, isn't it? And it's all very well for you, but I'm supposed to be going to university in October.'

'Yes, I know, but you don't want to go yet, do you? You said yourself in an ideal world you'd take a year off and travel. It's only your father who wants you instantly locked up and institutionalized again, so why don't you just defer it for a year? I'm not talking about for ever.'

I took a deep breath. 'Patrick, I can't just leave home like that . . .'

He shrugged and threw a pebble into the river. 'Fine, OK, don't. We probably won't see each other again though, will we?'

'That's not fair!' I cried. 'I deliberately chose St Andrews so I could be near you.'

'Oh, so what am I supposed to do – hang around on campus like some lovesick pillock waiting for you to come out of lectures – no, thanks. Look, all you want to do is write anyway, so what's the point of going there in the first place? Just fix yourself up with a pen and an exercise book, and get scribbling! Do you really think a few seminars on *Sir Gawain and the Green Knight* is going to help you write better poetry?'

'Concentrates the mind,' I muttered lamely.

'Rubbish, it just clouds the issue. Or perhaps it's the social life you're after, is that it? D'you secretly want to be part of Freshers' Week and join the Brass-Rubbing Society and the Drama Club and help organize the Rag Ball? Perhaps you'd like to have a crush on your English professor and cram like mad to get a first to impress him – or maybe it's the college scarf that attracts you, the whole "I'm a student" bit with your Railcard and your good luck gonk for exams and –'

'Oh Patrick,' I said impatiently, 'you're so cynical about anything remotely conventional. University doesn't have to be as squeaky clean as all that.'

'No, but it would be for you, Tess. That's the way you'd do it and you know it. You've been programmed from birth to do the right thing and if no one's there to stop you, you'll revert to type and run around organizing every committee under the sun, throwing yourself into lacrosse and basketball and –'

'What's wrong with that?' I snapped.

'Nothing,' he said patiently. 'There's nothing wrong with it at all, if it makes you happy. Oh, it'll certainly make your teachers happy and your father will be ecstatic and everyone will pat you on the back and say, "Jolly well done, Tess. Isn't she marvellous?" but what about *you*? What happens if you're standing there three years later with your mortar board on your head, a frozen smile on your face, clutching your bits of paper wondering if you've pleased everyone except yourself?'

I stared at him, unsettled.

He seized my hand abruptly. 'I dare you, Tess, I dare

you to be happy. Go on, pack a bag next week, leave a note for your parents and meet me at Heathrow. Yes, your old man will be livid; he may even follow us out and try and take you back, but you're eighteen now, you can do what you like. The point is, Tess, he'll get over it – but if you don't come, will you?'

I squirmed. 'It's . . . the deceit I hate, slipping out, leaving a note. You don't think if I just asked him . . . ?'

'Oh what, that he'd say, "Great idea, Tess, hang on a minute, I'll get my keys and drive you to the airport myself"?'

'N-no, but –' I struggled desperately, looking for loopholes. 'What if it doesn't work out?'

He threw up his hands in despair. 'What if, what if! Look, if it doesn't work out and we hate it, or hate each other, you can still go to St Andrews the following year. You can defer your place, can't you?'

'Ye-es, I suppose so, but –'

'So do it.'

I stared at him. He stood up and hauled me to my feet. He grinned. As far as he was concerned, it was settled.

'See you at Terminal One then. I'll get the tickets!'

'Oh, for God's sake, Patrick,' I snapped, exasperated. 'It's not as simple as that.'

He stared at me closely. 'It is if you want it enough. Don't blow it, Tess. You'd be surprised how rare this kind of thing is.'

For 'kind of thing' I suppose he meant love. But how was I to know that? I'd stumbled upon it so quickly and easily, how was I to know some people look for ever and never really find it at all?

I tried to meet him, I really did. Back home in Kent a week later I packed a bag, my tummy raging with butterflies, and left a note under my pillow in my bedroom. Then at the last moment, half an hour before I was going to leave the house, I told Laura. I think in my heart I knew she'd be far too scared to keep such a colossal secret to herself, that she'd tell Daddy. And she did. I sat motionless on the bed, waiting like a condemned prisoner, my bag on my lap, listening to the shout of rage in the kitchen as she spilled the Patrick beans, then the *thud thud thud* of footsteps coming up the stairs. The door flew open. It was late on a Sunday morning and Dad was still dressed in his cassock, his preacher's kit. His face was white with fury. I sat there, gripping the handle of my bag, as he towered above me like an avenging angel.

'Over my dead body!' he thundered.

A very ugly fight ensued and we both said things I'd rather forget, but never will. I'd never seen him so furious, so seething, so venomous. My mother, in a very brave moment, appeared behind him, and suggested that perhaps I should go for a week or two, just for a holiday, and that as a matter of fact she wouldn't mind coming with me as a sort of chaperone, she'd always wanted to see the frescoes – how about it, Ian? As he swung around to face her, I really thought he was going to hit her. He hustled her out and slammed the bedroom door behind them both and I threw myself on the bed and burst into tears. I sobbed into my duvet feeling utterly distraught, miserable and totally powerless, but – I sat up on the bed and blew my nose – if that were so, why was it then that there was just the merest hint of relief stealing over my soul? I stared through my tears at my bookcase, groaning with childish books, old teddies, a few rosettes on the wall above it. Was it because it had actually been too much of a big adventure? And now it was out of my hands? No longer my fault if I didn't make it?

I stayed up in my room all day while my parents talked in hushed tones below. Eventually, the telephone rang. My father called me down. Almost in a daze, I went slowly downstairs. Daddy was standing in the hall, dangling the receiver between his thumb and finger as if it were a piece of dog shit.

'Tell him,' he said, as I took it from him.

He stood over me as I explained, in a quivering voice, that I wouldn't be coming.

'Not ever?' asked Patrick, dumbfounded. 'Can't you meet me there later on, in a week or two? Give him the slip?'

'No,' I said, 'not ever.'

My father nodded, tight-lipped as I handed the phone back to him. I walked slowly upstairs to my room.

The following day I wrote to Patrick's mother and asked where he was living. Amazingly she wrote back and told me. I sent three or four letters to Florence, pleading with him to understand, to consider my position. He didn't reply. I suppose he simply couldn't believe I was so unlike him. So spineless, so timid.

That October I went miserably up to St Andrew's University. The first few weeks were the usual riot of frenetic activity with everyone rushing around joining societies, being personable and witty and madly collecting friends. I couldn't be bothered so I collected few. I withdrew into myself, worked incredibly hard and gained a reputation for being bright, but aloof and unapproachable, whereas in fact I was just plain lonely and miserable. Of course, as time went by I thawed and by the fourth year I'd made a few friends and even had a couple of flings, but nothing serious.

Then right at the end of my final year, I fell in love. I went to a party, met a law student and to my complete amazement, was totally bowled over by him. I sincerely believed lightning couldn't possibly strike twice, but this quiet, gentle man literally snuck up on me and persuaded me otherwise. Perhaps it worked because he was so different from Patrick, so laid back, mellow, kind and screamingly academic and intelligent. Perhaps I was just ready to try again. At the time he was debating whether to go on with his studies and do an MA at Cambridge with a view to becoming a don, or to join the Bar and make some money. Six months later the question was decided for him. I became pregnant and neither of us wanted to get rid of the baby. We married, very happily, and David became a barrister to support his new family.

Chapter Five

'Oh, for God's sake give her some Calpol!' snapped David as we sat in an horrendous traffic jam on the Hammersmith flyover, already an hour into our journey to Scotland and still only half a mile from home. In the back, Josie was sandwiched between our bored and fractious children, one of whom was already threatening to throw up.

'She feels *sick*, David. Calpol's not going to help!'

'No, but at least it'll knock her out and with any luck we'll have a bit of peace.'

'My God you have some strange ideas about bringing up children,' I snapped, thinking it was a bloody brilliant idea and wishing I'd thought of it, and, incidentally, thought to put the blinking stuff in the car rather than in my case in the boot. There was no way I was admitting to such gross inefficiency now though.

'No no,' I said brightly, 'we can't resort to drugging them just yet. I know, let's have a sing-song. After all, we are off on our hols, aren't we?'

David shot me an incredulous look. 'Hols?' he muttered. 'Jesus, you'll be getting out the ginger beer next.'

I ignored him and swung around to my equally incredulous children. 'Now,' I said beaming, 'what about *The Wheels on the Bus*?'

'What about them?' growled Hugo.

'Or *The Happy Wanderer*,' I persisted, ignoring David's

low moan. 'D'you know that one, Josie? Do they have that in Australia?'

She blinked. 'Not to my knowledge, but how about *Kookaburra*? We could do it in rounds.'

David went pale. 'Darling, please, I beg you,' he muttered, 'not *Kookaburra* in rounds. Perhaps past Stirling when we're absolutely desperate, but we haven't even got to the Talgarth Roundabout yet!'

'What do you suggest then?' I said irritably.

'A cup of black coffee and a browse through the *Observer* springs instantly to mind, but failing that, how about one of those God-awful tapes they torment us with sometimes?'

Another bloody brilliant idea and this time I took him up on it. I rifled feverishly through the glove compartment.

'Postman Pat or Funny Bones?' I threw over my shoulder. Fatal. Absolutely fatal, and me an experienced mother.

'Postman Pat!' yelled Clemmie.

'Funny Bones!' yelled Hugo.

'Postman Pat!'

'No, Funny Bones!'

'Postman – Oi! Ow!'

'Well, you thumped my leg! Mummy, she thumped my leg!'

'POSTMAN PAT! POSTMAN – OW! GEDD-OFF! MUMMY, HE'S HITTING ME!'

'*All right, that will do!*' I bellowed. 'We'll have Funny Bones first and then Postman Pat, all right?'

But of course it wasn't all right. Hugo crowed and Clemmie cried and a major fist-fight ensued across Josie, with me flinging in a few of my own right hooks from the front. At this point David let out a howl of anguish, performed an astonishingly dangerous U-turn in the middle of the Hammersmith flyover and belted down to King Street with his awestruck, silenced family around him. He screeched to a halt outside Rumbelows, ran inside, and two minutes later appeared with two personal stereos. He plugged both the children in while I rose to the occasion and shovelled a couple of spoonfuls of Calpol into their mouths – to quell the over-excitement, don't you know – and we crawled back into the jam again, now an hour and a half into our journey, even closer to home, and £75 worse off.

I groaned and slumped down in my seat. 'Happy holidays.'

David smiled and patted my hand. 'This is always the worst bit,' he said reassuringly. 'It'll be fine once we get there. We'll all relax – even you.'

'Don't bank on it,' I said grimly. 'All sorts of things will conspire to get on my nerves, like Penny and Piers for instance.'

David sighed. 'Oh God. Here we go.'

I ignored him. 'I wonder, for instance, just how much money Penny's spent on her house since I saw her last, hmm? What d'you think, David? Four thousand – five? I dare say those hideous gold towel rails have come in for a bit of re-plating, and I should think the shagpile's wearing a bit thin by now, they must have had it at least six months. Oh yes, I imagine the Credit Card Queen has been dealing her way all round Harrods and all because Piers is *such* a successful barrister, the implication being of course that you're not!' I ground my teeth.

'I don't think that's true,' said David mildly. 'You take everything so personally.'

'Because it's *meant* personally – you just never see it. God, last year he even told me, in a quiet and oh-so-frightfully-well-meant way, what an excellent barrister you'd make if you could just find that killer punch. I tell you, he damn nearly found it in his solar plexus right there and then, and *then* he had the audacity to say that he was surprised you had so many briefs!'

David smiled. 'What did you say?'

'I said I was surprised he had so many teeth.'

David threw back his head and shouted with laughter. 'Oh Tess, you do rise to him.'

'I can't help it. I mean, he staggers in every year with a groaning case full of work, never does any of it, of course, just shuffles it around under your nose and sighs over it at the desk periodically – what's he trying to prove?'

'He's just insecure, darling, you know that.'

'And bloody Penny tells me *constantly* how poor Piers is *s-o-o* busy and has to work every evening and every weekend because he's in such demand, and isn't it nice that you have so much time to relax . . . I mean, bugger off!'

'Barristers always like to appear busy,' said David, calmly overtaking a huge juggernaut in the middle lane. 'They have to talk it up.'

'But you don't, you never do!' I objected exasperated. 'People ask you what sort of work you do and you say – "Oh, crap mostly".'

'Well it is, mostly.'

'But you don't have to say so! Especially not in front of Penny and Piers – for my sake, darling, please.'

David raised his hand in thanks as he was let into the fast lane.

'David?'

'Hmmm?'

'Please, darling, don't talk yourself down in front of them, OK?'

'OK, OK!' he said. 'Stop nagging, Tess.'

'Well, they're so bloody competitive,' I said tetchily. I scratched my neck violently. 'God, she's bringing me out in a rash before I've even got there.'

'She's not that bad,' said David. 'You just handle her badly.'

'And it's not even as if I want to be like her!' I went on. 'I don't want her immaculate tasteless house on the Wentworth bloody estate, I don't want co-ordinating apricot hand towels with a nice gold P in the corner, or a sauna in the basement, or a *fountain*, for heaven's sake, in the conservatory . . . but what bugs me is that she thinks I do!'

'Oh God, Tess,' said David weakly.

'I don't want her homogenized, sanitized, ultra-hygienic home, thank you very much. I don't want to be forever flicking round my ghastly Lalique ornaments and my onyx ashtrays with a feather duster. D'you know, David, I once looked under the pepper-grinder in her kitchen and guess what I found?'

'What?' he said faintly.

'Nothing. Absolutely nothing. David, everyone has pepper under their grinder. She must be the only person in the history of the world who dusts *underneath* it! She is that anal, David.'

'She's your cousin, darling. Look, why don't you save

this for the end of the holiday? We've got three weeks to get through yet.'

I sighed, scratching my neck again. 'I know, I know. I just thought maybe if I got it off my chest now I might not be so rude to her when we get there. Incidentally, I've told the children to stop calling them the PPs. I just hope Perfect Child's taken a turn for the worse though, otherwise I might have to flush her head down the loo.'

David frowned in the direction of our less-than-perfect children in the back, who would have loved to have joined me in the disposal of PC – Penny's ultra-cute daughter – but a quick glance over my shoulder told me a soothing mixture of aural stimulation and Calpol was still giving them that lovely, vacant, open-mouthed glazed look. Josie was also tuned into her Walkman, a beatific expression on her lovely bronzed features.

'With any luck she'll have progressed from a perfect three-year-old into a normal, horrible four-year-old,' he soothed.

'Don't you believe it,' I said bitterly. 'If she could recite the whole of *The Owl and the Pussycat* last year while Clemmie was having trouble saying "ball", it's bound to be Keats or at the very least Shakespeare this year. D'you know, on the beach last year she asked me what I thought of John Major, and as I struggled for breath informed me that guinea fowl was very overrated. I nearly nose-dived her into the sand.'

David shook his head resignedly. 'I don't know why you let it get to you, Tess. You know Penny hot-houses that child, force-feeding her flash cards and God knows what else – she probably has her plugged into *Civilization* cassettes while she's asleep. She'll burn herself out by the time she's six, and you know you don't approve, so why get in such a state about it?'

I sighed. 'I know. Why am I in such a state?'

I looked out of the window and watched the country-side roll by. Penny and Piers had a lot to do with it of course, they always sent my blood pressure rocketing sky high, but there was an added irritation this year. Patrick's reappearance was more than anything else, annoying. I couldn't care less about him being there, but nonetheless I didn't want to bump into him looking like something the cat wouldn't even bother to drag in. It was irritating to think that I might have to bother to wash my hair more than once a week, or put on a dash of lipstick if I went into Invertarn, or even wear uncomfortable support pants, damn it, so that he didn't get the shock of his life when he stood behind me in the queue at the butchers and wondered who the low-slung woman in front wearing her bottom round her knees was, or struggled to recognize the female weight lifter, swearing and cursing as she dragged forty-two cans of baked beans – obligatory holiday fodder for Hugo – out of the grocers.

Yes, there was no doubt about it, twelve years and two children had taken their toll on my body, and if Patrick was going to even recognize me I'd have to walk around sucking in everything I possessed – tummy, bottom, all my chins – as if I had a cucumber up my bottom. Such a blinking *bore*. Or perhaps I shouldn't, I mused, watching the fields flash past. Perhaps that was the answer; perhaps I should wash my hair *less* often, abandon make-up altogether and let everything hang out, that way, he wouldn't recognize me at all. I could walk past him in the street in the perfect knowledge that he wouldn't have a clue who I was. I brightened. Yes, that was it. After all, he would have changed too, wouldn't he? So I might not even recognize him. We could be totally oblivious to each other. I mean, twelve years is twelve years – God, he was probably an accountant or something by now – a bald one, with a paunch. I snuck a look at David. At least one could say he was only vaguely thinning on top and he was still as slim as when I'd met him. I smiled. Comparisons, in this case, might be rather less than odious. I slipped my hand onto his knee and gave it a little squeeze. He slammed on the brakes and a coach damn nearly went up our backside. It honked furiously.

'What was that for?' David yelled.

'What!'

'You squeezed my knee!'

'I know! Affectionately, damn it – can't I do that?'

'Jesus.' David accelerated away from the bus, clearly ruffled. 'You gave me the fright of my life, I thought I'd missed a car pulling out or something.'

'For heaven's sake, David, I was just being friendly!'

'Well, don't – OK? At least not when I'm driving. It's too much out of character for you.'

We drove on. On and on, 582 miles to be precise, until finally, eight hours later, our car crawled slowly into Kilmarnoch's drive and crunched to a halt on the gravel. One by one, the surviving members of the Hamilton family emerged, exhausted, dishevelled, ratty and smelling very distinctly of sick. Clemmie, having threatened us with it for 580 miles, had finally delivered the goods half a mile from Kilmarnoch's front gates, giving us precisely two seconds to find the bucket, the one we'd so thoughtfully got ready just north of Slough but which was now buried beneath a mountain of sweetie papers. We didn't stand a chance. As we lunged hopelessly towards the Quavers packets, Clemmie retched and projected into Josie's – bless her – gallantly cupped hands. Having caught most of it, Josie then turned and threw it through what she thought was an open window, but sadly, wasn't. It was for this reason that at least two of the occupants of the back seat were now emerging from the car looking like a couple of Pizza Hut specials.

As we shuffled sheepishly up the front drive, the door swung back and there stood the Williams family; first (as always, to bag the best bedrooms), clean and tidy (naturally), and refreshed by a sensible overnight stay in York. Huge smiles of greeting were stamped on their well-scrubbed faces, but those smiles froze as they took in the Hamiltons. Then they dropped them altogether.

'Heavens, look at the state of you all!' gasped Penny. 'What happened?'

'I should have thought that was perfectly obvious to anyone with eyes and more particularly nostrils,' I snapped.

'Clemmie was sick,' said David patiently.

'But why didn't you stop?' she asked as Piers disappeared hurriedly down the hall, wrinkling his nose in horror.

'We thought it was more fun not to,' I said.

'No!'

'No, Penny, there wasn't time,' I said slowly. 'Otherwise, believe me, we would have done. She didn't give us any warning.'

'Well don't just stand there on the doorstep,' she said bossily, 'for goodness sake come in and get out of those clothes.'

The only reason we were standing on the doorstep, I thought gritting my teeth, was because she was barring the way into the house. We followed her in.

'In here, Clemmie – no, not in the drawing room, in the *kitchen*, child,' she shrieked, dragging poor Clemmie down the hall. 'We don't want it all over the carpet, do we? Now, strip off and then it's upstairs for a bath.'

She began with ruthless efficiency to strip Clemmie down to her pants. I sighed. I had to admit that Penny was the first one to give hands-on practical help while Piers was the first to disappear, but her no-nonsense manner always had the effect of reducing my children to tears. I could see Clemmie welling up even now.

Josie saw too and took Clemmie's hand. 'It's OK, Penny. I've got to go and have a bath too, so I'll take Clemmie with me and we'll get in together.'

I gave Josie a grateful smile as she led a sniffing Clemmie gently away.

Penny turned to me. 'Is that your nanny?' she hissed.

'Yes, why?'

'Did I *say* she could call me Penny?'

I groaned. 'Oh, for God's sake, Penny, she calls me Tess, d'you really want to be Mrs Williams all holiday?'

'Well, she might at least *ask*. It's a bit rich just to *assume* isn't it?' She bustled off down the hall. 'Anyway, let's go and get Clemmie some of Leonora's pyjamas, then at least you don't have to unpack.'

I followed her upstairs to the landing, watching as she rifled busily through the airing cupboard. She was just as buxom as she'd always been, but now in a much more matronly way. Her bust no longer rollicked happily around in low-cut blouses, popping out at the slightest provocation, but was strapped firmly into what surely must be a feat of engineering, so that it now resembled a large and sturdy shelf. You felt you could almost use it as a sort of bar, to lean on and chat to her, balance your drink on even, and still not be too rudely close to her face. Her blonde hair was cut to her shoulders now and neatly tied back in a band. The good-time girl with the big tits and long blonde hair was nowhere to be seen. And that was exactly the way Penny wanted it.

Since her introduction to Piers Williams six years ago, Penny had undergone a complete and miraculous personality and image transformation. So successful had it been that Piers – who came from a rather grand and pompous Gloucestershire family – had confided to me at their wedding reception that he was so terribly thrilled to have found such a fresh young gel like Penny, who for this day and age was so remarkably unspoilt and who had no – *ahem* – reputation to speak of – 'if you know what I mean, Tess.'

When I'd finally wiped my mouthful of champagne off his tie and taken my olive out of his top pocket, I nodded furiously, agreeing wholeheartedly that Penny was of course the most unspoilt girl I knew.

'So fresh,' he murmured.

'Couldn't be fresher,' I muttered back, thinking, blimey, so blinking fresh you had to literally tie her down, hold her back, because at the slightest opportunity Penny would *go*. With anyone really – doctors, dentists, builders, merchant bankers, merchant seamen, toy-boys, sugar daddies – I'll say this for her, she had no prejudices and no age limits; if it had a pulse it would do nicely and she just *went*. VROOM! In bedrooms at parties, in ploughed fields behind the wedding marquee with the best man, or the groom – or both – in the back of taxis, in the front of taxis . . . Given a man and an opportunity Penny was in there, rutting away as if her life depended on it.

Now quite how this had bypassed Piers I've no idea since most of London was acquainted with it – let's face it, most of London was acquainted with *her* – but blissfully ignorant he remained, which was all very well for Penny, but jolly taxing for the rest of us. This huge deception was an absolute minefield, and I was forever forgetting and saying things like – 'Oh come on, Penny, you *must* remember Charles, you went *out* with him!'

Penny would look at me sharply, glance quickly at Piers slumbering quietly over his brief, then stare thoughtfully into space, wrinkling her brow as if she were trying to remember.

'Oh y-e-s, Charles,' she'd muse eventually. 'I did once, didn't I – to the cinema, I think.' She'd glare at me through the frozen smile. 'Just a date.'

She was very keen on this 'date' word, conjuring up, as it did, a vision of a fifties-style Penny in a white cardy and gloves swinging her Etam handbag outside the Odeon, pecking her 'date' chastely on the cheek, whereas in truth she'd probably had her mini-skirt up round her ears, swinging her bra round her head whilst she sat firmly astride some bemused bog-brush salesman, joyously riding for England in the back of his Ford Capri.

Occasionally Piers would look up, frown and grunt something like, 'You went on an awful lot of dates, didn't you, darling?'

To which Penny would smile sweetly, lean across and murmur, 'An awful lot of boys were after me, darling,' at which point Hugo would leave the room, ramming two fingers down his throat in mock puke.

I looked at her now in her navy-blue skirt, Laura Ashley piecrust shirt, pearl earrings and velvet hairband with her nose in the airing cupboard, exuding not sex, but efficiency. It was a shame really. I actually much preferred the good-time girl who frolicked in the fields and was far less up-tight and inhibited, but then it was her marriage bed and she had to lie in it. Occasionally, especially on holiday, Penny would have a few drinks and let the mask slip and we'd have quite a laugh, because actually, when she wasn't being a pain in the tubes, Penny could be really good fun. I couldn't see much sign of a slipped mask right now, but as David had pointed out, we had three weeks to get through yet and it was crucial we at least started the holiday on the right foot even if we were at each other's throats by the end of it.

She handed me a pair of pyjamas. 'Here, these should fit her.'

I smiled. 'Thanks. Hey, sorry, Penny, I haven't even said hello properly yet. How are you anyway?' I gave her a hug. She instantly thawed and hugged me back.

'God, sorry Tess, I'm such an old bag I haven't given you a kiss either. I'm fine. A bit tired – I feel as though I've been preparing for this holiday for months now – freezing food and God knows what – but I'm bearing up. Have to, really. Piers hates whingers.'

I followed her back downstairs. 'It's all very well, but he'd whinge if he had to look after a four-year-old all day. These men don't realize how knackering children are.' I said this charitably, secretly thinking what a doddle it must be to have only the one – and Perfect Child at that. 'How is Leonora, by the way? I haven't seen her yet.'

'Oh she's fine, she's asleep.' Penny glowed. 'D'you know, she can count to a hundred already *and* write her full name and address and she's only just four, isn't that amazing?'

'Amazing,' I muttered, following her dispiritedly into the drawing room.

I flopped down into the huge armchair which was still exploding its usual quota of springs and stuffing, put my head back and gazed around. Suddenly I felt much better. Nothing had changed. I smiled.

It was a large room by any standards but the amount of furniture crammed into it was enough to make Crystal Palace seem snug. The two beaten-up old sofas were still either side of the fireplace, a couple of tatty leather armchairs were wedged in between, at least six hard wooden chairs were scattered elsewhere, and any surplus floor space was taken up by various coffee tables. The red threadbare carpet was thinner than ever, as were the rugs that covered the odd hole or stain that was really too disgusting to contemplate clearing up so was better covered. Above the fireplace hung the nondescript water-colour landscape with its unnaturally blue loch in the foreground and outrageously purple mountains behind, and around the other walls – in dire need, incidentally, of their five-yearly slap of magnolia – were those terrible drawings of salmon in various stages of gutting that Daddy had been conned into buying by some local artist years ago.

Down one entire side of the room was a waist-high bookcase, which was doing its usual melodramatic groan under the pressure of an eclectic half-hundredweight of books, all of which had been shoved in totally randomly, so that *Black Beauty* stood next to *Ulysses* which stood next to *A Cricket Pro's Lot* on top of which lay *The Secret Garden*. Just the other side of the room by the window, the huge mahogany cupboard was doing a competitive groan, creaking as it did with its boxes of Monopoly, Trivial Pursuit, Pick-up Sticks, Cribbage, Scrabble, jigsaws – most of which had at least one piece missing – and any number of table tennis bats, tennis rackets and balls. I sighed happily. It was, as David had said, relaxing in its timelessness, its dear familiarity.

At the far end of the room, opposite the fireplace, was a huge bay window with a window seat where Penny, Laura and I, years ago, had sat huddled for hours, clasping our knees, dreaming, plotting, arguing, laughing, and where our children now sat and did the same. The tatty chintz curtains still hung on a rusty rail around the bay. They were never pulled in case the rail collapsed – or the whole window, come to that – but then again, you'd never want to. Because the view from that window was breathtaking. Even now it dragged me up, tired as I was, from the armchair and pulled me across the room.

I rested my hands on the sill and gazed out. The lawn swept down from the house to the woods at the bottom, which in summer screened off most of the river. Just now and again though, you'd catch a glimpse of light, a bluey-grey flash of water. Rising up from the river on the other side was a steep bank, some fields, and then beyond that, the mountains. The light was fading fast now, but I could still make out the faint purple glow of the heather. I threw open the window and breathed deep.

'Aaah . . . that's better.' I turned and smiled at Penny. 'Still does the trick, doesn't it?'

'I'll say,' she said, wandering over, 'although these help too, of course.' She stood next to me and lit a cigarette.

I grinned. Piers was vehemently anti and had no idea his wife still smoked about ten cigarettes a day, another of Penny's little deceptions that gave one an idea of the state of Piers's brain cells and, incidentally, another bloody minefield. Penny was forever hastily handing lit cigarettes over as Piers walked in the room and then one had to go through a ghastly charade of: 'Oh – you mean this, Piers? Yes I had given up but I do have the odd one just now and then . . . yes, very silly I know . . . yes I know Penny's given up, isn't she marvellous?'

Piers obviously wasn't around right now because she was puffing away beside me like Thomas the Tank. I looked around.

'Where is everyone anyway? It's like the *Mary Celeste*.'

'They're all down at the river. First day enthusiasm – they'll probably still be fishing at midnight. Piers and David slipped down to meet the others when you arrived, they took Hugo with them for a breath of fresh air.'

'So who's here then, Mum and Dad?'

'Yep, and Laura and her new man.' She rolled her eyes expressively.

'She brought him – Edward?'

'She certainly did,' Penny said drily.

'Ah.' This didn't sound promising. 'So um, what d'you think?'

Penny tapped her cigarette ash out of the window. 'Well he's all right if you like white mice, I suppose. I mean, God – all I said was "Hello, you must be Edward", and he stepped back into the fire in fright. We had to spend the next five minutes stamping the carpet out. Where does she *find* these wet blankets, Tess?'

My heart sank. I had hoped that this one might perform just a little better than Gormless Martin had last year. 'I don't know,' I admitted. 'I really don't. Still,' I rallied, loyally, 'he might improve. It's only the first day and he's probably just a bit shy.'

'Don't give me that, Tess. You know damn well your sister's got extraordinary taste in men.'

'And your parents?' I went on, swiftly changing the subject. 'Are they here yet?'

'Sadly not,' she said in a small voice.

I looked at her quickly. 'What d'you mean? They are coming, aren't they?'

She shook her head, her eyes suddenly full of water. 'Not this year, I'm afraid. Daddy's taken a turn for the worse.'

She gulped and I threw my arms round her, hugging her hard. My own eyes welled up. I felt terribly, terribly sad. Penny's father, my darling Uncle Robert, had been in remission from cancer for some time. He'd battled against it for fifteen years now, when at the time they'd said he'd be dead in two. But he and Rachel had never given up.

'Is he in hospital?' I whispered.

'No. You know Daddy, he wouldn't hear of it. He's at home.' She blew her nose and laughed shakily. 'Mummy says he's even talking about getting over this little hiccup and joining us for the last week.'

'Well, there you are then!'

Penny blew her nose again noisily and shook her head. 'No,' she said quietly, stuffing her hanky up her sleeve. 'Mummy thinks this is really it now. But it could still be a few months, so they made me come up here. I'd much rather be with them, but for Leonora's sake . . .'

'Of course,' I said staunchly. 'You had to come, and if anything happens – I mean, if he gets worse – they'll ring, won't they?'

She nodded. 'And I'll fly back. I made Mummy promise she'd let me know the moment –' Her face suddenly crumpled. 'Oh God, Tess,' she gasped, 'I'll miss him so much!'

I clutched her close, as she fell into my arms, tears streaming down my face now. So would I. Oh so would I. Lovely, dear, kind Uncle Robert, with his mild manner and gentle ways, who always thought the best of anyone and would never hear the bad. Suddenly I felt frightened. I didn't like change. I wanted everything and everyone to stay just as they were, as they'd always been, like this house. It wouldn't be the same without Robert in it, hearing his voice as he helped Rachel wash up in the kitchen, or mended Hugo's bicycle in the hall. A quiet presence, so unlike my own father who couldn't enter a room without shouting, was preternaturally suspicious and generally thought the worst of everyone until proved otherwise. I jumped suddenly as his voice reached us through the open window. I looked over Penny's shoulder towards the river. I couldn't see anyone, but could hear Daddy's unmistakable tones rising above my son's wails. As I listened it took me sailing back. It could have been me, twenty-five years ago.

'Oh, for heaven's sake, Hugo, it's only a drop of water. Don't be such a ninny! If you're going to cry every time you get your feet wet there's no point in *having* a holiday by a river, is there? You might just as well stay in London!'

Out of the bushes emerged David, carrying a very soggy, tearful Hugo, followed by my father, hectoring away at him from behind.

'Now for goodness sake, brace up!'

I gave Penny a watery smile. 'Well some things never change, do they?'

Chapter Six

Supper that evening was the usual rowdy first night affair. We were down to eight without Robert and Rachel, but still managed to make as much noise and get through the usual staggering quota of Bulgarian Red. Piers brayed and roared and my father thumped the table for random emphasis as they both argued long and hard with David; two arch Conservatives against one rather lapsed, but essentially still socially conscious woolly Liberal.

'But it doesn't state anywhere that He didn't want women to become priests, does it?' persisted David.

'Of course it bloody doesn't!' exploded my father, 'because God never thought in a million years it would blinking well happen! Just as He didn't think it was worth jotting down that perverts can't become priests, or hamsters. I mean, some things just aren't worth wasting the parchment over. Some things you just take for granted! It never occurred to the Almighty that some idiot might one day think ordaining women was a *good* idea, otherwise He'd have put a clause in every bloody Scripture!'

David frowned over his glass. 'It's not the competition that worries you, is it, Ian?' he asked wickedly.

My father had unfortunately just taken a gulp of wine and couldn't answer this for seizing up with an outraged coughing fit.

Piers took up the mantle. 'OK David,' he demanded,

'how would you have felt about being married by a woman? Would that have bothered you?'

'Not in the slightest. In fact Clemmie was jolly nearly christened by a Deaconess in Putney but Ian felt so strongly about it we didn't do it in the end.'

'I'd rather she rotted in hell!' roared the Reverend, regaining his vocal cords and wiping wine off his chin with his napkin. He slapped the table. 'No grandchild of mine is going to be brought into the Christian faith by some jumped-up know-it-all female, because as far as I'm concerned, if she had, she'd still be a bloody heathen!'

Laura and I broke off our weighty debate on the pros and cons of Donna Karan's expensive, but effective, tummy-firming tights to raise our eyebrows at each other. Here we go again. Of course it was all academic because Clemmie was a heathen anyway. I glanced quickly round the table. Penny and Mummy were comparing carrot-cake recipes, Josie had retired early to bed, so that just left Edward who, with no one to talk to, had forged through his plate of roast lamb and was now trying to make a piece of broccoli last the ten minutes it would take everyone else to catch up.

I studied him surreptitiously under my fringe. I'd met him a couple of times before, once when he'd been to our house for a drink before going out to dinner with Laura and once when we'd all been to see a film, but the first time was brief and the second dark, so I'd never really had a chance to scrutinize him properly. He was blinking nervously behind his glasses, his rather sweet, boyish face pale beneath his freckles, his sandy hair flopping over one eye. God, he didn't look much older than Hugo and about a quarter as confident. I rifled around desperately for something to say. I'd already asked him if he enjoyed fishing, to which he'd blushed and replied he'd never done it before in his life, which of course put him at an immediate disadvantage since the rest of us had been flicking out straight lines with Farex on our trousers, and there's nothing quite so unsexy as a fumbling novice trying desperately to hoick his fly out of the gorse bush and then slapping it – *plop* – into the water followed by reams and reams of line flapping around like knitting wool. He caught my eye. I smiled warmly. He palpitated a bit behind the specs and smiled back. I smiled again. He smiled back. God, *say* something, Tess.

'Edward reminds me rather of Peter, that chap at the Chandlery, don't you think, Laura?' I said desperately.

Laura peered at her boyfriend as if she'd never seen him before in her life. 'No.'

'Oh come on, imagine him without the glasses.'

She peered again. Edward blushed and adjusted his glasses apologetically, as if he'd like nothing more than to smash them right there and then in order to look like Peter from the Chandlery. Anything to accommodate.

'No, nothing like.'

'Peter who?' demanded Penny, never letting man-talk pass her by.

'Peter who works at the Chandlery,' I explained patiently. 'I was just saying Edward looks a bit like him.'

Penny frowned at Edward. 'He's nothing like him. Honestly, Tess, you do talk rubbish. That chap's really tall and dark whereas Edward here's really –'

'No, not *that* one,' I said quickly, 'the other one, he works there on a Saturday. He's blondish with blue eyes and –'

'Oh, I know the one you mean,' said Laura suddenly. 'Yes, you *are* rather like him, Edward, around the eyes.' Edward inclined his head graciously, turning all the colours of a tropical sunset now, but clearly delighted Laura was reasonably pleased. 'Yes, he's got the same sort of thin hair as you. Penny, you must remember, you told us he's only got one –'

'More potatoes, Edward?' I said loudly, piling them on his plate and eyeing Laura sternly.

'One what?' asked Piers.

'Finger,' I said quickly. Laura had been about to say ball and I had the feeling Piers would want to know how Penny came by such classified information.

'Only one finger?' said Piers in surprise. Laura giggled. We spoke together.

'Frostbite.'

'Bacon-slicer.'

'Er, yes,' I went on. 'He was a very keen mountaineer and his fingers all got frostbite. They didn't actually drop off but they went a bit stiff and because they were so stiff he accidentally cut them off in the bacon-slicer.'

Piers stared. 'What was he doing with a bacon-slicer?'

'He worked in a butcher's.'

'Good grief. Sounds an odd sort of cove. Did you know this chap, Penny?'

'Not remotely,' Penny growled, looking thunderous. Laura was spluttering into her napkin.

'Plenty more veg, Edward. Here, have some broccoli.' I

beamed at what I could see of him behind the huge heap of vegetables I'd piled on his plate.

'Now tell me,' I went on brightly, 'what sort of a school d'you teach at, Edward? Is it one of those rather enlightened ones where you don't have to go to lessons if you don't want to, you just wander off and pick wild flowers and take recreational drugs?'

'Er, no I'm afraid it's a bit more structured than that.'

'Well, I should think from your point of view that's just as well. Imagine trying to round everyone up and detoxify them and –'

'I think I should like to have it off,' interrupted my mother abruptly.

We all looked at her, stunned.

'Mummy!' I gasped.

'I think if it were me, I'd like it off. The finger. So untidy, dangling like that.'

'Don't be silly, Daphne,' said my father. 'Much better to have one than none at all. I'm sure it was very useful, wasn't it, Penny? Who was this chappie, a boyfriend or something?'

Penny couldn't speak but she looked positively murderous now. Laura was crying into her wine as David quietly suggested all the ways in which it might be of use – hailing cabs, bidding at auctions, picking one's nose . . .

'Shut up, you two,' I said quickly. 'I'm asking Edward about his teaching.'

'He's at a comprehensive,' said my father, waving a fork in his general direction. 'I've already asked him,' he added as if Edward wasn't really with us. 'Can't get much out of him but I imagine it's one of those ghastly inner-city ones. Chap's probably a Communist or something, eh Laura?'

He turned to Laura for verification. She stopped spluttering and took a sip of wine. There was a silence. She blushed, as we'd both blushed for my father's blatant rudeness over the years. 'No, he's not,' she said shortly.

'But you're right, it is an inner-city school,' said Edward, rather bravely. 'It's in Tottenham.'

'Tottenham?' enquired my mother. 'And are you a fan?'

'Sorry?'

'Spurs – d'you support them?'

'Er, no.' Edward looked bewildered.

'Good. Bloody cad's game,' said my father. 'Well, that's one point in his favour, eh?'

'But I do support Sheffield Wednesday,' he added, even more bravely.

'Do you indeed?' purred my mother, as if he'd just said he had £300,000 a year and an estate in Gloucestershire. She gave him a twinkly smile. 'Good for you, Edward.'

My father harumphed. Piers was peering at Edward as if he'd only just noticed him.

'Is that where your people are?' he asked abruptly.

Edward jumped. 'My . . . people?' He had a dazed look on his face, wondering perhaps if Piers had somehow mistaken him for Big Chief Running Bull who'd left his people behind at the wigwam camp.

'Your family,' put in David kindly. 'Are they from Sheffield?'

'Oh! No, Streatham, mainly.'

'Really?' Piers raised his eyebrows incredulously then

inclined his head, mouth twitching. 'Well, I suppose some-one has to be,' he murmured.

'Teaching must be jolly hard work,' I went on, shooting Piers a venomous look and really, rather hating my family.

'Oh, er, it has its moments.'

'You must have to have infinite patience,' agreed David, helping me out. 'I'm sure I couldn't do it. I'd lose my rag with those kids in no time at all.'

'Actually you'd be brilliant,' I said, flashing him a grate-ful look. 'Remember when you wanted to teach? You were going to be a don.'

'That's a lot grander than teaching at a comprehensive,' said Edward, wildly turning his hand to a conversation.

'It may be grander but I should think it's a darn sight easier to teach a few nineteen-year-olds who are eager to learn than twenty rowdy fifteen-year-olds who haven't the slightest interest in anything other than skiving off school and playing football. I take my hat off to you, Edward. I imagine it's damned difficult.'

Edward began to glow under this sudden paean of praise for his chosen career, and even Laura began to look at him with renewed interest. 'Oh well,' he shrugged mod-estly, 'it's not too bad.'

'What exactly is it you specialize in?' I asked.

'Art.' He blushed some more. 'I teach art.'

'Really? Laura, you never said!' Laura shrugged, as if surprised it would be of any interest to anyone. 'Did you bring your paints with you? There's some fabulous scen-ery round here, you know.'

'I did, actually. I was hoping I might find time to do some sketching. Maybe even a few watercolours.'

'Ah well, Tess can show you all the best places for that, can't you, Tess?' said Penny slyly. 'All the etching hot spots?'

'Come on, Penny,' said David sharply. 'Get that port moving or we'll be here all night.'

'I shan't be,' said my mother, declining the port and dabbing her mouth with her napkin. 'I'm going to bed. I've got a lot to do tomorrow, especially if I'm going to find time to call on Madelaine Cameron.' She fumbled around on the floor for her handbag.

'Madelaine Cameron?' I said quickly. I looked at my father who'd gone a bit pale. 'Patrick's mother?'

'Yes,' she said, vaguely searching through the bag. 'Now her dreadful husband's died I thought I'd pop up and see her. Offer my condolences and all that. Now where did I put my reading glasses?' She began patting her cardigan pockets.

I could feel my colour rising. 'But why, Mum?'

'You'll do nothing of the sort, Daphne,' commanded my father suddenly. 'Leave well alone!'

'I certainly shall not,' she said quietly. 'Ah – here they are.' She reached into her skirt pocket, fished out her spectacles and made to leave the table. She smiled at the assembled company. 'Night, all.'

'I didn't know you knew her that well,' I blurted, aware that quite a few eyes, including David's, were on me.

'Oh yes, very well. We were good friends years ago, when she married that ghastly man, but we lost touch. Madelaine's a very nice woman. I shall ask her to tea next week.'

Daddy went puce. 'Daphne, I absolutely forbid it!'

'Oh, but it's undoubtedly the Christian thing to do, darling,' she said quietly, 'now that the poor woman's all alone.'

Daddy looked thunderous. 'She's *not* alone. She's got that wretched boy with her!'

'Ah, but not for long. I gather he's going back to Italy in a couple of weeks. He's become quite a successful artist over there, apparently. Has quite a following. There now, I think I've got everything. See you in the morning, and don't forget to turn the dishwasher on, will you, Penny dear?' She beamed at her niece.

'But Mummy,' I persisted, putting my hand on her arm as she made to leave the room, 'you can't just run up the hill and be her best friend after all these years!'

'Why not?' she said mildly.

'Because it'll look so . . . odd.'

My mother patted my hand. 'Not at all, dear. I think it's entirely natural to pay one's respects to one's old friends. It would look most odd if I didn't go. Now I'll hear no more about it from anyone, thank you!' And with that she removed my hand from her arm, gave her husband a pointed look and left the room.

A silence fell on the table as she went. Neither Patrick, nor his parents, had been mentioned for years in our family. Even my father was strangely quiet. I caught his eye, and he raised his eyebrows sheepishly. For once we were in agreement: we both knew there was no arguing with her when she was in this sort of mood.

Penny cleared her throat. 'Right, well I'm off too,' she said, getting up and clearing the plates. 'I'm knackered and I need an early night.'

I followed her out to the kitchen, bringing the rest of the plates with me.

'I'll do this, Penny,' I offered. 'You go to bed.'

'Sure?'

'Positive.'

She sighed. 'OK, thanks. I'm bushed, actually. I'll see you in the morning.'

When she'd gone I stacked the dirty plates in a pile by the dishwasher, and was about to put them in when I stopped and stared at them. Suddenly my eyes welled up, and for no reason at all except – oh God, everything really – I found I was fighting back tears. I took a deep breath and gazed out of the window into the dark night, biting my lip. Why did Mum have to go and stir everything up after all these years? To stir me up, more to the point. It was *my* past, the precious little there was of it, why couldn't she leave it alone? If she went to Gilduncan, Madelaine would undoubtedly come here and there was more than a chance I'd bang into Patrick. I'd certainly hear about him, for God's sake. And I didn't want to. Suddenly I felt afraid. I wanted to be back in Putney, tucking my children up in their own beds, to feel safe, secure. I didn't feel safe here. I felt as if someone was rattling my cage. Shaking my nest.

I picked up a plate and scraped it. Slowly I put them one by one in the dishwasher, trying not to think about what Mum had said. Just those few words had been enough to unsettle me. 'He's become quite a successful artist. Has quite a following.' I straightened up and gazed out of the window. So he wasn't an accountant after all. I tried not to, but I wondered what his studio was like. In

Florence, overlooking a square perhaps, one of those beautiful old, crumbling, terracotta buildings. High up, I saw Patrick hanging over the balcony, laughing, talking to someone below. It was a huge balcony full of sunlight and trailing bougainvillaea. Behind there were sunny, light rooms, full of friends, laughter, parties, flowing Chianti, pretty girls with long dark hair.

I crouched down and fished around under the sink for the dishwasher powder. The top came off in my hand and some spilled on the floor. Bugger. Still crouching, I stretched my hand up for a dishcloth in the sink and without looking, grabbed it, but the last person to use it hadn't washed it out and it was still covered in Clemmie's sick. I dropped it in disgust then tossed it into the bin. I got a new one out from under the sink, wiped the floor and tossed it back into the sink, not bothering to rinse it myself. I stared at it, lying there covered in dishwasher powder. And this was my lot, I thought, pursing my lips. This was the annual holiday I'd been so looking forward to. The absolute pinnacle of my year, my only release from the tedious routine of everyday life. Three weeks in Scotland with my bickering family who didn't even have the grace to make poor Edward feel welcome. Three weeks with Piers and his arrogant supercilious comments, with my father and his bombastic bullying ways, with Laura already abdicating all responsibility for her new man and hiding behind her silly giggles, Penny with her sly remarks, and now Mummy . . .

I shut the dishwasher door and turned it on. My mother. Most of the time so henpecked and browbeaten but just occasionally, like tonight, a complete law unto herself. An unguided missile that no one, not even my father, could stop. What was she up to? I heaved a great sigh. I for one had no idea. Oh well, only another twenty or so evenings like tonight to go. I bit my lip. Normally I looked forward to this holiday so much . . .

I shook my head as if to physically banish all rogue thoughts. The kitchen was tidy; I could go upstairs now – should go upstairs – but somehow I didn't feel like going to bed yet. Perhaps I could do with some fresh air? I walked slowly to the back door and hesitated. Who was I trying to kid? I knew I wanted to walk by the river in the dark, I also knew exactly where I wanted to go. And I knew why. To reminisce. I took my hand off the handle. No. That really would be madness. I turned back, and was about to switch off the lights and go upstairs when I spotted some ashtrays that needed emptying. I chucked the butts in the bin and took them to the sink, pausing as I did so to stare out of the window at the inky black sky. Perhaps just for a moment. Not right down to the river, just in the garden, and maybe as far as the woods. I quickly rinsed the last ashtray and turned off the tap. Suddenly I felt hands on my waist.

'Shit!' I jumped and dropped the ashtray in the sink. 'David, don't sneak up on me like that!'

'Sorry.' He looked surprised. 'I wasn't sneaking, I just came to find you. Everyone else has gone to bed. What are you doing down here on your own?'

'What does it look like?' I snapped. 'I'm clearing up. Someone has to, it doesn't happen by magic, you know.'

'Well, come on, you've done it now.' He took the ash-tray from me, seized a tea towel and dried it. 'Let's go to bed, it's gone midnight.'

'I will in a minute, I just want to wipe this floor. The children brought mud in from the river; it's filthy already – look.' I grabbed a cloth and bent down to wipe it, hiding my face.

'Josie can do that in the morning, can't she?' David put his arms round my waist and pulled me up from behind. He nuzzled into my hair. 'Come on,' he muttered. 'Put the damn dishcloth down and come to bed. We're supposed to be on holiday.'

I pulled my head away roughly. 'Oh, for heaven's sake, David – is that all you ever think about? Sex?'

He dropped his hands from my waist. I turned my head guiltily and saw his face. He raised his eyebrows, picking up an ancient copy of the *Spectator* from the table.

'Good Lord no,' he said lightly, 'hardly ever. How silly of me, I'd quite forgotten I'd had my quota for this month. I shan't be troubling you again until – oooh, the middle of September, or is that too soon?'

He tucked the *Spectator* under his arm and wandered out, but his back was rigid.

I groaned. 'Oh God, David, I'm sorry. I didn't mean to say that.'

He carried on walking.

'David!'

But he didn't turn back and I didn't go after him. I whirled round to the sink and threw in the dishcloth. Shit. Shit-shit-SHIT! I heard him going upstairs, then his foot-steps on the landing above me. A door closed. I stared blankly at some aubergines on the chopping board. Some-one had got them out and left them there to make into ratatouille in the morning. Suddenly I seized a large knife from the metallic rack and plunged it into the middle of one. Then I started hacking. I hack-hack-hacked away, spitting and snarling and cursing, until the whole work surface and most of the floor was covered in little bits of aubergine flesh. When I'd finished I felt a lot better. I threw the sad remains guiltily into the bin, wondering if I could blame the cat. Probably not. As I turned the lights off and went upstairs, I decided that if anyone asked, I'd just say I'd felt a bit peckish in the night.

Chapter Seven

Days passed and the holiday settled into its predictable routine. We fished, we ate, we fished some more, we ate some more, we played Scrabble and cards round the fire, we chatted, we went to bed. There was nowhere to go apart from the river or the beach, no television to watch and no dinner parties to attend. It was the perfect antidote to London life, and gradually our brittle urban nerves were soothed and softened as day after day we did little other than gaze into the dear familiar waters of the river Tarn and feel the warm breeze in our faces. We let the world slip by and we learned to relax. At least, most of us did.

For some reason I still felt restless. I felt as if I'd been doing all this for a thousand years and would still be doing it in a thousand years' time. I had a huge sense of here-we-go-again which irritated me because I'd been looking forward to this break. I did quite a lot of sighing and flopping down into chairs, was 'snappy' according to my husband and 'always in a strop' according to my children. Everything seemed to be such a huge effort, and all rather pointless. All that shopping in Invertarn for instance, heaving great bags of groceries home – and then all that cooking – and for what? Just so they could blinking well eat it! And all that washing and ironing and trekking down to the clothes line at the bottom of the garden with basketfuls of wet clothes – and again, for what? So they could wade in the river and frigging well make them dirty again!

When I expressed this sentiment to David, admittedly with a rather wild look in my eye on account of my third pre-dinner sherry, he regarded me over his *Times*, and murmured something about life being like that, really.

'Well perhaps I don't want it to be,' I snapped.

He gave me an odd sort of look and after that I learned to keep my own counsel. I went for a lot of walks and tried not to think too much. When I did think, I attempted to analyse my dissatisfaction and realized the problem was that I felt my life was marching on in a rather monotonous sort of manner. This shocked me a bit – heavens the last thing I wanted was a midlife crisis – so I tried to banish that rogue idea, but it would keep popping back. In the end I decided to consider it rationally. I racked my brains. Perhaps my life had always been monotonous and I'd only just noticed it? I rewound my lifespool back, three years, five years, ten. I sighed. No, I was sure that even then, even though I'd never exactly led a merry dance, I had at least pranced a bit, hadn't I? All right, shuffled. Perhaps not enough? Perhaps if I'd pranced and shuffled a bit more I wouldn't feel this bleak forced march so keenly?

My family, wisely, ignored me during these periods of introspection, and made Mummy's-in-one-of-her-moods faces at each other, presumably hoping I'd snap out of it, as indeed I hoped I would too.

There were other irritations too. In the space of a year Leonora's vocabulary had gone from strength to strength and now included words like *croissant* and *Wiener schnitzel*.

'I knew she'd be speaking French but I didn't expect

her to have German under her belt too,' I hissed in a paranoid fashion to David.

In the face of such fierce precociousness, my children instantly dug their heels in, went on strike and reverted to babbling babyhood, so that whilst Leonora was carefully winding spaghetti carbonara onto her fork, doing up all her buttons and saying please-may-I-leave-the-picnic-rug, mine were eating with their fingers, throwing themselves on sweetshop floors and holding their breath until their demands were met, peeing on the bathroom floor and generally acting like Vlad the Impaler.

'Hugo, for God's sake, aim!' I bellowed as I cleared up yet another puddle.

'I did aim,' he informed me. 'I was aiming at Leonora's shoes, but some of it must have leaked out.'

I stared, aghast, at the pair of urine-filled Mary-Jane Startrites, let out a Mohican-style shriek and sent him straight to bed, but nothing I could do or say would make them repent or change their course of action, which was, it transpired, to corrupt Perfect Child.

Hugo, who at eight was deeply anally fixated, would spend hours crouched beside her, furiously trying to teach her to fart, purple in the face from the exertion of demonstrating himself, and doing heaven knows what damage to his own sphincter, but all to no avail. Nature's trumpet would not sound.

'You're not pushing hard enough,' I heard him complain as he monitored her progress. 'I don't think you're even trying.'

'But if I push too hard I'll do a poo,' objected Leonora.

'Even better!' roared my son.

Poor Clemmie didn't fare much better. She wasted the best part of a morning patiently showing her pupil how to go through her mother's make-up bag, put powder on her face and quite a lot on the carpet, try on all the lipsticks and blunt them in the process and smother herself in Chanel No. 5. She then steered her over to Penny's jewellery box, decking her out in all her mother's pearls and losing an earring or two along the way – but Leonora simply refused to learn, and after a while wandered off to read her storybook or cut out paper-chain dollies. She was, it seemed, one of Nature's goody-goodies, a shattering revelation to two of Nature's baddy-baddies. I felt almost sorry for them as they crept into bed with me one morning and told me in shocked, whispered tones, how she didn't even like tomato ketchup, Mummeee, had never had a bag of crisps, didn't have a video and had never even heard of Mrs Goggins. The final straw came when she refused to raid the biscuit tin with them, at which point they gave up in disgust.

'You want to be careful, Penny,' I murmured, as we lay on the riverbank together, feeling the warm sun on our faces and vaguely keeping an eye on my two who were splashing around upstream. 'You'll turn that child into a freak. A social outcast.' I nodded over at Leonora, sitting quietly on her own listening to *Peter and the Wolf* on Hugo's Walkman.

'Nonsense,' snapped Penny. 'I'm teaching her to be an individual, not to slavishly follow the herd, that's all.'

'What does she do at parties then if she doesn't have jelly and ice cream and orange squash? Sit there with half an avocado and a Perrier?'

'She doesn't go to parties yet,' said Penny primly. 'She's only four years old. I'll cross that bridge when I come to it.'

'Doesn't go to parties? Good heavens, she's *already* a social outcast. Clemmie was on the party circuit at eleven months, she's been getting down to Musical Bumps since she could walk!'

'I dare say,' said Penny darkly, 'but then I'm not altogether sure I want a social butterfly for a daughter.'

'Had more of a cardiologist in mind, did you?'

'And why not?' retorted Penny.

'Why not indeed. I'm sure Leonora would make an excellent surgeon, I just can't help thinking if you push children too much they sort of burn themselves out, react against it, know what I mean?'

'Look, Tess, you bring up your children the way you think fit and I'll do the same – and incidentally, I'd be grateful if you'd restrain your son from inflicting his scatological obsessions on my daughter, it's not very –' She broke off in mid-rebuke to stare past me. 'Oh for God's sake look at that. It's pathetic,' she spat.

I sat up and followed her gaze upstream to where her middle-aged husband was teaching Josie and Edward to fish. Ostensibly he'd been teaching them both for the last four days, but in actual fact Edward's tuition had consisted of little more than a few cursory instructions yelled over Piers's shoulder. Josie's tuition, on the other hand, was far more demanding. She needed the full practical. Today her instructor had chosen to stand behind her, arms round her waist, hands gripping hers on the rod as he 'taught her from behind', quite a favoured method of his actually.

'Easy does it now,' we heard him coo as he nestled up close to her, cuddling into her rear. 'Take the rod back . . . gently, gently, and – flick!' The fly came down with a plop in the water followed by reams of tangled line.

'Oh I say, that was awfully good!' brayed Piers.

'Ah sheet! That was terrible!' shrieked Josie, going into peals of laughter.

'No no no! *Au contraire*,' gushed her instructor, 'I think you're definitely getting the wrist action. Now, let's try again, shall we? Only this time . . .' he eagerly clasped her again, legs pressing against her bare brown thighs in their high-cut denim shorts, 'this time, give it a bit more of a – flick!'

The fly came down again, still with a plop, but perhaps not quite so deafening.

'That's it! That's it!' chortled Piers, jumping up and down on the bank, clapping like an overgrown schoolboy. 'Absolutely first class!' He gave her a quick congratulatory squeeze round the waist. She shrieked with laughter. He moved in again, perhaps for another playful little hug, but as he did so, he caught the cold eye of his wife further downstream. His hands flinched off Josie's slim young waist as if it were molten lava, and one of them hoisted itself into the air in a nervous wave.

'Hello, darling,' he called.

'Good morning, Piers,' she responded coolly.

He came galloping over with a silly grin on his face, looking distinctly flushed. He flopped down next to us, panting a bit. 'Having a lovely time, my darling? Nice and relaxing?'

'Reasonably relaxing, Piers, but as you can see we do

seem to be looking after the children, which wasn't actually the idea since Tess did bring a nanny along for just that purpose.' She smiled thinly. 'But she seems to be otherwise engaged.'

'Ah yes, your nanny!' He turned to me. 'I say, *super* girl, Tess, *super* girl,' he enthused, somehow missing Penny's shovel-load of irony. 'Really – well – *jolly*. So much more fun than that Hungarian shot-putter type you brought last year.'

'Yes, but then the Hungarian shot-putter was frightfully good at other things, like cooking and cleaning and shovelling food in mouths and clearing up sick,' I said sweetly, 'but I do agree, not quite so *jolly*.'

'No, not at all. This new one's a real, well – treasure!' He turned eagerly to his wife. 'You're always banging on about getting some help, aren't you, poppet, and goodness knows, you girlies work so hard you really deserve it. How about asking Josie if she's got any nice friends, hmm?'

'Now don't you worry your head about my domestic arrangements,' purred Penny, patting his hand. 'You leave all that to me. I've got a nice Miss Mason coming back for a second interview when we get home. She's a bit deaf, but sweet, spinsterish. I think you'll like her and after a while you won't even notice her facial warts.'

Piers went a bit green. 'Ah ha ha,' he laughed nervously, scraping back his hair. 'Marvellous, terrific,' he muttered. 'Still, must get on – lots to do. Toodle-oo, my darling!' And he scampered hastily back to his pupil.

'Over my dead body,' said Penny darkly, lying down next to me again. 'Honestly, Tess, you must be mad having that creature in the house. David must walk around with a permanent hard-on.'

I grinned. 'God, you're insecure, Penny. Are you seriously telling me you wouldn't employ a pretty nanny in case Piers fancied her?'

'I certainly wouldn't want Claudia bloody Schiffer mincing down to breakfast in her baby-doll nightie, I can tell you that. I mean, look at her, Tess. A pink vest with no bra on, nipples sticking out like marbles, bottom spilling out of those shorts, it's positively indecent.' She folded her arms behind her head. 'But then I suppose you don't really care any more, do you?'

I frowned and turned my head towards her. 'What d'you mean?'

'Well, you don't really care who David fancies or whether he's frustrated or not. You've lost interest in that side of things, haven't you?'

I sat up, horrified. 'Penny! What on earth makes you say that?'

She shrugged. 'Intuition.' She shaded her eyes against the sun and stared at me. 'It's true, though, isn't it?'

'Of course it's not bloody true,' I spluttered, my eyes darting away from hers. 'David and I have a marvellous sex life, thank you very much.'

'Balls,' scoffed Penny. 'I bet you do it about twice a month, and that's because you feel you have to, just to keep things ticking over.'

'Oh, and I suppose you and Piers are swinging from the rafters every night, are you?'

She considered this. 'No, not every night, but we're still pretty active. Three or four times a week at least.'

'Three or four times a week!' I gasped. 'Good heavens, Penny, what are you on?'

She looked at me sideways. 'Lust. Remember that?'

I threw back my head and laughed hollowly. 'Lust! Crikey, yes, vaguely, somewhere in my dark and distant past. Before I spent my life looking after small children and wiping floors and tables and noses and bottoms and God knows what else. Wasn't it something to do with feeling a strange tingling sensation in your loins that spread all over your body and then doing a lot of panting and not being able to get up the stairs fast enough before you could tear your clothes off?'

'Thought it might ring a bell.'

'Only a very dull and distant one.' I smiled. 'No, Penny, I have to say, lust is fairly low on my list of priorities now. It's quite hard to fit it in between rag-rolling the kitchen, belting off to do the school run and doing battle in Sainsbury's.' I lay down again with a faint smile. So she was still just as keen to get her rooty-tooty, eh? Still got her brain lodged firmly between her legs.

'And you're not planning on experiencing it ever again?'

I looked across at her. 'What?'

'Lust. That's it then, is it? For ever – end of story?'

'Well no,' I blustered. 'We still have sex, we still love each other –'

'Not quite the same though, is it?'

'As what?'

'As it used to be. Bit stale and boring really, isn't it? Bit predictable.'

I stared at her. 'I'm not quite sure I know what you mean, Penny,' I said carefully.

'Oh, I think you do. But you don't really care. You've written it off. Been there, done that, on to the next thing. Something more grown up, like gardening. Or stencilling. Lust is for adolescents, isn't it?'

'Well, I –'

'You know what you need, don't you, Tess?'

'Penny, I don't know how or why we even embarked on this conversation, but to be honest I really don't want to discuss –'

'You need a damn good affair.'

I sat up and stared at her. 'Oh, don't be ridiculous!' I scoffed.

'Don't pretend it hasn't occurred to you. You blush every time his name is mentioned.'

I blushed obediently. 'Whose name?'

'Patrick's, of course.'

'As usual you're talking total crap,' I muttered.

'Am I?' She sat up next to me. 'Listen, Tess, if you ask me it's just what your marriage needs – a damn good kick in the butt. A bit of extra-curriculum wham-bam would do you the world of good. Let's face it, you've been thinking about him ever since you got here. Why don't you just go and do it, get it out of your system? You'll go back to David feeling amazingly sexy and rejuvenated and so incredibly guilty you'll be plying him with sexual favours, practising all your new techniques. I promise you, he won't know what's got into you but he won't give a damn because he'll think it's so terrific. It'll do you both the world of good.'

I stared at her, fascinated. 'Is that what you do then, Penny, when you're feeling a bit down? When the dusting gets a bit much, or the Hoover breaks down or you've OD'd on pyramid-selling jewellery parties? Go and learn a few new techniques?'

'Oh no,' she smiled smugly. 'I got all that out of my system long ago. I've had all the men I need; I'm quite satisfied with my husband now. You, on the other hand, have only ever been to bed with two men, haven't you?'

'Oh, for heaven's sake,' I groaned, 'if we're going to start counting conquests we'd better get a ruddy calculator out for you. You're being particularly childish now.'

I shut my eyes, pretending to sleep. I wished she'd be quiet. It was past midday now and the sun was burning. I could feel it hot on my eyelids. I stretched out on the grass and pulled up my skirt, letting it scorch my thighs. I tried not to think about Penny's idiotic ramblings and switched my mind instead to something else, tonight's supper for instance. I wondered if Coronation Chicken might be nice for a change, we hadn't had that yet and there was plenty of cold chicken in the fridge. With a salad.

'Anyway,' she murmured after a while, 'it's not really cheating, is it?'

'What?'

'You've done it with him before so it doesn't count. And you know what actors say – it doesn't count on location either, so there you go, you've escaped on two counts. Added to which, he'll be going back to Italy in a few weeks and you'll be off to London, so you'll never see him again. Perfect!'

I swivelled my head and stared at her. Her eyes were shut; she had a slight smile on her perfectly made-up lips.

'What are you, the devil dressed up as a Wentworth

housewife? Talk about stuffing the poisoned apple down my throat!'

She shrugged. 'Just trying to help. Just trying to save your marriage.'

'Penny, there's nothing wrong with my marriage! Just because I'm not salivating behind the front door waiting for David to get home from work so I can wrest his brief-case from his hand, rip open his suit, tear the shirt from his back and savage him on the doormat doesn't mean my blinking marriage is on the rocks!'

'No, not on the rocks, but shallow water I'd say. Sand-banking, perhaps.' She shrugged. 'It's not serious. All you need is to get your eye back on the ball again.' She giggled. 'Get a taste for it again. The problem with you, Tess, is you don't think sex is important. You'd rather be pruning your roses or making a bloody Coronation Chicken or something.'

I blinked. Coronation Chicken . . . Christ, how on earth had she –

'And what you don't realize,' she went on, 'is that those are the incidentals. The fillers-in, the things we're supposed to do to pass the time when we're not making love.'

'Oh, far out Pen, pull up a beanbag, what about giving peace a chance too?'

'Mummy!' Leonora called to her from further along the bank. She was having trouble getting her boots on.

Penny stood up. 'Oh, you can scoff, but you'll see I'm right in the end. You're just papering over the cracks at the moment, but something will give, it's bound to.'

'Oh really? And pray, tell me, when am I supposed to have this tempestuous affair, the one that's going to cement my marriage up like the Great Wall of China? In between making the cheese rolls for lunch and giving the children their bath, perhaps?'

'*Mummy!*'

Penny brushed her skirt off at the back. She smirked. 'Ah, well now you're talking How, and not If, Tess.' She winked. 'I'll leave the logistics to you.' She walked briskly off to help her daughter. 'Coming, darling!'

I stared after her. For a moment I felt a bit dazed, then I shook my head. I smiled. Dear old Penny. Quite the philosopher today, wasn't she? Fancy thinking sex with another man would help my marriage . . . Wasn't that just so typical of her? Who else, I wondered, would come up with a solution like that? As if I even *needed* a solution! There was nothing wrong with my marriage. I was just feeling – well, a bit down, that was all.

I watched as Penny helped Leonora on with her boots. She took her hand, then striding up to where Clemmie and Hugo were fishing with nets, shepherded them both briskly out of the river and sat them all down on a rug to have their lunch. I should have gone over and given her a hand, but somehow, I couldn't face the arguments over who wanted jam and not ham in the sandwiches, and counting who'd had the most biscuits today. Anyway, Josie was around. She could help for a change.

I got up and quietly slunk away in the opposite direction, along the riverbank. I rounded the bend and found a rock to sit on. I drew up my knees and rested my chin on them, smiling to myself as I watched the water rushing past; clear, bright and fast as it hurried over its bed of grey pebbles. Yes, dear old Pen. So naive, so simplistic, so convinced that sex was what made the world go round. She hadn't given a thought to loyalty or love or duty, or honour, or any of those rather more taxing words, but then Penny wasn't one to be taxed unless she had to be, was she? I envied her that in a way. She was a simple creature, at the mercy of her animal instincts. She saw an erotic opportunity and went for it, without considering the repercussions. I threw a pebble in the water and watched the water ring out around it.

What about the lies, the deceit an affair would involve – had she given a thought to that? And then afterwards, the guilt, the regret, the shame. But of course there wouldn't be any of that with Penny, would there? It wouldn't eat away at her afterwards because she had no moral sensibility. But I did. I was – well, I was more complex, I thought smugly, more cerebral if you like, and certainly more moral, and it was because of that that I'd no more have an affair than fly to the moon. I simply couldn't live with myself afterwards.

I pulled up a strand of grass and chewed it. And what about the old marriage vows, eh Pen? Forsaking all others and keeping only unto thee? Good heavens, Penny had never forsaken anyone in her life and she'd kept unto thee, thee and thee as a matter of principle! Before she was married, naturally. I was pretty sure she was telling the truth when she said she didn't indulge now, but as she pointed out, she didn't need to: she'd had her fill. She was full up, as it were.

I frowned and smoothed a bit of rock with my finger, gazing down at the shiny granite. Was there anything in that, I wondered? Was that why I was feeling a bit melancholy these days, because I hadn't indulged myself enough in the past? I stared into the bright water. No, of course not, and I wasn't about to indulge myself now either – and not because I hadn't satiated my appetite in the past like she had but because I didn't *want* to, didn't *need* to have an affair, thank you very much.

Suddenly I flushed. The very idea! Betray my lovely, loyal David, make a cuckold out of him, break my solemn promise, and for what? A quick roll in the hay? And me, a wife, a *mother* no less – what on earth was she thinking of? And she, practically my children's *aunt*, suggesting their mother took a lover! Suddenly I was angry. Angry that she'd even had the nerve to suggest it, had presumed to know what went on in my marriage bed. How dare she? Why had I let her talk to me like that? Instead of laughing it off and thinking 'dear old Pen' I should have told her where to get off, in no uncertain terms. And I would too, I determined, later on tonight. I'd have a quiet word with her in the kitchen, or a noisy one if need be, and tell her to mind her own bloody business. It wasn't as if I even *wanted* to go to bed with Patrick Cameron. The whole idea was absurd. I was quite happy going to bed with my own husband, thank you very much.

As if to prove it, I flashed up a quick picture of David and me in bed together, recalling the last time, which would have been – ooh, a couple of weeks ago. Yes, that's right, a Saturday morning while the children were downstairs watching *The Flintstones* and very nice it had been too. A warm glow came over me as I remembered. Hmm, lovely, apart from Clemmie bursting in like that at the last minute and asking me to mend her doll's leg – '*Now* please,

Mummy.' Other than that it had been just fine, no complaints whatsoever.

I smiled. I know, just for fun, just for Penny's sake, why not summon up another little snapshot, one of Patrick and me together? Where should we be . . . in a hayloft, perhaps? Would that be rural and tacky enough for her? Lots of tickly straw, was that what she had in mind? We'd both have to be semi-naked, of course, lots of hastily discarded clothing, and I suppose we'd be writhing around a bit, locked in some kind of athletic embrace, skin on skin, bodies hot, wet and – *Whooooosh!* I gasped as a bucketful of adrenalin suddenly shot up the back of my legs. I wobbled and clutched the rock. Crumbs, that had been a bit more than a warm glow, hadn't it? I looked around nervously. Talk about wiping the smile off my face.

I blinked, adjusted my skirt and settled myself on the rock again. Blimey. I wouldn't be trying that again in a hurry . . . or would I? I bit my lip. Perhaps I should take another look, just to make sure I wasn't mistaken, that it hadn't just been my tummy rumbling? My mind needed no further prompting: it fled guiltily, back to the hayloft scene. Ah yes, there was Patrick, lying propped up on one elbow now, his chest bare – I made sure he had his trousers on this time though – and he was smiling down at me, fondly, but not too lecherously. I paused, testing my reactions. OK, Tess? Yes, fine, I was fine, carry on. So – there he was, leaning over me in the hay, pushing a strand of hair out of my eyes, smiling, stroking my face with the back of his hand. His fingers traced slowly down my neck, moving towards my bare shoulder, pausing, slipping downwards, caressing my – God, it was happening again!

This time I jumped clean off the rock because as well as all that adrenalin sloshing around I had a tingling sensation in my loins which was spreading to the rest of my body and – heavens, I was *panting*! Any minute now I'd be sticking my tongue out like a dog. I felt hot, flustered and very excited. Unnerved, I sat down abruptly on the grass and listened hard to my body. My heart was thumping away madly now and the dull bell that had rung so faintly recently was suddenly clanging loudly and very persistently indeed. Lust!

Abruptly I swung around and stared at the river. A moorhen was dipping and diving amongst the reeds on the other side. I gazed intently, knowing it was very important to keep that moorhen at the very forefront of my mind. Was it looking for fish, I wondered? Where was its warren, or whatever it was it slept in? What were its mating hab– no! I mean its migratory habits? Gradually my heart stopped pounding and my pulses ceased throbbing. I got unsteadily to my feet.

At *my* age, I thought as I brushed off my skirt. At my age, lust! What was I thinking of? Well, sex, clearly, that's what had done it, but really, after eight years of marriage and two children, it was a little *outré* to get in such a state, wasn't it? I walked on.

Or had I, I wondered after a while. Perhaps the sun had just been a bit much for me . . . It was remarkably warm for the time of year, wasn't it? I felt my forehead – hot, yes. And I'd had no lunch of course, an empty stomach always made me feel a bit dicky. Silly to think it might have been anything else. And there again Penny's idiotic ramblings hadn't helped much either . . .

As I rounded the next bend I came across the main pool at the top of the river. This was where the real fishermen gathered. Standing on the bank today were my mother, Laura and Willie, son of the old gillie, Hamish, who'd handed over the running of the river to his son a few years ago. Further upstream I spotted Hamish too, a huge, grey-haired old man gazing intently into the river, watching for signs of life. It was Hamish who'd really taught me to fish. Years ago, when Laura and I were children, he'd stood on the bank for hours beside us, watching us cast, quietly instructing us, and whereas my father had always given up with a shout of irritation after we'd tangled our lines for the millionth time, Hamish didn't. He patiently unravelled them and encouraged us to have another go, until eventually we flicked out something resembling a straight line. Although he'd retired now he still came to help out now and again, particularly when us Fergussons were fishing. It was as if he were unable to let the river go, and perhaps my family with it. I crept up quietly and stood behind them. These were serious fishers. I was glad I'd found them: it gave me something to fix on.

I watched Mum and Laura as they stood a few yards apart in the sunshine, even from the back, so alike. The way they stood, one leg resting, the tilt of their heads, both small and yet both so elegant. Mum, with her silver hair pushed up under an old felt hat of Dad's, and Laura, effortlessly stylish in a Barbour but with a baseball hat pulled firmly over her blonde hair, as if to cock a snook at being too green-wellied.

Willie stood next to my mother, looking on approvingly as she cast expertly upstream and let the fly drift down. He towered above both the women, tall, broad and fair. He could only have been in his early thirties, but his face was already weathered by years of working the river, tending the fish, supervising the rods.

'Caught anything?' I whispered.

'Not a sausage,' murmured my mother. 'If you ask me the river's empty although Willie assures me otherwise.' She grinned in his direction.

'Och, there's fish there orright,' he affirmed. 'It's just catching 'em that's the bugger. And this hot weather dinny help much either.' He looked at the sky. 'What we need's a drop o' rain.'

I smiled. Every year since I could remember we'd have this conversation with the gillie and spend the whole of August, when most people were desperate for sun, praying for a drop of rain to swell the river.

'Ah well, if you will work on a spate river, Willie,' I teased.

'I dunno none better,' he retorted, rising to the bait as usual. 'I'd rather work this one than some bloody river where it don't matter what the weather's doing – where's the fun in that?'

'Where indeed,' I agreed, although I secretly thought there might be quite a lot of fun in actually catching a salmon or two now and then. We stood in silence. A dragonfly whirred off in the bulrushes in front of us.

'Children all right?' murmured my mother, after a while.

'Fine. They're with Penny.'

I watched as she cast out again, straight as a die, over to the other bank.

'Mum?'

'Hmmm?'

I kept my eye firmly on her fly. 'Did you ask Madelaine Cameron to tea in the end?'

'Yes – why?'

'Oh, no reason.' I paused, waiting for her to elaborate. She didn't.

'When's she coming?'

'Tomorrow afternoon.'

I watched the fly drift downstream. It got caught in the rushes.

'Damn.' She gave it a tug but it was stuck fast. 'Why, darling?'

'Oh, I just wondered.'

I turned and walked for home.

Chapter Eight

David frowned into his Bran Flakes. 'Tess, I do think at the very least you should check him out. We can't have her tearing around the countryside with any Tom, Dick or Harry.'

'I agree,' said Piers staunchly, stabbing his boiled egg with a soldier.

'David, it's none of our business where Josie goes or who she goes with. She does what she likes in London when she has time off, so what difference does it make up here?'

The men were hurt. Feathers had been ruffled. Josie had met a boy in a pub, a young boy, and by all accounts he was taking her out tonight.

'But a bike boy,' muttered Piers peevishly.

'Vrmmm vrmmm!' I giggled.

'All I'm saying,' said David patiently, 'is that we should meet him first, find out a bit more about him, that's all.'

'Ask him what his intentions are? David, she's your nanny, not your daughter, but I dare say he'll pick her up from here tonight on his Harley-Davidson, you can just flip up his visor and ask him what the devil he thinks he's up to.'

The men flinched at this allusion to the bike, conjuring up as it did visions of youth, freedom, irresponsibility, power throbbing between still-taut thighs, black leather and undoubtedly, more hair.

At that moment, Josie popped her own tumbling blonde mane round the breakfast-room door and a palpable frisson ran through the assembled male company.

'I've dressed the kids, Tess – is there anything else you want me to do? Otherwise I think I'll have a bath.'

At the mention of his goddess, supine and naked in warm water, Piers swooned visibly, swept back his own thinning head of hair and fixed her with mad, lustful eyes.

'No, you go ahead, Josie. I'll clear up here and when you've had your bath perhaps you could give me a hand with the picnic.'

'Sure, no problem.'

'I should think so too,' muttered Penny who was sitting next to me. 'Oh, and Josie . . .' She reached into a Boots carrier bag at her side and handed her a packet. 'On your way up, put these in the upstairs loo, would you?'

Josie stared at them. 'Sure, what are they?'

Penny gave a thin smile. 'Medicated disposable lavatory-seat covers, of course.'

'Penny!' I gasped in horror.

'It's no good looking like that, Tess. You really can't be too careful these days, you know.'

'Oh, for heaven's sake, Penny,' I spluttered, 'we're family!'

'Edward's not, is he,' she hissed, 'and who knows where he's been? Laura has after all had an awful lot of boyfriends and I'm not convinced this one's in the best of health. He does a hell of a lot of scratching and his personal body odour lends itself more to rotting cabbage than – Ah, good morning, Edward. We were just talking about you!'

Edward sidled nervously up to the table scratching his

head and dislodging a certain amount of dandruff. It spiralled around in the beam of sunlight coming through the window.

'Morning,' he muttered.

'Morning!' barked Piers and David in unison as a wall of newsprint went up. They didn't like talking at breakfast at the best of times and Edward, in his bobbly Fair-Isle woolly, blinking sheepishly behind his specs wasn't much of a replacement for the fair Josie, it had to be said.

'Good morning, Edward,' I said cheerfully. 'Come and sit down.' I patted a chair beside me.

He slipped in gratefully, smelling, I had to admit, distinctly ripe.

'Now,' I went on, 'there's the usual toast and cereal, or if you can stomach it I made some lumpy porridge earlier. It's over there on the hotplate, but don't feel you have to.'

'Sounds delicious!' He got to his feet eagerly, keen to please, and lunged towards the sideboard where he began to clatter around with bowls and lids.

'Ow!' There was a resounding crash.

'The lid's hot,' I murmured.

'Sorry, dropped it!'

The newsprint didn't flicker for an instant but my mother, nearest the sideboard, slipped out of her chair and got up to give him a hand. She retrieved the lid, put it back and picked up the bowls. Then she took one, filled it with porridge and handed it to him.

'Looking forward to giving you a good thrashing on Saturday, Edward,' she murmured.

Edward leaped as if he'd been stuck in the buttocks with a pin and as he did, the bowl of porridge leaped too, jerking out of his nervous grasp, flying up into the air, somersaulting, then crashing down onto the floor, splattering everywhere.

'Dear dear.' Mummy reached for a cloth.

'What did you say?' he gasped.

'On Saturday. We're playing you at Villa Park in the League Cup. Don't think you've got a leg to stand on myself.'

I suppressed a giggle as Edward tried to regain his composure. There was porridge on the hotplate, the wall, the window, my mother's shoes, her skirt and all over the floor. At the table, no one even murmured. They might have been a clutch of Trappist monks sworn to silence.

'Oh! Oh yes, right! Er, should be a good game. Gosh, I'm so sorry, Mrs Fergusson. What a mess. Here, let me –' He looked around desperately for another cloth.

'No dear, that's Penny's headscarf.' Mummy quickly seized the square of Gucci silk from his sweaty hand and I felt Penny freeze next to me.

'Here, just take your porridge,' she ordered, 'and eat it while it's hot, there's a good boy. I'll clear this up.' She turned him round by his shoulders like a child and pointed him at his seat, raising her eyebrows at me in despair.

'So Edward,' I began cheerfully as he shuffled in beside me, 'going fishing again today? Looking forward to landing your first salmon?'

He reached forward for the orange juice and emptied the carton into his glass. 'Oh yes, I'd love to,' he said eagerly. 'I'm not sure I'd have the expertise to land it, but – oh!' He peered into the carton. 'Oh I say, I'm awfully sorry, I've taken all the orange juice. Um, would anyone like some – some of mine? Or can I get some more from the kitchen?' His bottom came up once more and hovered over his chair. 'I'll do that then, shall I? I'll just slip out and –'

'Edward, just sit down,' I said exasperated. 'We've all had ours. Now, what about going up to the top pool today, where Laura was yesterday? I'm sure she'll show you where it is. Where is Laura, incidentally?'

'I'm not sure. Actually I was going to ask you.' He blushed.

'Is she up yet?'

'Er . . . to tell you the truth I've no idea.' He blushed some more and spooned away at his porridge.

Oh hell. They clearly weren't even sharing a room now. Had Laura moved out? What was going on?

'She was up early,' muttered Piers from behind the *Telegraph*. 'She's gone fishing with your father.'

'Ah!' exclaimed Edward and I in unison as if we'd hit upon the Holy Grail. 'Oh well,' I went on brightly, 'if she's gone with Dad, how about fishing with me today?'

'Er, well, actually I thought I might take my sketchpad out, do some drawing, if – if that's all right?'

'Marvellous idea,' I said quickly, flooding with relief. 'Lovely day for it.'

Lovely day for sitting on your own having been abandoned by your girlfriend and thrust in the midst of her not particularly friendly family, I thought as I cleared the plates.

As soon as Edward had been dispatched with sandwiches and a flask of coffee like a small boy and the real children organized with buckets and spades to go to the beach with Josie, I hurried off to find Laura. Sure enough, she was at her favourite spot high up at the start of the river. Dad was ten or fifteen yards downstream of her standing right in the middle of the water in his waders. He waved and I waved back. I strode up to my sister.

'Edward's been looking for you.'

'Well, here I am,' she murmured, casting towards the opposite bank. 'He can come and find me, can't he?'

'Oh, that's really friendly, isn't it,' I snapped. '"He can come and find me, can't he." What's the matter with you, Laura? Why are you treating him as if he's got the plague?'

'I told you in London, I've gone off him.'

'Why did you bring him then?' I said, exasperated. 'You always do this, Laura.'

'He wanted to come. Said he'd been looking forward to it. Thought everything would be all right once we got here – once I'd relaxed, as he put it. I knew it wouldn't, I knew it would be worse, but he pleaded, so I let him come.' She calmly drew her line back and cast again.

'So now you've chucked him out of your room?'

'Not at all. I merely suggested he might like to sleep next door.'

'But that's so em*barr*assing for him, Laura. Everyone *knows*. Couldn't you just lie next to him, keep up the pretence?'

'No, I couldn't. I find him physically repulsive. If you must know, I was finding it hard to go to sleep without puking on him.'

'Oh, don't be so melodramatic! You must have fancied him at some stage.'

'I think I must have been drunk.'

'What, permanently? You went out with him for two months, didn't you?'

'Clearly.'

'Clearly what?'

'Clearly I was permanently drunk,' she said lightly.

'Laura, you're being deliberately obtuse. Why do you always *do* this?'

'Do what?'

'This. Bring some poor chap up here and dump him the moment you arrive.'

'I don't *always* do it.'

'Well, you did last year. Remember the cringing chiropodist?'

'He was clinically insane,' she said calmly.

'And before that, Toby with the one eyebrow that went from ear to ear, and Clive the enthusiastic potholer who brought all his kit up thinking the Highlands would be full of holes – oh, and that tubby one, Martin, who laughed before you could even get the joke out, and –'

'Oh, all *right*!' Laura suddenly flung her rod down. 'All *right*, Tess, so I make a mess of my love life. Fine, OK, I admit it – what do you want from me?'

'Nothing, I'm just –'

'Just pointing out my shortcomings in the boyfriend department, my propensity to pick no-hopers, my lack of a proper partner, my inability to find Mr Right – yes, well I know all that, thank you very much, OK?' She glared at me. There were two very bright pink spots in her cheeks.

'Laura,' I said patiently, 'I'm doing nothing of the sort. I'm merely trying –'

'Oh, it's all right for you, isn't it?' she broke in angrily.

'You, who've only ever had two love affairs in your whole life, both of which were the ultimate, both of which were perfect! The first one lodged neatly in your memory for you to look back on fondly and the second one by your side for the rest of your life – well, lucky you! But life's not like that for the rest of us, you know. It's a bloody jungle out there. There are so many predatory bastards trying to lure you back to their lairs it's not true, and while you're tiptoeing past those you get snared by another type, the ones lying low, the ones who've disguised themselves in beards and anoraks, the quiet shy ones who on the surface seem terribly kind and nice but underneath are so horribly weak and insecure they've got even more hang-ups than you have!'

'Oh, come on, Laura, there must be something in between.'

'*Find* me one, Tess, and I'll believe you. You're so bloody sure and smug, you just *find* me one.'

She picked up her rod and wound the line in furiously. She cast again. I watched her.

'Those bastards that you're so terrified of,' I said after a while. 'What are they like?'

'You want me to pick a bastard?'

'No, I'm just saying, since you insist there are only two types of men and you religiously bring home the anorak type which seems to end in tears, what about giving the bastard type a go? You never know, you might find one with a soft centre.'

There was a silence.

'Like Dad, you mean?'

I stared at her. 'What d'you mean, like Dad?'

'Tess, if you think I'm going to let some tyrannical bully boss me around for the rest of my life just because now and again there's a flash of humility, you're wrong. I'm not going to spend my life waiting for the odd flash.'

I groaned. 'God, Laura, I had no idea we had a psychological problem here!'

'We do *not* have a psychological problem and there's no "we" about it. This is my life, thank you very much, and if you don't mind I'll sort it out for myself!'

With that she reeled in her line, seized her fishing bag and stalked off down the river. I chased after her.

'Laura! Laura – wait, don't be so bloody silly!' I caught up with her and grabbed her arm. I swung her around to face me. She had tears in her eyes. She stared past me, over my shoulder.

'It's all right for you,' she sniffed, 'but oh God, Tess, you have no idea! I'm so terrified of getting it wrong. Of making a mistake.'

I put my arms round her and hugged her hard. 'You old silly,' I murmured. 'Why on earth would you do that?'

'Well, Mum has, hasn't she?'

'Has she?' I was shocked. It struck me, not for the first time, that Laura and Mum were very close.

She nodded. 'I think so, and I think she thinks so too.' She pulled back, fished a hanky out of her pocket and blew her nose. 'Come on, Tess, how would you like to be married to Dad?'

I glanced across at him, legs apart, up to his thighs in water, cap pulled right down over his eyes, mouth set in a determined line. 'Well, no, but – well, he's just our dad, isn't he? We can't change that.'

I'd never really thought about it. It wasn't as if Mum ever complained; she was always so – stoical. Laura clenched her fists.

'But you see, I don't *want* that! I don't want my children to think – he's just our dad – I want them to adore him! I want him to be perfect!'

I shook my head in amazement. 'Laura, this is no way to fall in love. You're not out there choosing a piece of furniture. You don't take a cool, calculated look from all angles and wonder if he's going to make a good husband or a good father. You don't try the drawers, examine the hinges and then say, "Yes, that'll do nicely, I'll take it." You meet someone, the thunderbolt hits you splat between the eyes and wham bam you fall in love!'

Laura gave a hoot of derision. 'Oh, don't make me laugh. In Mills and Boon books, maybe, and maybe even in your life, but take it from me, the majority of us mortals struggle on out there without even feeling half a volt, let alone a thunderbolt.'

'But you won't let it happen, Laura,' I urged. 'You've got to stop tiptoeing around, you've got to be open to the so-called bastards once in a while, just in case. I mean, for God's sake, you're beautiful, you're intelligent, you could have anyone. You can't just keep playing it safe and hanging around with doormats or you'll never fall in love, and apart from anything else it must be so depressing!'

She bent down and started putting her flies away in her tin. She picked up a rather beautiful one, peacock blue with a gold streak, and stared at it. 'It is,' she said in a small voice.

'Well then, for God's sake be true to yourself! Make

yourself available to the hunks, the sexy ones with the chiselled chins and smouldering eyes – so what if he's got a Porsche, a pad in Knightsbridge and a Gold American Express Card – you'll get over it! You'll struggle through the dinners at le Gavroche and the nights out at Annabel's; you'll maybe even get used to the yacht in the Bahamas. I promise, once you get the hang of it, it'll be a breeze!'

She was sniffing again. I bit my lip. Stop it, Tess. She was unhappy and I was getting into my Mickey-taking stride, enjoying the sound of my own acerbic tongue. Why did I always do that? She straightened up and I gave her a guilty hug. 'Sorry,' I muttered.

She sniffed into my hair. 'No, you're right. Someone has to say it. I'm a coward. An emotional coward. A scaredy-cat, as Hugo would say.'

'Sitting on an Edward doormat.' I clapped my hand to my mouth, horrified at the vision. 'Oooh Laura,' I groaned, 'I don't know how you can.'

She gave a wry smile and swung her bag over her shoulder. 'Oh, I just think of it as charity work. Administering to the needy, the less fortunate.'

We wandered back downstream together arm in arm. For a while neither of us said anything. Eventually I broke the silence.

'And have you really never felt anything like I described?' I said tentatively.

She sighed. 'Oh yes. Once.'

I looked up quickly. 'And?' I knew better than to make that, 'Who?'

She shrugged. 'And it wasn't reciprocated.' She smiled perceptibly. 'I made a complete fool of myself, if you must know.'

I nodded and left it at that. She wouldn't elaborate, I knew. I wondered if Mum would know anything about it? I'd ask her. Sometimes I got so wrapped up in my own life and my own children I forgot about Laura. Except on holiday, of course, when I lectured her. I sighed. More guilt.

'Oh well,' I said brightly, 'at least you know you *can* feel like that – that's a start, surely? I mean, better to have loved and lost than –'

'Oh please, Tess,' she widened her eyes in mock horror, 'spare me *that*!'

I grinned back. At least she was smiling again. 'OK. No clichés, but listen, no more doormats either, all right? Promise me that at least. I'd rather you were celibate than doing charity work with another of those wallys who shake your hand like a piece of jelly.'

She giggled. 'OK. No more wallys.'

'But,' I wagged a finger schoolmarmishly, 'in the meantime you could at least be civil to the wally you've brought on holiday. You don't have to sleep with him but you could at least bare your teeth at him occasionally, toss him a civil word or two. It wouldn't hurt to –'

Laura put her hand on my arm. 'Sshh! Talk of the devil,' she murmured.

I looked up, horrified. Sure enough, just around the next bend, slightly hidden from view amongst the gorse bushes was Edward, perched on a little collapsible stool sketching the mountains. His knees were practically touching his chin on the ridiculous seat and he looked like a little gnome.

'D'you think he heard?' I hissed.

She shook her head. Suddenly he glanced up and saw us. I nudged Laura in the ribs. Her hand shot up in the air.

'Hi there!' she called.

Edward looked surprised, then flushed with pleasure. 'Hi!'

He stood up – too eagerly – and knocked his stool over. As he turned to pick it up he kicked over his open flask. He made a desperate lunge to stop it soaking his sketch pad, but as he did so, his glasses slipped down his nose, off his face and into the drink. He seized them and, clearly not wanting to be at any more of a disadvantage – like blind – rammed them back on again, coffee and all.

'Give me strength,' muttered Laura as it dripped down his face.

'Be *nice*,' I counselled her.

She grinned and galloped gallantly over to help him pick up his things, wipe his glasses and calm his nerves. I watched her raise a hopeful smile from him and even – good grief – a laugh, then I turned and made for home.

It was all very well, I thought to myself as I strode through the woods back to the house, this bossiness, this sorting out of other people's lives, this preaching the word about being true to oneself . . . but how true was I going to be to myself, eh? I strode up the gravel path. Answer me that one, Tess. I didn't, because I had a sneaky feeling that, 'Too true,' was the answer, but at this stage I was damned if I was going to admit it. Least of all, I thought as I pushed open the back door, to myself.

Chapter Nine

'Tess, this is Madelaine Cameron.'

I stopped mid-stride. I was making my way down the hall to the rod room to relieve myself of my wet boots and clothes and had to backtrack a bit to peer through the open drawing-room door. My mother and another woman were sitting either side of the fire drinking coffee.

'Oh!' I stared in surprise. 'I – I thought you were coming for tea.'

Madelaine smiled broadly. 'I was, but at the last minute something came up so your mother invited me to lunch instead.'

'Oh!'

'Darling, don't just stand there dripping water. Go and take your boots off and come and join us,' admonished my mother.

'I will. I'm just . . .' Just staggered by the sheer beauty and elegance of this woman who was absolutely nothing like I'd imagined.

In the first place she wasn't hefty and tweedy, dressed from head to toe in lovat green with a headscarf covered in horsy paraphernalia and a couple of black Labs at her heels, and in the second place she didn't have a commanding thigh-slapping manner and a county accent. This woman was slim, petite, expensively and elegantly dressed in a nut-brown cashmere polo neck and a camel knee-length skirt. Her legs were slim, encased in sheer silk and crossed at the ankle, her ash-grey hair waved softly behind her ears, her skin was almost translucent and her eyes were clear and blue like Patrick's. She looked about forty but must have been more like sixty, but what was even more staggering was that she was clearly French.

'Tess,' said my mother again uncomfortably, as I gaped.

'Yes! Right! I'll be back in a minute.' I hastened to the rod room and was back a moment later.

'Sorry for staring,' I said as I came back in, extending my hand towards her and hoping it wasn't too grubby, 'but you're not a bit like I imagined.' Either I came clean, I'd decided, or she'd forever think I was an open-mouthed, gormless nutter.

Madelaine laughed and shook my hand. 'Ah, I think you were expecting someone a leetle more traditional? A leetle more English, yes?'

I sat down, noticing that Mummy had managed to give her the exploding armchair and that the springs were even now attacking her expensive cashmere arms.

'Well, yes, or Scottish I suppose, but I'm very relieved to find you're not. I should think there are quite enough people round here who can trace themselves back to Bonnie Prince Charlie and permanently reek of haggis. They must regard you as a breath of fresh air.'

She shrugged and grimaced. 'Too fresh, I theenk. You know, unless your ancestors went to school with Macbeth you will always be a stranger in these parts.' She smiled ruefully. 'But of course I didn't discover that until I married.'

At the mention of her marriage I remembered. 'I – was sorry to hear about your husband,' I said quickly.

She inclined her head in acknowledgement. 'Thank you.' She reached down into her handbag and took out a packet of Gauloises. I watched as she lit one and blew a thin line of blue smoke high into the air. I was impressed, having only ever seen cool French adolescents indulge before, but then, Madelaine was, I decided, essentially cool. She uncrossed her slim stockinged legs and regarded me quizzically with her bright blue eyes.

'And you, if I may say so, my dear, are not at all as I imagined either.'

I flushed and instinctively pulled David's fishing jumper down over my thighs. This was the *quid pro quo* of course and I was at a distinct disadvantage. I'd assumed I'd have time to wash and change before she arrived at teatime; as it was, my hair hadn't seen a shampoo bottle for a week and I must reek of the river. I brushed a tangled lock out of my eyes.

'Oh, er, really? In what way?' Knowing, of course, that she could only mean in the unattractive, ungroomed, smelly sort of way.

She frowned. 'I had imagined you would be more of a cringing violet.'

'Oh! Er, d'you mean shrinking?'

'Exactly! You are more forthright, more self-assured. I thought you'd be rather . . .' she searched for a word and tried one '. . . demure?'

Mum laughed. 'I don't think anyone could call Tess demure.'

'I was once,' I said abruptly. I knew what Madelaine was

talking about. 'When I was younger. I didn't always have the courage of my convictions.'

'Ah, but sometimes it is more courageous to do the right thing, than rebel and do the wrong thing, you know,' she said softly, meeting my eye.

There was a silence. Her hand slipped towards the coffee table and picked up a photograph. 'We've been looking at your lovely family, Tess.'

I glanced across. Mum had obviously found some pictures of Hugo and Clemmie.

'They're beautiful,' she went on. 'I am very envious of Daphne having grandchildren anyway, but to have such divine ones is too much.' She shook her head ruefully.

I waited, wondering if this would be the moment for her to bring up Patrick, to rebuke him for not providing her with a daughter-in-law, grandchildren.

'And this is your husband?' she went on, peering closer.

I leaned over to see. Oh, for heaven's sake. David appeared to be asleep in a deckchair with his mouth wide open and Clemmie and Hugo had clearly taken advantage of this to put a half-empty bog-roll in his mouth and an old loo seat round his neck. They were doubled up behind him, holding on to each other, crying with laughter. I cringed.

'Mum,' I hissed. 'Where did you get that from? It's awful!'

'I took it in the garden last summer,' said my mother in surprise. 'I thought it was rather fun.'

'Ah yes it is, it is!' insisted Madelaine. 'Such a feeling of –' she waved her hands expressively – 'of family! Of *joie de vivre*!' She poked a manicured finger at it. 'This ees the picture the designers really want for their perfume ads, the ones with the beautiful people cavorting on beaches with young children, yes? But they never seem to capture the essence! The *esprit*!'

Personally, I wasn't convinced that Giorgio and Calvin would be lining up to trade in their supermodels for an aging barrister dressed as a lavatory flanked by his guffawing children, but then she was probably just being polite. What must she think of us? I wondered.

I looked across at Mum, who although always elegant was pretty shabbily dressed as usual in an ancient jumper and skirt. When was the last time she'd bought any new clothes? I wondered. I glanced quickly around the room and for the first time saw it for the mess it was. Toys littered the floor, old roses drooped in vases, books lay open everywhere. Madelaine's Parisian chic seemed to highlight everyone and everything. I blushed. Couldn't Mum at least have tidied up a bit? Thrown some of the old newspapers away, emptied a few wine glasses, chucked Barbie and Ken into the toy box and shoved their revolting dream kitchen and chalet-style bungalow behind the door? Madelaine's eyebrows suddenly shot up.

'Ah! Is that them?' She turned eagerly towards the window. 'The children? How enchanting!'

Childish shouts were undoubtedly coming from the garden and I moved quickly towards the window, keen to beat her to it, to shove my bulk between her and anything too enchanting. Would the little darlings be killing the cat perhaps, or Leonora even? I held my breath and peered out nervously. Happily, an unexpectedly tame scene met my eye. Down on the lower lawn, Piers was playing chase with Hugo and Clemmie. The children were shouting with laughter as he ran after them and he'd even blown up some balloons which they were tossing around in the air. Madelaine clapped her hands ecstatically. 'Ah! *Regardez! C'est tellement agréable!'*

I was pleased and very surprised. Piers didn't often play with my two – in fact, I'd go so far as to say never. I watched as he and Hugo raced towards the house.

'Yes, they can be rather sweet,' I agreed indulgently.

Hugo leaped the little box hedge and made it to the terrace. He flashed by our window, grinning from ear to ear and waving a balloon. We smiled and waved back, but suddenly my hand and smile froze, it wasn't a balloon he was waving at all, but an inflated condom. A second later Piers flashed past too, purple in the face, steam pouring from every orifice.

'Come back here, you little bastard!' he roared.

Mummy tutted. 'So competitive,' she murmured.

'Er, more coffee, Madelaine?' I said hastily, steering her away from the window and back to the table.

'*Non, merci.* I've had plenty, and a most delicious lunch too. Your mother really is a wonderful cook, Tess. I must get that recipe from you, Daphne, chocolate roulade is so difficult and yours was perfection. And what lovely lilies.' She paused to admire the only vase of surviving flowers in the room.

'Yes, beautiful,' agreed Mummy, 'but not frightfully well arranged, I'm afraid I'm a bit of a plonker.'

Madelaine frowned, perplexed. 'A bit of a – ah! Ian, how lovely!' Suddenly her face cleared, she beamed and we all turned to witness my father tiptoeing past the open door, boots in one hand, rod in the other, obviously hoping to make it to the rod room at the end of the passage without being seen. He froze in mid-creep, foot poised high in the air like a pointer. The foot wavered for a moment, then dropped. He knew he was trapped.

'Madelaine, how delightful!' He gallantly swept his hat off his head and advanced with a fixed smile, hand extended stiffly.

Madelaine took it and also planted an elegant peck on each of his cheeks too. He managed not to cringe or rub them off, but nonetheless stepped smartly back, out of range for any more. His chin jutted out.

'I was um, sorry to hear about Marcus!' he almost shouted, as if he was determined to get it out. He twisted his flat cap round and round nervously in his hands.

Madelaine smiled. 'Thank you, Ian.'

'It um, must be very difficult for you,' he bellowed.

'I'm bearing up.'

'Yes, yes,' he nodded hard. 'My – my sincere condolences. Er, anything we can do, of course, delighted. Don't um –' his hat was spiralling now as if it might take off like a propeller at any minute, 'don't hesitate to er –'

'Thank you, Ian, but I'm fine, really. Daphne has been most kind and cooked me a delicious lunch. I just hope she will come to me next time.'

She reached for a chocolate-brown throw hanging on the back of a chair and swept it round her shoulders. She gave a dazzling smile. 'But now I really must be going.'

'Oh.' I was dismayed. 'So soon?'

'I'm afraid so, my dear. I have to take the car to the garage. Another bleenking gasket has blown or something, that's why I couldn't come at teatime. Such a bore.'

'Ah, yes, cars, too tedious. Well, if you'll excuse me.'

Daddy reversed out of the room at top speed, half nodding, half bowing. 'Lovely to see you, Madelaine, delightful,' and he escaped down the hall.

'You too, Ian.' She smiled to herself, then turned to me. 'Tess.' She gazed for a moment, then suddenly leaned forward, resting her hands lightly on my shoulders. She kissed me on both cheeks. 'It was so good to meet you at long, long last.'

I gazed back at her and for a moment couldn't speak. She turned to my mother. 'Daphne, such a treat, thank you so much.' They kissed warmly and walked towards the door together, arm in arm, away from me.

'We must do it again some time.'

'Yes, we must, it's been too long.'

'Far too long. I'll give you a ring and —'

'How's Patrick?' I blurted out suddenly.

They stopped and turned back to me in surprise.

'Oh, he is fine,' said Madelaine. 'Yes, very well.'

Both women were staring at me now. I felt my colour rise. 'Good. Good,' I said faintly, feeling foolish.

Madelaine was charm itself. She came back towards me, carrying the conversation, smiling, letting me recover.

'His painting is going so well now, you know. He is really making quite a name for himself, he's had four or five exhibitions in Florence and one in Rome. I went out to see the one in Rome for myself and my goodness, I felt quite important — the mother of the artist, you know! And in just two weeks' time he 'as a one-man show in London, at the Pierre Boulavère gallery in Cork Street, very prestigious, I believe. But still,' she sighed, shaking her head, 'still he ees not settled. Still he 'as no wife, no family, and he is so secretive, tells me precisely nothing.' She appealed to Mummy. 'Are your girls the same, Daphne, or is it just the boys, you think?'

Mummy had been watching me carefully, but she turned her attention to Madelaine now. 'Laura's certainly secretive,' she admitted. 'She never tells me anything about her love life, about how she really feels anyway.'

'But you meet them, her menfriends? She brings them home?'

'Oh yes, we meet them all right, but they're all,' she struggled, trying not to be disloyal, 'well, a bit dreary, I'm afraid. They're all out of the same mould, the trainspotter type.'

Madelaine was mystified. 'Trainstopper? You mean on the tracks? They throw themselves?'

'Sadly no,' murmured Mummy. 'No, it's a type, Madelaine. It means timid, really.'

'Ah.' She shrugged. 'Ah well, we have to let them find their own way, I suppose.' She turned back to me and smiled. 'The problem with my boy is, I think, that he never really got over you, Tess.'

I stared at her. Gulped. Couldn't speak. She patted my arm. 'So lovely to meet you, my dear.' Then she turned and went.

I managed to wait till she'd left the room, then my hand shot to my mouth, stifling a gasp. She couldn't know, of course. She couldn't know that that was like tossing a sweetie to a child who's been deprived for years, that I would throw myself on those words so hungrily, devour them so voraciously. I watched from the window as Mum saw her to her car. I could almost feel the blood pumping through me, pounding in my fingertips, in my toes. 'The problem with my boy is, I think, that he never got over you.' I savoured the words, rolling them around in my mouth. '*Never got over you.*' My blood surged and my heart beat faster, I glowed with guilt and delight. They were the words I'd been waiting for and I knew it.

I watched Madelaine get into her car, heard it crunch slowly down the drive and as it went, a secret smile spread over my face until I thought the bottom half of it might drop off. For the first time in ages I felt wide awake, alive. Madelaine had unwittingly lit the blue touch paper and my advice to everyone now was: *stand well back.*

On a sudden impulse I slipped out to the hall and ran upstairs before Mum came back through the front door. There was something I wanted to do. I hurried along the landing to our bathroom and as I pushed open the door, almost tripped over a pile of washing. I kicked it, exasperated. It was a bundle David had put out, presumably in the vain hope that if I fell over it, it might get washed. Lying on top was a shirt I'd given him last Christmas. The sleeve was flung out at an angle as if waving at me, flagging me down, reproaching me. I seized it angrily and chucked it in the linen basket. No, I would *not* be reproached, I would *not* be frowned on, and apart from anything else, I thought, slamming the door shut, I hadn't even done anything yet, had I? I refused to feel guilty about a crime I hadn't even committed, and maybe wouldn't commit either! I mean, maybe I just wanted to feel this warm glow for a bit, to fantasize, to know that there was someone out there thinking about me, someone who'd – and I quote – *never got over me*. Yes, that's right, me. I stared at my flushed reflection in the mirror, Tessa Hamilton, mother of two, housewife from Putney.

Quickly I began unbuttoning my shirt and peeled off my clothes. There was no lock on the door, but I was pretty sure nobody was about right now. I got down to my socks and bra and knickers and hopped over the pile of clothes to the full-length mirror in the corner. Hmm, I pursed my lips. Very pop socks and white M&S undies. I took the pop socks off and then whipped off my bra too, throwing it on the floor with a flourish – there! Then I shuffled closer to the mirror and peered in. Good Lord. Where on earth had my boobs gone? Apart from the odd cursory glance in the bath it was ages since I'd inspected these two properly; they seemed to have turned into a couple of small tea-bags. My eye travelled nervously down to my tummy, which far from disappearing had, in the absence of my critical eye, taken the opportunity to spread itself rather luxuriously. Perhaps that's where my boobs were, somewhere in my tummy? Had they relocated without me even realizing it? I looked like a duvet that had gone thin at the top and fat at the bottom. I needed to be seized by the ankles and given a damn good shake.

Panic-stricken, I lay down. Perhaps that would help, if I shifted everything around a bit? I swivelled on the cold lino floor and craned my head to look in the mirror. There was a definite improvement in the tummy and thigh department, but my boobs seemed to be pointing the wrong way now. What was the attraction of my armpits, for God's sake? I sat up, alarmed. Would he notice? Would he find me very altered? Well, of course I was altered! I'd given birth twice, breastfed twice, failed to keep up my post-natal exercises twice, cheated on my pelvic floors twice and eaten vast quantities of Jaffa Cakes and abandoned fish fingers every day for the last eight years. All that was bound to take its toll on a girl, but would it matter? Would it put him off?

Suddenly I reached across and grabbed my eyeliner from the bathroom shelf. Ah yes, the pencil test – always the acid test of droopy boobs at school. Could I still pass it, or would I have to go and hang myself from the nearest netball post? I hoicked a tea-bag up and stuck the pencil underneath. It clung like a cling-on. I wiggled around a bit but it stayed resolutely put. Damn. I gazed sorrowfully at my reflection. Oh well, I reasoned, boobs weren't everything, were they? I mean, look at my legs. They were still pretty terrific, weren't they? Still long and thin. I stuck one in the air and waggled it. Not bad. I'd go so far as to say amazing even, except – wasn't there something a bit odd about the consistency of those thighs? Weren't they looking a bit *porridgey*? I poked one and it wobbled violently. Hell's teeth. I slapped my leg smartly to arrest the slipstream and then all of a sudden, rather rudely, it dawned.

The gym. Of course! So *that's* why all my friends went there so religiously, three or four times a week sometimes – toning up, slimming down, doing weights, pumping iron, sweating buckets, charging up and down imaginary steps like lunatics and I'd always thought it such a narcissistic waste of time, such a vain, navel-gazing obsession. I'd always rather smugly claimed to prefer a good book, to be doing something about the bit on the *in*side rather than the bit on the *out*side . . . Why hadn't someone let me in on the secret? That the *real* reason I needed to look after my body was not that I might need it some day, that I'd live longer, feel better for it, have a better quality of life and blah blah blah – no, the *real* reason was that someone *else* might need it some day. Someone *else* might be requiring a toned thigh, a tiny waist, a firm bust, a taut tummy – and we're not talking your ever-loving here either.

I sat up and sighed. Oh well. Too late to do anything about all that now and anyway, I reasoned, there were other, more subtle charms on offer too like, well, arms, for instance. I twirled an undeniably slim one ruefully. Oh, and my smile, of course. I quickly changed the rueful one in the mirror to a seductive one and discovered a tea leaf. I picked it off thoughtfully. Oh – and my laugh – that couldn't have changed much in twelve years, surely? I experimented with a girlish tinkle: 'Ah ha ha ha!' Hey, not bad, and that thrownback head certainly minimizes the chins, Tess. Have another go. 'Ah ha ha – shit!'

The door flew open and two heads appeared, David's at the top and Hugo's at the bottom.

'Here she is!' cried Hugo. 'Why are you laughing and why is there a pencil under your bosom? Are you drawing on them? Can I have a go?'

I grabbed a towel. 'No, you bloody well can't.'

'Are you all right?' said David. 'We heard you laughing – you sounded a bit delirious.'

'Yes, of course I'm all right,' I said shortly. 'I was just

doing some – some exercises, if you must know! And I was laughing at something –' I thought wildly – 'something Penny said.'

'What?' demanded Penny, pushing the door open and barging in too. 'Oh, there you are, Tess, we've been looking everywhere for you. What did I say?'

'When?'

'You just said I said something funny, I heard you.'

'Yes, what?' demanded Hugo.

'Oh, nothing really,' I said, scrambling to my feet and pulling the towel around me. 'Just something you said down at the river, made me smile, that's all.'

'Laugh,' corrected my son, 'really loudly, and she was doing exercises in the nudey-wudey.'

'What was it?' persisted Penny with a smile, always keen to imagine she was amusing. 'What did I say, go on, what?'

'Oh, you *know*,' I said, winking and pretending we shared a private joke, desperately trying to think of anything Penny had ever said that was remotely funny.

Penny frowned, then her eyes grew wide. 'Oh, you mean about You Know Who!'

I gasped, suddenly realizing what she meant. 'No!' I said quickly. 'No, not that, something else.'

'My goodness, you old devil.' Penny nudged me, eyes shining. 'You're going to do it, aren't you? Exercising in the nude eh, getting yourself in shape – you old dog.'

'May I enquire as to what all the hilarity is about?' asked David who'd been quietly filling the bath for Hugo who was once again soaking wet from the river.

'No, you may not,' I snapped. 'I don't know what Penny's talking about.'

'What?' shrieked Hugo, jumping up and down in his wet clothes. 'What are you going to do, you old dog, WHAT?'

'NOTHING!' I screeched back, grabbing my clothes off the floor and barging past them out of the room. 'God, sometimes I feel like Greta bleeding Garbo!'

'Did she exercise in the nude too?' asked Penny.

'No, but she wanted to be alone!'

I ran down the passageway but Hugo was right on my heels. I flew into the loo at the other end, and locked the door smartly behind me.

'WHAT?' screamed Hugo, hammering on the door. 'What are you going to do, tell me you fat belly farty MUMMEEE!! TELL ME-E-E!'

I sank down on the loo seat knowing I'd have to sit this one out but jumped up smartly as I hit the medicated seat cover. Bugger Penny, bugger her! I'd only just made up my mind to consider this blinking affair, only just allowed the idea to filter into my own consciousness, and now suddenly my whole bloody family wanted to discuss it – Jesus!

I folded my arms and leaned back on the wall, knowing a battle of wits was about to commence out there. I wouldn't move until Hugo moved and he wouldn't move until I did, except – hello, hang on. I put my ear to the door and heard footsteps padding away. Tentatively I placed my hand on the handle, but – no, wait: footsteps were padding back, accompanied by – clink, clink, clink – oh no, a bucket of Lego! I groaned. He was setting up camp out there, I could be in here for *hours*. I tightened my lips and folded the towel around me decisively. Not bloody likely. I turned the key, opened the door and stepped smartly over boy and Lego. Hugo was up in an instant.

'Mummy! Mummy what! What are you going to do, tell me please!'

I rounded on him. 'Go and have your bath immediately!' I thundered.

'But —'

'NOW Hugo!'

'But why? I —'

'Because I am the mother!'

'So?'

'So I outrank you!'

I stormed off, pretending I hadn't heard the muffled, 'Bugger,' behind me. I didn't often pull rank but when I did, it was curiously effective.

I marched into my bedroom, slammed the door and flopped down on my bed pulling the pillow over my head. Damn and blast the lot of them.

I didn't encounter Penny again until I joined her at potato-peeling hour in the kitchen that evening.

'Thanks very much,' I said tartly as I walked in and grabbed a knife from the draining board. I began peeling furiously.

'What?' she giggled. 'I was only —'

'Only suggesting I might commit adultery when my husband and son were both in the room. Yes, thanks a bunch.'

'Well, are you?' she asked eagerly.

I stared at her incredulously, put my knife down. 'No, of *course* not, Penny. I wouldn't dream of it.' I shook my head despairingly and resumed peeling. 'You really do say the most ridiculous things sometimes, you know.'

'Don't fib.'

'I'm not bloody fibbing.'

'You bloody are, Tess. I can tell, you were definitely up to something in there, lolling around on the floor with nothing on and simpering in the mirror. I know when you're guilty, you get all cross and defensive and start swearing a lot. I remember that summer with Patrick, you used to shout "Bollocks" a lot and – God what's that?'

A huge roar happily interrupted her quaint reminiscences, making us both jump. Through the kitchen window we saw an enormous motorbike loom up the drive; it turned and skidded to a halt outside and a spray of gravel hit the window. A youth encased in black leather and a red helmet gave us the benefit of his back, and then a bit more throttle.

I went to the kitchen door. 'Josie!' I yelled up the stairs.

He gave a couple of toots on his horn and sat waiting for her.

'Too cool to knock at the door, I suppose,' snapped Penny, glaring out of the window. 'Who does he think he is, tearing up our drive like that?' Penny did so love to play the Lady of the Manor.

Seconds later Josie stuck her head round the kitchen door. 'Bye then, Tess. I've got a key so don't bother to wait up.'

I gazed at her in wonder. She looked terrific. Long blonde hair, a real waist and slim brown legs, a very small proportion of which were encased in a short red skirt, white T-shirt and red jacket. She could knock any model I'd ever seen into a cocked hat. I felt almost proud of her.

I grinned. 'Bye, Josie, you look amazing. Have a good time.'

'Crikey,' muttered Penny, equally awestruck. 'I'd forgotten she wasn't even trying during the day.'

We watched, unashamedly now from the window, like the couple of has-beens we were, clutching our potato-peelers, wanting just a little sniff of the action, wanting to breathe in just a hint of our lost youth. Josie ran out to greet him. She flipped up his visor and kissed him playfully on the nose, then swung a long brown leg over the back of his bike and snuggled up close, clutching him round the waist. He turned back to check she was on properly, and as he did so, I saw his face for the first time. His bright blue eyes met mine and crinkled up in a smile. My jaw dropped, my eyes glazed, my potato-peeler fell with a resounding clatter into the sink. It was Patrick.

Chapter Ten

'Bloody hell!' squawked Penny. 'Did you see who that was?'

I was still staring out of the window as if I'd seen a ghost. I'd lost all control of my vocal cords.

'It was Patrick! Didn't you recognize him, Tess?'

'What the – how did they – where did they –' I floundered. My brain was spinning and I was having huge trouble with basic English.

'Oh, so it must have been *Patrick* she met in the pub,' breathed Penny. 'How extraordinary. Isn't that weird, Tess?'

My mouth was still moving, but no coherent sounds were coming out. Josie and Patrick? Surely not – no, it was too outrageous, it was obscene, it was – suddenly, my mouth connected with my brain.

'It's sick!' The words erupted from my lips like Mount Vesuvius. 'How *dare* she! What the hell does she think she's playing at!'

'What d'you mean?'

'Well, he's *far* too old for her!'

'Well not really, Tess. I mean she's what – twenty-two – and he's early thirties; that's not such a huge age-gap. But I know what you mean,' she mused. 'Because he's our age and she's so young and pretty, it does seem as if she's from a different generation, doesn't it? Well, different *planet*, actually, ha!'

This had the effect of rendering me speechless again and I damn nearly grappled her to the floor and stabbed my potato-peeler into her throat.

'I don't care what bloody planet she's from,' I spluttered. 'She's my nanny, for God's sake, my employee. I won't have it, I just won't have it!' I leaned heavily on the draining board for support. I was in danger of hyperventilating here.

'And how dare *he*!' I muttered, staring into the sink, my eyes boggling down the plug-hole as the situation became clearer by the minute. 'How dare he roar up our drive and whisk her away like that, right in front of our noses. The cheek! The – the nerve!'

'Do you think he knows she's your nanny, then?' said Penny. 'I suppose he must have gathered by now – he definitely saw us at the window.'

'She's deceived me,' I seethed, 'betrayed me, the little hussy, the little tramp, the little two-bit jumped-up, brainless, braless, knickerless harpy!'

Penny frowned. 'Now hang on a minute, Tess, I'm not her biggest fan, but that's not really fair. She wasn't to know, was she? And anyway, I thought you said at breakfast yesterday she could go out with who she liked?'

'Yes, but within reason,' I spat. 'I don't particularly want her poaching my ex-boyfriends! Did you see her skirt, Penny? Up round her *arse*!'

I was totally out of control now, in the grip of a violent, homicidal rage, my potato-peeler seemed to be stabbing wildly at my chopping board.

'And all that *make-up!*' I brought the knife down savagely, gouging a hole in the wood.

'I don't think she was wearing make-up actually, just a bit of lipstick perhaps, a touch of blusher . . .'

But I wasn't listening. I was in another world – the one Othello no doubt inhabited for a while.

'And as for him,' I ranted on, 'a motorbike! I mean I ask you, at his age – who does he think he is – James sodding Dean? He's thirty-four, for God's sake!'

'Well not all thirty-somethings want a Volvo with a couple of baby-seats in the back, you know. I thought he looked quite cool actually.'

'Cool? Penny, he looked sad. A sad old sugar-daddy cradle-snatching a gold-digging bimbo!' My voice rose hysterically. 'The whole thing is repulsive. I won't have it, I won't!' I stamped my foot.

Penny put her arms round my trembling shoulders. 'All right, all right,' she soothed in the kind of voice one reserves for the mentally deranged contemplating a leap off Beachy Head. 'Now you come and sit down here and I'll pour you a nice big drink. You're just upset, that's all.'

'Upset?' I muttered, allowing myself to be led to a chair. 'Who's upset? I'm not upset, don't be ridiculous.'

'Of course you are, and it's understandable. As far as you're concerned he's still your property,' she went on in her caring, counsellor tone, 'and you can't bear to see him with someone else – especially someone as young and beautiful and perfectly formed as Josie because you know you can't compete. It's perfectly natural,' she soothed.

My teeth snapped manically at this and she damn

nearly lost her nose, but at the last minute I got a grip and sank them into my hand instead.

'Don't be silly,' I croaked, forcing a laugh, and knocking back the glass of wine she put in front of me. 'I couldn't care less!' I piped in a high, unnatural voice.

She sat next to me. 'Of course you could. You and I both know you secretly entertained hopes of, well, how shall I put it – turning back the clock? Revisiting old pastures, shall we say?'

'No we shall not!' I snapped. 'God, you're revolting, Penny. How can you be so tacky? I had no intention of revisiting anything with Patrick, I'm merely concerned for my nanny's welfare, concerned she doesn't make a fool of herself, the little –' It was no good, the venom was rising again, it was in my throat, my mouth and – 'TART!' I bellowed. 'The little hussy, harlot, painted bloody Jezebel, Judas sodding Iscariot!' I clenched my fists.

Penny refilled my glass. 'Drink,' she ordered.

I swiftly obeyed, knocking it back in one.

'And she's a hopeless nanny,' I spat. 'Hopeless! All she does is sit around on her arse watching spot-the-brain-cell quiz shows and reading bonk-busters all day. She's crap at ironing, hasn't a clue how to sew a button on – God, I even had to teach her how to make oven chips! I'm going to sack her,' I went on in a quiet, mad sort of way, 'tomorrow. No, why wait? Tonight, when she comes back – the moment she sets foot through the front door.'

Penny frowned. 'But I thought you said she was good. I distinctly remember you saying –'

'I don't care what I said, she's going, she's as good as

gone. That girl is history, she's on the next train back to London in the morning.'

I turned and seized Penny's arm urgently. 'I can do that, can't I Penny? It's not against the law, the trade descriptions act or anything? Or do I have to give her notice? What about just a huge wodge of money, hundreds, thousands – I know, what about my gold Rolex, d'you think she'd like that?'

'Tess, you can't sack her just because she's seeing your ex-boyfriend!'

'It's got nothing to do with that,' I hissed. 'I told you, she's going because she's useless and the children hate her.'

My fingers wound round the stem of my empty glass like snakes; any minute now my tongue would fork too.

'Oh, what rot, the children adore her, you know they do.'

As if on cue, Clemmie ran into the kitchen in her pyjamas and picked up the cup of warm milk Penny had put out for her on the table. I seized her wildly.

'Clemmie darling, you hate Josie, don't you? Secretly? Yes? Tell Mummy, she's mean to you, isn't she? Makes you eat your horrid sprouts?'

Clemmie frowned and wriggled free. 'No, Mummy, I love Josie. Mummy, are you still my mummy?'

'She's lying,' I hissed between clenched teeth, letting her go. I gulped my wine.

'Mu-mmy!' Clemmie plucked at my arm. 'Are you still my mummy, only I haven't seen you all day and if you're not careful I might have to divorce you like that boy in the papers did. Will you read to me?'

Where would they go? I wondered. Along the cliffs for a moonlit walk? To the sand dunes?'

'MUMMMEE! Read to me in bed.'

I glanced down. 'Hmmm? Oh no, darling, not tonight. Daddy will read to you, Mummy's tired. Now run along.'

I drained my glass. Or would they go to the river, where we used to go? Lie side by side on the bank?'

'No, you blinking fat MOO!' roared my daughter.

'Clemmie!' I bellowed. 'Don't you speak to me like that. Go up and find Daddy immediately. Go on, up those stairs this instant!'

Rather fortuitously, David appeared at that moment in the doorway, bearing a bundle of washing. Clemmie promptly burst into tears and ran to him. He scooped her up.

'I'll give them their tea, bath them *and* put them to bed then, shall I?' he enquired. 'And then shall I do this pile of washing that's been sitting on the bathroom floor for three days?'

'Oh, for God's sake, David, don't give me that sexist demarcation crap. I'm on holiday too, you know!'

'Of course you are, my darling, and don't we know it.' He flung the washing down on the floor and marched upstairs with a howling Clemmie in his arms.

'Damn. Damn, damn, damn!' I refilled my glass.

Penny got up from the table, raising her eyebrows at the heavy marital scene and then at the almost-empty wine bottle. 'Um, Tess, I know I said have a drink but d'you think you should drain the thing dry?'

'Yes, I do,' I muttered, clutching the bottle possessively, cuddling it almost.

Penny silently resumed her potato-peeling at the sink. I gazed at her disapproving back. It seemed to be going in and out of focus quite dramatically. One glass was generally enough to make my eyes go squiffy, two tended to make them rotate, how much would it take to drink myself into oblivion, I wondered? I whimpered slightly at this. Oh God, was I hitting the bottle? Here I was experiencing all the repercussions of an extra-marital affair – heavy drinking, neglected children, parental rows, resentful husband – and I hadn't even bloody *had* one!

I heaved a great sigh. Nor would I have, at this rate. I sank back miserably in my chair. The shock was abating slightly but it was being replaced by a tidal wave of self-pity. Where were they now, I wondered. Arm in arm somewhere, staring at the stars? And what would they talk about? This cheered me slightly. Yes, what exactly *would* a grown man talk to a twenty-two-year-old nanny about? Who was doing what to whom in *Neighbours*? Whether or not Take That would ever re-form? I mean, it was hardly likely to be *À La Recherche du Temps Perdu*, was it? I gave a hollow laugh and poured myself another soupçon of wine. It had to be a soupçon because that was all there was left. Oh yes, I reasoned, having a great body was all well and good, but without the grey matter to back it up . . . I tapped my temple smugly, but suddenly my fingertip froze. *Hang on a minute*. I had a nasty feeling . . . hadn't Josie mentioned something about a degree when I'd first interviewed her? Now what was it? I racked my brains furiously – table tennis, needlework or – oh, hang on, it was coming to me now . . . Yes, that was it: *History of Art*.

My eyes glazed. History of Art! Shit! So they'd be

talking paintings, introspection, Impressionists, light formation . . . they'd be snuggling up on the beach together making plans – great galleries we must visit! My chest felt strangely tight. Good God, what had I hired here? Was I out of my mind? I'd only gone and hired Brian bloody Sewell masquerading as Claudia blinking Schiffer! Why hadn't I gone for a Rumanian weight-lifter with enough space in her head to park a brace of caravans? Oh God!

I moaned low, slumped forward onto the table in defeat. I lay there with my head on its cold Formica surface. Penny ignored me and carried on peeling. I groaned again, pitifully. Still she ignored me. I shut my eyes painfully. I could hardly see now and my head seemed to be in the grip of a centrifugal force, but funnily enough, it was strangely comforting. I abandoned myself to the mind-numbing headspin but after a few minutes I heard the back door fly open.

I opened my eyes bleakly. Laura was standing there, grinning from ear to ear and carrying a huge, shiny, dripping salmon.

'Look!' she cried. 'How about that!'

'Oh, well done!' cried Penny. 'That's our first, isn't it?'

'It certainly is,' beamed Laura proudly, 'and what a whopper – eight pounds two ounces. Have you got anything planned for supper, or shall we have it tonight?'

'No, I've only done some vegetables, let's eat it. Oh, you are clever, Laura. Here, let me help you.'

Together they manhandled the salmon over to the work surface and eagerly began cleaning and gutting, chatting away happily as they worked. I watched blearily through my hair, my head feeling like a lead weight on the table. Eventually Laura glanced around. I shut my eyes tight. She whispered something to Penny. Penny whispered back.

'*No!*' I heard Laura gasp. 'Really?'

I peeped and saw Penny nod expressively. Laura glanced over again in my direction. I quickly shut my eyes.

'And is she a bit . . . ?' she murmured. 'You know . . . about it?'

'More than a bit,' muttered Penny.

'More than a bit what!' I barked raising my head abruptly. 'You old witch, you old spleen dragon, what vicious lies are you whispering, what filthy muck are you spreading about me now!'

Laura stared at me, astounded.

'Tell me, Penny,' I spat, probably looking rather like that attractive little girl in *The Exorcist* whose head managed a 360-degree turn. 'Tell me exactly what you said or I'll boil your silk pyjamas!'

'I was merely explaining to Laura why it is you're a little upset,' she said soothingly.

'For the last time,' I thundered, 'I am not upset!'

Just at that moment my father came through the back door. 'Laura, Willie tells me you've got a salmon!' He rubbed his hands together gleefully. 'Marvellous news – I was beginning to give up hope.' He crossed the room and gave her a hug. 'I rather thought this might be our first year when we didn't catch a thing, and that was starting to depress me somewhat!'

He laughed, patted Penny on the back, then turned and caught sight of his elder daughter, hair askew, eyes rotating, swaying slightly at the kitchen table, hugging an empty bottle of Chardonnay to her bosom. His smile froze and his eyes went cold.

'What's wrong?' he demanded. 'Why are you drinking, Tessa? What's happened?'

'Oh, for heaven's sake,' I said, stifling a burp, and getting up and making for the back door. 'Making' was about right, since my first attempt landed me in the larder.

'I'm thirty years old,' I said as I fought my way out through baskets of vegetables, skidding on a rogue tomato. 'Can't I even have a drink if I feel like it?' I lurched past them all, eventually finding the back door. 'I'm going for a walk. You can stuff supper!' I blundered out into the garden.

I stumbled down the first lawn, jumped the little hedge, somehow landing on my feet, then ran down the second and plunged into the woods beyond, crashing through them blindly, scratching my face on brambles and tripping over roots. I still felt extremely woozy but the fresh air was reviving me slightly and I didn't stop running until I reached the water's edge. The last thing I wanted to hear was my father's footsteps behind me, his booming voice, catching up with me, seizing my arm and demanding to know what the devil was going on.

I ran and ran, along the river path, over the little bridge, and across into the heather, to the round, clear pool I always liked to sit by. I sank down on the shingle at the water's edge, panting. My heart was hammering in my chest now. I flopped on my back and gazed up at the still blue sky.

A dragonfly, making the most of the last minutes of daylight, whirred around above me and higher still, a pair of swallows swooped in formation back and forth across the water. Suddenly I felt a bit sick. I sat gingerly up. The trees span around me, then stopped, casting their long evening shadows across the water. I grabbed a handful of pebbles and threw them angrily at their reflections. The water peppered, the trees wobbled a bit, then slowly cleared to their still reflection again.

I sighed. Thirty years old. Yes, I was thirty years old. And he was thirty-four. And what a difference, eh? I gave a hollow laugh. Here was I, pissed off, careworn, body a mess, responsible for just about everything and everybody, and there was he charging around on a Harley-Davidson with a babe on the back, not a care in the world and not looking a day older than when I'd first met him. I chucked in another handful of stones. And what a babe. I thought of Josie, stretched out sunbathing in our back garden at home, tiny waist, firm boobs, long athletic legs just the way he liked them; 'built for speed' he'd say. Then I thought of my own sad reflection in the mirror this afternoon. I shuddered. Perhaps after all I'd had a lucky escape? Perhaps I'd spared myself the embarrassment, the look of disbelief on his face as he recoiled from me in horror? I picked up another handful of shingle and threw it savagely in the water.

'Hey! What d'you think you're playing at!' barked a voice behind me.

I swung around quickly. A huge figure loomed from behind a tree, but the low evening sun was right in my eyes and at first I couldn't see who it was. My heart pumped a bit, but then I relaxed.

'Oh God, it's you, Willie. You gave me a shock!'

'Yull be shockin' those fish too, I shouldn't wonder. What are you tryin' to doo, stone them to death? Are you lot that desperate for fish?'

I blushed as he towered over me. 'Sorry.' Disturbing the river was distinctly frowned on. 'Is anyone still fishing?'

He sat down next to me. 'No, but that's ney the point, is it? You're upsetting my charges, disturbin' their beauty sleep!'

He grinned and I tried to grin back but failed. He looked rather thoughtfully at me and I quickly looked away.

Willie leaned back, resting on his elbows, eyes narrowed. There was silence. I knew he was watching the river, he always was, never seemed to take his eyes off it. I observed him out of the corner of my eye, a huge mountain of a man, but so serene, so at ease with himself. But then he had his lifestyle to thank for that, didn't he? Day after day, month in month out, he led a solitary existence, taking care of the river and the wildlife it supported, except for a few months each summer when harassed townies like us would descend on him, desperate for just a couple of weeks of his own particular brand of contentment, for just a small slice of the inaction that he called normal life. What cares did he have? What pressures? I followed his eyes to the opposite bank but couldn't see anything.

'There,' he said quietly, pointing.

I stared. 'Oh yes.'

A young water rat was inching its way cautiously out of a hole, poking its nose out nervously then popping back in, until finally, it decided the coast was clear and slipped like a snake into the shallows.

'Did you see it?'

I nodded. His moss-green eyes crinkled in satisfaction and the wind ruffled his sandy blond hair. His eyes darted along the bank again, looking for other signs of life. I sighed, envying him his peace, his calm. I'd known him since he was a child; we'd all played together. I used to think he was shy but now I knew he just liked his own company. He was sure of himself in the truest sense, which was more than I could say for me. Another mammoth sigh unfolded from my boots.

'So what's up then?' he asked softly, following a dragon-fly now.

'What d'you mean?'

'Why are you sitting here on your own throwing stones and sighing like that?'

'Oh, I don't know, Willie. Just life in general, I suppose.'

'Dunny give me that.'

'What?'

He didn't answer.

'What? Don't give you what?'

He shrugged. 'It's none of my business.'

I swallowed hard. 'All right then, more than just life in general. It's something . . . something I thought might happen . . . which won't, now.'

He chucked down his blade of chewed grass and picked another one. 'Oh ay? Somethin' you'd been looking forward to, like?'

I nodded, not trusting myself to speak. My nose, God-damnit, appeared to be filling up with water.

'What was it, a treat or somethin'?'

In spite of myself I couldn't help thinking this was a quaint way to describe a sex romp.

I gulped and nodded. 'It might have made a nice change,' I squeaked – oh God, talking about it was fatal. Tears were threatening to break ranks any minute. I desperately fished up my sleeve for a non-existent hanky. *Don't cry Tess, don't cry!*

He sat up next to me and a comforting arm about the size of a tree trunk went round my shoulders. 'Hey, hey now, whatever it was can't have meant that much to you.'

'It did, it did!' I bawled, and that was it. The dam burst. 'It *did* mean a lot to me, and now it's all *spoilt*,' I sobbed into his soft Viyella shoulder. 'Nothing ever goes right for me any more and all I wanted was this one little thing and even *that*'s been taken from me!' I knew I was behaving like a four-year-old but somehow I couldn't help it.

'Och now, there there,' he soothed, giving me a huge hug. 'Come on now, come on.' I'd heard him talk in the same way to his dogs who adored him, licked his boots, and now I knew why. I felt like licking them too.

'I *can't* come on,' I sobbed pathetically. 'I'm sick of coming on and bracing up and being strong and keeping a stiff upper lip, I'm sick of catering for everybody else's needs except my own!'

'Of course you are, of course,' he crooned, stroking my hair. 'It's only natural.'

'Just this one little thing,' I sobbed dramatically, 'of my own! For me! That was all I wanted!'

I was vaguely aware I was getting terribly out of control now, even perhaps wallowing in it a tiny bit, but then Willie didn't know what I was talking about so it didn't really matter. And it was so nice having my shoulder hugged like that and my hair smoothed like a child and being able to sob and bawl and lean my cheek against his soft shirt which smelled of grass and fresh air and – well, him, I suppose.

Gradually though, my sobs subsided and I began to feel a little foolish. I kept my head flat to his chest, sniffing quite a bit, not wanting him to see my tear-stained face. I did feel an awful lot better for my outburst though, if a little weak. Crying always had such a debilitating effect on me, so much so that there wasn't a lot I could do about the fact that he was still stroking my hair, and actually, my neck too. Couldn't move a muscle. Or a finger. Oooh . . . that was lovely, bit lower – perfect. He tucked my hair back behind my ear and dropped a soft little kiss on the top of my head. Mmmm . . . a comforting, brotherly sort of kiss, you understand. I shut my eyes and nuzzled dreamily into his shoulder, wondering if it would happen again. Ah yes – there, lovely. As I leaned against him with half-closed eyes, I started to turn to goo inside. I felt so warm, so relaxed – rather like a hot water bottle, in fact.

Still he stroked and kissed and still I couldn't move, but little by little I began to realize that there was more on offer here than just tea and sympathy. But then again, I reasoned, eyeballing his Viyella checks rather nervously, I hadn't actually participated yet, had I? Hadn't done anything wrong? I stared at the small clear buttons on his shirt and watched his chest rise slowly up and down. Nerves turned to excitement. My tummy began to churn and presently, the moment came when he couldn't conceivably carry the show on his own any longer. Circumstances demanded he took my face in his hands and tilt it up towards him. I succumbed to the tilt and gazed, mesmerized. His moss-green eyes were soft, kind and enquiring, and his lips, when they came towards mine, so warm and comforting, and his tongue, so huge and hypnotic, that to be honest, there was damn-all I could do about it except fling my arms round his neck, lock them firmly together and pull him down roughly on top of me in the long, sweet grass.

Another soft kiss unfolded and another, and then he paused, possibly for breath, but also perhaps to search for that vital green light, the one that would give him the All Clear. What he got was more of a continental traffic cop, all beckoning white gloves and frantic whistles.

'Yes!' I gasped wantonly, then, lest there be misunderstanding, 'Yes, come on!'

After a few minutes I began to feel faint and realized I hadn't inhaled for a while. I came up for air and simultaneously felt a howling gale whistling around my midriff. I seemed to be losing some clothing.

'Not here,' I gasped. 'Too risky!' Not, notice, get off me right now, you mad fool, I must get home to my husband and children.

Willie nodded, and without so much as pausing in his exploration of my tonsils, scooped me up in his arms, Tarzan style, and strode determinedly off down the river. It was at this moment, I'd like it recorded, that a very small piece of conscience did actually raise its tentative head to wonder what the hell I was up to. What on earth was I doing? Was this a good idea? For a moment I wasn't sure, then – wait; yes I was. I'd been planning on doing it with Patrick, hadn't I? What difference did it make if I did it with Willie the gillie instead? In the face of such brazenness that small, lone voice shrivelled and died, leaving the new, sex-crazed fallopian-tube-throbbing me to be carried into what I can only describe as a rude sod hut.

Willie kicked open the door and threw me down masterfully on a bed with a sheepskin rug on top. I caught a whiff and wasn't convinced the original owner had enjoyed rude health so I breathed through my mouth.

'Where are we?' I gasped, kneeling up on the bed and hastily unbuttoning my shirt.

'In the hut,' panted Willie.

His hands were quicker than mine and his shirt was off in a flash, then in an even quicker flash, his pants and trousers. He stood before me, huge, totally naked and unbelievably, gigantically, priapic.

My hands froze on my buttons, my eyes bulged, transfixed.

'Good God!'

He frowned. 'What?'

'Nothing! I'm just – religious!' I gasped, trying to tear my eyes away from what I imagined would make a very serviceable pogo stick. 'Good God bless us and keep us,' I went on, crossing myself and adding quickly – 'you too, Willie!' I really wished I hadn't said that. I was sure he was used to the sound of his own name but somehow under the circumstances . . .

He smiled and came towards me. 'Ay, I forgot you were a vicar's daughter.'

'Oh yes. Very much so!' I gulped, sounding more like a football manager now.

Still we didn't make contact. Perhaps it was a pogo stick after all? Perhaps he was just going to have a quick hop around the room then we'd sit down to a cosy cup of tea?

But such were the subtleties of dramatic effect; quite lost on me. A moment later he'd dropped to his knees on the bed in front of me, seized me in his arms, smothered me in frantic kisses, and from that moment on a cup of tea was clearly out of the question.

A dark and steamy tussle ensued with my own, recently much maligned body giving the performance of a lifetime – or a year or two at least. Zones which I'd imagined had long since ceased to be erogenous and hitherto had had to be jump – or even kick – started, roared into life with a momentum all of their own. I fizzed, crackled and spat with so much sexual energy it's a wonder I didn't spontaneously combust. Now and again, as we snaked and writhed, I'd catch a rather surprising glimpse of myself – a sleek thigh perhaps, or a snappy waist, a tight calf, a pleasantly rounded buttock turning swiftly in the moonlight and I'd gaze in wonder and think – good heavens, are those bits mine? Do they really belong to me, or am I having an out-of-body-and-into-someone-else's experience here?

It was then that it dawned on me. Of course. This was clearly the answer. Feeling a bit fat? A bit flabby? A bit unconfident? Simple, just hop into bed with the biggest man you can find, ideally the Incredible Hulk, because

162

comparatively, you're bound to look petite, aren't you? At all costs though, I decided as I launched myself at Willie from the other end of the bed, I would avoid jockeys. That, I was sure, would be a serious morale basher. I wondered, as I rolled around wantonly in my particular Hulk's arms, if Robbie Coltrane might make himself available next year? After all, he was Scottish wasn't he? Or that huge man from *Whose Line Is It Anyway?* or any of the England scrum or – suddenly I froze. I went stiff in Willie's arms. What on earth was I talking about? What was I *thinking* about? I drew back. Was I seriously considering making a habit of rolling around in the sack with sixteen-stone giants by way of sexual therapy? By way of boosting my morale? I rocked back on my heels and stared down at Willie beneath me. He blinked up at me, flat on his back on the bed.

'What?' he panted. 'What's wrong?'

I shook my head. 'Willie, I – I can't!' I gasped.

Slowly he smiled. 'Och you're playing all provocative and hard to get now, aren't you? I know you London women with your sophisticated whip-lash ways, yull be tying me to the bed post and tickling me with yer feather duster next, come here, you little sex-machine, you little temptress you –' He made a grab for me but I shied away, jumping clean off the bed and taking the sheepskin with me for protection.

'No, Willie!' I gasped, clutching it to me.

He sat up and frowned at me in the moonlight. 'What is it? What's the matter?'

'Look, I'm terribly sorry, but I'm not sure I can go through with this.'

He stared at me. 'Not much more left, Tess, to tell you the truth. It's damn nearly over, bar the shouting.'

'I – I know, and I feel awful calling it off at the last minute, it's just that – well I don't think I can. Do it, I mean. I – think I've lost my bottle.'

I stared at him. Our eyes locked and suddenly he looked awfully huge sitting there stark naked in the moonlight. My heart began to hammer. I might have lost my bottle but I was damn sure he hadn't lost his, in fact I wondered if he might just have a handy one under the bed he could reach for and cosh me over the head with. Or perhaps he'd use his salmon-bashing implement? Or strangle me with his extremely able hands? He was after all a Scotsman and they weren't exactly renowned for their even tempers were they? I clutched the rug to me, trembling very slightly now, backing away.

'Talk about the eleventh hour, Tess.'

'I know, I know,' I whispered.

He gazed at me for a moment, then suddenly he smiled. He reached out for my hand. 'Och now don't be silly,' he said in a gentle voice. 'It's not important. Don't you go upsetting yourself over a little thing like sex.'

I blinked and stopped backing away. 'Really?' I whispered.

'Really.'

Slowly I took his hand and let him draw me down next to him. I sat on the bed beside him still wrapped in the sheepskin. 'You mean you're not – cross?'

'Of course not.' He shrugged. 'If you've changed your mind you've changed your mind, these things happen.'

I breathed in relief, squeezing his huge hand, 'Oh Willie, you're so sweet not to mind!'

'Och now don't push yer luck. I didn't say I didn't mind I just said I wasn't cross.' But he smiled. 'Come here.' He put his arm around my shoulders and kissed my cheek. We sat there companionably together for a moment. After a while he began to nibble my ear.

'Are ye quite sure now?' he mumbled.

I smiled but brushed him away. 'Quite sure.'

It was true too. My libido, which only moments before had been revving up like nobody's business, had sunk right down to join my heart, which all this time had been quietly watching from the sidelines, a spectator rather than a participant.

Willie sighed and abandoned my ear. 'Shame,' he reflected. 'Just what you needed really.'

I raised my eyebrows. 'A damn good seeing to you mean?'

He chuckled. 'Well, that was what you were after anyway, wasn't it? Only not with me?'

I opened my mouth to protest, but suddenly, couldn't be bothered. I smiled. 'Perhaps. I'm glad I didn't though.'

He shook his head wearily. 'You London women,' he mused. 'Yer like tight bloody springs when ye come up here, yer all so wound up with yer dinner parties and yer children and yer husband's office politics, you dinny know how to relax any more.'

'And you're the man to show us how are you, Willie? To uncoil our springs?'

He grinned at me sideways. 'Just yours, o' course.'

I smiled. 'Of course.'

I wondered, as we sat there together on the edge of the bed, just how many highly strung London women Willie had indeed worked his magic on. And whether he was right. Yes, maybe I would have felt better if I'd gone through with it, particularly if the warm-up had been anything to go by, but in my heart I was glad I hadn't. I'd gone much too far already. I looked around for my clothes.

'I must get back.'

He held on to my shoulder, gently but firmly. 'Och now don't be running off just yet, Tess. Just because you got cold feet doesn't mean you have to scuttle away like a frightened rabbit. Lie down next to me for a few minutes and let's at least couch up and keep warm together for a bit, eh? Come on, we can still be friendly, don't leave me here on a sour note.'

I glanced across at him doubtfully. His eyes were warm and gentle. I wasn't convinced our definitions of friendly totally coincided since mine didn't usually extend to lying around stark naked with strange men in huts, but since his clearly did, it seemed rude not to somehow. I lay down hesitantly. Just for a moment or two. And anyway, I reasoned, he'd probably be asleep in a few minutes. I could slip away then.

I turned my head and glanced at him. Sure enough his eyes were closing rapidly, his chest expanding like a pair of giant bellows and his mouth dropping slowly open. A moment later he was fast asleep. I smiled. There was no way I was falling asleep, I had to get back. The trouble was I felt so damn sleepy all of a sudden. I sighed and started to raise myself up onto my elbows, but inexplicably, sank back again. My head seemed so thick and heavy, and totally opposed to movement. Perhaps I should stay and rest a moment longer? After all, it was so delightfully peaceful here in this little wooden hut by the river and I did feel so warm and relaxed and well — *safe* now that Willie was asleep. I turned my head — God, it was an effort just to do *that* — and gazed out of the grimy window to the huge pale moon that was coming up over the horizon, casting its path of milky light. Outside the birds were still singing determinedly and I could hear the river rushing by next to us. It was all so gloriously restful that I did just pull the rug up to my chin, curl my legs up and snuggle down. Slowly, gratefully, I shut my weary eyes. Just for a moment, of course.

Chapter Eleven

'No, she's definitely not here,' called a familiar voice.

'Let's walk along to the bridge and then come back on the other side,' came an equally familiar, but rather strained response. 'And then I think I'm going to ring the police, it's almost midnight.'

I opened my eyes blearily and blinked. David? Had that been David's voice? I frowned. What on earth was he doing wandering around shouting about the police – particularly if it was midnight? Why wasn't he here in bed with me? I flung my arm out for the light on the bedside table and as I did so, my hand froze. Suddenly I went cold. I sat bolt upright and the curtain came up on the nightmare. He wasn't here in bed with me because I was still in the rude sod hut with that rude sod Willie! A horrified eyes-right at the vast, inert, snoring mass beside me confirmed this terrifying truth. So David must be – I yelped silently – outside! Looking for me, searching for me, with my father. Shit! I damn nearly did. I sat for a moment, rigid with terror, then hurtled into action. I flew out of bed, and shot behind the door, waiting for the urgent rattle of the door handle for the commanding, 'Open up!' For basically, my comeuppance.

Seconds passed. Nothing happened. Nothing? No white-faced husband, no quivering, accusing finger, no fire and brimstone from the vicar? With a heart beating like a bongo drum I realized I was in some sort of reprieve here and I had to take advantage. I got a grip. First I gripped my shirt, then I gripped my pants, and then I ran for cover under the only window in the hut. I coaxed my trembling arms into my shirt-sleeves, willed my legs into my knickers, and slowly came up under the sill in silent prayer. I peered out. Oh please God, please don't let them be right outside peering in. Don't let our eyes meet! I hadn't quite grown accustomed to the dark and the window was thick with grime but after a moment, I could see that my prayer had been answered. Certainly there were a couple of shadowy figures out there wielding long sticks in the grass, certainly they did resemble my father and my husband – but thank the Lord, they were incontrovertibly *on the other side of the river.*

Oh thank you God, thank you, thank you! I fell to my knees in yet more prayer and as I did, spotted my skirt, hastily abandoned under the bed, and bent to put it on, just as David's voice rang out again across the water.

'You don't think she could be in the hut, do you, Ian? It's shallow here, I could just about wade across.'

My leg froze, poised as it was to plunge through the waistband of my skirt.

'Bound to be locked,' responded my father rationally. 'And anyway, we can try it on the way back. Come on, let's walk up to the bridge first.'

Oh bless you, Daddy, bless you and keep you in radiant health now and for ever more for dissuading David from taking that retrograde step across the water and saving me from subsequent divorce proceedings!

I threw the rest of my clothes on any old how, fumbled

with my buttons, managed a couple but gave up on the rest, and hastened to the door. I was off, I was out of here as they say in the movies, but as I reached for the latch, my hand stopped short. *Wait a minute, Tess.* What if they came back here and woke up Willie? I glanced over my shoulder at the huge, slumbering lump on the bed, face down, spreadeagled and snoring like a demon. What if he came round in a haze, rubbed his eyes sleepily and mumbled something like – 'Hmmm? Tess? Oh yes, she was here a moment ago. I should know, I was about to give her a damn good rogering!' Oh no, that would never do!

I grabbed his shoulder and shook it violently.

'Willie!' I hissed. 'Willie! You've got to wake up!'

I thumped him with all my might between the shoulder blades and then again in the kidneys, but I was as a flea to an elephant. He didn't so much as break the rhythm of his snores. Oh God! I looked around frantically for something to whack him with – an implement, something hard with spikes preferably. All I could see was a brace of pheasants hanging on a wall. A smutty rhyme about not being the pheasant plucker but the pheasant plucker's mate sprang inconveniently to mind and only served to make me more desperate than ever to wake this pleasant fuc– this bastard up!

'Willie, for God's sake wake up!' I flung myself on top of him, straddling his back, bouncing hard, gripping with my knees in true Pony Club style.

'Willie, are you deaf? Are you dead? Wake up, will you!' I said, as loud as I dared in his ear. I bit the lobe savagely just for good measure.

'Eh, wha—?' he responded sleepily as I tugged hard at his hair.

'Willie, my husband's outside,' I gasped. 'He's got a gun!'

'Mmmm,' he mumbled. 'Not yet, Tess, later maybe.' He gave a faint sigh, smacked his huge chops and fell back to sleep, muttering something about 'insatiable bloody urban wenches'.

I clapped my hand to my mouth in horror. Oh God, this was exactly the sort of incoherent mumbling I was terrified of, I had to do something – fast! I thought wildly for a second, then leaned over and cupped my hands to his ears.

'Poachers!' I hissed.

Willie's arm instinctively shot under the bed, he grabbed his gun and then rose up backwards like a monster from the depths, shaking me off his back like a drop of water. I fell with an almighty thump on the floor, landing smack on my coccyx.

'Ouch!' I yelped, as Willie strode stark naked to the door.

'Where?' he barked.

'No! No, not really!' I shrieked, flinging myself at his ankle and just managing to tackle it before he could push open the door and blow my husband's brains out. He tried to shake me off but I sank my teeth into his Achilles heel.

'Ow!'

'Then listen!' I pleaded. 'Not poachers, Willie, David! He's out there with my father – they're looking for me.'

Willie frowned down at me from his gigantic height.

Slow thought processes began to engage. He scratched his huge, giant's head.

'David?'

For a moment I wondered if I wasn't in fact addressing Goliath here and I was about to get a front-row seat at a very modern stoning.

'Yes, David, my husband, you stupid great berk!' I croaked, very nearly croaking comprehensively right there and then on the floorboards. My heart seemed very weak; I wasn't sure if it could take much more of this. Then I heard a truly terrifying sound. *Running footsteps.* And the voice accompanying the footsteps belonged to my husband.

'There's someone in the hut!' he shouted.

Willie and I stared at each other.

'Quick, under the bed,' Willie hissed, suddenly very much alive to the situation.

Sadly I was very much dead, paralysed from the brain down. Willie seized me and with his huge paws, folded me in half like a camp bed then shoved me under, just managing to kick a recalcitrant leg out of sight as the door flew open.

'Oi!' roared Willie as my husband and father flew in. 'What's going on?'

'Willie,' panted David, 'we're looking for Tess. Have you seen her?'

'Fock me, I thought you were poachers,' bellowed Willie convincingly enough, still stark naked and handily brandishing a gun. 'Nearly wasted the pair of ye!'

'Have you seen Tess?' demanded David again.

Under the bed I shut my eyes tight, pressed my nose

hard into the floorboards and prayed to Almighty God that the rampant, nervous diarrhoea that was threatening to engulf me didn't, nor that my legs, which seemed to be twitching convulsively, would shoot out and kick my husband inadvertently on the ankle, thus giving the game away.

'Tess?' said Willie. 'No. Why, is she lost?'

David's voice when it came was harsh and unnatural. 'Been gone since teatime,' he said. 'Terrified she's fallen in the river. So dark.'

Oh my poor love, my poor love! I shed silent, guilty tears for my stricken, fearful husband. 'I'll make it up to you,' I sincerely promised an earwig that was trapped down a crack in the floorboards. Oh David, David, David, I'm so sorry. I'll make it up to you, I swear!

'Och noo, no danger of that,' soothed Willie. 'I've been up and doon this river all evening, had a feeling there was poachers about, ye see. Thought I'd kip in here to make sure and came in about half an hour ago. I'd know if there was summat amiss. If you ask me she's fallen asleep somewhere. Had she been drinking?'

'Well, yes,' David admitted, 'she had.'

'She'd had a whole damn bottle!' barked my father. 'Willie's right, she's asleep in some blasted field somewhere, and she won't come to till dawn with all that alcohol inside her. I'll tell you something, when she does, I'll give her a piece of my mind!'

I quaked silently under the bed.

'Well, I hope you're right.' David sounded slightly reassured.

'Tell you what,' suggested Willie. 'We'll try yellin' for

her. You go off in that direction towards Frenche's Farm, I'll go back upriver, and you mark my words if we don't find her in some haystack or trip over her in a ditch or something.'

I hadn't actually taken a breath for a full, terrifying forty seconds now, but as things did seem to be reaching some sort of a climax, I allowed myself a brief inhalation lest I fall into a coma. This achieved, and still staying perfectly still, I swivelled my eyeballs up from the floorboards and right. Just eighteen inches away were my father's black boots, to the left of those, David's green ones, and completing the triangle, Willie's bare feet. I saw Willie's hand come down. He reached for his trousers, pulled them on, then seized his own boots and set them upright, dextrously flipping the white bra strap that was hanging decoratively out of the side of one inside and trampling it down with his foot. I whimpered silently to the earwig.

'Come on then, off we go, no point hanging about,' Willie ordered. 'We're not going to find her in here, are we?' And with that he ushered the search-party out of his hut.

This struck me as being a particularly sick joke, but I blessed him from the bottom of my overworked heart, knowing he was doing a damn good job of saving my bacon. I counted shakily to a hundred and when it was clear the posse of men would not be coming back with a search warrant, I crawled out from under the bed.

Still feeling very wobbly, I crossed over to the window and peered out just in time to see them disappear round the bend; Willie in one direction, David and my father in the other. With a last furtive look around in case I'd left something, I too slunk out. I tiptoed round the back of the hut, found my shoes where I'd kicked them off in a joyful moment in Willie's arms – thank God they'd missed those – and hastily slipped into them. Then I scurried off on very shaky legs in the direction of home and hopefully, safety.

I scampered along in the dark, my heart hammering high in my oesophagus. Dad and David were heading off to Frenche's Farm which meant I had to run like billyo to a destination somewhere in between there and the house so they could neatly trip over me on their way back, that much was clear. I hurtled along, leaping ditches, hurdling low stone walls and eventually came to the footpath I knew they'd take to get home. With a thumping heart I sank down in a ditch. This would have to do. This was just about the route they were bound to take back. I drew up my knees and hugged them hard, shivering wildly, my eyes huge with horror.

Let's get this straight then, Tess. You've just had a sexy romp with Willie the gillie, is that right? Interesting departure from the norm, but we'll discuss that later. For the moment though, here you are in a ditch. In a field. In the middle of the night. How on earth had this happened, I wondered in amazement. How on earth had this situation even *begun* to arise, let alone escalated into this? Right at this moment it just didn't bear thinking about. What did though, was how to successfully extricate myself from it. I had to keep my head, that much was clear. There'd be plenty of time for horror and remorse later.

Five minutes went by, then ten, until finally, I heard footsteps again. Numb with cold and terror, especially since my renown as an actress is not great, I began to make strange mumbling noises. As the footsteps got closer, I stretched my arms above my head and gave what I hoped was an accurate rendition of a sleepy yawn, but actually had more of a ring of a deranged harridan about it. The footsteps halted.

'What's that?' said David.

'What?'

I yawned and mumbled again.

'Over there, I heard something!'

I stretched widely this time. '*Ohhhh* . . . goodness gracious me. What a lovely sleep . . . mmmm, lovely.'

'Tess!'

In a moment the footsteps were a running stampede and in another, I was being scooped up into my husband's arms.

'Tess! Thank God!' He hugged me close.

'David? What?' I rubbed my eyes.

I hoped he wasn't hugging me close enough to notice that my heart was pumping unnaturally fast for someone who's just been raised from a deep, soporific slumber.

'What the hell happened to you? We've been looking everywhere for you!'

'You've got some explaining to do, my girl,' barked my father.

I cringed, but somehow this was infinitely preferable to David's relieved tones. Oh yes, give me a hair shirt right now, and knickers to match. I'd slip them on and wear them for ever.

Hating myself, I gazed at David and feigned a puzzled stare.

'Hello darling, what are you doing here?'

'I'm bloody looking for you, that's what I'm doing here,' he burst out, relief quite rightly turning to outrage. 'I'm tramping up and down this sodding river all night wondering if my drunken wife has fallen in leaving two motherless children, that's what I'm bloody doing!'

I rubbed my eyes. 'Mmm, I must have fallen asleep. I came out for a walk and sat down here in the ditch and it was so lovely and peaceful and the stars were so beautiful, I must have drifted off . . .' I looked around in amazement. 'Goodness, it's pitch dark.'

David took me fiercely by the arm. 'Well, it would be, wouldn't it, it's one o'clock in the morning! Come on. We're going home.'

'I'll go and tell Willie,' muttered my father angrily. 'You *stupid* girl, Tessa.'

And with that he strode off in the other direction to tell Willie what he already knew.

David and I started for home in silence. He held on to my arm as I stumbled along in the dark, tripping over tufts of grass. I glanced up. His face was white and his lips very tight.

'Sorry, darling,' I said tentatively. 'I didn't mean to worry you.'

David's mouth remained tense. He looked straight ahead.

'David?'

'Unless you want to be on the receiving end of a torrent of abuse,' he snapped, 'I should bloody well keep quiet and let me seethe in private, OK?'

'OK,' I mumbled.

We walked quickly and quite soon were crossing the back lawn up to the house.

'The lights are all on,' I said in surprise.

'Well of course,' said David with scarce-disguised sarcasm. 'Piers is poised to ring the undertaker, Penny's planning her funeral outfit and your mother's choosing the hymns.'

'Oh David, I'm so sorry,' I gasped. 'I didn't realize I'd worried everyone so much.'

The back door swung open as we approached and Mummy peered out, white-faced in her dressing gown.

'Thank God!' she whispered, giving me a hug.

'Sorry, Mummy,' I murmured into her shoulder, feeling truly, deeply appalling now. 'I – I fell asleep.'

'Where?'

'In a field.'

'Darling!'

Penny and Piers were sitting at the kitchen table in their pyjamas. They gave me a pair of withering looks, then got up, yawned ostentatiously and made for the stairs.

'Sorry Penny, Piers,' I muttered after them. They didn't reply.

Mummy patted me on the shoulder, recovering slightly. 'Never mind. At least you're safe, that's all that matters.'

She smiled and rather shakily picked up her *Telegraph* from the table. She followed the others upstairs, using the banisters for support, I noted, rather more than she would normally. I gulped, mortified.

'Come on then,' said David gruffly. 'Let's go up too.'

We went upstairs together in silence. When we got to our room I went on through into the bathroom.

'I'm going to have a quick bath,' I muttered.

'What now?' he demanded. 'In the middle of the night?'

I nodded miserably as I peeled off my clothes and threw them at the foot of the bed.

'I must,' I whispered. 'Won't be long.'

I lay back in the hot, bubbly water and stared numbly at the bathroom ceiling. Great waves of shame and self-disgust swept over me. How awful. How completely despicable of me. How could I have done such a thing? Jeopardized my marriage, my family like that – and for what? A quick roll in the hay with a man I'd never even really noticed before, let alone fancied? Jesus, when you think about it, it could have been anyone, couldn't it – Edward, Piers – whoever had just happened to be strolling on by that night. *Oh, hello Tess, fancy a quick one? Sure, why not?* What was I, a tart or something? I groaned and sank down in the water, Bade-das, shame and revulsion washing over me.

What on earth had got into me? Well, drink, obviously, a whole bottle in fact, and rejection too, of course. Patrick and Josie zooming off like that had really got my blood up, but – good grief, Tess, that's no excuse. I shouldn't even have been thinking about Patrick in the first place! I was a married woman. Suddenly I seized the soap. I had to be clean, really clean. I soaped and scrubbed every inch of myself, employing flannels, sponges, whatever cleaning equipment came to hand, a Brillo pad would have done nicely, but then just as suddenly, I stopped. I dropped the flannel in the water and sank down miserably into the bubbles. What was the use? I'd never be truly clean again, would I?

179

The full implications of what I'd done hit me. I'd cheated. I'd betrayed David. I'd had – not a fling, because that sounded so impulsive, so carefree – and not an affair because that sounded more serious, more intense, two people completely at the mercy of their romantic impulses . . . no, what I'd had was casual sex. Not all the way, granted. Happily I'd had the sense to resist that temptation, but quite a lot of the way nonetheless. I wondered, tentatively, if this made me, not a fallen woman but just a stumbling one? Since I hadn't actually gone the whole hog? Just a half hog?

I shivered even though the water was piping hot. No, that was undoubtedly a blessing but it was no mitigation. I still had a hell of a lot of explaining to do. Oh dear God, I muttered silently, please forgive me. I eyed the ceiling nervously. It was a long time since I'd addressed Him properly, rather than just angrily in passing because I'd tripped over the carpet or lost my car keys. No, I hadn't prayed for a long time, chiefly because I always identified Him with my father. In fact, it seemed to me that even now, floating above me, was not an old man with a long white beard and a staff, but a middle-aged man with a bristling moustache and a dog collar. The Reverend Ian Fergusson. I winced.

Dear God, I struggled on, I'm well aware I've made a complete and utter pig's ear of things tonight, but I swear that I'll make amends. From now on I am determined to devote myself entirely to my husband and family. To be nothing more than a good wife and mother. I took a deep breath. I intend to darn socks rather than throw them away. I intend to make puddings rather than chuck yoghurts on the table and demand to know what's wrong with that? I intend to make plum jam – David's favourite – to fingerpaint, to throw away all the children's videos, particularly those Disney ones that immobilize them for a blissful eighty-six minutes, and instead I intend to read them storybooks for eighty-six minutes. I winced slightly at this but staunchly continued. I intend to indulge in frequent bouts of imaginative play with my children, to be Robin to Hugo's Batman, to be Barbie's pony, to neigh, whinny and trot on command and to indulge in frequent bouts of imaginative sex with my husband – not all at the same time, you understand, but I think you get the general idea. In short, I intend to subjugate my own wishes to those of my family and this, dear God, is something that I want You to know I do willingly. When I think how close I came to losing them, to ruining everything – oh dear God, it simply doesn't bear thinking about! With this I sank back in the water and covered my face with a flannel.

I lay there motionless for a while, when suddenly I heard a noise. I whipped the flannel off. There was a sort of rustling sound coming from the bedroom. I sat up. Good heavens, was David still awake? Was he waiting for me? Reading perhaps? Crikey, I'd been ages! I quickly hopped out of the bath and rubbed myself dry with a towel. I did hope he wasn't waiting to interrogate me or something, I'd rather hoped he'd be sound asleep by now. I stopped still for a moment and listened. No, it was all quiet again now, it must have been the sheets rustling as he turned over. He wouldn't interrogate me anyway, I thought gratefully, it wasn't in his nature. He always believed people, always thought the best of them. I wrapped a dry towel around me and crept back into the bedroom. Yes, my darling husband, he didn't have a suspicious bone in his body, he –

'David!'

I stopped dead in my tracks. My darling husband stood at the foot of the bed peering very suspiciously into my underwear.

'What's all this sheep's wool?' he enquired, picking up my shirt. 'Look, it's everywhere.'

I gazed down. All over the carpet and inside my clothes was indeed a huge amount of white fluffy stuff. I gulped. 'Ah, that'll be the sheep,' I croaked.

'What sheep?'

'The one I fell asleep on.'

'You fell asleep on a sheep?'

'Not a live one.'

'A dead one?'

'Er . . .' There didn't seem to be another option. 'Yes. A dead one. I didn't realize at the time, of course. Just thought it was a nice cosy pillow.'

'But . . . the field we found you in didn't have any sheep in it.'

'Ah, no, I moved. When I realized. Hopped over a wall into a different field.'

'Good God. And went back to sleep?'

I hung my head and shook it miserably. 'I was very, very drunk, you know.'

David briefly tore his hair. 'Clearly. God, it must have reeked.'

'Oh it did, and that's why I wanted a bath so much,' I went on quickly. 'To get rid of the pong.'

David dropped my clothes hurriedly. He shook his head in disbelief, sighed and got into bed.

'Why are you still awake?' I mumbled, climbing in next to him and quickly turning out the light so he couldn't see my flaming face.

'Because I wanted to tell you something.'

'What?' I sat up in alarm, my heart leaping into my mouth. He was leaving me. He'd seen through the whole charade.

'Peter rang when you were out.'

'Oh!' I relaxed. 'Your clerk?'

'Mmm. There's some case that's come up, he wants me to fly back and do it.'

I lay down again. 'Oh, what a bore. When?'

'Tomorrow.'

'Tomorrow! What did you say?'

'I said I would. I have to, Tess. It's a Court of Appeal thing that was supposed to have surfaced ages ago and didn't. Now it's suddenly reared its ugly head again.'

I lay there, realizing I didn't have a leg to stand on. Normally I'd be incensed, argue long and hard about how his work was yet again ruining the only family holiday of the year and how on earth was I supposed to cope with the children on my own, et cetera . . .

'So you'll go tomorrow?' I said meekly.

'After breakfast. Just thought I'd mention it tonight in case you fancied a lie-in after your hectic night out with your dead sheep and woke to find your husband had packed his bags and gone. Just thought I'd let you know it's nothing personal,' he said grimly.

'Ah!' I laughed nervously. 'Righto, darling. Thanks for letting me know.'

'My pleasure,' he said darkly, before finally falling asleep.

Chapter Twelve

The following morning I awoke late to find that David had already gone. The covers on his side of the bed were thrown back and a couple of wet towels lay abandoned in a heap on the floor. Normally I'd smile, stretch lazily and think how nice it was to have the bed to myself, but on this particular morning I badly wanted to see him there next to me. The empty pillow looked at me reproachfully. I sighed, hating myself already, but although my conscience hurt like hell it was nothing to the physical state I was in. My head was throbbing like a New Wave disco, my mouth was desert-dry and my bladder so fit to burst I had to get out of bed that very second, and since our bathroom didn't possess a loo — that would be far too convenient — make my way as fast as possible down to the one at the end of the corridor.

I lumbered along the landing like some rough beast with my eyes half-shut and my hands already outstretched and groping for the door, when Penny suddenly stepped out in front of me, in true paparazzi style. She'd clearly been loitering around the airing cupboard for some time, waiting for a chance to doorstep me, to get an exclusive. Her eyes gleamed alarmingly as she barred the way with a mountain of ironing in her arms. I stumbled to a halt in front of her.

'Oh, good *morning*,' she chirruped, 'and how are we feeling today?'

'Er, fine, thanks Penny,' I lied. 'Has David gone?'

'Yes, Piers took him to the airport. We thought you might need a lie-in after last night.' She raised her eyebrows. 'Quite an adventure, eh? David said something about a dead sheep. Really setting your sights high this time, aren't you?'

'Ah, yes. Um, that was kind of Piers. To take David, I mean.' I tried to sidle past her but she sidled with me.

'Wasn't it?' she said beaming broadly, obviously on the brink of whipping out her microphone and asking one of her most probing questions.

'So tell me, Tess, what exactly – oi!'

With one quick flick I knocked the pile of ironing clean out of her hands and sidestepped around her.

'Oops, sorry, Penny! Hand slipped! Can't stop now, emergency!'

I sprinted on past her, but as luck would have it, arrived at the loo at precisely the same moment as Josie, whose bedroom was next door. Our hands simultaneously went for the handle.

'Sorry, go ahead,' I muttered.

'Oh hi, Tess. What happened last night?'

'Oh well, you know, this and that,' I said, grinning manically and hopping around from foot to foot. God, if I could just have a pee, was that too much to ask first thing in the morning? The place seemed to be swarming with budding interrogative journalists. Couldn't they organize a press conference later or something?

'Um, are you –?' I jerked my head towards the loo.

186

'No no,' she insisted. 'You first.'

'Thanks.' I dashed in. Oh, the relief . . .

When I came out she was still waiting. She smiled. 'My evening didn't amount to much either,' she said.

I stared at her blankly for a moment, then remembered. Of course, Patrick.

'Oh yes, how was it?' I asked politely. As if I cared! God, I never wanted to so much as *talk* to another man aside from my husband as long as I lived!

'It was OK,' she said, nodding without much conviction.

'Really?'

'Well,' she grimaced, 'maybe not. In the end we only went for a quick drink. I was back here by ten.'

'Oh!'

'Yeah,' she scratched her chin. 'He'd forgotten he had some phone calls to make to Italy, about his work. Galleries, that kind of thing.'

'Oh, right. Did you mind?'

She shrugged. 'Nah, not really. To be honest I think he's a bit old for me, or maybe I'm too young for him. Actually I don't even think he's that interested, I think he just thought I'd look good on the back of his bike.' She grinned good-humouredly.

That was what I liked about Josie, she had such refreshing Aussie candour.

'Well, you certainly did,' I said warmly. 'You looked great. I saw you go off.'

'He saw you too,' she said. 'Hey, I had no idea you two were an item?'

'Oh, er, yes. A long time ago.'

'Yeah, he said.' She folded her arms and leant on the wall as if we might be there for some time. 'In fact, he said —'

'Um, listen Josie,' I interrupted, unwilling to discuss any more of my menfolk, past or present, with anyone else on the landing that morning. 'I've got something I must do this morning. It's quite important. You wouldn't mind having the children on your own for a few hours, would you? I know you're due a morning off, but —'

'Nah, it's fine. We'll go down to the beach, go crabbing.'

'Oh thanks, you're a brick.'

She was. There was no malice in Josie's heart, and I shuddered as I remembered how I'd maligned her last night. And then I shuddered some more as I remembered everything else about last night too . . . Still, that was all in the past now and would be firmly entrenched there for ever if I had anything to do with it.

I threw some clean clothes on and went down to breakfast. Thankfully, most people appeared to have eaten already. Piers had taken David to the airport, Penny, thwarted in her attempts to cross-examine me, was about to go shopping, and Mummy and Laura had gone fishing. Only my father and Edward remained, and I soon found out why. Daddy was in full swing, furiously brandishing the *Telegraph* and ranting away to poor Edward about some vicar who'd got more or less every girl in his parish pregnant. Happily he was far too incensed to remember anything about last night, let alone berate me. I slipped quietly into a chair, blessed the randy vicar from the bottom of my heart and began to butter some toast.

'Makes me spit!' he thundered, poking his finger at the

newspaper. 'And it's not as if they'll even *do* anything about it, he probably won't even get his wrists slapped! Oh no, in all probability what he'll get is a nice spot of therapy, a caring shoulder to cry on so he can lay all his misdemeanours at society's door and explain exactly why he felt it was his bounden duty to knock up every single girl in the parish and all, mark my words, at the wretched tax payer's expense! Oh yes, the National Health Service will foot the counselling bill and then all the pregnant wenches will stagger into National Health hospitals to have his bastards and then they'll all be sent to bloody state schools, and who's paying for all that, eh?'

He glared at Edward who blinked nervously.

'I am, that's who and you, too, Edward! What's more you'll probably have to *teach* the bastards too! And all because a vicar, a man of the cloth, a *servant of God*, dips his wick in every passing fecund wench he fancies! MAKES MY BLOOD BOIL!' he bellowed.

Edward quaked into his porridge.

'He should be strung up, made an example of, eh?' He glared at the pair of us but I'd already propped up the *Guardian* Arts section on the Frosties packet and was well and truly unavailable for comment.

'Oh yes sir, definitely sir,' muttered Edward timidly.

'He should be setting an example – *noblesse oblige* and all that. Has he no concept of duty, of – where are you off to, Tess?'

I paused, halfway out of the door with a piece of toast in my hand. Damn. Thought I'd timed that rather nicely, actually.

'I have to go and see Willie.' Best not to lie.

My father raised his eyebrows enquiringly. 'Oh?'

'Yes. I left some of my best flies down by the river yesterday and I think he's probably picked them up.' Best to lie.

'Hrmph. Well, you won't find him at the river today, it's his day off. He'll be at home.' He frowned, suddenly remembering. 'Now then Tessa, what on earth was last night all about, eh? David and I spent the best part of two hours looking for you. Your mother was worried sick!'

I took a deep breath and was about to embark on an elaborate explanation when my eye suddenly lit on the same offending article in the *Guardian*. Marvellous. I screwed my eyes up quizzically.

'Oh look, there's a picture of that vicar in here too. Did you know him, Daddy?' I asked innocently.

My father glanced across at the unfortunate man's mug-shot and came rapidly to the boil again.

'Makes me spit!' he roared, spitting indeed, a small piece of toast right across the table and hitting Edward squarely in the eye. He flinched in terror.

'No, I didn't know him, thank God! Dirty little scumbag, he was no friend of mine – but then that's hardly surprising, is it? A family man like me with no extra-marital affairs to speak of like most of the clergy – no prizes for guessing why I won't be the next Bishop of Durham, eh? No good at all to the modern church am I, eh? What?' He glared at the only person who hadn't dared to make an escape like everyone else.

I tiptoed out.

'Er, no sir, I mean yes sir, I'm sure you are sir,' I heard poor Edward mumble as I slipped down the hall.

My car keys were on the hall table. So Willie would be at home today, eh? Even better, even more private. I'd go and see him there. It was probably totally unnecessary but I wanted to make things crystal clear to that man. Warn him off. I was quite sure he knew how the land lay, that it had been a drunken mistake, I cringed – a never-to-be-repeated foolish escapade . . . but it wouldn't do any harm to make sure.

I ran down the stone steps into the drive and realized it looked remarkably empty. Damn, no cars. Piers had taken his to the airport so Penny had obviously taken mine shopping. That left Daddy's, which I wasn't convinced I was insured for. I was about to go back and ask him when I spotted the bicycles in the front porch. I paused. Yes, why not? I didn't particularly want to encounter Daddy again, and apart from anything else a cycle-ride would do me good. Blow the cobwebs away. When was the last time I'd had any decent exercise? Apart from last night, of course.

I wheeled a pretty ancient-looking contraption out into the drive and inspected it. No gears, naturally, but it appeared to have two wheels, a saddle and at least one brake, and it wasn't as if I was going to go very fast, was it? Anyway, Willie didn't live too far away. If I got sick of it I could abandon it in a hedge and pick it up later. I got on, wobbled precariously, then pedalled unsteadily down the drive. I went through the gate, round the corner and set off in the direction of Willie's house.

The first half-mile was easy enough – a doddle, in fact, I thought cheerfully as I gently pedalled along the lanes enjoying the fresh air. But then a hill appeared, followed by another and then another, and all of them went up, rather than down. I'd been past Willie's house once before in the car but I certainly hadn't remembered it enjoying quite such an elevated position, being quite so much in orbit as it were. God, I'd be on a different planet soon. On and on I pedalled and puffed, onwards and upwards, my legs going not so much like pistons as shivering lumps of cellulite. Finally I dismounted and pushed the wretched thing up the hill, once more bemoaning my lack of aerobics classes. Good grief, I'd need an oxygen cylinder soon. Surely no more hills? Just the one, a vertical one as it happened, around the next bend, and then just as I thought I might give up and collapse in a heap in the hedge, Willie's little bungalow came into view. It was clustered amongst ten or twelve other identical white bungalows – for moral support, almost – on this vast mountainside, looking as if just one little shove from behind would cause the whole lot to slide off down into the valley below.

I threw my bike down outside, boiling hot now and in a muck sweat, and fumbled gratefully with the garden gate. I was keen to be inside where there seemed less danger of plummeting into the abyss. I rapped smartly on the front door and as Willie opened it, realized I'd been so taken up with my epic journey I hadn't the faintest idea what I was going to say.

'Hi!' I gasped, discovering that actually I couldn't speak anyway. I bent double, clutched my knees for support and fought for oxygen.

Willie looked down at me in surprise, dressed as he was

in nothing but a green towelling dressing gown with a piece of toast in one hand, a mug of tea in the other.

'Tess! What on earth are you doin' here?'

I made some vague hand-movements to try to convey that I couldn't actually speak right now but would endeavour to do so just as soon as was humanly possible.

Willie looked over my bent back at my bike in the hedge. 'Good God, you didn't cycle here, did you?'

It was rather like being in the dentist's chair with half a ton of steel equipment in one's mouth and an invitation to speak at length on a chosen subject. He ushered me in and I followed, still speechless but boiling to death under my Guernsey after all that exertion.

'Just a second,' I panted, struggling to pull the wretched thing over my head. When I emerged from its woolly depths, a rather alarming light was gleaming in Willie's eye. 'Changed your mind, eh, Tess? Fine by me! Hang on, I'll just get rid of my breakfast and then I'll get my kit off too.'

He stuffed a whole piece of toast in his mouth and went for his dressing-gown cord. I recoiled. Oh no! He thought I'd come to finish the job! Thought I'd cycled feverishly up a mountainside to get to grips with his naked person only hours after I'd left it in the rude sod hut!

'No!' I shrieked. 'No, Willie. I —'

Too late. The cord was being loosened. I instantly clapped my hands over my eyes.

'Put it away,' I hissed. 'For God's sake, didn't you get enough of that last night? I know I did, now put it away!'

There was a pause.

'Has it gone?' I demanded.

'Well, I certainly can't see it,' said a female voice, 'unless it's very, very wee.'

I gasped in horror and swung around. A pretty dark-haired girl with freckles and a cheeky grin popped her head out from the other side of the sofa where she'd clearly been reclining.

'Oh!'

'Tess, this is Kirsten,' Willie informed me, a wicked smile on his face. His dressing-gown was still firmly wound up, like me I realized. I blushed.

The girl swung her brown legs round, stood up and came towards us. Long dark hair, a waist, the shortest of denim skirts and a red gingham shirt tied in a knot above her midriff. I was old enough to be her mother, but probably far too ugly. She grinned at me.

'Don't mind me, I was just off.'

'Oh! No! Well, you don't have to,' I blustered, pushing my sweaty hair out of my eyes. 'I mean we weren't – I mean there's nothing –'

She winked. 'I should pick up where you left off last night if I were you. Bye Willie, have fun!'

She tapped him playfully on the cheek and sauntered out. I listened for a scream, hoping she might fall over the precipice but no such luck.

'Who was that?' I asked faintly.

'Kirsten,' said Willie with a grin. 'She . . . um,' he wrinkled his brow thoughtfully, 'she came to borrow some tea-bags.'

I stared at him. 'Oh yeah? Well, she forgot to take them with her, didn't she, unless she stuffed them in her handbag.'

'Yes, she did actually.' Willie calmly bent down to pick a couple of empty coffee mugs up off the carpet. He straightened up and looked at me. 'Kirsten's my cousin, Tess. She lives down the road.'

I flushed. 'Oh! Gosh, I'm sorry Willie. It's none of my business anyway.'

Willie went behind the breakfast bar to turn a whistling kettle off. 'Och, it's only natural,' he grinned. 'You don't want to feel one of many.'

'No, I don't! I mean, it doesn't matter if I am or not, if you see what I mean. That's what I came to tell you. What happened down by the river shouldn't have, should it? Well, I'm – sure you know that already, but I just thought I'd better come and make sure.'

He poured the boiling water into a teapot, watching me. Silent.

I licked my lips and laughed nervously. 'Come on, Willie, help me out here. I mean it was just a one off, wasn't it? Great fun and all that but it was a mistake, *my* mistake, and I don't want it to happen again,' I said decisively.

He put the kettle down and looked at me carefully. 'Aye, but it will though, won't it?'

'What?'

'Happen again.'

'No! Certainly not. That's what I –'

'Och, I don't mean with me, necessarily, but I'm pretty sure that's not the end of your extra-marital activity.' He smiled. 'Let's face it, Tess, up until you got cold feet you were absolutely panting for it.'

I flushed. 'How dare you! I was not!'

He laughed. 'Och now, don't get excited. Nothing

wrong with being keen; nothing wrong with enjoying things, is there?' He winked.

'Certainly there's something wrong if it's outside the marriage bed,' I stormed piously. 'You can't just go around doing it with whoever takes your fancy, not when you've got responsibilities, a husband and family like I have. People could get hurt.'

'Of course,' he agreed, 'and that's why it's so much better to do it with me than with anyone else.' He twinkled knowingly at me. 'Especially the person you originally had marked out for the job.'

I flushed. 'What d'you mean?'

'Come on now.' He handed me a cup of tea. 'Don't give me that. I knew damn well you'd been thwarted in some way yesterday. I also knew Patrick was back.'

'What's that got to do with it?'

He leaned on the breakfast bar and sighed. 'Tess, this is a small community. Everyone knows everything about everyone else. Everyone knows you had an affair with him years ago, everyone knows you never got over each other and everyone knows he's back. And so are you. Perhaps not everyone knows he chose to take your nanny out on a date late last night though.' He sipped his tea, regarding me thoughtfully over the top of his mug.

'That's got nothing to do with it,' I exploded. 'I was not looking for anything with Patrick, I was –'

He raised his eyebrows. 'Just looking forward to a bit of a treat, wasn't that what you said?'

I bit my lip and looked away. I could feel my face flaming.

Willie chuckled. 'Och Tess, I'm not laughing at you,

really I'm not. Not unkindly anyway.' He came round from the other side of the bar and put his arm round my shoulder. 'And you're right, this is a serious business. That's why I'm tellin' you.' He turned me round to face him, his expression grim. 'Think carefully before you mess around with the likes o' Patrick Cameron.'

'What d'you mean?' I whispered. 'Not that I intend to,' I added quickly.

'What I mean is you might not be able to extricate yourself from his arms quite so easily as you did from mine.'

'I haven't the faintest idea what you're talking about,' I said sharply, shrugging his hand off my shoulder.

He sat down on a bar stool next to me and sipped his tea. 'Look at it this way, Tess. Sex with me is safe, isn't it?'

I laughed hollowly. 'I'm not so sure, judging by the amount of women flitting in and out of your life.'

'What I mean is,' he went on, 'that you can almost regard me as a sort of service industry.' He flashed me an infuriatingly attractive grin. 'A bit of a meals-on-wheels if you like, or a mobile library. You have a need and I fill it, but with no strings attached. Certainly no heart-strings. It's just good old-fashioned lust, isn't it? But you fill that need with Patrick Cameron and mark my words, it'll be a whole new ball game. All those repressed emotions you two put the lid on years ago?' He shook his head. 'You open up that can of worms again and you won't know what's hit you.'

I smiled a superior smile. 'Willie, thank you for your concern but I assure you I have no intention of opening anything.' I took a gulp of tea. It was scalding hot and I burned my mouth.

He grinned. 'Oh good. I'm not sure I believe you, though. I still think you have a need.'

Suddenly I bridled. How *dare* he cross-examine me like this? I drew myself up haughtily.

'Yes, well, thank you so much for these pearls of wisdom about my life, Willie. I'm indebted to you, really I am, but rest assured I do *not* have a need and I certainly don't have one that requires filling with yours, or anyone else's "services" as you so quaintly put it. I require neither meals-on-wheels nor sex-on-tap which is, I take it, what you were offering. What happened last night was not only totally out of character but happened entirely under the influence of alcohol, something I do not generally indulge in. I want you to remember that.'

His mouth twitched. 'Och aye, I'll remember all right.'

'*That* is what I came here to tell you and that is all I have to say on the matter.' Was it my imagination or did I sound like Margaret Thatcher? 'Thank you for your concern but it's not necessary, do I make myself clear?'

He wrestled with a smile. 'Crystal.'

'Good.'

'Sorry if I spoke out of turn.'

'Not at all.'

'You're too kind.'

I turned away exasperated and drained my tea in silence. How did he manage to make me feel such a fool? It was infuriating! I was the educated, urbane, sophisticated one, wasn't I? He was just a blinking gillie, for heaven's sake . . . a keeper. What did he know about life in the real world?

The one that went on beyond the trees and the fields and the river, the one that thinking, chattering people lived in? This wasn't real life, damn it, this was a ruddy Utopia, a holiday camp. What did anyone who lived like this know, aside from which pools to fish and what the weather would be like tomorrow? A silence fell. Eventually Willie cleared his throat.

'So what happens now?'

I looked up, miles away. 'What? Oh, yes.' I stood up. 'I must be going.'

'No, no, I didn't mean that, I meant in your life.'

I frowned. 'Sorry?'

'Well, you're married now, you've had your bairns, your second one's about to start school, you've got your nice house in Putney, presumably you've more or less finished tarting it up, painting the dado rails, quarry-tiling the floor, adding a conservatory and you don't need a country cottage 'cos your dad's got this place . . . so what happens next?'

'Why does anything have to happen next?'

He shrugged. 'It always has done, hasn't it? Up to now? You've always had something to occupy you, to look forward to. A wedding, a bairn, another bairn, a house – so what's next?'

I sighed and folded my arms, regarding him narrowly. 'Why is it, Willie, that I get the distinct impression we're back to sex again? You mean an affair, don't you?'

'It's either that or an art appreciation course, or Silk Screens Made Easy, or Opera for Beginners perhaps, and I know which I'd rather do!' He grinned.

I shook my head wearily and stood up. 'You really are

incorrigible, and I don't know where you get your information about London women from, but you're woefully misinformed.'

Willie stood up. 'First-hand knowledge, Tess, not information. I see women like you all year round – and no, I don't sleep with them – but I observe them. Get a glimpse of their lives, their frustrations. I sympathize, really I do.' He put his arm round my shoulder as we walked to the door.

'Well gosh, Willie, I'm sure the entire female population of South East England will be truly comforted to know your thoughts are with us. That we can rely on your sympathy and understanding as we go about our boring, mundane lives.'

He chuckled, then as we reached the door, turned me around to face him. 'Seriously though, all I'm saying is that these are dangerous times.'

I raised my eyebrows at him. 'Oh really? For who?'

'For you, of course. At this stage in your life you're very vulnerable.' He bent down and kissed me on the cheek. 'Take care, Tess.' He stroked my cheek. 'I shall worry about you, you know.'

I smiled. He really was quite sweet. If a little simplistic. 'OK, I'll take care,' I assured him, humouring him.

He kissed me on the other cheek. 'See that you do.'

'I will, I will!'

He kissed me on the side of my mouth, softly. 'No, but really Tess,' he murmured, 'I mean it.'

'Yes, yes I mean it too,' I murmured back as he kissed me again. Heavens that was nice, all warm and soft and . . .

No! I pushed him away, angrily, furious with myself. Willie was laughing, his eyes dancing. 'You see?' He wagged his finger. 'Very, very dangerous!'

'No, I do not bloody see!' I stormed, wrestling with the doorknob. 'I haven't the faintest idea what you're talking about and if you'll excuse me I've got a million things to do today. I've got shopping to do, meals to cook, washing to do – art appreciation – ha! I wish! Opera for Beginners – Jesus, if only I had time! What happens next? Good God, I haven't got time for what happens *now*! For your information, Willie, I am always on the bloody go, I never sit still, there is never a moment in my hectic life that is not catered for and – Oh for God's sake open this sodding door and let me out of here before –'

'Before?' he enquired mildly.

'Before I wring your neck,' I hissed.

He laughed, reached up and pulled back the bolt at the top. I fled down the path to my bike.

'Pedal carefully now, Tess,' he warned, watching as I lifted the bicycle out of the hedge and swung my leg over. 'Don't go charging up a tractor's backside in your hot and bothered state.'

I wobbled precariously. 'Who's hot and bothered!' I cried. 'I've never been so blinking calm in my life!'

'Oh, by the way – catch!' He threw something and a rather grey bra landed on my head. 'I found this bit of erotica in my boot!' I grabbed it furiously and stuffed it in my pocket. I didn't look back but out of the corner of my eye I caught sight of him, head thrown back, laughing like a drain as I took off down the vertical slope with a vengeance.

I sped off. How dare he! How dare he take the mickey out of me like that! How dare he presume to know me so well, to judge me – after one drunken night! Bloody nerve, bloody men – bloody typical! Give them an inch and they take half a bloody mile. And him, a hick from the sticks – what did he know? What did he know about running a household, about the incessant demands of a family, the constant juggling that went on – he was just a man on his own living in the middle of nowhere!

I pedalled furiously, round one bend, round the next one and on down the hill. Oh, I knew what he thought all right. He thought I was a frustrated housewife who spent her entire life rolling around with gillies and plumbers and washing-machine repair men. He probably thought last night had been just another in a long line of blue-collar interludes – Jesus!

My feet were going like pistons now, and it was only on the third bend that I realized the folly of this. I was on a more or less vertical slope here. One did not pedal furiously on such a slope, one did not give oneself a flying start down an incline of this nature. One got enough of a flying start from the angle itself. I desperately tried the brakes, I mean brake, but quickly realized it wasn't a brake at all but just a decorative feature on the handlebars bearing absolutely no relation to what was going on with the wheels.

The scenery was whipping past like a speeded-up video now and I felt quite sick with fear. How on earth was I supposed to stop the wretched thing? I hurtled down, quite out of control, each hairpin bend becoming more difficult to negotiate than the last and it seemed that no sooner had one been accomplished than another was upon me. Shit! Should I stick my feet out onto the road, I wondered, or would that send me catapulting high into the air? I gripped the handlebars tight, the wind whistling past my ears, my hair streaming out behind me. Suddenly I knew there was no way on earth I could possibly negotiate another corner. I'd have to go for a crash landing. Ahead of me was a field, to the left, another hairpin bend. Better to shoot straight across the road, crash into the field and collapse on the grass rather than veer round the bend and crash on the lethal Tarmac, I decided.

'*Ahh, ahh ahhhhh!*' I shrieked in terror, as I shot across the road Kamikaze-style, as just to my left, a car appeared up around the bend. I don't remember much, but I do remember the sickening crunch of metal on metal. I also remember flying through the air, somersaulting over the car and registering that it was red. Then the last thing I remember, before I fell with a thump in the field, was Patrick's shocked eyes over the steering wheel. After that, all I recall was the blackness.

Chapter Thirteen

As I opened my eyes Patrick was leaning over me. His hand snaked furtively up under the blanket, his face was close to mine, his breath on my cheek. I froze.

'Don't even think about it, Patrick Cameron,' I snarled. 'I wouldn't sleep with you if you were the last man on earth.'

He blinked. 'I was just checking to see if you were breathing, Tess.'

'And if I wasn't you'd have had me anyway, would you? Dead or alive?'

'Don't be silly, you must be delirious. You've had an accident.'

'Oh, don't give me that. Wh-what? An accident?' I clutched the blanket to me in panic, only I could see now that it wasn't a blanket, it was somebody's coat, and I couldn't be in a bedroom because there was far too much fresh air about, too much sky. A convalescence home, perhaps? By the sea?

'How long have I been like this?' I imagined months, years, a prolonged coma, paralysed from the neck down. Perhaps I was an old woman, with grown-up children? I imagined Clemmie and Hugo, middle-aged, coming to visit me in the twilight home, bearing grapes and bored, fidgeting grandchildren who were mesmerized by my teeth in a glass.

'About thirty seconds so far.'

'Is that all?' I sat up. 'Am I all right?'

'I don't know, you tell me.'

I clutched my head. 'Oooh, God no, that hurts like hell.'

'Well, at least you can sit up. Can you move everything?' he asked anxiously, crouched down beside me.

Despite the pain in my head and the general shock I couldn't help noticing that although I hadn't seen him for twelve years he really hadn't aged that much. Certainly not in a portly, hair-thinning sort of way anyway. There were a few extra lines fretted around his eyes but they were still as clear and blue as a summer sky, and although his hair had touches of silver at the edges, the majority was still jet black. He was as tanned as ever and in some ways, looked even more ruggedly handsome than ever. I noticed he was staring at me in much the same way. Digesting the changes. Rolling back the years. Finally he broke the silence.

'Tess?'

'Hmmm?'

'Can you move?'

I came back to life and concentrated hard on waggling bits of my body around. 'I think so,' I said doubtfully as I rotated my head. 'At least my neck's not broken and my arms are OK but – ouch!' I gasped. 'My ankle!'

'Broken?'

'No, I don't think so. I can move it but it's bloody agony!'

I've never been frightfully good at pain, shrieked the place down in childbirth in fact – very lower-class, apparently – and I had a nasty feeling I was about to be very lower-class again. I clenched my teeth and moaned low, trying to quell the scream.

'At least it's not broken,' said Patrick, rather heartlessly I thought. He jumped up. 'I think in that case we'll get you into the car. It'll take for ever to get an ambulance out here, I'll call the doctor from home.'

'No!' I cried, as he swiftly scooped me up off the grass and deposited me in the back seat of the car. 'Patrick, what are you doing? What about my bike and whose home are you talking about anyway?' I felt alarmed: events seemed to be galloping out of control here.

'Mine, of course,' he said as he threw the tangled bike in the boot and slammed it shut. He got into the driver's seat. 'The house is just over there, behind that hill. I was literally coming out of the back drive when you flew out like a bloody bazooka. We'll be there in a second and Mum can look after you until the doctor comes. She used to be a nurse, you know.'

He started the engine. I looked around quickly. Of course, this was probably all Gilduncan's land. I'd forgotten it stretched so far, but – I didn't want to go there!

'No!' I yelped as we pulled off. 'No, take me home. I don't need a doctor, or a nurse for that matter. Patrick, take me home!'

I scrabbled frantically for the door-handle but by the time I'd found it we'd already turned into some stone gates and were doing about twenty miles an hour up the back drive.

'Patrick, this is abduction!' I squealed, my voice slightly hysterical now.

'Don't be ridiculous. What makes you think I want to

abduct you? I just don't particularly want to leave you lying on the side of the road for the rabbits to nibble, that's all. If the doctor says you're all right I'll take you home, OK?'

Suddenly I felt rather foolish. I cleared my throat. 'Uh, right. Thank you. Sorry. Um, must be the bump on the head,' I muttered.

He smiled at me in the rearview mirror. 'It's me who should be apologizing, but to be honest I just didn't see you. You seemed to come out of nowhere and the next thing I knew you were flying over the roof of the car. Lucky for you, you landed on the grass. If you'd hit the Tarmac it would have been a great deal messier. What on earth were you doing cycling around up there anyway? No one in their right mind attempts that hill on a bike.'

'I'd been to see Willie,' I muttered.

'Oh, really?' There was a pause. 'Any particular reason?'

I sighed. 'I thought he might have picked up some of my flies down by the river.'

'And had he?'

'No.'

We rode on in silence. God, this driveway seemed to go on for ever. He might just as well have driven me home. Panic began to rise in my breast again.

'Long way to go to get some flies,' he observed.

'They were particularly nice ones,' I replied tartly. Why on earth did I have to explain myself to him?

Finally we swept up the side of the house then around in a semi-circle to the front. We crunched to a halt on the gravel and I stared up at the façade of Gilduncan as it towered above us. I'd never actually been here before, just glimpsed it through the trees as we'd sped past the front gates in the car. As a girl the very mention of its name had been enough to make my heart perform backflips and triple somersaults and now here I was, about to enter it, and my heart was still energetic, but for different reasons.

It was a huge, greystone Baronial place, more of a castle than a house in fact, complete with turrets and most probably a drawbridge tucked away somewhere. I glanced warily at the slitty little windows at the top of the turrets. Any beady-eyed archers up there I wondered? I half expected a hairy man with bagpipes to appear on the battlements and blast out my arrival but instead, the oak front door swung back and two enormous lurchers flew down the steps, hurling themselves in a frenzy of delight at Patrick's shoulders. Following in the lurchers' enthusiastic wake was Madelaine, drop dead elegant in cream silk and pearls. She looked surprised.

'Patreek darling, what on earth are you doing back so soon?'

Patrick came round to open my door.

'I ran into Tess – quite literally actually. Knocked her off her bike at the bottom of the back drive.'

'*Ah, ma pauvre chérie!*' Madelaine was all consternation as Patrick revealed me in all my cringing glory.

'I'm perfectly all right, honestly,' I said, shakily attempting to get out. 'I don't know why Patrick didn't take me home.'

'She's sprained her ankle badly and she's got a nasty bump on her head. I'll call Dr McKlellen.'

'But I don't *need* a doctor,' I protested. God – had everyone gone deaf? Why wasn't anyone listening to me? 'And

I certainly don't need to be carried,' I objected, as Patrick lifted me bodily from the car. 'Patrick, put me down this instant!'

Patrick ignored me as I thrashed vainly in his arms and marched up the front steps. He seemed to have an iron grip to match his iron will, but as we swept through a grey, flagstoned hall, he suddenly paused and looked down at me, lips twitching.

'Is it my imagination, or have you put on a bit of weight, Tess?'

'Put me down!' I spluttered.

'Now where shall we have you,' he mused, looking around thoughtfully. 'In my bedroom, perhaps?'

I stared at him in horror. 'No!' I gasped.

'Only joking,' he grinned. 'I'll put you on the sofa in the drawing room.'

He shouldered open the huge double doors in front of us to reveal an enormous light room that seemed to stretch the entire length of the house. He marched in, bent down and gently lowered me onto a cream sofa.

'I'll take you up to my bedroom later,' he whispered in my ear, 'and have my wicked way with you then, dead or alive!' He gave a melodramatic Vincent Price cackle and rolled his eyes manically. 'You will be mine, all mine!'

I glared at him. 'You're enjoying this, aren't you?' I spat. 'You haven't changed a bit, Patrick Cameron!'

He raised his eyebrows in mock injury. 'But it was your idea, Tess,' he said, 'back there on the road, don't you remember? Jabbering on about sleeping with me, dead or –'

'I know what I said,' I snapped, 'and I haven't the faintest idea what got into me.'

I blushed as he stood over me, grinning. 'Can't help you there, but a psychologist would probably say that before you got your bonk on the head you had another sort of bonking on your mind!'

'Don't be ridiculous!' I snorted. God, today had turned into a non-stop nightmare. Was this all part of my punishment?

'Now, Patrick, don't tease Tess,' said Madelaine, bustling in with a First-Aid box. 'She's had a nasty shock and the last thing she needs is you wittering on – oh my dear, you're shaking!'

She was right. For some reason I was in the grip of a rather embarrassing spasm. I couldn't stop it.

Patrick threw a tartan rug over me. 'It's just shock,' he said cheerfully. 'She'll be all right.'

You're damn right it's shock, I thought, teeth chattering. Shock of seeing you again, probably. My breath was coming in short sharp bursts now, my cheeks were wobbling violently and I couldn't control my shoulders which were shuddering like a pneumatic drill.

'I'll phone Dr McKlellen,' said Madelaine, regarding me anxiously. She put the First-Aid box down and hastened away again. Patrick perched on the arm of the sofa and watched me, which frankly was all I needed as I shook, rattled and rolled away like some kind of possessed washing machine in final spin. After a while however, the shaking subsided and came to a gentle tremble.

'How are you feeling now?' he asked kindly.

'Pretty groggy actually,' I whispered truthfully.

'The doctor will be here soon.' He patted my hand.

Stupidly I flinched away, which of course implied that

it was far more than a friendly pat. He looked at me in surprise, then got up and walked over to the fire. He stood with his back to me, his hands clasped behind him.

A silence fell. I bit my lip. Oh, well done, Tess, I thought bitterly. That's really gone and opened up the chasm, hasn't it? The one that's absolutely brimming over with all those nice juicy memories. It was his fault, I reasoned, for being nice to me. It had been so much easier when he'd teased me and we'd snapped and sniped. I wondered how long it would be until we could get back to doing that again? It was infinitely preferable to this uneasy silence. I cleared my throat and tried to think of a suitably acerbic opening gambit, but what do you say to someone you haven't seen for twelve years when practically the last thing you declared was undying love? 'How's your life been?' 'What have you been up to all these years?' Mercifully, Madelaine returned and retrieved the situation, delivering us back to normality, to social graces, to the present.

'I got him on his mobile – he's at the McTavishes' in the village,' she announced. 'Isobel's just had her baby and he said he'll be up here as soon as he's finished. What a stroke of luck. You can wait hours for a doctor around here!'

I smiled weakly. Madelaine had restored the equilibrium and the air was clearer, but physically I was feeling decidedly rough now. Patrick came back from the fire and sat down on the sofa with his mother as we waited for the doctor. They chatted away but I felt too queasy to join in. Everything in the room seemed to be moving around, conspiring to make me feel sick. Patrick and Madelaine's faces swam in and out of focus and quite often merged together in a rather surreal way before separating again. Occasionally I made a stab at coherent conversation but judging by the bemused expressions on my hosts' faces I was clearly talking utter gibberish.

'Try not to talk for a while,' said Madelaine kindly.

Well, if that wasn't a hint. Please God I hadn't been instructing Patrick in no uncertain terms to desist from ravaging me again. I shut my eyes and had just enough nous to tell myself to shut my mouth until the doctor arrived.

When the tweedy, grey-haired, Dr Finlay lookalike did indeed materialize, he poked, prodded and tutted quite a lot, before diagnosing a badly sprained ankle and mild concussion.

'Bed-rest for at least a week,' he announced, snapping his case shut and removing his stethoscope from his ears.

He eased himself up from the edge of the sofa where he'd been perching and looked down at me sternly.

'And then take it very easy indeed, young lady. If you get any blinding headaches or see flashing lights, let me know immediately. And keep that ankle up at all times.'

'Yes, Doctor,' I said meekly, thinking there was fat chance of that with two young children to look after.

'Well, you'll get no rest at all with two children to look after,' said Madelaine, uncannily echoing my thoughts. 'You'd better stay here.'

'Oh no,' I laughed. 'That's out of the question. No, I'm perfectly all right. I'll just totter off home now and –'

'You'll do nothing of the sort,' interrupted the doctor,

'and you certainly can't run around after children. Madelaine's right, you should stay here.' He smiled at her. 'She was an excellent nurse in her day, I'm sure she'll look after you splendidly. You really mustn't move at all for the present.'

'But I'm fine,' I protested, making a vain attempt to demonstrate how fine I was by trying to get up off the sofa and failing miserably. 'If I could just use the telephone –'

'I'll telephone,' said Patrick, striding off to the hall. 'I'll let them know where you are.'

'Tell them to pick me up,' I squeaked desperately. 'Ask Laura to come, or Penny.'

He disappeared and I flopped back into the pillows feeling totally helpless. Patrick returned a few minutes later.

'Laura agrees with me,' he announced. 'You should stay here for a few days to recover.'

'No!' I cried. Then, realizing it must sound terribly ungracious to Madelaine: 'I – I mean under normal circumstances, I'd love to of course, but –'

'Tess, I insist,' said Madelaine firmly. 'Please, I'll hear no more on the matter.'

I stared up at the three determined faces thronged above me. 'What about the children?' I said faintly. 'David's gone to London – they'll be all alone.'

'Josie's there, isn't she?' said Patrick.

'Oh yes of course,' I said grimly, 'you've met Josie, haven't you?'

'Briefly,' he grinned. 'Nice girl. So that's all organized then. Oh goodbye Angus, are you off?'

He turned to shake hands with the doctor who was keen to be away. Madelaine went to show him to the door.

'No, it's not OK,' I hissed at Patrick. 'I want to go home!'

'Look, Tess,' he said patiently, 'you go home and you'll be hobbling around on that ankle as soon as you get there, your head will be throbbing and you'll feel ghastly, you know you will. Stay here just for a day or two and then go home when you can at least walk, OK? Penny's coming over with some clothes for you.'

'Got everything organized haven't you?' I said bitterly, but actually, my resistance was fading fast. I didn't feel like going anywhere for a moment – in fact I felt quite sick again.

I gulped hard and shut my eyes. Oh please God, don't let me throw up all over Madelaine's immaculate creamy sofa. Please don't let me disgrace myself quite so comprehensively! I ignored Patrick, kept my eyes firmly shut, breathed deeply and counted to a hundred. When I opened my eyes again I felt a bit better. I looked around. Patrick had disappeared. On the telephone again, no doubt, arranging for all my worldly goods to be sent over forthwith, thereby ensuring I didn't leave for months.

I groaned. How on earth did I get myself into this mess? Talk about crashing into the lion's den, and what about the children? My poor babies, fatherless since this morning and now motherless too! Perhaps they could come and see me here tomorrow? I looked around and winced. Maybe not. The thought of Hugo and Clemmie jumping all over me and the cream sofa demanding chocolate biscuits and picking up everything in sight and me not having the wherewithal to spring up and whip priceless *objets d'art* from their grubby hands made me feel even iller. Perhaps they could come in a couple of days, when I felt a bit better. I cocked an enquiring eyebrow at myself. A couple of days eh, Tess? Got yourself ensconced here for that long already, have you? Didn't take much arm-twisting, did it?

I snuggled back into the sofa. Actually I had to admit that if one was going to be ill, this was certainly the place to do it. This room was supremely relaxing. I gazed around: Madelaine had done it beautifully. Whilst not exactly ignoring the uncompromising stone floors and walls, she nevertheless hadn't pandered to them either. There were no gruesome stags' heads sticking out of walls here, no crossed swords hanging above the fireplace and the place wasn't swathed in aggressive tartans either. Instead, she'd gone for cool creams and blues which complemented the cold granite beautifully. Faded duck-egg drapes hung at the tall French windows that ran the entire length of one wall, beyond which was a fabulous view of the mountains. No leaping salmon adorned the walls either; instead, beautiful and no doubt highly valuable Impressionist paintings hung from the picture rail, together with tapestries, perhaps Madelaine's own, which had also been made into cushions and were scattered over the sumptuous sofas. Yes, I thought dreamily, one could sink into one of these sofas and never surface again. I felt my eyes closing. How strange, I suddenly felt incredibly weary.

I must have fallen asleep because the next thing I knew, someone was knocking on my head. I opened my eyes.

No, it wasn't my head, it was the door, but not the door to the drawing room. I was in a different room now, a rather pretty lemon-yellow bedroom, with sprigged curtains and a view of the mountains. I sat up. How on earth had I got here? More embarrassing weight-lifting from Patrick again? I groaned, imagining myself lying heavy in his arms, head lolling back, mouth open, perhaps a nice trickle of dribble coming out of one side. Terrific.

The knock came again, only this time, the handle turned. I quickly reached for the covers, pulling them up to my neck.

Penny popped her head around the door. 'It's only me,' she whispered, creeping in. 'Are you all right?'

I relaxed. 'Yes, I'm absolutely fine. I just can't *move*, that's all. It's maddening.'

'What on earth happened?'

'Patrick knocked me off my bike, that's what happened.'

'And now you're laid up here. What a lark!' She perched on the side of the bed grinning. 'Gosh, you jammy thing, I wouldn't mind lying in bed for a few days, especially in this place, it's like a blinking palace. And so quiet, no children running about. D'you get waited on hand and foot? I saw a couple of uniformed maids downstairs bustling around with silver dishes – bit different to Kilmarnoch, eh? What's the food like?'

I stared at her incredulously. 'Penny, this is Patrick's house, not a hotel and I haven't had any food. I'm sick, for heaven's sake!'

'Are you really?' She glanced furtively at the door. 'Or did you just kind of wait for his car then accidentally on purpose wobble out in front of it? I won't tell, honestly.'

'Penny!' I was aghast. 'How can you even suggest such a thing!'

'Well, when was the last time you went for a bike-ride, eh? Coincidentally passing the bottom of his drive?' She nudged me and winked. 'Kind of convenient, wasn't it, and now here you are, prostrate in his house, ordered not to move by the doctor, David in London and Josie on permanent duty with the children – marvellous! Tess, I really take my hat off to you, I think it's ingenious. It's sort of, literally flinging yourself at him, isn't it?' She laughed a merry, tinkling laugh.

I clenched everything I possessed under the blankets, speechless with rage. Eventually I found my vocal cords.

'If you don't shut that revolting mouth of yours I shall scream! I do not want to be here, they forced me, against my will, to stay and if you really think I threw myself under the wheels of his car – God, I might have been killed! Has your sewer-like mind considered that possibility?'

'All right, all right, don't get excited. It was just a thought.' She reached down and rustled around in a plastic M&S bag while I glared at her, breathing heavily.

'I brought you some clothes – jumpers, jeans, oh and a pair of pyjamas in case you want to wear something in bed.' She raised her eyebrows. 'But perhaps you don't?'

'I most certainly do!' I snarled, grabbing them from her.

She giggled. 'Oh, and I found this in my drawer.' She held up a tiny black, diaphanous nightie. 'Any good? For those warmer, balmy evenings perhaps?' Then seeing my face she went on hastily: 'Well, you decide. I'll just leave the bag here by your bed, OK? There are some shoes at the bottom and a couple of magazines Laura found. Oh, but I'll take this back. You won't be wanting this, will you?' She removed my make-up bag from the top.

'Why not?'

Penny frowned. 'Make-up, in bed? You, an invalid? Surely not.'

'Well I might just manage the occasional hobble downstairs, mightn't I, and I wouldn't want to frighten the servants. Just put it back, Penny, and stop being such a cow!'

She grinned. 'All right, all right, keep your hair on. I'm going now anyway, they've asked me to stay to lunch.'

She got up and smoothed her jumper down, sniffing the air speculatively. 'Mmm . . . salmon *en croûte* if I'm not very much mistaken, on the terrace apparently, and I saw some rather expensive-looking bottles of white wine going out too.'

'Really,' I said drily, gritting my teeth and wishing she'd go.

She sauntered round the room picking things up and putting them down again, then sat down on the stool at the kidney-shaped dressing table and peered at her reflection. She whipped her lipstick out of her bag, applied an extravagantly thick layer then set about combing her hair.

'I say, he's still awfully attractive, isn't he?' she murmured to me through her reflection. 'I went strangely gooey when he was talking to me downstairs. He's still quite wild and gypsyish, of course, but not so crazylooking. Seems to have mellowed a bit with age, although he's still got that frightfully dominant manner, which is terribly sexy. I went all weak at the knees when he absolutely insisted I stayed for lunch. He was quite adamant, you know. Honestly, Tess, I really wouldn't say no myself and you know how loyal I am to Piers, so I wouldn't blame you, really I wouldn't. And it's not as if anyone would find –'

'Out!' I cried, pointing to the door with a quivering finger. 'Get out of here Penny, you're making my head ache!'

She raised her eyebrows at me in the mirror. 'Phew! What a nasty temper.' She fiddled around with her hair again, then put her comb back. 'All right, all right, I'm nearly ready.'

She stood up and preened again in the mirror, pressing her lips together to set her lipstick, then reached in her bag for her Chanel No. 5 spray and gave herself a quick blast behind the ears.

I moaned quietly. Would she ever be gone? Finally she bustled to the door, almost tripping over the black négligée which had fallen out of the bag.

'And take that with you,' I ordered.

'Sure?' She picked it up, grinning wickedly.

'Out! Now!'

She giggled and left, but then just as I was about to sink once more into the pillows, her hand came back around the door, hanging the nightie on the handle.

'Just in case,' she whispered, then beat a hasty retreat.

I groaned and thumped the bed with clenched fists. Oh *God*! Now I'd have to go and *get* it, before someone came in and wondered what on earth it was doing there! Slowly I began to manoeuvre myself out of bed, cursing Penny, when – bugger, too late. There was a quick rap on the door and Patrick appeared. I quickly flopped back, pulling up the covers. He glanced down at the nightie swinging gaily from the handle.

'What's this?' he asked, picking it up gingerly.

'It's Penny's. She left it behind. You might hand it back to her over the lunch-table.'

'But why bring it here?' he asked, bemused.

'Well, apparently she'd heard you had a rather attractive gardener, so she thought she might tempt him with it. You know Penny, dib dib dib, be prepared and all that.'

He grinned. 'God, she hasn't changed, has she? Well, she's been sadly misinformed. I'm afraid our gardener's nearly ninety.'

'Yes, that'll be the one,' I said grimly.

He laughed, then as the laugh faded, he leaned against the doorframe, just sort of looking at me. I raised my eyebrows enquiringly.

'Oh,' he straightened quickly. 'I, er, just came to tell you we're about to have lunch. D'you want anything brought up?'

I shook my head. 'No thanks. Still feel a bit queasy. Maybe later on.'

He nodded. 'I thought as much. Oh, and I brought you this.' He handed me a mobile phone. 'Thought you might want to ring your husband, tell him where you are.'

'Oh! Thanks.' I met his eye briefly as I took the phone and for some reason found myself blushing.

'He's called David, by the way,' I muttered.

'Ah.' He nodded. 'We've met then.'

I started. 'Where?'

'When I took Josie back. He came to the door.'

'Oh! Right.'

A silence fell. I gazed at the phone, twiddling the digits. Patrick cleared his throat.

'I'll be off then. If there's anything you need, just yell.'

'Will do.'

I smiled but couldn't help thinking you could scream yourself sick in this vast house and no one would hear. Patrick turned to go.

'Patrick –' I said suddenly. He turned back. 'I haven't been very . . . well, grateful. And you've been very kind. Thank you.'

He smiled. A proper smile. 'It's no trouble. In fact it's lovely to see you again, Tess.'

With that he closed the door and went down to lunch.

Chapter Fourteen

When he'd gone I stretched out in bed and stared at the mobile phone lying face down on the duvet. My hand twitched towards it, then unaccountably away, then back to it again. I grasped it firmly. Of course, once David knew where I was they'd have to let me go. He'd insist. It would be straight back to Kilmarnoch for me, and a good job too, I told myself sternly. Best place for me. Yes. Right. Go on then, Tess, punch out the number. Finally I did so and his clerk put me through.

'David Hamilton.'

'Darling, it's me.'

'Tess! I've just this minute walked in. How's things?'

'Not so good, actually. David, don't be alarmed, but I've had a bit of an accident. Not a bad one, but I've got a knock on the head and I've sprained my ankle pretty badly.'

'Good Lord. How on earth did you do that?'

'Well I was, um, knocked off my bike.'

'Your bike? What bike?'

I sighed. 'It's a long story, but basically the cars were all spoken for and I didn't have any choice so I cycled. I think I'm a bit rusty actually, I wobbled out in front of a car.'

'Good heavens! Are you badly hurt?'

'My ankle throbs like hell and I can't walk, but it's nothing serious.' I cleared my throat and braced myself.

'Actually, it was Patrick Cameron who knocked me off. I'm at his house now.'

'Patrick Cameron?'

'Yes, you remember. He and I –'

'Yes, I know,' he said quickly.

There was a silence.

I hastened on. 'You see, I was very near his house when the accident happened, that's why he brought me here, but it's so ridiculous, darling, there's absolutely no reason why I can't go home. I'm perfectly all right, but everyone's making such a stupid fuss. They say I have to stay here with my leg up till I'm better. It's maddening.'

'Has the doctor been?'

'Yes, and he said I should stay because I wouldn't get any rest at home, but what the devil does he know about my domestic arrangements? The whole point of bringing Josie was to give me a bit of a break and she's quite capable of looking after the children on her own, it's absurd!'

The line went quiet.

'David?'

'Yes, I'm still here, I was just thinking.' He sounded a long way away. There was another pause and I was about to say something when he spoke.

'You know, on balance I think the doctor's right. You'll get precious little rest at Kilmarnoch with the children running in and out of your room and I know you, you'll get up and start hobbling down to the kitchen to cook supper like a martyr, it'll drive Penny and Laura mad. I think you'd better stay put for a bit.'

I gawped. 'What d'you mean, for a bit? How long?'

'Until you're better. How long will your ankle take to recover? What did the doctor think?'

'He said I'd be flat on my back for a week,' I scoffed. 'I told him that was out of the question, but —'

'Then that's what you must do,' he interrupted firmly. 'It's no good getting up and making it worse. These things have a habit of recurring later if you're not careful.'

'But David, why can't I be in bed at Kilmarnoch?' I felt panicky. 'There's no earthly reason why I have to lie around in Patrick's house, is there?' I said 'Lie around' and 'Patrick' quite loudly in the hope that alarm bells might ring in what passed for his brain at the moment, but apparently he didn't hear them.

'There's every reason if it gives you a chance to rest,' he said briskly. 'The children will be fine with Josie. Just relax and take advantage of it, for heaven's sake. You're always banging on about how you never get a break from them, well now's your chance. Have you got something nice to read?'

'Yes, but —'

'Good. Darling I must go now, I'd love to chat but I'm due in court in a few minutes. Give me your number . . .'

I reeled it off in a daze.

'Right. I'll give you a ring tonight, OK? Now rest please, I don't want an invalided wife stumbling along behind me on a Zimmer frame!'

'But David —'

'Bye Tess, give my love to the children.' And he rang off.

I stared incredulously at the receiver. Good Lord. Did he have no idea? Did he not have a brain? He was supposed to be a barrister – an intelligent, probing man. Had he no grasp of the situation? Of the implications? I blinked. Or perhaps he did. Perhaps he wanted me to have an affair, perhaps it was some kind of kinky fantasy of his, to have me holed up with my ex-lover, trapped in his castle, bolts on all the doors, drawbridge raised, no possible means of escape. Perhaps he was hoping I'd be tied to a four-poster with a bit of bondage thrown in for good measure? I chucked the phone down in disgust.

That was the thing about men, I reflected, they were such simple creatures, so trusting. Any sensible, reasonably alert woman would have had sirens wailing and warning lights flashing within seconds of discovering my whereabouts, but not David, oh no. He just wondered if I had something nice to read. I gave a hollow laugh. It was quite clear he didn't think there was the slightest chance of me being tempted by Patrick or vice versa, which if you thought about it, was rather sweet. I smiled. Simple, but sweet. I turned around and plumped up my pillow. Not that there *was* a chance now, of course, I reflected – not after Willie. I snuggled down into the crisp linen. Yes, thank God for Willie. If it hadn't been for him, things might have been very different. I might have been lying here feeling deliriously happy about finding myself holed up in Patrick's spare room, unable to believe my luck. I might be preening myself even now, slapping on the fake tan, reaching for the mascara, working out the logistics of getting my one serviceable leg over – hell, what do I mean *might* be, WOULD be more like! I mean, let's face it – up until very recently I'd thought of nothing else. I shuddered. Well, I'd certainly had enough extra-marital activity to last me a lifetime. Oh yes, great fun and all that, but I couldn't be doing with all that guilt and shame that went with it, thanks very much.

In which case, I asked myself thoughtfully, was there any real harm in my being here? Whatever plans Patrick might harbour, I knew precisely where I stood, so was I therefore in any danger? I blinked as this radical thought dawned. No, none whatsoever. So why not just relax and enjoy it then? Why bother to resist? Why not, as everyone was so vehemently insisting, have a rest, put my feet up, and treat it as a holiday? After all, apart from one disastrously wet weekend with David in Dorset, this was the first break I'd had from the children since Clemmie was born. Why not make the most of it?

With this rather reassuring thought in mind, I pulled the white bedcover up to my chin, yawned hugely and sank down into the gloriously sumptuous bed. For the first time I took a good look around the room, noting the beautiful paintings on the walls and the antiques that were scattered liberally around what might have been a spare room to the Camerons but was more like the size of your average bungalow. This wasn't so much faded grandeur as out-and-out unadulterated luxury, and for a couple of days at the most, would do very nicely, thank you.

I fingered the crisp white bedlinen. It was so sharp you could almost cut yourself on it and I couldn't help thinking it must be hell to launder, but then I didn't imagine that was Madelaine's problem, likewise the picking and arranging of that deep vase of flowers placed strategically in that pool of light over there. Their very presence struck me as extraordinary since surely no one could have had any idea that this room would be occupied? But then perhaps Madelaine insisted on flowers in every room, occupied or not? This was clearly a house where no expense was spared, a house that revolved around comfort. I had no doubt that in winter the heating would be on twenty-four hours a day, with windows open for fresh air if necessary, because this was not your average Scottish pile where you froze your goolies off, had cold baths and put on a third jumper if you were cold. Oh no, this was as close as Madelaine could come to transforming a Highland castle into a villa in the South of France, and whilst that might not appeal to the purists, in my present condition, who was I to complain?

Suddenly I frowned, listening. I craned my neck and tried to peer out of the window. I couldn't quite see, but I was almost sure I could hear splashing down there – did they have a pool? And if so, how many days a year did they use it? My eyes boggled in astonishment. I mean yes, OK, we were having a warm spell now, but it must be the one week out of fifty-two, surely? What an extravagance! I could almost hear my father's reaction. 'A swimming pool,' he'd scoff, 'in Scotland? They must be mad!' I smiled. Mad or not, I found the whole sunshiny hedonistic environment very reassuring right now.

My ankle was beginning to hurt a bit so I leaned back and shut my eyes, propping up the heavy bedclothes with my healthy foot to stop them pressing against the bad one. I lay there, listening to the muffled sound of chatter below on the terrace. I didn't mean to fall asleep, but I obviously did, because when I opened my eyes again my ankle was throbbing like crazy and Penny was standing by my bed poking me hard in the shoulder with her fingernail.

'Tess, Tess! Oh good, you're awake.' She was swaying and her eyes looked very pink. 'I didn't wake you, did I? I just came to tell you I'm going now.'

'Eh?' I struggled to focus. The pain was excruciating. Someone seemed to be driving a stake through my ankle.

'I'm going,' she repeated breathlessly. 'I just came to tell you we had the most marvellous lunch, by the *pool*, would you believe! We sat there, drinking champagne under one of those glorious white Conran umbrellas and Tess, we were *waited* on by a couple of uniformed maids! God, I felt like a film star, and it wasn't salmon it was lobster which is my absolute favourite and oh, Tess, Madelaine is simply heaven!' Penny clasped her hands ecstatically then staggered and clutched the bedpost, clearly highly intoxicated. '*So* unbelievably chic – she's French you know, Parisian in fact, with an outrageous accent, and she's lent me these fabulous sunglasses . . .' Penny put them on and pouted, giving me the benefit of both profiles. 'She said I could hang on to them because they're old and she's got hundreds of them, but they're Yves St Laurent, for God's sake!' she squeaked. 'Look!' She waggled them around in my face so I could see the label, banging my nose with them.

'Penny,' I gasped, stretching past her for my painkillers which I couldn't quite reach on the bedside table. 'My ankle . . . You couldn't just –'

She flopped down on the side of the bed, knocking the pills out of my hand just as I'd managed to grasp them. I groaned as they fell to the floor.

'Honestly, Tess, these people are *simply* delightful,' she exclaimed breathlessly. 'I can't think why we haven't got together with them before. It's all our parents' fault, of course, fancy falling out with a family like this. Think of the fun we could have had here! Swimming parties, skinny-dipping, drinking – dancing even, Madelaine said they'd had some wild parties here with jazz bands and rose petals all over the pool. It sounded like something out of *Gatsby*! And as for Patrick – oooh!' She swooned and clutched her heart dramatically. 'Tess, he has *changed*!' she hissed, 'beyond *belief*! He is simply divine now and the perfect host, so considerate – shifting my chair into the shade and all that sort of thing because he thought I was going a bit pink – look.' She jumped up and unbuttoned her shirt to reveal a pair of enormous bright-red bosoms which had no doubt been out on permanent display. 'See my mark? And I was only in the sun for an hour or so.'

She left her blouse open and seized my hand playfully as I made another valiant attempt to reach my pills on the carpet.

'Oh – and Tess, he's so *funny*! You didn't tell me he was funny, did you, you sly old thing.' She waggled my wrist playfully and the pills slipped once again from my desperate grasp.

'He's *hysterical*! I nearly *wet* myself laughing at some of his stories, and you know how I *L-O-V-E* funny men.' She rolled her bloodshot eyes extravagantly. 'In fact, at one point he was being so hilarious and looking so mind-bogglingly handsome sitting there in his faded denim shirt with his tan and his bright blue eyes that I damn nearly threw down my lobster, leaped on his lap and told him to roger me senseless right there and then in front of his mother!'

'Well, you can tell him now,' I croaked. 'He's right beside you.'

Penny turned and giggled as Patrick came in, not remotely abashed. 'Oh hello, Patrick.' She linked arms with him and did a quick snuggling-up dive into his armpit. 'I was just telling Tess how you've changed. You used to be such a surly, aggressive chap and you've turned into a really lovely man, quite the hunk!'

He grinned. 'Why thank you, Penny, I'm glad I've turned out all right, and may I return the compliment by saying that you haven't changed one little bit?'

Mistakenly imagining this to be a huge compliment, Penny simpered girlishly and squeezed his arm, but Patrick was frowning. He leaned over and peered closely at me.

'Are you all right, Tess? You look awfully pale.'

I shook my head. 'Ankle,' I whispered. 'Agony.'

'Where are your pills?' he said quickly.

'Floor,' I managed, pointing down at Penny's feet.

He picked them up and went quickly to the bathroom for some water. My cousin, swaying violently without Patrick's support, bent down to peer at me. As she did so her bag slipped off her shoulder and bashed me hard on the side of the head. I yelped in pain.

'Yes, you do look a bit peaky, Tess,' she agreed, leering at me, hair all over her face, her breath reeking of booze. 'You should have been out by the pool getting some sun on your face instead of skulking away in here like a flipping killjoy. We had a marvellous time out there, didn't we Patrick? Honestly, we didn't stop laughing once. God, I was on form. Oh, and what was that *terribly* funny joke I told when your mother was banging on and on about getting older and being on her own and – oh yes! What's the similarity between a dog turd and an older woman? The older they get, the easier they are to pick up – HA HA! God, it was funny – although I'm not sure your mother appreciated it, Patrick. She looked a bit po-faced to me, and I was only trying to cheer her up. Maybe it's because she's no spring chicken herself, or perhaps it's the language barrier or –'

'Here.' Patrick brushed Penny rather roughly aside as he came back with the water. She overbalanced and clutched at the bedpost, just managing to stay upright, clearly not just a bit pissed but catastrophically drunk. He handed me the pills. 'Take these.'

Patrick supported my back and I guzzled them greedily. I hoped to goodness they'd work soon. My teeth were going through the Irish linen like a tatty old sponge and the pain was going to render me embarrassingly vocal soon.

'Come on.' Patrick turned to Penny and jerked his head. 'Tess needs some rest, I'll take you home.'

'Oh, we're not going, are we?' she asked, pouting. 'I was just limbering up for a nice little *digestif* – a touch of Calvados, perhaps. I bet your mother slips that down a treat eh, Paddy, being French and all that! Hey,' she whispered, grabbing his arm confidentially, 'has she got any lovers yet? Any toy-boys?'

I gasped at her, shocked despite the pain. 'Penny!'

'It's no good looking at me like that, Tess. You know what these Latin women are like, no sooner have they got their husbands safely stashed six feet under than they're swinging their Louis Vuitton bags over their shoulders and are off down the Champs Élysées sniffing around for a bit of *Jacques le garçon*! Ha ha! Know what I mean?' She elbowed Patrick in the ribs. 'How's about that Calvados then eh, Paddy? Don't be stingy!'

'Er, some other time perhaps,' said Patrick, hustling her quickly out of the room. 'Back in a bit,' he threw over his shoulder to me before they left.

I nodded weakly, in no position to argue.

A while later he was back, alone. He sat down gently on the side of the bed, taking care not to jar my ankle.

'How are you feeling now?'

'A bit better,' I gasped.

It was partly true, the pills had worked fast, but not quite fast enough. I hadn't realized quite how comprehensively I'd hurt myself.

He nodded. 'You must take these pills every six hours, that's what they're for. I broke my shoulder a few years ago so I know what it's like. It's not funny, is it?'

'Not remotely,' I whispered, 'and I'm afraid I'm a bit of a coward.'

'Don't worry – this is the worst bit. You'll feel better in the morning and then increasingly so every day.'

'Promise?'

'Scouts' honour.' He flashed me a gentle smile.

I gulped and turned away. Don't you flaunt those blue eyes at me, Patrick Cameron. Talk about taking advantage of a weak defenceless woman. You just wait till these pills start doing their stuff; there'll be no sitting on the side of my bed giving me those crinkly-eyed smiles then. Oh no, it'll be over to that chair in the far corner and nothing more than a tight little grimace, please. For the moment, however, I reflected, wincing again at the pain, he could stay.

'How's the head?'

'Not too bad.'

There was silence.

'Is talking difficult? D'you want me to go?'

I shook my head. A big mistake, it began to throb, but I didn't want to be on my own.

Patrick got up and strolled around the room, hands deep in his pockets. I watched as he peered at all the pictures and then at the view out of the window, almost as if he'd never been in this room before. But then perhaps he hadn't. The house was so flipping big, perhaps there were great wings he didn't even know existed. He paused at the round tripod table by the window, picked up a magazine and flicked through it.

'Did you ring David?' he asked casually.

'Yes.'

'What did he say?'

I laughed hollowly. 'Oh, he agrees with everyone else around here, says I should stay until I get better.'

Patrick looked up from the magazine in surprise. 'Ah well, there you are then. If your husband says you should stay . . .'

'Quite,' I said grimly.

He put the magazine down and gazed out at the mountains. Silence prevailed for a bit. After a while he turned.

'Does he . . . know about us?'

I looked at him squarely. 'He knows we went out together, if that's what you mean.'

'Ah.' He nodded.

I sat up a bit in the bed. The pills were working after all. My leg was easing up and I felt a lot stronger.

'Let's get this straight, Patrick,' I said calmly. 'There's nothing *to* know about us. Nothing more than the simple truth, which is that twelve years ago, we met on a beach and had a holiday romance – OK? There are no deep dark secrets waiting to be discovered, no nasty skeletons lurking in cupboards. Of course David knows about you, we don't have secrets from each other. He told me about his old flames and I told him about mine – husbands and wives do that, you know. In fact, an old girlfriend of his even came to our wedding. I would have asked you too,' I said lightly, 'but I wasn't sure how to get hold of you at the time.'

Patrick stared at me incredulously. Then he threw back his head and gave a shout of laughter.

I widened my eyes. 'What's so funny?' I enquired politely.

'Your wedding! Yes, well, that would have been um . . .' he searched for a word and nodded. 'Memorable.'

'Yes it was, very memorable. A fabulous day, happiest day of my life actually.'

'Really?' he grinned.

'Yes,' I snapped. 'Really. Never looked back.'

'If that's the case I couldn't be happier for you.'

'Yes of course it's the case, I just said so, didn't I?' I glared.

Patrick looked at me for a moment. He came over to the bed. 'Why are you being like this, Tess?'

'Like what?'

'All sort of – chippy. Defensive.'

'I'm not defensive, Patrick, but when I told you David was happy for me to be here you instantly asked me if he knew about us. As if there was something that perhaps he didn't know. Something that, had he been privy to it, might have made him think twice about encouraging me to stay.' I stared at him. 'Am I right?'

Patrick chuckled warmly. 'What an active mind you have, Tess. What an extraordinary supposition! I simply asked if he knew the situation.'

'And I'm simply telling you,' I said coolly, 'that there is no situation to know about. If there ever was a "situation" it ended twelve years ago, got it?'

'My God, Tess, you haven't lost any of your old fire, have you? To be honest I was being entirely selfish. I didn't want to get into a cosy fireside chat with your husband and be on the receiving end of a "how do you know my wife?" enquiry, but since you've obviously made things crystal clear there'll be no danger of that, will there? Phew!' He mopped his brow and backed away towards the door, reaching for the handle and rattling it frantically, pretending he couldn't open it.

'Let me out of here,' he pleaded, 'she's gone mad! Penny, come back and rescue me, I'll do anything you want. Roger me senseless in front of my mother!'

I giggled in spite of myself. 'Shut up, you fool.'

'What?' he gasped, wrestling with the doorknob. 'You said you're sorry?'

'No, I didn't.'

'Did you say, "I'm sorry, Patrick, I overreacted" – is that what you said?'

'No, I bloody didn't, but –'

'But what?' He pounced, delighted.

I licked my lips. 'But – well, all right. Maybe I did over-react. Slightly. But I'm not sorry,' I added defiantly.

He grinned. 'Fair enough. I'd call that quite a capitulation for you.'

We eyed each other warily like a couple of prize fighters, sizing each other up, trying to get the measure of each other, both trying to weigh up the changes twelve years had made. In his case very little. Looks-wise he was much the same and – yes, I thought, shifting out of the glare of his steely blue eyes, mentally, he was just as I remembered too. Fiery, sparky, argumentative, irritating, amusing, challenging, exhausting but – invigorating too. No, he hadn't changed a bit.

'You haven't changed a bit, Tess,' he said quietly.

'Really?' I arched my eyebrows at him in surprise. 'How extraordinary – you have.'

He looked momentarily taken aback, then burst out laughing. As he left the room he was still chortling and I could still hear great hoots of mirth as he went off down the stairs.

Chapter Fifteen

The following morning the telephone woke me. No one seemed to be answering it downstairs so after a few demanding rings I picked the one up by my bedside.

'Hello?' I enquired politely.

'What on earth are you doing *there*?' Laura's voice screeched into my ear. I instantly held the phone a couple of inches away. 'I mean – in Patrick Cameron's house, of all places!'

'I thought you might have heard by now – I fell off my bike,' I explained patiently.

'Oh yes yes, I know all about that, but it's a bit dodgy, isn't it? I mean what with you and him having been lovers, what with all that steamy rampant sex by the river and everything?'

'Yes all *right*, Laura,' I stopped her before she declined to mince her words further, 'thank you for pointing out the subtleties of the situation to me, they hadn't actually escaped me, and believe me – I would much rather have fallen off in Mary McTavish's front garden, or – outside the Campbells' house perhaps, but it just didn't happen like that, OK? Now I'm doing my level best to recover and get out of here, without, I might add, much co-operation from my family who seem to want me to be incarcerated here for as *long as possible*!' My voice at this point rose to an hysterical shriek.

'The sooner you're out of there the better,' she intoned

darkly. 'I can remember a time when you two couldn't keep your hands off each other and you know what you're like when you're ill. You get all pathetic and vulnerable. Your defences are right down at the moment and who knows what else might follow . . .'

I fumed silently for a moment at her tacky insinuation, but eventually found what I hoped was a calm and level tone.

'Thank you for that supreme vote of confidence. However, you seem to have forgotten that not only is my leg in a bandage and my head throbbing like a pneumatic drill, but that I am also a married woman! I would have thought at least one of those tiny details might ensure my personal safety, wouldn't you?'

'Possibly,' she said doubtfully, 'but I'm not convinced. Personally I think you should be heavily chaperoned. I'm coming over.'

'Fine, fine,' I muttered weakly. 'Do what you like.'

'I'll be there in twenty minutes.'

'Terrific. Can't wait. Oh – and Laura?'

'What?'

'Bring the children with you, would you?'

'The children?'

'Yes, Hugo and Clemmie, my offspring, fruit of my loins and all that, remember? If it's all right with you I'd like to see my babies!' My voice quivered a bit at this because damn it, she was right – I *did* get rather pathetic when I was ill. It was my huge yellow streak, you see. I always feared the worst, sensed my mortality. Chickenpox, flu, it was always the same, even post-natal piles had had a seriously debilitating effect on my morale.

'All right, all right,' she said hastily. 'Don't worry, I'll bring them.'

'Thank you,' I bleated, and put the phone down.

I lay back on my pillow and sniffed a bit. My babies. My poor motherless little babies, missing me desperately, no doubt. I blew my nose and stuffed the hanky under the pillow. I sighed. That was the funny thing about children, I reflected. When you're with them all day long you dream of being without them; of having a cup of tea without having to share it with dolly; or taking a solitary trip to the loo without a captive audience demanding to know why you haven't got a willy; or having a house that looks like something out of *Homes and Gardens* rather than something out of Beirut, but then the moment they're not there – there you go, missing them like crazy. Their dear little faces, their winsome smiles, their . . . ooh dear! I reached under my pillow again for the hanky and gave in to a good old blub. When I'd finished I felt considerably better. I blew my nose sternly and stuffed the hanky back again.

It also wouldn't hurt, I decided, for Patrick to see them with me too. Yes, let him see what I'd done in twelve years, see what I'd produced. I couldn't help thinking that however badly the little darlings behaved they'd knock a few poxy watercolours into a cocked hat. Ha! Yes, put that on your palette and paint it, Mr Cameron. I bit my thumbnail thoughtfully. It was a shame I couldn't spirit up David, too, the devoted husband. Have the whole idyllic shooting match gathered round the bed in true *Hello!* style.

I was just wondering what the devil I was supposed to do about breakfast when my maid appeared – my *maid* for heaven's sake – to draw the curtains and deliver my bacon and egg. I made a big show of struggling to sit up and help with the tray, thanking her profusely, but knew full well that after a couple of weeks of this treatment I could quite easily be giving her a curt nod and demanding to know why the hell my egg wasn't sunny side up. She departed and was followed ten minutes later by Madelaine to check I'd taken my painkillers.

'And how are you feeling, my dear?' she asked anxiously as she bustled over to check that the maid had delivered all that Madame required.

'Oh much better, thank you,' I beamed, wiping my eggy mouth with my napkin. 'I really think I might be able to go home soon.'

She sat on my bed and patted my hand. 'We'll see. Rather selfishly I am not in so much of a hurry, you know. It's been a while since I had some company.'

I flushed, mortified. 'Oh! No, I didn't mean I was in a hurry, it's wonderful being here, it's just – well, my children, you know.'

'Ah, my dear, of course.' She clapped her hands in consternation. 'You must ask them over.'

'I have already, actually, if that's all right. With Laura. I hoped you wouldn't mind.'

'But of course not. They'll stay to lunch?'

Try and stop them, I thought grimly, but smiled. 'I'm sure they'd love to.'

'Splendid!' She got up hastily. 'I shall tell Cook immediately. So much to do.' She hastened to the door.

'Oh, Madelaine, I'm sure a sandwich, or a what d'you call it – a Croak Monsieur would be fine. Please don't go to any tr–'

But she'd gone, hurrying off no doubt to get the haunch of venison out of the cellar, slinging it over her shoulder and staggering up to the kitchen, or maybe she'd even go out onto the moors to kill it first with her own bare hands, because there was, it seemed, no end to the lavish hospitality of these Camerons. They were like frustrated hoteliers, thwarted for years by a lack of guests but with a sudden chance to fill up all those barren bedrooms and empty dining chairs. Well, if that was the case, they'd picked the right family. I was quite sure my lot would need absolutely no encouragement to lap it up.

After a while there was a crunch of gravel, a car door slammed and great shrieks of delight drifted up from below, followed by the thump-thump-thump of tiny feet up the ancestral steps. I smiled. The little dears, they'd arrived. I sat up a bit, adjusted my pyjamas and clasped my hands together, smiling expectantly – maternally even – at the door.

Minutes passed and I was still smiling maternally at the door. I frowned. Oh well, perhaps they were having an orange juice in the kitchen. My children always seemed to need orange juice more or less intravenously the moment they set foot anywhere, and that, of course would prompt a biscuit, which would in turn prompt another, so we were probably talking – I glanced at my watch – ooh, a good five minutes now.

I glanced idly at the stack of books placed thoughtfully on my bedside table. *Persuasion*, *Vanity Fair* and *Middlemarch* – how extraordinary, three books I'd always meant to read at some stage but had never got round to. What a treat. I reached eagerly for *Persuasion* and scanned the blurb on the back.

Nineteen-year-old Anne Elliot falls in love with Captain Went-worth but is forced by her snobbish father to refuse his offer of marriage. Seven years later he makes a dramatic reappearance in her life, passions are rekindled and — Bloody hell!

I chucked the novel back on the table like a hot coal, wishing I had a crucifix handy, or perhaps a clove of garlic to rub on the cover. Had he put it there deliberately d'you suppose, hoping I'd pick it up, read it, consider the similarities of plot and — oh for heaven's sake, Tess, stop being so paranoid! What a thoroughly suspicious mind you have. He probably couldn't care less whether you were holed up in his spare room or not. He's probably longing for you to recover so he can get shot of you and your wretched family as soon as possible, have the house to himself and get a bit of peace and quiet — speaking of which, where *were* those children?

What on earth could be keeping them? Why weren't they hurrying hot foot to see their poor injured mother? Had they been kidnapped too? Was this some hideous plot? I strained to listen. Ah, no, it was OK, I could hear them now. A gust of childish laughter drifted up from the terrace below my window. I heard Patrick's voice, then Laura's, laughing. They must be on their way. I settled back and rearranged my pillows and yet again, my smile, anticipating their worried little faces, their anxious enquiries, preparing to reassure them, to open my arms to their warm hugs.

Then I heard a splash. And another splash. Then shrieks of delight. I gasped. Good Lord, they weren't in the pool, were they? What, without even coming to see me first? But there was no disguising those whoops, those

splashes, those cries of: 'Come on, Clemmie, there's a diving board up this end!'

Suddenly I knew exactly how poor old King Lear had
felt, and how much sharper it was than a serpent's wotsit
to have a thankless child. And my sister too, encouraging
them! The Goneril, the – the Vegan, I seethed, getting my
Shakespearean characters in a vegetarian twist. God, she
couldn't even be bothered to shepherd them up here first!
I mean yes, OK, there was no disputing the fact that
Hugo and Clemmie were thoroughly sybaritic, always had
been, took after their – no, I couldn't possibly blame
David on this count. Who could I blame? Yes! Took after
their aunt probably – but you'd think she'd at least encourage them to see how Mummy was, to – what was that? I
sat up. I could have sworn I heard a loud 'pop!' Despite
the pain I threw back the covers and hopped furiously on
one leg to the window.

Down below, on a sun-drenched terrace, Patrick was
pouring an overflowing champagne bottle into the greedily outstretched glasses of Laura and Edward, both of
whom were already in their swimming costumes – Laura's,
I noticed, being extremely minimal – and both of whom
were already stretched out on bloody sun-lounger things.
Aaargh!

I hopped furiously back to bed, teeth gnashing rhythmically. Oh, have fun won't you, I spat between the
grinding molars. I mean, be my sodding guests! I flopped
down on the pillows and stared at the ceiling. You bastards! You're only here because I'm here, remember?
Would it be too much to ask you to pop up and see how
the invalid is first? Jesus! I fumed silently, listening to the

merriment from the holiday camp below, until finally it became too much and I reached for a box of tissues. I stuffed one manically in each ear. I just don't be*lieve* it, I seethed. Yes, Victor Meldrew was now playing King Lear.

Precisely forty-six minutes later, there was a thump-thump-thump up the stairs. A second later Hugo burst into my room in a wet bathing suit closely followed by Clemmie. Their smiles were radiant and their eyes shone, and as usual, I couldn't resist them, damn it. I sat up and they flew into my arms, soaking me comprehensively and then Clemmie sat squarely on my bad leg.

'Owww!' I screeched, as Laura sauntered in after them in her swimming costume and sarong, a glass in hand.

'Hey, Hugo, Clemmie, mind Mummy's leg,' she admonished vaguely, waving her hand a bit.

'Bit late now,' I gasped.

'Sorry,' she muttered with slightly more consternation as no doubt my face went green.

'I suppose it didn't occur to you to usher them quietly into their crippled mother's sickroom?' I hissed, wincing from the pain.

'Oh God, sorry Tess. Come on you two, get off Mummy's bed and sit here, look.' She patted a little chintz sofa at the foot of the bed.

'It's all right,' I said, recovering slightly. I curled my arms around each waist as they plonked themselves on my pillows. Clemmie kissed my cheek. I thawed and grinned.

'It's lovely to see you again, you little horrors.'

'Mummy, there's a pool!' said Hugo.

'So I gather.'

'And a lilo and a boat like a dolphin and a slide that goes

zooming into the water and I went down it and Clemmie was too scared.'

'Was not!'

'Yes, you were!'

'No I wasn't, but, Mummy, he was going to push me, I know he was!'

'I was not!'

'You were, you –'

'All right, that will do!' I bawled.

Immediate silence. Nice to know I still had it in me.

'Now.' I went on calmly, 'Are you having a nice time at Kilmarnoch? Are you doing everything Josie says?'

Hugo stuck his finger up his nose and dug deep. 'No, not really, but she doesn't mind because you and Daddy aren't there to see. There aren't any rules really, it's great, like being an orphan. Everyone's nice to us, even Aunt Penny. I think I'd like to be an orphan.'

'Would you, Hugo? Yes, well I'm sorry I didn't oblige and go the whole hog, it's just the leg, I'm afraid.' I clasped my hands and smiled at them both. 'Now. Would you like a treat?'

'Oh yes!' Hugo and Clemmie leaped up in unison, eyes shining.

'If you look in that drawer –' they ran as one and yanked it open – 'you'll find some nice writing paper and some pencils. How about doing some drawing while you talk to me?'

'Oh.' They gazed in disappointment in the drawer.

'I thought you meant chocolate,' said Clemmie.

'Oh yuk, drawing. No thanks, we're going in the pool again, aren't we, Clem?'

245

'Y-E-SS!' she shrieked, and they tore out together, for once united in their pursuit of fun. It seemed that even my children were able to share an Olympic-sized swimming pool without civil war breaking out.

'Yes, well, lovely to see you too, darlings!' I called after them.

'You can't really blame them,' said Laura, sauntering over to the window and smiling down. 'This place is like a veritable pleasure dome for them. They really have got the most fabulous set-up here you know, Tess. You should see the pool – it's huge! What a bore you have to stay up here and miss it all.'

My lip was curling up like a brandy snap. 'Well don't let me keep you from your pleasure dome, Laura,' I bridled. 'Yes, perfectly well thank you, ankle throbbing like a traction engine, head about to explode, but other than that fine, absolutely fine. Off you trot!' I shooed her away with my hand.

She looked surprised. 'Oh, don't be like that, Tess. I'm not going yet and I was about to ask how you were. How are you?'

'In . . . great . . . pain,' I said in a measured voice.

'Ah.' She nodded and sat on the end of my bed. 'Does seem a shame though, doesn't it, that you're up here? I mean, I know it hurts and all that, but it's only a sprained ankle. Couldn't Patrick carry you down or something, then at least you could sit in the sun.'

'Only a sprained ankle,' I echoed. 'Laura, I was catapulted through the air at eighty miles an hour. *I nearly died.* And no, I do not want to be draped languidly in Patrick's arms, thanks very much. I don't think it's entirely fitting.' I declined to add that I'd already been languid and unfitting at least twice.

'OK, what about Edward then?'

'Edward! Good God, I should probably end up carrying *him*! What did you bring him for anyway, Laura? This isn't open house, you know.'

'Mummy made me. She said I'd been ignoring him too much lately, and anyway, Madelaine doesn't mind at all. She told me to bring anyone I wanted next time.'

'Next time? What is this, a permanent poolside arrangement?'

'Madelaine said to come every day, until you're better. To keep you company,' she added quickly. 'D'you think you'll be here for a while yet?' she asked hopefully, surreptitiously sneaking a bottle of suntan lotion from the dressing table and applying it to her legs.

'Well now let's see, how long would suit everyone? A couple of weeks, perhaps?'

Laura looked up eagerly from the backs of her calves. 'Oh yes, that would be –' she began brightly, then saw my face. 'Er, no, no, of course not. We all hope you'll be back with us long before that.'

'Don't bank on it,' I said darkly. 'Hugo is keen to be an orphan and I might get so depressed I respect his wishes.'

'Don't be silly,' she said briskly, screwing the top back on the Ambre Solaire and popping it back. 'You'll be right as rain in a couple of days. Now, can I get you anything? Piece of toast? Glass of water, perhaps?'

'Laura, it's my leg that's the problem, not my digestive system. I'm sure I'll be having the same lunch as you.'

'Oh really?' She looked surprised. 'Potted shrimps and

Dover sole then, only Madelaine mentioned something about chicken soup for you.' She glanced at her watch. 'Actually I must go, she said it would be ready at one and I don't want to be late.'

'Yes, run along, you wouldn't want to miss the hors d'oeuvres,' I gnashed.

'Well, quite.' She hastened to the door, somehow missing the bucketload of sarcasm. 'I'll pop up and see you later then. Bye!'

And without a moment's hesitation she'd gone, just like that, her sarong whisking after her around the door.

I sat for a moment, fuming silently, listening to her bare feet padding down the corridor. Potted shrimps? I *adored* potted shrimps.

'Laura!' I bellowed.

She padded back and stuck her head round the door. 'What?'

'I'm coming with you.'

I threw back the covers and swung my good leg round, then holding my bandaged one carefully in my hands, swivelled it around and down to join the other.

Laura hovered nervously. 'Oh Tess, d'you think you should? Didn't the doctor say —'

'I don't give a damn what the doctor said. If you think I'm sitting up here while you lot quaff champagne and guzzle exotic sea food down there in paradise you've got another think coming. Now, hand me that shirt in that Sainsbury's bag — there, the red one, that's it — and that wraparound skirt thing . . . Now, tie it up for me . . .' she helped me into my clothes '. . . perfect! Now you'll have to kind of . . . that's it!'

She put one arm round my waist and I slung one of mine round her shoulders. Together we hobbled towards the door.

'Tess, how sensible is this?' she panted. 'We've got a flight of stairs to get down yet and you must be in terrible pain.'

'Just keep going,' I said through gritted teeth. 'The smell of the Dover sole is doing wonders for keeping it at bay.'

Together we somehow hopped and struggled downstairs, with much yelping from me as the dagger in my ankle went too deep and much shrieking from her as she nearly dropped me. We staggered down the hall, out through the conservatory and finally emerged on the terrace where – oh look, a champagne bucket! My morale soared. I felt rather like John Mills and his cronies as they stumbled into the bar in *Ice Cold in Alex*.

'Made it!' I called out triumphantly.

All heads swivelled.

'Tess!' cried Patrick in astonishment as he sat chatting to Edward by the pool. 'What the hell are you doing?'

'Fancied a change of scene,' I gasped, feeling ready to faint. The pain was quite dreadful now and poor Laura was having a job to stay upright. Any minute now we'd be in the pool.

'Here!' He jumped up and seized me from her and in one deft movement I was languid in his arms again, damn it. He glanced towards a sunbed. 'Edward!' he yelled. 'Drag that bed over here please.'

Edward jumped, instantly recognizing a command from a being higher up the evolutionary chain than himself.

He made haste to assist with the bed. Patrick laid me gently upon it.

'You bloody idiot,' he muttered, 'what the hell are you playing at? Why didn't you call me? I'd have brought you down.'

'Sorry,' I muttered, trying to avoid his rather scrutinising gaze. His nose was inches from mine.

'So you should be. Here, hang on while I drag you out of the sun.'

'Sun's fine,' I said, quickly digging my good heel into the terrace.

'Really? And d'you think you should be drinking that?' Laura had surreptitiously slipped me a glass of champagne.

'Oh I do, I do.' I held on to it firmly and beamed up. 'Numbs the pain, Doctor.' I settled back on the bed. 'Ah, that's better!'

I took a sip of champagne and gazed around. Gosh, this really was terrific, wasn't it. Just look at the size of that pool! It stretched out before me, yards and yards of it, sparkling bright blue in the sunshine and contrasting wonderfully with a glorious wall of red bougainvillaeas that flanked it at the far end. How on earth did Madelaine do that in the Scottish Highlands? Did she have a private solar system or something? All around the pool, ancient urns spilled over with drifts of pale blue plumbago, and up on the slightly raised terrace area where we were sitting, steamer beds were dotted conveniently about, covered in pristine white towelling like something out of an expensive Caribbean hotel. I half expected a little punkah wallah to slide silently out of the shadows and fan me. Bliss.

'Your health!' I raised my glass merrily to one and all, ignoring Patrick's rather censorious gaze.

'And yours too,' he said sternly. 'Take it easy, Tess.'

It occurred to me to wonder who the hell he thought he was to tell me to take anything easy, but then this was his house so I let it pass. His house. I sipped my drink thoughtfully. Yes, I suppose it was now that his father had died. Quite an inheritance, eh?

Madelaine bustled around getting the children organized on a little table of their own. She seemed to be doing such a marvellous job I left her to it.

'Children,' she called, clapping her hands. 'Lunch!'

I watched in amazement, as without so much as a hint of prevarication, my offspring dutifully left the pool and sat quietly at their table whereupon they were immediately waited on by a maid, who, trying desperately to keep a straight face, served them fish fingers and chips from a silver salver. The pleases and thank yous flowed, albeit in hushed, overawed tones. Being treated like kings was having a curious effect on my children. They were displaying manners hitherto unheard of – in fact, I haven't the faintest idea where they found them.

'Tomato ketchup, Clemmie?'

'Yes please, Hugo. Thank you, Hugo.'

I half expected to hear, 'Not at all, Clemmie,' but that really would have been scary.

'This is clearly where you're going wrong,' Laura said *sotto voce*. 'You should be mincing round your kitchen dressed as a French maid doing silver service instead of screeching at them like a fishwife.'

'Quite,' I murmured back. 'I'm surprised Penelope Leach hasn't thought of it.'

Out of the corner of my eye I saw Patrick looking on with approval and was secretly and immoderately pleased. By God, if only he knew the blood that was spilled at home.

The second sitting then took their places and Madelaine fussed happily around finding me something to rest my foot on.

'This is so kind of you, Madelaine,' I murmured as I slipped my gammy leg under her white linen luncheon table, greedily counting the courses the array of silver suggested.

'Nonsense my dear, for me this is a rare treat! It's so wonderful to have some company. Usually you know I eat alone, which for someone who lives to eat is terrible.'

'Patrick doesn't join you?'

'Ah, Patreek. Usually he is painting. He goes out in the fields promising faithfully to be back for lunch and just about makes eet for supper. He gets lost you know, absorbed.'

'Really.'

I glanced across at him. He met my eyes and I chickened out, diverting my gaze to Edward instead. Heavens, what a contrast! I almost jumped. His face was pink from too much sun, and his broken glasses slid around precariously on the beads of sweat on his nose. He'd put a polyester short-sleeved shirt on for lunch and it was clearly the one he'd deployed on every family holiday since he was about twelve. It gripped him firmly everywhere, particularly in the damp patches under the arms. I smiled, I hoped, kindly.

'All right, Edward? I say, you look frightfully hot.

Crumbs, you've got socks on,' I said, suddenly noticing. 'You must be boiling.'

'I am a bit,' he admitted. 'Would anyone mind if I took them off?'

There was a silence. Why would we mind?

'Of course not,' I said quickly.

Laura was looking at him rather as one would a flasher who'd lost his nerve. Around the table the potted shrimps were ready for eating, but Madelaine was waiting for Edward. We watched as he bent down and carefully undid his Docksiders – something I've never before seen anyone do – peeled off a pair of damp grey socks, retied his Docksiders, rolled the socks into a neat little ball – and panicked. Perhaps he thought dropping them on the ground might be construed as litter? Who knows, but instead, he placed them carefully on the table, next to his side plate, nuzzling gently against the knife Madelaine was about to employ on her potted shrimps.

There was a nasty little pause. Just long enough, in fact, for the pong to make it from socks to nose. By golly, it was noxious. I held my breath and out of the corner of my eye saw Laura give him a look that was enough to freeze your underpants off. The tension mounted as everyone stared thoughtfully at the socks. How to get them off the table without thoroughly embarrassing Edward was the question. Suddenly, a hand appeared as if from nowhere and a maid slipped them onto her salver. She covered them gravely with a domed lid but before she slid away, she gave Edward a look of withering magnitude that clearly said she recognized a social incompetent when she saw one.

'OK now, Ed?' said Patrick jovially, giving him a pat on

the back. 'All sorted out? Ginny will look after those for you. Now, how about some wine?'

Lunch finally began, and despite Edward's gaucheries was a huge success. Everyone seemed determined to enjoy themselves and Patrick was at his most amusing and cavalier. Laura and Madelaine roared with laughter as he gave an hilarious account of the volatile nature of everyday life in Italy where it seemed a simple hello could be misconstrued and result in a punch-up. I was determined not to laugh too uproariously but his stories were so hilarious that in holding back I found myself doing all sorts of unattractive nasal snorts and at one point even shot a mouthful of wine across the table.

As I surreptitiously mopped it up I watched the raconteuring continue. Laura, beside him, was shaking with laughter and Madelaine was wiping tears from her eyes. Of course, I reasoned, as I sipped my wine thoughtfully, he really couldn't fail with this audience, could he? A girl who hadn't spoken to a real man in years, his mother who clearly adored him, a mouse masquerading as a man, and me who – yes, well, me. He caught my eye and I was about to look away, when I grinned. OK Patrick, point taken. You're still as funny and irreverent as you ever were.

Later, when we'd all eaten and drunk too much we flopped down on the beds to snooze. At least, the women and Edward did. Patrick excused himself and withdrew to his studio to paint. As I lay on my bed watching him go, I found myself feeling faintly disappointed. Surrounded by other people I felt comfortable talking to Patrick, even joking and flirting with him. It was safe, and somehow it wasn't so safe when we were alone.

Ah well, I thought turning over on the bed, perhaps it was just as well we weren't all laid out here together. I was still lily white and in no condition to bare my body, but without his blue eyes boring into me, was daring enough to pull my skirt right up to my thighs and undo a couple of buttons on my shirt. I swivelled my head to look at Laura. Stretched out beside me she was altogether a different story. Her gold one-piece was cut high at the sides and had tiny shoe-string straps going up over her slim shoulders. With her shiny blonde hair and light tan she looked like a slim nugget of burnished gold lying next to me.

Beside her was Edward, still in the terrible shirt, lying on his back and peering at her longingly through half-closed eyes. He'd draped the *Telegraph* over his shorts but for all its careful positioning I couldn't help noticing that it peaked dramatically in the Sports section. I smiled and turned over. Poor chap, she must be driving him wild. The children sloshed noisily around in the shallow end with Madelaine supervising, enjoying her role as surrogate granny for the day. I shut my eyes. Marvellous. Perfect peace. I made a mental shopping note for Putney. One frustrated grandmother, one swimming pool, and one maid, and with that simple memo in mind, drifted off down the dark lanes of sleep.

Chapter Sixteen

When I opened my eyes I found there had been yet another dramatic scene change. This time, I was in the drawing room. I groaned inwardly. What was wrong with these Camerons? They weren't just frustrated hoteliers, they were frustrated flipping body-snatchers too. I only had to lower my eyelids and breathe regularly and they were sneaking up on me and hustling me off to a new location. How on earth had I been spirited in here? From the other side of the room a newspaper rustled. I looked across as a broadsheet lowered. Patrick smiled, folded it, and got up out of a pale-blue wing chair. As he crossed the room I glanced down – oh God, my skirt was still up around my knickers and my shirt was practically undone to my navel! I frantically sorted myself out, cursing Laura or anyone else who might have had the decency to make me look presentable. When I looked up, Patrick was standing over me.

'You're awake,' he said gently. 'How d'you feel?'

'Fine.' I hurriedly did up another button. 'A bit groggy, though. How did I get here?'

'Ginny and I wheeled the sunbed in. It started to get a bit chilly out there; we thought you'd be better off in here.'

I struggled to raise myself up onto my elbows.

'Chilly? The last thing I remember was blazing sunshine. How long have I been asleep?'

He consulted his watch. 'Ooh, about five hours. It's half-past seven now.'

'Five hours! Good grief.'

'Well, you obviously needed it. That bump on the head is not to be taken lightly, you know. You're still recovering.'

I peered around. 'So has everyone gone?'

'Yep, they all piled off about an hour ago, but we decided not to wake you. Mum gave the children tea in the kitchen and then sent them home loaded with Smarties and other teeth-corroding goodies, I'm afraid. You'd better watch out, she'll be knitting for them next.' He perched on the arm of a chair next to me and grinned. 'I must say they're lovely children, Tess. They're a credit to you.'

I beamed with pleasure. 'Thanks. Although I have to admit, we're talking best behaviour today.'

In fact we were talking totally unheard-of and unlikely ever to be seen again behaviour, but I didn't admit to that. Patrick was sitting quite close to my shoulder and he'd clearly had a bath and changed into some cotton trousers and a clean blue shirt. I suddenly felt foolish lying on a sunbed in the middle of the drawing room. I longed to wash my face and get out of these rather grubby clothes. I pretended to itch my cheek with my shoulder but surreptitiously sniffed my pits. Well, at least I didn't pong, that was something, but I still felt thoroughly disadvantaged. I sat up, hugging my good knee with my back towards him slightly. At least I could sit, I thought defiantly. I didn't have to lie around like a flipping invalid, did I?

'This is a beautiful room,' I said lightly, trying to deflect the attention away from me. It was the pale blue and cream drawing room I'd been brought into when I'd first had the accident.

Patrick glanced around surprised. 'Yes, I suppose it is. I've lived here for so long I've never really noticed. Mum's got quite a good eye for colour though.'

'She has, and I just adore her pictures. They're so . . .'

'What?'

'Well, fresh. And original. Landscapes can be a bit dull and drab but there's a lot of light and colour in these. You just want to keep on looking at them.'

'Really?' He stared up at the one just above us.

'Yes, they draw the eye. So many pictures are just wall-coverings.'

'And these aren't?'

'No, they're vibrant, like that seascape over there with the sailing boats. It's –' I stopped suddenly. He was grinning.

'My God. They're not yours, are they?'

He scratched his chin. 'Well, actually . . .'

'Bloody hell, Patrick, did you do these? They're fantastic!'

He inclined his head in a mock bow, colouring slightly. 'Why, thank you.'

I sat up, delighted. 'You've gone all coy! I can't believe you're blushing, Patrick. Patrick Cameron, are you blushing?' I peered at him as he cleared his throat, recovering.

'Of course I'm not,' he said gruffly, 'but I suppose I was a bit nervous about you seeing them.'

'Why?'

He shrugged. 'Don't know. Value your opinion, I suppose.'

'Oh!' I was surprised. 'Thanks. Well, they're good. Very good. D'you exhibit a lot?'

'Quite a bit. Got a one-man show coming up in Cork Street in a couple of weeks actually.'

'Really?' I gazed around at the pictures. 'Hey, who's that?'

My eye snagged on a huge portrait at the far end of the room. It was of a rather voluptuous nude, Rubenesque at the top with a huge bosom, but tapering down to a tiny waist, snake-like hips and long slim legs which curled gracefully on a sofa. She had masses of long dark hair tumbling over her shoulders and the face of an angel. She looked very young. Patrick glanced over.

'Oh, that's Luciana,' he said casually.

'You know her? Or she just sat for you?'

'Oh I know her, she was a girlfriend. For a while anyway, a year or so.'

'Heavens! She looks like a film star. Are they all like that?'

He laughed. 'You make it sound as if I've got a stable full!'

'But are they?' I persisted.

'Well, I suppose they've all been pretty, yes. I'm afraid I suffer from a curious condition which makes me allergic to unattractive women. I come out in a rash.'

'Patrick!'

He grinned. 'Terribly chauvinist, I know, but call it the artist in me. I have to be surrounded by the aesthetically pleasing.'

'That's no excuse.'

'I wasn't looking for one.'

A silence fell as I gazed up at the picture again.

'Like Josie, I suppose?' I said abruptly.

'What?'

'I was just thinking, most of your girlfriends would be like Josie. Sexy young au pair types.'

He frowned. 'You make them sound rather frivolous.' His mouth twitched. 'Young Josie has a degree, don't forget. Just because she's attractive doesn't mean she's an airhead. Think of all the Miss World contestants who've striven for world peace.'

'Yes, of course,' I said quickly, dimly aware he was winding me up, 'I know she's got a degree. What I meant was, I suppose most of them have been, well – young.' I wasn't at all sure where this line of questioning was getting me or why I was pursuing it, but I was finding it hard to resist.

He shrugged. 'I suppose they have.'

I smiled, satisfied. 'Ah. I thought so.'

'And what's that supposed to mean? "Ah, I thought so"?'

'Nothing.'

'Come on, Tess, what are you getting at?'

'All right, why is it that men like you don't go for women your own age? It's always the dolly birds, isn't it? What's wrong with a thirty-something like yourself? Too past it? Or are you trying to recapture some of your own youth with a nineteen-year-old?'

'Not at all,' he said calmly. 'It's just that there aren't many thirty-somethings left. Most women of my age are married with children, and the ones that are left tend to be hardened career women who frankly aren't my type.'

I pounced. 'Why's that? Feel threatened by them, do you? By their proper jobs? Their power suits?'

'No, I just find them rather tough and competitive. I prefer my women softer.'

'More pliable.'

'No,' he said evenly, 'just softer.'

I thought for a moment. He definitely meant pliable.

'That's rubbish anyway,' I said abruptly, 'what you said about career women. It's just a hackneyed old cliché. You can't possibly generalize like that. I mean – look at Laura. She's successful, got a terrific job, but she's not remotely tough.'

He stood up and walked over to one of his pictures on the wall. He thrust his hands in his pockets and stared up at it.

'Ah, but Laura's a totally different kettle of fish, isn't she?' he murmured. 'She's one very mixed-up young lady.'

I stared at his back. 'What d'you mean?'

He turned and gazed down at his shoes. He shook his head. 'Nothing.'

'No, go on, what the hell d'you mean?'

He looked up sharply. 'Do you really want to know?'

'Of course I want to know!' I spluttered. 'And apart from anything else, there isn't anything I *don't* know. She's my sister, for God's sake!'

'Well then, you'll know that she's still a virgin, won't you?'

I stared at him in amazement. 'Oh don't be ridiculous,' I scoffed. 'Laura, a virgin. She's had heaps of men!'

'Hanging on to her arm, yes, but in bed,' he shook his head. 'I doubt it. What d'you think she's doing with that creepy Edward?'

'Well yes, OK, he is a bit wet, but there have been others –'

'Who were cast in much the same mould, I bet.' He raised his eyebrows. 'Am I right?'

I frowned. 'I suppose on the whole they have been a bit dim, but what's that got to do with her being a virgin?'

'Because a guy like Edward will expect precisely nothing from a girl like Laura. God, I bet he can hardly believe his luck just hanging around with her. He'll be happy just to be seen with her, be grateful for a hug, a chaste kiss on the cheek, then he'll go back to his room and do the rest himself.'

'Patrick!'

'I bet they're not even sleeping together.'

'Well, not now, but at the beginning of the holiday they were.'

'To keep up appearances, no doubt. Then after a couple of nights she told him to push off. You see if I'm not right, Tess. Edward is happy to stick with it in the vain hope that he might get somewhere one day, but he won't, just as no one before him has.' He went over to the sideboard and poured himself a couple of fingers of whisky from a decanter. 'Of course, she has to go for that type because no normal guy would stand for it, but with guys like Ed, she's safe.'

I stared at him. 'But why on earth wouldn't she want to, you know . . .'

He shrugged. 'Who knows? And if you don't, I shouldn't think anyone else does. You must be about the closest person to her, aren't you?'

'Yes, but –'

'Well then, why don't you ask her? I'm surprised none of this has occurred to you before.'

'Why should it have, for God's sake?' I was upset now.

'Well, you must have thought it odd that she went out with these no-hopers, a stunner like Laura?'

'Yes, I've asked – of course I have.'

'And?'

I desperately tried to remember. 'She just says . . . that she hasn't found the right man. That she's still looking, I think.'

He shrugged. 'Well, there you are then. Perhaps that's all there is to it. I don't know, Tess, I'm just hypothesizing here. She's certainly changed though,' he commented, swilling his whisky around in his glass. 'Much more kind of deep, broody.'

'Oh Patrick, what would you know,' I muttered, unnerved by all this. 'You knew her as a child of fourteen, played games with her on the beach. Of course she wasn't deep and broody then.'

I frowned. It was true though. She'd become far more introverted. When did she get like that? Why hadn't I noticed?

'Oh no, I've seen her since then.'

I stared through the French windows, past the pool, to the mountains beyond. Suddenly his words registered. I swung round.

'What?'

'I said I've seen her since then.'

'Don't be ridiculous, when?'

'Oh, I don't know.' He paused to think. 'How old is Clemmie?'

'Four – why?'

'Then it was four years ago. You were just about to have her.'

My mouth fell open. 'You saw Laura then? Where?'

'I ran into her at a wedding in London. Recognized her immediately.'

'But I thought . . .' I was stunned. 'I thought you were in Italy!'

'Yes, sure, I live there,' he said impatiently, 'but it's not beyond the wit of man to get on a plane occasionally, is it? I do have friends in England, you know.'

'But . . . she never said.'

He shrugged. 'Why should she? You were practically in labour as I remember. She probably forgot all about it in the excitement.'

'Yes, but *never* to mention it . . .' It was extraordinary. 'Even later on.' I turned to him sharply. 'So you just saw her that once, at the wedding?'

'No, we went out for supper a few times. I was over for a couple of weeks.'

'No!'

'Yes. Why not?'

'Well, no reason, no reason at all,' I spluttered, 'but – well, my gosh, it just comes as something of a surprise, that's all. That she never said!'

'Why, do you talk to her about me then?'

I felt him looking at me carefully and blushed furiously. 'No, of *course* not!' I didn't, as it happened.

'So why should she mention it?'

Happily Madelaine hurried into the room at that moment and saved me from answering.

'Oh, there you are, Patreek. I've been looking everywhere for you. I hope you haven't been bothering Tess, she needs all the rest she can get. How are you, my dear?'

'Much better, thank you,' I said, feeling rather dazed.

'Oh good, I'm so pleased. Now, we're going to have supper soon, but I thought perhaps you might just like some soup in your room? Lunch did seem to knock you out rather. I wonder if Dover sole and champagne wasn't just a leetle bit ambitious?'

I smiled. 'Far too ambitious, but delicious nonetheless and I wouldn't have missed it for the world. But you're right, I do feel a bit delicate now, and soup in my room would be perfect. But this time,' I said, wagging my finger sternly at Patrick, 'I'll get there under my own steam. I do not need to be lifted – Patrick, I said I do *not* – Patrick, put me *down*, will you? For God's sake, you're driving me mad!'

But it was no good, he'd swept me off the sofa and was even now marching upstairs. I kicked my bedroom door open viciously.

'I don't *need* this. I feel like the little woman, and I am *not* a little woman.'

He grinned as he dumped me on the bed. 'No Tess, that is not an accusation that could ever be levelled at you. It's simply that it's safer and more expedient to carry you up than to let you spend ten agonizing minutes hobbling up on your own, OK?'

I gritted my teeth. 'I suppose so,' I muttered ungraciously.

He stood over me as I lay on the bed and our eyes seemed to lock, whether in combat or not I'm not sure, but it was too borderline for comfort and I looked sharply away. I could feel him watching me for a moment, then he walked over to the window. A silence fell. He fiddled with the catch on the casement.

'Your window doesn't close properly,' he remarked at length. 'I must do something about that.'

I watched his back. 'Yes, I suppose this is your house now. Your responsibility.'

'Effectively, yes. Mum doesn't want it, she only comes for a couple of months a year. Prefers hotter climes.'

'So . . .' I hesitated. 'Will you live here?'

'I don't know.' He turned around. 'It's too big for one person really. Needs a family. Children.'

'Perhaps you'll have some one day,' I said lightly.

'Perhaps.' He stared at me and I felt what lightness I'd managed to summon up drain away. We both looked away at the same moment. There was a long pause.

'Umm, Patrick,' I mumbled eventually, staring at the duvet, 'could you tell your mother to forget the soup, only I'm really not hungry. I think I'd much rather just read and then go to sleep.'

I'd had more than enough eye-contact with Patrick for one day, and there was always the chance he'd deliver the soup personally and perhaps embark on some more extremely personal and frighteningly acute observations about my family. Perhaps even about me, I thought nervously.

'Sure.'

He moved towards the door. Halfway out though, he stopped and glanced down at the books on my bedside table.

'What are you reading?'

'*Bleak House*,' I said firmly.

'Ah.' He smiled and left the room.

When he'd gone I picked up my book. I stared intently at the words on the page but nothing seemed to register. I put it down and opened a magazine instead: perhaps something more frivolous would distract me. But even as I flicked through, gazing unseeingly at the debs and their delights my mind kept flying back to Patrick. I put *Harpers & Queen* down and gazed out of my open window. Not for the first time I tried to imagine what his life in Italy might be like. In my mind's eye I saw that apartment again, the one in Florence, high up, overlooking a piazza, with marvellous views across the city, the ancient duomo, the terracotta rooftops and down towards the river and the Ponte Vecchio. I saw a large roof garden, full of light and flowers with geraniums and jasmine tumbling over the railings. I imagined hot summer nights out there, with the city bustling and twinkling down below. Then I saw Patrick, on his terrace with friends, earnest young men, fellow artists perhaps and writers, with beautiful young girls on their arms, perched on their knees, slim arms flung around necks, chatting, flicking back reams of long silky hair, laughing and talking late into the night. I saw a girl chatting to Patrick, her back to the balcony, elbows resting on the rails, a slim, beautiful girl with dark, wavy hair and laughing brown eyes. The girl in the picture, Luciana.

By day, I imagined, he painted her and by night, slept with her, in a cool dark bedroom at the back of the apartment with the windows thrown open to the hot night, the sheets flung back. I tried not to think about how he'd be with her, how he'd lie with her in his arms, their dark heads together on the white pillows. Instead, I moved quickly on to the morning. I saw Patrick, on the terrace again, leaning over the balcony in a white towelling robe, listening to the bustle of the city below as it hummed into life, basking in that misty, soft-focus haze that heralds another baking hot Mediterranean day. Then I saw the girl, padding softly out onto the terrace in her own white robe, her hair long and loose, her feet bare. She leaned over, kissed him lightly on the cheek before sitting down to breakfast on the terrace in the sunshine; the Italian papers, fresh bread, orange juice, strong black coffee. She'd laugh as he read bits out of the newspaper to her, they'd chatter softly in Italian.

Later I saw her get up from the table, disappear back into the apartment and return ten minutes later in a stunning cream linen ensemble, short skirt, baggy jacket, long brown legs. 'Ciao.' She'd drop a kiss on the top of his head and waft back through the apartment. He'd lower his newspaper and watch her go, listening to her closing the front door, tapping lightly downstairs. Then he'd get up and lean over the balcony as she appeared beneath it. She'd look up, wave and smile, before disappearing into the crowd, turning back to wave once more, blowing him a kiss, looking like something out of Italian *Vogue*.

I sighed. Gosh, how wonderfully civilized. How blissfully romantic. Rather ruefully I then envisaged a comparable scenario in Pelham Road, Putney. An average morning might go something like this: I'd probably wake up in the grip of an affectionate stranglehold administered by my daughter, turn blue, wrench her off, glance at the clock, shriek with alarm, stagger downstairs and reach blindly for the coffee as the children banged spoons on the kitchen table demanding Hula Hoops for breakfast because you did once, Mummy, remember?

I'd lie that I remembered no such thing, fling Coco Pops in bowls, reach into the fridge for the milk bottle – empty – snatch the cereal bowls back and reach into the bread bin – empty – throw the Coco Pops back on the table and bellow, 'Don't be ridiculous they're delicious with water,' before blundering into the airing cupboard searching for school clothes, clean clothes, dirty clothes, *any* clothes. I'd quickly recycle a dress of Clemmie's by picking egg off the collar, get cornered by David in boxer shorts and socks enquiring if a clean shirt was out of the question for the *second* time that week, snap that this wasn't a flipping Chinese laundry, snatch one from the tumble drier, hastily iron the collar and cuffs and hand it back telling him it was a cold day and he was unlikely to take his jacket off, now was he?

I'd stalk back to the kitchen to let the-cat-who-refused-to-use-the-flap out of the back door for a poo, then realise there was little point because she'd already done it and it was even now squelching up between my bare toes. I'd shriek, curse, kick the cat, grab kitchen paper and bend down to mop up my feet and the floor, only to be booted in the backside by the back door opening and nosedive onto the terracotta tiles. Get up, turn around and see the Unigate milkman apologizing for being late and bearing three pints, but also, a strange excited gleam in his eye. I'd realize I'd been up-ended wearing David's nightshirt with no knickers on underneath and resolve to switch to the Dairy Crest milkman immediately.

Then I'd dress the children, throw jeans and a jumper on over my nightshirt, tear around the house looking for car keys, hurtle out of the front door telling the children to *hurry up* or we'll be late *again*, dash down the path and be abruptly seized by my usual if-only-I-hadn't-had-that-last-cup-of-coffee desire for the loo. Hover at the gate, racked with indecision, buttocks clenched, the children waiting – will she or won't she chance it – then dash back into the house to be enthroned for the next five minutes with an audience of two urging me to, 'Push, Mummy, push, or we'll be late!'

After a degree of success I'd run out of the house with my trousers undone only to bump into the *other* milkman at the garden gate and see *his* eyes gleam too. As I pulled up my flies I'd realise, with a sinking heart, that my only option now was to buy the sodding milk myself.

I'd then drive dangerously fast to respective schools, dump the children in empty playgrounds, spy diligent children of organized mothers already crayoning away through lighted windows, dive under the dashboard in an effort to hide from Hugo's headmaster who already regards me as frivolous and beat a hasty retreat, only to be ambushed at the school gates by a new boy's mother who for some reason thinks I'm just the person to enlighten her on the opening times of the Natural History Museum (don't know) the whereabouts of the Philosophy for Children Centre (don't care), and the possibilities of cuboid maths tutoring (don't even know what it is). I'd then talk education for ten solid minutes until I felt I was going to pass out, excuse myself on the grounds of having left the cat in the oven, tear home, screech to an emergency stop outside the corner shop, run in, and make for the cake counter to secure a box of Mr Kipling's Fondant Fancies for the children's tea.

On arriving home I'd flick on Richard and Judy, rip the Mr Kipling box apart, devour the cakes, spy a huge pagoda of washing up and feel guilty but not guilty enough to spring up and do it but also relieved that Josie was doing the Sainsbury's shop and not around to see me playing Lady Muck. I'd then spray cake all over the carpet as she appeared in the sitting room having returned for her keys. I'd help her look, discover I'd picked them up by mistake in the mad, pre-school search for my own, apologise, mutter something about rampant PMT making me forgetful, guiltily offer her a Fondant Fancy, Richard and Judy, comfy sofa, grab my own car keys and dash off to do Sainsbury's myself, whence I would emerge an hour later looking bowed, bloodied, broken, and absolutely nothing like something out of Italian *Vogue*.

I sighed and sank back into my pillows, gazing out of the window to the mountains beyond. I chewed my lip reflectively and dredged up another deep sigh. It wasn't that I wanted a life like Patrick obviously had; I wasn't dissatisfied with my lot or anything, it was just that now and again I wouldn't mind savouring a *bit* of it. Just a week perhaps – not even that, a weekend . . . God, even half an hour would do. I wasn't jealous as such, no no, I wouldn't swap my lifestyle for a million years – I mean, who'd want Florence when they could have two children, a husband and Putney High Street, eh? Yes . . . well . . . I bit my thumbnail. One shouldn't make comparisons.

I opened *Bleak House* and tried again. '*London. Michaelmas term lately over, and the Lord Chancellor was sitting in . . .*'

I looked up. And then there was Laura. What about all that, eh? Could Patrick possibly be right about that? Could he possibly have an insight into her that had completely passed me by? I put *Bleak House* down and this time, imagined Laura's life. Laura at home, in her flat in South Kensington, where I never really saw her because I was always too busy to go there . . .

I imagined her waking up in her pale blue toile de Jouy bedroom. Was she alone? Somehow I couldn't see Edward's head on those White House pillows. I saw her slip her silk dressing gown on, make filter coffee in her galley kitchen, flick Classic FM on the radio, then sit, with a croissant, at the round table in the bay window overlooking the garden square. I tried to see Edward there with her, sitting opposite her perhaps, eating, what – cornflakes? Slurping them a bit? I shook my head. Somehow I couldn't see it; she still seemed alone.

I saw her take a quick shower, slip into something French and expensive, then run lightly down the stairs, out into the sunshine and into London's bustling streets. She'd walk across the park to work, arrive at her building, take the lift to her floor, then settle down at her huge desk; beautiful, composed, self-contained, efficient. Would Edward ring? Maybe. Maybe I could see her talking to him on the telephone, and maybe later, he'd – what, meet her from work? No, I shook my head. No, I couldn't see him anywhere near her smart modern offices, or having a drink with her colleagues either, and certainly not at any of the smart cocktail parties she went to, so – when then? When did she see him? Later on, perhaps.

Yes, maybe later she'd make an excuse, slip away from

her drinks party, hop into a taxi and arrive at a rather unfashionable, out of the way Italian restaurant and there – yes, there, finally, I could see Edward. I imagined him waiting for her at a table in the window, in a mac, blinking behind his specs, reading *What Car?* I saw Laura slip into a seat opposite him, apologize for being late and I saw him flush with pleasure. She'd toy with a salad, drink Perrier, stare out of the window as he struggled to make conversation. She'd smile at him occasionally, distractedly; with him in body, but not really there at all.

Then I saw her look at her watch. He'd get the bill and up they'd get; he'd try to help her on with her coat but she'd already have it on and be halfway out of the door. Outside, Edward would look around vainly for a taxi but Laura would be the one to stop it, hail it, and then they'd trundle off in the direction of South Ken. But then this was the rub. Would he get out of the taxi? Would he come in? I hesitated. Certainly I hadn't been able to see him staying the night, waking up with her in the morning, sharing her breakfast table, but would he come in late at night for – you know, coffee?

The taxi door slammed. On the steps, Laura turned, waved and went into the white stucco block on her own. The taxi purred by the pavement for a moment, then drove away into the night. I frowned. Was that right? I wondered. Was that how it really was, or did he go up too? Could they hardly get up the stairs and into the flat for ripping each other's clothes off and making mad passionate love?

I sighed. Oh well, who knows. I certainly didn't, but one thing was for sure. I was going to – tactfully – find out. If Laura had some problem, some hang-up about sex, I wanted to know about it and I wanted to know the reason why.

The mobile telephone on my bed rang suddenly, making me jump. I stared at it for a moment. Was that for me? I was never quite sure in this place whether there was a switchboard somewhere, some lone operator in the basement putting calls through to my room. I picked it up nervously.

'Hello?'

'Darling?'

'David! Oh how lovely!'

'You sound surprised.'

'Well, I was rather.'

'Pleasantly, I hope?'

'Of course!' What a funny thing to say.

'How's the leg?'

'Much *much* better. I think I'll go home soon, maybe even tomorrow.'

'Well, don't . . .' The line began to break up, I strained to hear.

'What? Are you in the car?'

'Yes, sorry, on my way home. Terrible line. I said don't go until you're completely better.'

'No, OK, but –'

'No buts, Tess. You promised – OK? You're to stay put until you're completely well, until you're back on your feet again, all right? Promise me that now.'

'I promise,' I said slowly.

There was a pause.

'How's work?' I asked. 'When are you coming back?'

'Not just yet, I'm afraid. I'm up to my eyeballs here and the case is still going on. Tess, this line's appalling, I'll ring again in the morning.'

'Why not when you get home?'

'Well, you'll be going to sleep soon, won't you?'

I looked at my watch. Gosh, it was nine-thirty. He was coming back late from Chambers. 'Um, yes. I suppose so.'

'So I'll ring tomorrow. How are the children?'

'Fine, they came over today.'

'Good, good.' The line crackled. 'Bye then, Tess.'

'David —' But he'd gone.

I put the telephone down slowly, staring at it as I did so. Was he behaving oddly, or was it my imagination? How weird that he kept insisting I stay here. And no kiss. He always blew me a kiss if we were away from each other. He hadn't even minded that the children had been here. I'd wondered if he'd be angry that they'd been here, in Patrick's house. Oh, don't be silly Tess, I told myself. It's just David — he's such an innocent in many ways, thinks the best of everyone — and why shouldn't he, come to that? What was there to feel suspicious about? And of course he was rushed off his feet at the moment with all that work . . . Wistfully, for the third time that evening, I picked up *Bleak House*. I read precisely four lines, then fell asleep.

Chapter Seventeen

I was woken the following morning by a tremendous banging outside my door.

'What the – who's that?' I sat up and rubbed my eyes as Patrick stuck his head round the door. He grinned.

'Just testing them out, making sure they're sturdy.'

'What?'

'These.' He threw open the door and limped noisily in on a pair of ancient-looking crutches.

'Found them in the barn. They must be years old but there's nothing wrong with them apart from a bit of wood-worm. Think you'll be able to handle them?'

He stood at the side of my bed grinning down at me. I pulled the covers up, irritated. It was extraordinary the way he just came barging into my room all the time without so much as a tap on the door.

'They look as though they're out of the Ark.'

'Doesn't matter, they're still functional. Come on, get up, you can't lie around in here all day. I'll be back in half an hour to take you for a walk.'

'Don't be ridiculous – a walk? I can't even –'

But he'd gone, limping noisily away down the corridor, whistling merrily to himself.

'Don't shut the door, will you,' I muttered, hopping out of bed and slamming it shut.

In the bathroom I grumbled to myself about the complete lack of privacy in this bloody place and the fact that I was supposed to need rest but didn't actually seem to be getting any. Yesterday I was told not to move at *all* – but today I was urged to get up and run a blinking marathon! Nevertheless, I managed a quick shower balancing on one leg and even attempted to wash my hair. I found a bag of fresh clothes Laura had brought me and was just towelling my hair dry when the door flew open again.

'Ready?'

'Suppose I hadn't been dressed!' I shrieked.

'Oh, I knew you would be. I gave you at least half an hour and you're not the titivating type. Coming?'

'Patrick, if you think for one moment I'm going anywhere on those crutches you're mistaken.'

What did he mean, I wasn't the titivating type? I could titivate for hours if I felt like it. Did he think I had nothing to titivate?

'Fine. How about we discuss it downstairs?'

'There's nothing to discuss.'

'Ah right, so you'll be staying up here all day, will you? Room service again, madam?'

He made to go. I hesitated.

'Come on, Tess, don't be wet. Just give it a go, eh?'

I narrowed my eyes and grabbed the crutches. 'Wet? Who's wet! I'll show you how to use these things, Patrick.'

I stuck them under my arms and clumped noisily out of the room. I had to admit, it was pretty easy once you got the hang of it and more to the point, it made me much more independent. I stomped down the passageway and turned at the top of the stairs.

'OK, I'll use them, but on one condition. You let me

hop downstairs under my own steam, all right? We'll have no more heroic muscleman displays. If I can go for a walk I can get down the stairs on them.'

He grinned. 'Be my guest.'

I hesitated for a moment. The staircase was huge and sweeping and this time there wasn't the smell of Dover sole to entice me down it. I held on to the banister with one hand and then using only one crutch, made a gradual and slightly painful descent, conscious that Patrick was hovering behind me all the time. Finally I reached the bottom.

'There.' I felt rather elated. 'Nothing to it. Now,' I beckoned, 'my other crutch, please. Oh, and I'll need my purse if we're going out. It's over there on the hall table.'

His eyes widened. 'I say, Tess, you're getting rather used to the idea of servants, aren't you? Just call me Mellors,' he croaked, shuffling over and handing me the crutch and my purse. He doffed an imaginary cap. 'And consider me to be at your service, ma'am.'

I rested on the crutches and stared at him thoughtfully. 'You're full of the joys of spring this morning, aren't you?'

'And why not? It's a beautiful day!' He threw open the front door to demonstrate and the sun streamed in. 'Come on, Tess, stop bellyaching and get down those steps. We can go to the river for a bit.'

'Oh yes, what a splendid idea,' I said sarcastically, limping through the hall after him. 'Stony footpaths, lots of nice deep water for me to topple into, plenty of gorse bushes to manoeuvre. Terrific.'

In actual fact I was quite keen on the river idea. I tended to get withdrawal symptoms if I was away from it for too long in Scotland, but for some reason I didn't want to appear over-enthusiastic about anything Patrick suggested. If we were to go for a walk together I somehow felt it was terribly important I was a complete pain in the tubes. As vile as possible, in fact.

I manoeuvred the steps and then hobbled over to where Patrick was holding open the passenger door of a red Mercedes convertible.

'Oh Patrick, how delightfully obvious – a red sports car! Precisely how long is it now? How much has this added to it?'

He laughed and helped me in. 'You can't live in Italy and not own a red sports car – and don't pretend you don't like them. All girls like the wind up their skirts, it makes them feel young and sexy.'

'Balls!' I spluttered as we roared off down the drive, my head catching up with my neck a few seconds later. 'That's the ad man's propaganda to lure the rich and brain-dead into the car showroom and you fell for it eh, Patrick? You were their number one mug. Well whaddya – hey, slow down, will you! Just stop showing off!'

But he paid no attention and we sped off down the winding country lanes that he knew so well at what seemed to be an extraordinarily dangerous speed. The rush of wind in my mouth did at least put paid to my stream of invective, which perhaps was the idea.

It was already a gloriously hot, sunny day and I had to admit it took years off me as we hurtled along under a clear blue sky with the yellow bracken beside us and the purple mountains making a stunning backdrop behind. Damn him. I felt young and – I hastily clutched my skirt which was billowing up – well, young. I snuck a sideways glance at my chauffeur. His arms were resting in denim shirt-sleeves on the car door and his blue eyes were narrowed against the wind. His face was lean and tanned. He caught my eye and grinned. I quickly looked away.

As we whipped around a corner and were about to make the descent down to the river, Patrick suddenly swung into the side of the road and stopped the car. He turned the engine off.

'Hey! I thought we were going to the river?'

'We are. But just look at that for a moment.'

I followed his eyes to the vista that stretched out before us. Down below in the deep well of the valley the river snaked and glistened, licking its way through the heather. On the valley floor, dotted with sheep, lay a bed of soft green fields, the sides of which rose gently up to rolling hills which rose in turn to majestic purple-topped mountains, soaring into the bright blue sky. I caught my breath.

'Oh God, it's heaven.'

He smiled. 'Isn't it just? Pure heaven.'

We were silent for a moment, just sitting, gazing out. Suddenly Patrick reached across. I jumped, absurdly, but his hand went on to the glove compartment and he pulled out a packet of cigarettes. He lit one and exhaled slowly, still looking straight ahead.

'Awful lot of questions you were asking me last night, Tess,' he said softly.

I blushed. 'Was I? Sorry, must have been the champagne.'

'Doesn't bother me, I just feel slightly disadvantaged.

Haven't a clue what you've been up to for the last twelve years.' He took another drag and looked at me sideways.

'Oh, not a lot,' I muttered. 'Couple of babies, couple of houses, nothing very exciting.'

There was a pause.

'Do you work?' he asked at length.

'Oh yes,' I said with a hollow laugh, 'I work.'

'Really?' He turned, interested.

'Yeah, from home.'

'The writing? Great! What – articles, that sort of thing?'

'No, not the writing. I'm a mother.'

'Ah.' He smiled. 'I see.'

'Do you?' I raised my eyebrows. 'I think what you actually meant, Patrick, was do I earn, and the answer to that is of course no. My work is entirely voluntary and unpaid. In fact, I'm thinking of registering myself as a charity.'

He laughed. 'OK, OK, so why don't you earn, if that's the way you want it put? I mean, you could, couldn't you? You've got a nanny.'

'I've got a twenty-two-year-old au pair, not a surrogate, and neither would I want one, thanks very much,' I said tartly.

He exhaled. 'All right, all right, I was only asking.' He paused and stubbed his cigarette out. 'But there are other ways, aren't there? Of – you know, child-minding?'

'You mean a crèche? A sort of upmarket orphanage with pretty pictures on the walls, the only difference being that the children get to go home and sleep in their own beds at night? No thanks.'

'Wow, you're prickly about this, aren't you? To be honest I couldn't care less whether you worked or not!'

'Ah, but you could, Patrick. It was your first question and believe me, it always is and I've sat at enough dinner parties to know that, "No, I'm a mother" is not a riveting-enough reply. It does not prevent the eyes of the man sitting next to you from glazing over as he summons up the energy to politely enquire which school little Johnny attends, although of course he's not remotely interested because he's got his own little Johnny at home and has quite enough child-rearing chat with his own wife, thanks very much. No, what he *really* wants to know is whether he should get into aggregates, or whether those Aerospace shares were a good buy, or what your latest marketing campaign is so he can immediately lean back and launch into his.'

'Oh come on, Tess, there are other things to talk about besides work.'

'Like what?'

'God – I don't know – politics, religion, art, sex . . .'

'Yes, but those don't tend to be opening gambits, do they? Those subjects tend to crop up a bit later on, when you know someone quite well. It's that first, ever-so-mild, but ever-so-probing initial enquiry I'm talking about – *What do you do?* And it doesn't matter how scintillating you make child-rearing sound, you've instantly been pigeon-holed into a nice girl – because of course men like women who stay at home and look after kiddies, they tend to be softer, you see, Patrick, more pliable . . .' I gave him a beady look '. . . but on the interest scale you don't begin to score. In their eyes you're a cypher.'

'Rubbish!'

'I said in *their* eyes, Patrick, that's all.'

282

'Well, if that's how you feel you're perceived, why don't you do something about it?'

I shook my head and smiled ruefully. 'Can't. I'm trapped. It's the old cleft stick, I'm afraid. You see, I refuse to let someone else bring up my children – which, let's face it, is what it amounts to. Not that they wouldn't necessarily make a damn fine job of it – God, some of my friends work and have marvellous nannies and marvellous children come to that. Who knows, Hugo and Clemmie might even benefit from it, learn a few manners, but there's always a risk, isn't there?'

'What risk?'

'That they might turn round to me one day, aged about fifteen and say, "And where the hell were you when I needed you, Mummy?"' I shook my head. 'Frankly it's a risk I'm not prepared to take.'

Patrick scratched his head sheepishly. 'Look, Tess, if you want to bring your children up yourself that's fine by me, I'm certainly not asking for an explanation.'

'Yes, but I want to give you one, Patrick,' I said urgently, twisting round to face him in my seat. 'You're not just some stooge I'm sitting next to at a dinner party – and, to be perfectly honest, I don't care if most of them think I'm a flipping basket case – you're someone who knew me when I was young and enquiring and – *intelligent*, damn it. I *want* to explain to you why it is that I can only talk about my pottery classes, or my plans for my garden. There is actually a reason, you know. I don't want to be brain dead, it's just force of circumstances, and yes I *do* feel bad about it, I feel I've betrayed my intellect. It's not just the working mothers who feel guilty about leaving their children behind, you know, it's the home-makers who feel guilty about leaving their brains behind. I left mine in that maternity hospital eight years ago and I haven't been able to lay my hands on them since. And that's another thing,' I ranted, well away now, finger wagging vigorously.

Patrick clutched his head with his hands. 'No, spare me, spare me,' he moaned.

'Not only has my mind deteriorated beyond belief, but my body has, too.'

He gasped in mock horror. 'No!'

'Oh yes.' I nodded vehemently, a trifle wild about the eyes now. 'Childbirth,' I raved, 'has left me with a body that even now has room for two. I'm stretched in places you can't imagine were designed to stretch, I'm overloaded at the bottom and underloaded at the top – God, even a Wonderbra has its work cut out doing wonders for me – so don't let anyone tell you breast-feeding doesn't affect your bust, Patrick, because it's a damn lie!'

'Thanks, I'll bear that in mind,' he muttered. 'Er, is this something else you've always wanted to say at dinner parties, Tess? Because I have to warn you, unless everyone's really tanked up on the old port it might not –'

'I do not keep fit,' I swept on, 'I keep fat, and aside from lugging shopping bags around and picking up bits of Lego from the floor I do no exercise whatsoever. My thighs move independently of my legs when I walk and I wouldn't be at all surprised if everything falls out at the bottom one day because let me tell you something that very few people know, Patrick,' I hissed. 'When I was supposed to be doing my pelvic floors, I cheated!' I nodded triumphantly.

Patrick's eyes were wide. 'No! Your pelvic floors? I'm telling.'

'Don't you mock me, Patrick Cameron. These are intimate and serious shortcomings I'm admitting to here and yes,' I nodded solemnly, like some new recruit at Alcoholics Anonymous, 'yes, I know it's all my fault. I know I should take myself in hand and arrest the decline, go jogging, go to the gym, but I just can't bring myself to join that depressing queue. D'you know something, Patrick, twenty years from now our children will be shown videos of people in the 1990s, furiously stomping up and down imaginary steps, grimly riding imaginary bicycles, sweating like pigs in a mock-up of a hamster wheel, twenty to a room, each locked into their own cycling shorts and their own little egos, and they'll think we must have been completely bonkers. I went to one of those places once, just to see, and I thought it was the second most depressing room I'd ever been in.'

'The first being?' He nervously took the bait.

'The crèche.'

'Ah yes, of course.'

'So there you have it, Patrick, I am not the girl you knew. I have no job, no figure and have done absolutely nothing that you would regard as interesting with my life.'

Patrick cleared his throat. 'Personally, Tess, I've always thought that having children must be the most fulfilling thing a woman –'

'Oh, spare me the soft-soap crap!' I snapped.

I swung away from him and stared angrily out at the view. My teeth were clenched and I tried hard to control my breathing, to stop my nostrils from flaring. It was extraordinary, I mused, heart hammering hard, how I'd managed to get so worked up about this. I actually didn't recognize myself. Was this me talking? To be honest I'd never really given a fig what people thought of me, couldn't care less if some pompous stockbroker wrote me off as a simple homemaker, so why did it suddenly matter so much now? Why, all of a sudden, did I mind that I hadn't done more with my life? Was it because Patrick reminded me of my youth? Of the plans I'd had for myself at nineteen, the travelling, the writing, the success, of all that potential that I'd willingly poured down the drain? Perhaps I was, rather late in the day, mourning the loss of my once more than adequate brain. I'd never questioned my decision to stay at home before because as far as I was concerned, it was all to do with instincts. My instincts kept me with my children, other people's took them out to work, so why then, suddenly, did I wish that just for the purposes of this conversation, I'd gone against my instincts? Why did I secretly wish I was sitting here as Head of Editorial at *Vogue* looking like I'd just Garboed out from between its covers? Why did I want to prove myself to this man?

'Why are you telling me all this?'

I jumped. 'What?'

'The warts and all stuff.'

'Don't want you to be under any illusions, I suppose.'

'Why should it matter what I think?'

I licked my lips and felt my colour rising. 'For the same reason, I imagine, that you valued my opinion about your pictures.'

There was a silence. We both looked straight ahead.

A curlew was circling overhead, calling to its mate. I kept my eyes very firmly on that curlew.

'Tess,' he said at length, 'I have to admit I wasn't under any illusions about you. I didn't actually imagine that when you weren't stirring the baked beans you were moonlighting as a captain of industry or the first housewife in space, and I do have eyes enough to see that you don't have the body of a supermodel.'

'Or even an Australian au pair.'

He frowned. 'Comparisons are always odious.'

'You can bet your life they would be in this case,' I muttered.

Patrick turned the key in the ignition. 'Come on,' he said, 'let's go down to the river.'

We drove the rest of the way in silence and as we roared along I tried to make sense of my mood. Why was I being so awkward? So defensive? I rested my head back and sighed. I wasn't exactly sure, and even if I had a vague idea, I felt nervous about pursuing the matter. Instead, I abandoned myself to the feeling of the wind rushing through my hair, only this time, I didn't feel quite so young, quite so lighthearted.

When we arrived at the river we were nowhere near the beach my family usually used because we'd had to go somewhere reasonably conducive to crutches. I looked around. I didn't recognize this place at all. Patrick came round to help me out, but I hopped out before he'd got there, declining his offer of an arm. No, if the idea was that I could manage this myself then manage I would. He strode off down the caked mud path that had been beaten smooth over the centuries along the riverbank and I limped slowly after him. Sensing my desire for independence, he didn't turn around and wait for me but when I arrived at a reasonably clear, grassy stretch, I saw him sitting at the water's edge. I flopped down next to him, chucking my crutches away.

'Phew! Made it,' I cried triumphantly.

He turned and smiled, chewing some grass. 'Knew you would.'

'These things aren't too bad once you get used to them actually,' I panted, patting my now trusty sticks. I lay down on my back in the long grass.

'Bliss! Listen to the river, and those birds. This is just what I needed, Patrick.'

'Thought it might be.'

I shut my eyes and let the sound of the water flow over me as it rushed over its bed of pebbles, licking at the bank. The lapwings called to each other, backwards and forwards across the river, and far away a woodpecker was tapping out its faint Morse Code. The sun was beating down on my face and I could smell the warm gorse and heather as it basked in the sunshine around me. Heaven. I could stay like this for ever, I thought. I did for a while, until I heard a different noise. Someone was laughing, a man. I sat up.

'What was that?'

Patrick quickly turned to me and put his finger to his lips. He was sitting up, his eyes narrowed, staring down to where the bank on the opposite side fell away and flattened out to fields, and then beyond to where the woods began.

'It's Willie.'

'Where?'

'In those woods over there,' he pointed.

I strained my eyes, following his finger. 'Oh yes. What's he doing in the woods, d'you think?' I lay down again. 'Besides talking to himself.'

'He's not talking to himself, he's got someone with him.'

I sat up again and shaded my eyes. 'Where?'

'There, look, just going into that copse. Keep quiet or they'll hear us,' he whispered.

I followed his gaze and sure enough, a girl's laugh rang out, shrill and clear. Whoever it was had her back to us. She was wearing jeans and a pink T-shirt and suddenly, the T-shirt rippled up and flew off over her head. The girl appeared from under it, shaking out a mane of blonde hair. She laughed again and turned around, bare-chested.

'Good God, it's Penny!' I gasped.

Patrick grinned. 'Well well well,' he murmured. 'The old devil.'

We watched as she ran skittishly through the bracken at the edge of the wood, swinging her T-shirt around on her finger, bouncing around spectacularly, clearly imagining she was some kind of heavily breasted wood nymph. Patrick's eyes were on stalks.

'Bloody hell!' he gawped.

Willie gamely played along, chasing after her like her swain, but looking somewhat bemused it has to be said. She turned and laughed girlishly, then disappeared into the wood, only to pop her head out from behind a tree a second later and beckon him on with a coy little smile. Then off she darted again, skipping and prancing around in the bracken. As they finally disappeared from sight Patrick gave a great guffaw of laughter.

'Oh, good for you, Willie,' he hooted, 'good for you! Blimey, she's unreal though, isn't she? She's like something out of a *Carry On* film! And did you see those socking great –'

'I can't believe it,' I breathed incredulously, eyes boggling, 'I mean Penny, of all people. I just can't believe it!'

Patrick wiped his eyes, still chuckling. 'Oh I don't know, she always was a bit of a goer, wasn't she? And of course Willie makes a point of bedding all the attractive London women who come up here every year.'

I swung around. 'No!' I gasped.

'Oh yes. And why not? Does them the world of good, a bit of *al fresco* rumpy pumpy with a great big hairy Scotsman. Must make a refreshing change from Peter Jones sheets and a balding merchant banker, don't you think? I'm surprised he hasn't tried you, Tess!'

'Don't be ridiculous,' I stuttered, flushing. 'The very idea!'

He grinned. 'Well no, perhaps not, he does tend to go for the more obvious types. She's not the first girl this week though, he had one in the hut a few days ago.'

I gazed at him, speechless with horror. My mouth felt dry, my throat tight.

'How d'you know that?' I whispered.

'I saw them, late one night. It was after I'd taken Josie out for a drink actually.' He lay back in the grass, clasping his hands behind his head. 'I didn't feel like going to bed so I wandered over for a dram with Willie. I do occasionally.' He grinned. 'Unfortunately, he was otherwise engaged. I was just about to open the door when I heard a girl's voice whooping away in there. Whooping and moaning actually, very vocal whoever it was, lots of Ooohs and Aaahs – "*Ahhh, Willie, oooh – ahhhh . . . yes – YES!*"' he chuckled.

'How d'you know it wasn't Penny?' I croaked, feeling rather sick.

'Peeped through the window.'

'No!' My hand flew to my mouth. I sank my teeth into it.

He grinned. 'Couldn't resist it. Couldn't see much because it was so dark, but whoever it was had a whopping great bottom, much bigger than Penny's.'

My hand stayed firmly on my mouth. I froze and my eyes glazed over. 'Bigger than . . . Penny's?'

He chortled. 'Gives you some idea of the scale, doesn't it? We're talking *huge* here!' He illustrated the broadness of the beam with hands wide apart, like a fisherman demonstrating the size of his catch.

'Really?' I breathed as casually as possible, teeth gritted.

'Yes, and she was throwing it about like nobody's business. I must say, whoever it was had guts. If I had a bottom like that I wouldn't take it shopping let alone chuck it about like a beach ball – ha ha!'

My lip was curling uncontrollably now. 'Is that so?' I said. 'But perhaps it was the light? – perhaps you were deceived? After all, you did say it was very dark?'

He shrugged. 'Yes, OK, it was a bit dark, hard to tell I suppose. God, don't go all sisterhood-ish on me, Tess, I'm sure she was a very nice girl, heart of gold and all that. Just had a big bum, that's all.' He peered up at me. 'You look a bit sort of white and tense, are you all right? What's the matter, are you in shock? Doesn't this sort of thing happen in Putney?'

'Yes – yes of course it does!' I laughed nonchalantly. 'Happens all the time.' Bigger than Penny's! Wouldn't take it shopping! Bloody hell! I snarled inwardly but struggled on, forcing a bright smile. 'I'm just a bit surprised at Penny, that's all.'

'Well, I wouldn't go broadcasting it to the nation, no harm done. It's just a quick bonk, no point in rocking the marital bed. I expect she's having the time of her life right now – oh look, talk of the devil, she's back!' He sat up. 'Good heavens, that was quick – but no Willie. Has she left him for dead, d'you think? Ravished him rotten then spat him out?'

We watched as Penny tripped gaily out of the woods, T-shirt on this time but still frolicking girlishly, skipping along in the long grass, throwing back her blonde hair like Miss Piggy. Giddy with sexual gratification no doubt.

'Ah no, here he is,' grinned Patrick, 'the man himself, looking a bit worse for wear though.'

Willie staggered out of the woods after her. His hair was all over the place and his tongue and his shirt were both hanging out – the latter, I'd hazard, even from this distance, short of a few buttons. He looked distinctly dazed and I could have sworn he had scratches on his face.

'Looks like she's put him through his paces,' I murmured.

Patrick looked horrified. 'God, it's a terrifying thought, isn't it? I mean, if that's what she's done to a strong man like Willie in a matter of minutes, no wonder poor old

Piers looks like he's not going to make it through the afternoon.' He scraped his hair back nervously. 'I tell you what, that man's gone up in my estimation. She's a flipping Rottweiler on heat.'

I giggled. 'Oh look – there's her car. Gosh, talk about obvious, she must be very sure no one's coming out this way.'

We watched as she skipped back to her car parked on the edge of the wood, turning and blowing kisses to Willie all along the way. So much for getting all that out of her system before she got married, I thought grimly. This was one leopard who hadn't remotely changed her spots. She got in, and we heard the engine turn over.

'There she goes,' murmured Patrick as the car pulled away, 'back to Pukey Piers – oh, and there goes Willie, back to Kirsten no doubt.'

Willie tucked his shirt in, adjusted his trousers and swung his leg over his bike. He grinned and waved to Penny then pedalled slowly, and it has to be said breathlessly, off up the hill that led to Invertarn.

I frowned. 'Kirsten? You mean the girl who lives down the road from him? She's not his girlfriend, she's his cousin.'

Patrick laughed. 'Cousin my eye! No, Kirsten's his regular bird when he's not going off piste with the holiday makers. I think she's under the impression he might make an honest woman of her one day, but I have my doubts. Willie's got enough wild oats in his sack to sow a blinking prairie. He's into anything that moves.'

'Really?' I said with a tight little smile. 'Is that so?' My teeth, behind the smile, began imperceptibly to grind.

Patrick saw my face and grinned. 'My, what a sheltered

life you've led, Tess. Still very much the vicar's daughter, eh?'

'Yes,' I laughed airily. 'Yes, I suppose I am.'

Up until last Thursday night that is, I thought grimly, when the vicar's daughter was throwing her whopping great bottom around with the man who's got enough wild oats to sow a blinking prairie. Thank God I'd stopped short of the seed sowing though, I thought with a surge of relief. That at least was a mercy. I wouldn't have been one of many, I'd have been one of flipping millions, and not only that but those flipping millions now included my cousin Penny. It was outrageous, the man was a sex fiend, unfit to be roaming the fields, he should be . . . oh well, what's the use? I caved in suddenly. Forget it, Tess. Stop ranting and forget it. What's done is done.

I lay back and breathed deeply, slowly, trying to calm myself down. I wondered if I could remember any of the breathing exercises I'd been taught at ante-natal classes designed to lower the blood pressure and – joke – relieve the pain. (And if that doesn't work we'll pop back and paralyse you from the waist down, OK?) Sort of – in through the nose and out through the mouth, wasn't it? Yes, something revolutionary like that. I practised for a while feeling the sun beating down on my face. I'd probably got a red nose by now but I couldn't be bothered to do anything about it. I breathed a bit more, and slowly, surely – amazingly – felt the irritants of the world slip away. Sod Willie. Sod Penny. Sod everyone, in fact. Gosh, yes, this was working, how marvellous. I breathed on.

So Willie had an insatiable sex drive – so what? So Penny was still a goer – what did it matter? So I had a big – no, steady Tess, don't think about that, keep breathing. Hard. Better. I began to calm down again. Yes, what did anything matter when I could lie here and listen to that bullfinch calling to its mate? Or to that woodpecker, tapping out its persistent message and wasn't that a kingfisher? How marvellous, now that really took me back. I hadn't heard a kingfisher for years, not since . . . Slowly I opened my eyes. I raised myself up onto my elbows and gazed around. Yes, of course, I thought slowly, how stupid of me. Not since the last time I'd been here, twelve years ago. To this exact same stretch of river, except that we used to sit, or rather lie, on the opposite bank . . . and it was always dark . . .

Slowly I turned around. Patrick was watching me closely, had been watching me closely all this time, no doubt. My mouth dried.

'Patrick, why have you brought me here?'

'Why d'you think?'

'I – don't know.'

He smiled but there was an odd look in his eyes. 'Oh, I think you do, Tess. It's very simple. I brought you here to tell you I still love you. Always have done, actually. There's never been anyone else and at this rate,' he gave a strange half-laugh, 'I don't suppose there ever will be.' He shrugged. 'Sorry to be inconvenient, but there it is.'

Chapter Eighteen

My senses dazzled for a moment. I stared at him in horror. On one level I was totally stunned; but deeper down it didn't come as a complete surprise somehow. Of course. He'd waited for me. After all these years he'd waited for me to come back, and I hadn't even realized. The writing must have been graffitied on the walls in letters ten foot tall, yet somehow, I'd missed it. I turned and reached shakily for my crutches.

'Patrick, I – must go now. Take me back, please.'

He put a hand on my arm.

'Tess, just hear me out. There's no need to leap around like a frightened rabbit, I'm not going to jump on you or anything, I just want you to consider something. You don't have to give me an answer now, you can take your time. God, I've waited twelve years, any more won't make much difference, but please, let me speak, OK?'

He looked at me gently, kindly even.

I gulped and put down my crutches. 'Well, what is it then?' I whispered.

'I'd like you to think about coming to live with me. It doesn't have to be in Italy, I can see that might be inconvenient, but I'd like you to consider living with me here, in Scotland. With the children, of course.'

For a moment I couldn't believe he meant it, he was so

cool, so – unemotional. Then I looked into his eyes, there was nothing cool about those, they were absolutely loaded with emotion. Oh yes, he meant it all right.

'Good God, you're mad,' I muttered.

'Why? Why am I mad? Because I know what's right? Because I can cut through the crap and say – look, this is how it should have been? Here are two people who loved one another and for reasons beyond their control – outrageous fortune, your father, whatever you want to call it – were kept apart. Why is that mad?'

'Because – because, Patrick, I have a family now,' I spluttered. 'Haven't you noticed? Have you no eyes in your head? You're twelve years too late. I have children, a husband, it's out of the question!'

Patrick stared into the middle distance and dragged on his cigarette.

'Well, I'd call that encouraging,' he said at length. 'It's not that you don't want to, it's because you can't. Because it's not possible.' He stubbed his cigarette out in the grass. 'And that in itself is not a problem, Tess, because any-thing's possible. It's just whether or not you want it enough, or are brave enough to make it happen. And there's certainly no such thing as too late.'

'Oh, don't talk nonsense, of course there is. Get real, Patrick, we're not a couple of lovestruck teenagers any more, we're adults! Middle-aged adults, and you may not have any responsibilities, but I certainly do!'

'Responsibilities,' he echoed, seeming to mull the word over in his head. 'Yes, that's about pleasing other people, isn't it? About putting other people's happiness before your own, like you did when you were eighteen. You pleased your father then, remember? Felt a responsibility – duty – towards him, and now when you have a chance of real happiness the second time around, you're prepared to please your husband and children instead of yourself, is that it?' He looked at me sharply. 'Because let's face it, you're not really happy are you, Tess?'

'Of course I'm happy!' I burst out. 'What a thing to say!'

'Really? Can you honestly look me in the eye and say you've never wondered what might have been? What life might have been like for the two of us together?'

'Well,' I blustered, 'well all right, I might have *wondered* occasionally, but – that's only natural, our relationship was so unresolved, but I've never for one moment wanted my life to be *other*wise, if that's what you mean!' I stared at him defiantly.

'Really?'

'Yes, really! Damn you.'

He dragged on his cigarette a bit. Then: 'Tell me, why did you marry David?'

'Because I loved him of course,' I said quickly.

'And because you were pregnant?'

I swung around. 'How did you know that?'

'I read *The Times*. I read about your engagement and then nine months later I read about the birth of your child. You don't have to be Einstein to figure that one out.'

'Yes, all right, I was pregnant. But I still loved him, OK?'

'So you'd have married him anyway.'

'Yes,' I cried. 'Yes, I'd have married him anyway! God, what do you want from me, Patrick?'

He shrugged. 'The truth, I suppose. Do you love me?'

I gazed at him, appalled. 'What, now?'

'Yes, now.'

'Patrick, what a question! I mean, years ago *yes*, of course, but now – no, no I don't! God, I haven't seen you for twelve years.'

'You can't separate people from their passions, Tess.'

I turned on him. 'And that's the problem with you, Patrick. As far as you're concerned, it's all about passion. Well, there are other types of love, you know, that are equally important. Love of children, parents, spouses –'

'*Spouses!* Is that how you think of your soul-mate? It's hardly romantic, is it?'

'Life isn't romantic,' I hissed. 'It isn't about travelling around hot countries, painting here, writing there, living off your trust fund in a sybaritic style under a sweltering sun, it's about domestic routine, schools, friends, mortgages . . .'

He shrugged. 'The children could go to school here. They'd have a marvellous life, they'd soon make friends, they'd –'

'They wouldn't have their father!' I shouted. 'You're talking about *taking them from their father*, Patrick!'

'Of course I'm not. All I'm saying is that they could have the same life up here as they do in London, only better. Think of them by the river every day, on the beach, think of the freedom. Children adapt, Tess, they –'

'Don't you dare plan a life for my family. Don't you dare mention my children again,' I said in a low, trembling voice.

'Why are you so angry?'

'Why am I so angry?' I stormed, tearing my hair briefly. 'God, you're asking me why I'm angry when here you are, questioning me, grilling me, asking me to justify my marriage, my whole existence, the very infrastructure of my life! You want to know if I'm deliriously happy, and if I can't tell you absolutely unequivocally that I'm quivering with joy every single second of the flipping day you want to know why it is I won't just up sticks and waltz off into the sunset with you. Well, I'll tell you why, *because you're twelve years too late, you stupid bastard*!' At that I broke off, and to my absolute horror, burst into tears.

For a while I just sat there sobbing, quite violently actually, and whilst I was horrified, it was such a relief. To do it, to get it all out. Thankfully he didn't try to comfort me or to stop the tears, he just sat next to me, and after a while as the sobs quietened into shuddering shoulder shakes, passed me a hanky. I took it gratefully, wiping my eyes. Then I blew my nose noisily.

'All right?' he asked gently.

'Yes, fine thanks,' I muttered. 'Sorry.'

I sniffed and wiped a bit more. We sat there, side by side, staring out at the water.

'It's funny,' he said eventually. 'I was so sure you'd come. It was such a shock, seeing that engagement announcement in the paper one morning. I couldn't believe it.'

'Yes, well you always were a cocky bastard,' I said, sniffing. 'I bet the only reason you're sitting here now is because I'm the only girl that's ever turned you down. And what exactly stopped you from coming to see me, eh? What stopped *you* getting on a plane?'

He shrugged. 'I didn't see the point. You knew where I was, you wrote to me –'

'And you never replied!'

'Of course I did. I wrote to you every bloody day, asking you to come, sent you enough frigging tickets –'

'What tickets?'

'Plane tickets. You didn't . . .' He stopped.

I shook my head, stunned. 'Daddy must have intercepted them.'

We were silent for a while. Remembering.

'Well,' I said at length, with another almighty sniff. 'That's that then.' I made to get up.

'That's a no then, is it?' he said quietly.

I turned. 'Yes, it's a no.'

He stared at me, slightly pale under his tan perhaps, but otherwise very composed.

'What did you expect?' I said, exasperated. 'I haven't seen you for twelve years and then you spring this on me as cool as a cucumber. I mean it's not even as if you're asking me for a quick roll in the hay here, you're asking me for total commitment, for a complete change in my life, it's unreal!'

'You mean you'd have considered a roll in the hay?'

I flushed. 'I didn't say that.'

He looked at me closely. 'You would, wouldn't you?'

'Don't be ridiculous!'

'How interesting. A brief interlude in your otherwise rather mundane life.' He gave a slight smile. 'Yes, perhaps I should have considered that. Perhaps I should have got you tipsy, snuggled up to you on the riverbank, whispered in your ear, reminded you of old times, slipped my hand round your waist, up your jumper – yes, we could have had an affair, couldn't we? And then when you were up to your neck in the quicksand, I could have just grasped you by the ankles and,' he gave a quick jerk down with his fist, 'pulled you under.' He smiled ruefully and shook his head. 'Sorry, Tess, I'm afraid that's not my style.'

'No, Patrick, I know. You're far too arrogant for fore-play.'

'No, it's not that at all, I just couldn't bring myself to do it. Smacks of dishonesty to me. Of lulling you into something messy until you're in too deep to get out. No, this is something that needs a good, long, calculating, clear view. You think twelve years is a long time, but you've got another fifty odd to go, you know. You want to get those right, don't you?' He paused. 'Think about it. You never know, you might change your mind. Take a couple of years if you like.'

I stared at him in amazement. 'And meanwhile you'll do what?'

He grinned. 'Oh, I won't save myself for you if that's what you mean. I'll carry on as normal, but in my heart I'll be monogamous. A bit like a swan really – they mate for life, you know. We found each other and it was right; that's an undeniable truth, isn't it, Tess? Whatever else has happened in the meantime, we were a perfect match, weren't we?'

His eyes were clear and bright. I met them briefly, then looked away.

'Yes, we were,' I murmured. That was all I was pre-pared to admit. I cleared my throat. 'But I'm not a frigging swan, Patrick, and that was then and this is now. And fortunately for me, I fell in love again, a few years later. Unfortunately for you, you didn't.' I looked him straight in the eye. 'David and I are also a perfect match, you see. And now I'd like to go home, please.'

He gazed at me for a moment and I met the anguish in his eyes head on. Held it. Then it was his turn to be forced to turn away. There was a terrible silence.

After a while I slowly manoeuvred myself to my feet. He didn't offer his hand and I didn't look for it. He quickly got up and walked on ahead. I limped after him watching his stiff back. When I reached the car he was sitting in the driver's seat, staring straight ahead. The passenger door hung open for me. I limped round, threw my crutches in the back and slipped into the seat, slamming the door behind me. I knew that my last remark had been aggressive, brutal, even, but I also knew that it had to be said if I was to protect myself and my family. I couldn't afford to be soft, not for one moment. We drove back very fast to Gilduncan in silence. Five minutes later we crunched to a halt on the gravel.

'I think I'd better get your things from upstairs and take you back to Kilmarnoch, don't you?' he said in a gruff voice.

I nodded. 'Yes. I'd like to go home.' Why had I stayed so long? Why had I stayed at all? Deep down, I think I must have known all along. Known and half enjoyed it? I shook my head miserably.

'Patrick, I'm so sorry.'

'Don't, Tess,' he said, quietly. 'Let's leave it at that, shall we? I had to know if there was ever going to be a chance, and now that I know there isn't, I'd rather not prolong the discussion. No amount of damage limitation from you is going to make things any better.'

I nodded sadly. 'I'll get my things,' I offered.

But he was already out of the car. 'No, stay there. I'll ask Ginny to get your clothes.'

He disappeared into the house.

I stared down at the long treelined driveway. Sorry to be inconvenient . . . but I love you, I always will. I blinked. Patrick's cigarettes were in the open glove compartment. I pulled the packet out, fumbled for one and lit it with a shaky hand. They were strong, Italian, and I hadn't smoked for years, not since I was about eighteen but it didn't seem to have any effect on me. My senses seemed dazed, numb almost. I dragged in great lungfuls of the pungent smoke, then threw the butt out onto the gravel. It lay there, smouldering. A few minutes later Patrick reappeared. He chucked my Sainsbury's carrier bag in the back and jumped in without looking at me.

'I ought to say goodbye to your mother,' I faltered, 'thank her, at least.'

'She's not there,' he said briskly. 'You'll have to write to her.'

He started up the engine and off we flew. As we roared back down the lanes Patrick lit one cigarette after another, all of which lasted only a minute or so in the fierce wind. It was the only indication of any turbulence, any emotion beneath his set face. That, and the way his hand shook slightly as he lit them.

We roared up Kilmarnoch's driveway and screeched to a halt outside the house. Without wasting a moment

Patrick jumped out and hoisted my bag out of the back seat. He carried it up to the top of the steps, dumped it there and then leaped down the steps again. I levered myself out of the car, my ankle throbbing painfully, and limped heavily up to the door.

'There'll be someone in, I take it?' he asked shortly, from the bottom.

'Oh yes, Penny's car's here . . .'

'Right, I'll be off then.' He jumped back in.

'Patrick –' As he started the engine, he glanced up and for the first time since we'd left the river our eyes met properly.

'I'm terribly sorry,' I whispered.

He shook his head briefly, indicating that I shouldn't say any more. His eyes were full of something dangerously close to water. He didn't speak. In a moment he'd turned the car around and I watched as in a cloud of dust and gravel it sped off down the drive, round the corner and away into the distance. I stood there on the step gazing out at the empty lane, stayed there for quite a few minutes. Then, with a sigh that seemed to come from the depths of my very soul, I picked up my bag and shouldered open the door.

The house seemed still, quiet, empty. I dumped the carrier bag down by the umbrella-stand and limped listlessly down the dark hall. Halfway down I paused. I could hear strange muffled cries coming from the drawing room. I limped on, stuck my head around the door and saw Penny, lying on the sofa with her head in a cushion. She didn't see me but her body was heaving, racked with sobs. It occurred to me that the last time I'd seen her, a few hours ago, she'd

305

been tripping merrily through the bracken, bare-breasted, swinging her T-shirt round her finger. Had Piers found out? Had there been a dreadful scene? Had he left her? Oh God, I really didn't think I could cope with all that just now. I made to limp on but she heard my crutches, looked up, saw me. She threw down the cushion, jumped up and ran towards me, sobbing. Before she collapsed in my arms I saw that her eyes were full of pain.

'Daddy died!' she gasped into my neck.

Chapter Nineteen

Penny's sobs echoed in the silent house. I led her gently back through the drawing room and over to the window seat. She clung to me as we sat there together, sobbing into my neck. I rocked her gently and gazed over her head to the view of the mountains beyond. The view he loved. Tears filled my eyes. Uncle Robert. Dear, kind, lovely Uncle Robert, my father's beloved younger brother who was as mellow and calm as my father was sharp and irascible. Now, finally, after years of clinging to the wreckage, he'd gone, and with him such a large part of my childhood.

A great sigh engulfed me and the tears fled down my cheeks as I realized, with a jolt, that I'd never see him in this room again, at that table playing cribbage, in that chair with a book, or standing, laughing, with his back to the fire, warming his legs. A huge, clever, quiet man, not an opinionated bellower like my father, but a quiet, let's-get-on-with-it doer; a calming presence, and such an influence on me when I was younger.

When we were children it was always Uncle Robert who'd sit for hours with bicycle repair kits in the dark hall, fixing yet another inner tube, or a fishing net, or untangling a rod. I could see him there now, surrounded by children, with bits of twine and nails in his mouth and his Swiss Army penknife, patiently going through the rigmarole of showing us every single blade – including the hoofpick – before he could get on with the job in hand. It was Uncle Robert who'd sit doing all the sky in the jigsaw while we got on with the interesting bits and Uncle Robert who, when we were too tired to walk home from the river, would scoop all three of us up at once with a great roar, one riding on his shoulders, one under each arm, with my father crossly telling us to brace up and not be so feeble and us shrieking with laughter.

Later, after tea, when the other grown-ups were snoozing or reading books, Uncle Robert was the one we used to pounce on and drag protesting from his armchair, a child at each arm, another pulling his jumper, demanding he play round-the-table ping-pong, or come to the beach with us to collect mussels because the tide had gone out, or to the river on bikes because we weren't allowed to go without a grown-up . . . 'Now, *pl-ea-se*, Uncle Robert, *pl-ea-se*!'

Later, when we were older, he'd sit and help us with our CVs, get them typed for us, offer advice, work experience in his accountancy firm, anything, in short, that he could do in the way of practical hands-on help for his nieces – a course of action that was completely alien to my father. As far as he was concerned, we had teachers to help us with all that, and as for his niece, well, she had her own father, didn't she?

Daddy, I thought with a sudden lurch of pity. How on earth must he be feeling now? His adored younger brother and the perfect foil for him, if he did but know it. For Robert was the only person who could really temper Daddy's furious outbursts, who could admonish him to lower his high moral tone, who could reason with him to be more tolerant, more compassionate, as no one, not even my mother, could. What agonies must he be going through now?

And Penny. I looked down at Penny's fair head. Penny, who'd lost such an adored and adoring father. A man who'd unquestionably spoiled and pampered his only child, but who at the same time was the only one who could really keep her in check, curb her tantrums, her foot-stamping, her extravagances, her petulance, as surely her husband couldn't. Robert's was the only reproof that really shamed her.

But it was for my aunt that my heart really broke, for theirs was not a marriage to be taken lightly. When she was young, my mother had told me, Rachel had been so beautiful – a debutante, the society girl of her age, and bright, too – that she could have had almost anyone. But she chose Robert and later, once told me that if she couldn't have had him, she wouldn't have married at all. Theirs was the perfect match. Patrick's words came back to me. Yes, if anyone had found the real thing, they had, and now he'd gone, leaving his other half behind.

I bent my head on Penny's and the tears rolled down my face. Suddenly my heart ached for my own childhood. I longed to look for rock pools again, to hold on tightly to my uncle's hand as he led me cautiously over the barnacled rocks and slippery seaweed in my bare feet, when all that mattered was how many crabs I had in my bucket and whether my fish were bigger than Penny's and Laura's. I longed for simpler days.

Eventually Penny's sobs subsided. Her head lolled onto

my shoulder and her eyes were half-closed. She looked almost weak from crying. I glanced up as my mother came quietly into the room. Her face was very pale. My eyes filled up again and we exchanged sad little smiles.

'Come on, Penny darling,' she said gently, 'come and have a lie down.'

'Not upstairs,' whispered Penny. 'Not on my own.'

'No no, dear, here, on the sofa. Tess and I will be close by.'

She led her to the vast red sofa in front of the fire, laid her down like a child and put a blanket over her. I sat on the floor beside her, holding her hand, listening to her sobs gradually subside to the point where she was just catching her breath, watching her eyes close. Mummy sat behind me, perched on the arm of the sofa, her hands tightly clasped in her lap. When eventually Penny's breathing became regular, I turned and looked at her. She nodded and we tiptoed from the room.

In the kitchen we hugged each other hard.

'How's Dad?' I whispered.

She sat down, or rather lowered herself into a chair, and I suddenly thought, with an awful pang, how thin and frail she looked herself.

'Terrible,' she said sadly. 'I've never seen him like this, not since – well. Not for years. He won't speak to anyone, won't let go, just walks around the garden pretending he's pruning roses looking white and stricken.'

'Where is he now?'

'Still outside.'

'I'll go and –'

'No, Tess.' She put a hand on my arm. 'Give him a moment. He wouldn't want it, really.'

I sighed and nodded. 'OK. And the children?'

'Josie and Laura took them to the beach.'

'Do they know?'

'Oh yes, we told them. Hugo and Clemmie are all right, I mean they were upset, but they knew he'd been terribly ill and after all they only saw him once a year and death is so hard to grasp at that age, but Leonora . . .'

'Her beloved Grandpa,' I said softly.

'Quite. Who would have been such a good influence on her, don't you think?' she said quietly, looking up at me.

I nodded, knowing exactly what she meant. That she didn't always get the best of influences from her parents.

I put my hand on hers. 'Rachel will always be there for her.'

'Of course,' she rallied, 'and more so now. She'll put what's left of her heart and soul into that little girl.'

I blinked back the tears I wanted to cry for Rachel. For lost love. I sat down next to Mummy at the table and she grasped my hand. We sat still, remembering, in silence.

'Is Penny very upset that she wasn't there when he died?' I said eventually.

'Of course, but you know,' she glanced quickly at the door, 'I think Rachel would have wanted it this way. Penny would have been – well, upset, understandably.'

'Hysterical.'

'Exactly. This way, they could say their goodbyes quietly, alone.'

I nodded. A final, peaceful, loving goodbye. For a while we were quiet again. My mother rallied first. She straightened up and looked at me, as if seeing me for the first time.

'And how are you, darling? You're on crutches, I see – that's good. How's the ankle?'

'Better, much better.'

'And the head?'

'Fine.' I patted her hand, smiling. 'Don't you worry about me.'

'And the heart?'

I looked at her sharply. Her eyes held mine firmly.

'That's – all right,' I faltered in astonishment.

'Good.' This time she patted my hand.

She got to her feet. 'Now,' she said briskly, 'we must think what's the best thing to do. Have a plan of action. Penny will want to go back to London, of course, and your father too, I'm sure . . .'

She moved around the kitchen putting cutlery back in drawers, folding up tea towels, wiping surfaces, discussing the options. I watched her as if in a dream. Not so silly, my old mum. Not so silly at all. Why did I always under-estimate her? Was it because Dad was always such a huge presence, such a main player? Because she was so often the background to his foreground?

'. . . so I think the best thing would be if you, Josie and the children stayed on with Laura and Edward for a bit, don't you? No sense in everyone dashing back immedi-ately, the funeral won't be until next week and it seems a shame to cut short the only holiday the children have. Robert wouldn't have wanted that.'

'What?' I looked up at her, still dazed. 'Oh – no. No, you're right. And David will come back to drive us home, I hope.'

'Oh darling, of course, you can't drive. Well, Josie

would do it surely, I mean if David doesn't want to come back?'

'Oh don't worry, I'm sure he won't mind, you know David. Anyway, I was thinking, I might let Josie go with Penny, sort of – loan her out for a week or two. I think Penny could probably do with the help and Leonora knows Josie so well now.'

My mother turned and smiled properly for the first time. 'Oh Tess, that would be so kind. Piers seems totally incapable of dealing with hysterical women, not to mention his sad little daughter. It's such a long drive home. Josie could play games with Leonora in the back and it would give Penny a chance to grieve quietly without upsetting Leonora.'

'Exactly.' I stood up, pleased to have done something positive. 'Does David know?'

'Yes, your father rang him earlier. We tried to get you at the Camerons' but you were out.'

'Yes, we – I was at the river.' I declined to meet her eye. 'I'll ring David now.'

'Oh, he's not in Chambers. His clerk said he'd taken the day off to do some shopping.'

I turned to her, incredulous. 'Shopping? David? For what? I thought he was supposed to be so busy?'

She shrugged. 'Don't know, darling.'

I sighed. 'Oh well, I'll ring him later.'

I plucked an apple from the bowl and limped out into the garden. I sat down on the step that led down from the terrace to the lawn and ate it slowly in the sunshine. Down at the far end of the garden I could see my father, bobbing around in the bracken in his khaki hat. He had an old scythe in his hand and was swiping away at the brambles like a man possessed. The scythe was blunt and rusty and the brambles so thick and tangled it was a thankless, futile task. There was something pathetic about the spectacle. Once or twice I was sure he'd seen me but he didn't stop flailing away, didn't acknowledge me.

I drew up my knees to my chest, resting my chin on them. I gazed down at the old York stone that we'd played hopscotch on for hours as children. I knew every square of that stone, every line, every crack, just as my father probably did, and Robert too. Tears welled again. But it was funny, I mused, brushing them away, how on one level my heart ached for Robert, but on another, purely selfish level, I was grateful to him for his timing. By mourning his death, I didn't have time to think about my own life, about Patrick. Sorry, I could tell myself, but I haven't got time for all that heart-searching now: my uncle's died, you see. Yes, how weird. I looked up at the mountains. It was almost as if Robert was still around, still helping me out somewhere out there.

As I sat gazing into the distance, two very small, very familiar figures gradually came into sight. My face broke into a smile as I watched them race along the valley floor, Clemmie yelling for Hugo to wait, Hugo forging ahead, competitive to the last. They disappeared from view in the wood at the bottom of the garden for a second, then popped up again just below my father. He ignored them as they scrambled past him, racing up the lawn towards me.

I hugged them both as they flopped down beside me. 'Hello, pixies,' I murmured, kissing their heads hard.

'Uncle Robert's dead,' panted Clemmie. 'He's a dead man now, Mummy.'

'I know, darling.' I pulled her close.

'Is he with God? Up in heaven?'

'I'm sure he is.'

'No,' piped up Hugo. 'No, Mummy, he might be down –'

'Thank you, Hugo, that will do.'

'But he can't fly!' said Clemmie with anguished eyes. 'What will he do?'

'Oh Clem, he'll manage.' I squeezed her.

'Will God lend him some wings?'

'Well . . .'

'Like you said He would when Pericles and Roderick died?'

'Oh. Yes, probably.' Clearly I'd peddled that particular line of drivel when our pair of smelly homosexual guinea pigs had died so there was no going back now.

'And will Uncle Robert share a room with Pericles and Roderick?'

I laughed. 'Darling, I'm not sure there are rooms, as such, in heaven.'

'What then? Where will they sleep?' Her eyes were like saucers.

'Well . . .' Clouds sprang immediately to mind and I realized I hadn't actually updated my own view of heaven since I too was a four-year-old.

'Not at the airport!' she cried.

I frowned at her. 'No,' I said slowly, shaking my head, 'no, not at the airport. I'm sure they'll sleep – yes, in a room.' I nodded firmly, unable to think of a suitable alternative.

'With on sweet bathroom and sea view?'

I stared at her in amazement.

'Cuntimental breakfast? Balcony and beeday?' she demanded.

I blinked. Good heavens, what a bourgeois child I'd raised! Balcony and bidet? How on earth did she even know what a bidet was?

'Yes, I expect so,' I said comfortingly.

'How lovely,' she breathed. 'Hugo, where's your sword?'

'Upstairs,' he muttered into the York stone, engrossed in the capturing of an ant. Clemmie raced off.

'Ow! It stung me!' he yelled, brushing it off with his hand.

'Hugo, where did she get all that heaven stuff from?' I asked. 'What have you been telling her?'

'Not me,' said Hugo, sucking his wounded finger. '*Wish You Were Here*, on the telly. That fat lady with the yellow hair shows you a hotel on a beach and then says it's heaven.'

'Oh!' I breathed. So we had Judith Chalmers to thank for this warped view of the after-life, did we? Terrific. No doubt Clemmie also thought wings would be available from reception for a quick flit around the bay followed by a barbecue on the beach with the heavenly host. Doubtless she expected the Angel Gabriel to meet her at the airport in full nightie and halo regalia before standing at the front of the coach with a microphone saying: '*On your right we have the Copa Cabana disco . . .*' I groaned.

Clemmie was back in a twinkling, brandishing Hugo's sword. 'Hugo,' she ordered. 'Kill me.'

'Brilliant!' Hugo sprang up off the grass. 'No, hang on

Clem, I'll strangle you if you don't mind. I'll just go and get my dressing-gown cord.'

'You'll do no such thing!' I roared.

He stopped in his tracks and turned. 'But she said –'

'I DON'T CARE! Now inside the pair of you, it's teatime – and take off those wet sandals before you go in, Hugo.'

'But I want to die,' said Clemmie, her lip quivering. 'I want to do beach sports with Uncle Robert, just let me die!'

'Come on, Clemmie.' I tried to lead her in by her arm.

She went limp in my arms. '*I want to die!*' she bellowed at the top of her voice, dragging her legs behind her.

'Where's Josie?' I demanded, lugging my infant prima donna towards the house and looking around wildly. God, I'd only been back two seconds and already I was panting for the au pair.

'Upstairs, changing Clemmie's bed,' said Hugo. 'Clem tried to hatch some eggs last night. Thought if she lay on them all night she'd have some chickens in the morning.' He sniggered. 'But all she got was egg up her bum.'

'Oh Clem,' I sighed, 'you didn't, did you?'

She stood up. 'That's what hens do, isn't it?' she demanded.

I groaned. 'Oh God, I'd better go and give Josie a hand. Now listen, you two. Go inside and find Granny – take her in, Hugo – oh, and be very nice to Leonora, please. She's a bit sad today.'

'I gave her some of my old Easter egg,' sniffed Clemmie, wiping her eyes. 'It had gone all white but she didn't mind.'

'And I didn't put sand in her knickers like I usually do when she takes them off to put her swimsuit on,' said Hugo proudly.

'Excellent, excellent,' I muttered weakly. 'That's the spirit, darlings, that's real progress.'

I trudged wearily upstairs thinking, not for the first time, how easy it would be to commit infanticide, particularly with one's own offspring.

I found Josie in Clemmie's room making a valiant attempt to get half a dozen eggs out of a mattress. The room smelled violently already. I perched on the bed opposite, held my nose, told her she was doing a marvellous job and then as casually as possible floated the Penny loan scheme with her. She paused and sat back on her heels, J-cloth in hand. I could see her hesitate and I didn't blame her. Leonora was a doddle of course, an absolute dream child to look after, but Penny, who got through about sixteen cleaners a year, was without doubt the employer from hell.

'All right,' she said finally, 'but for one week only, OK? That's my absolute limit. Otherwise I can see myself taking the bread-knife to her.'

'Absolutely,' I said quickly. 'One week only, you're a brick, Josie. And don't forget, you're still working for me, she's just borrowing you so don't take any, you know –'

'Shit.'

'Quite.'

We smiled at each other. She put the cloth down, folded her arms and looked at me squarely.

'So how was Patrick?'

I swallowed. Not ones to beat about the Outback, these Aussie girls, were they?

'Fine,' I said, smiling broadly. 'He was fine.'

She grinned. 'He's still crazy about you, isn't he?'

'Oh!' I shrugged. 'Well, yes, I suppose he is. A bit.' I nibbled the skin around my thumbnail. 'How did you know?'

'Oh, he more or less told me. More or less admitted that's why he'd asked me out. He wanted to make you jealous, let you see what you'd given up. Said he knew it was childish but he wanted to ram home the comparison – you know, there you were, middle-aged, jaded, careworn and all that, and there he was still young, free and single.'

I gulped. Clearly it was a comparison Josie could relate to too. 'Yes, well he did that all right,' I said, remembering my seething jealousy. 'He told you that, did he?'

'Yeah.' She dipped her cloth in the bucket and resumed her scrubbing. 'I could see he wasn't a bit interested in me so I asked him what he was up to. He came clean.' She laughed. 'I liked him all the more for it actually. We had a bit of a laugh after that, cleared the air. Had a game of darts in the pub then he took me home.' She looked up at me coyly. 'Not that I would have said no, though, Tess. I mean, Jeeze, that man is absolutely knockout.'

I blinked. 'Really?'

'Oh *what*?' She dropped her cloth incredulously. 'Tess, he's drop dead GORGEOUS, you must know that!'

'Er, yes.' I nodded. 'Yes, I suppose I do.'

She shook her head in amazement. 'He must really

have been something else when he was younger. I'm surprised you didn't –' She broke off.

'What? Didn't what?'

'Nothing.' She bent her head and resumed her scrubbing. 'Don't think I'm gonna shift all this egg you know, Tess.'

'Oh, just soak it in Fairy Liquid and turn the mattress over. No one will ever know.'

She wrinkled her nose. 'It'll honk for ever, won't it?'

I shrugged. 'So what? Most people who stay here are so pissed by the time they fall into bed they'll just think it's all that salmon and port repeating on them.'

She giggled and I wandered out, leaving her to it. I walked slowly downstairs, chewing my nail. *I'm surprised you didn't pick him instead of David,* was what she'd been about to say. I paused on the landing halfway down and ran my finger round a picture frame, collecting a neat pile of dust. Well of course she would think that, wouldn't she? From a twenty-two-year-old's point of view Patrick was the obvious choice; attractive, wild, loaded, funny, whereas David – I smiled wryly. David was more of an acquired, sophisticated taste. Wouldn't appeal to a youthful palate at all. I grinned. More of a jaded, careworn old bag's palate perhaps.

As I hopped the last few steps into the hall I saw Piers through the open front door, packing up his car. I went out to him. He turned as he saw me and rather wearily put down the case he'd been struggling with. I gave him a big hug. He squeezed me gratefully. Piers had adored his father-in-law but it occurred to me that there would be no room at all for his grief. Penny's would be all-encompassing. I told him about Josie and he looked hugely relieved.

'Oh, thanks so much, Tess. I tell you, I wasn't looking forward to the drive back, or the next week or so, come to that. At least I won't have to worry about Leonora.'

'Exactly.'

'Just the week though?' he said hopefully. 'I couldn't persuade you to part with her for any longer?'

I hesitated, 'Well you could, but –'

'But she's not prepared to put up with my wife for any longer, and who can blame her?' He grinned. 'Just the lifetime of servitude for me, of course. Uh-oh, talk of the devil.' His expression softened as Penny, her face streaked with tears, came slowly down the front steps.

'All right, my darling?' he said gently, taking her arm.

'Yes, thank you,' she whispered. 'Are we off soon?'

'Just give me ten more minutes to organize the back of the car and then we'll be away,' he promised.

'OK,' she sniffed. She turned and disappeared back into the house.

'You're going now?' I asked in astonishment.

'Apparently,' he muttered. 'Don't ask me, Tess, I'm just following orders here.'

'Blimey. I'd better tell Josie.' I dashed back into the house and in the dark hall, collided with my father carrying a suitcase. His eyes were hollow with pain, his face white and contorted. It buckled as he looked down at me.

'Daddy!' I flew into his arms and felt his body stiffen as he tried to keep control. I hugged him hard.

'Cry,' I urged. 'Just cry!'

'Will do,' he said in a strange, strangled voice. He patted me on the shoulder. 'In my own good time, Tess, in my own good time.'

He disentangled himself and moved quickly on past me to the front door. I watched him go down the steps to the drive, his back as stiff as a door. I turned sadly and went off in search of Josie.

Finally, about an hour later, both parties left. Piers, Penny, Leonora and Josie – looking very doubtful – in one car, and my parents in the other. Laura and I stood on the steps and sadly waved them off. It wasn't the usual jolly Invertarn departure at all. There were no tooting horns, no children hanging out of windows waving, no jibes to 'beat you back to England!' just the gentle purr of the cars going down the gravel drive. Laura and I linked arms tightly and watched as they went round the corner, down the winding lane and disappeared off into the distance. Then we turned and walked slowly back into the house.

Laura sighed. 'So unfair, isn't it?'

'Well, life's a bitch, et cetera. You must know that by now.'

She nodded. 'I certainly do.'

That evening I rang David. We had a sober commiseration about Robert then I told him of Josie's departure.

'Are you mad?' he said irritably. 'How are you going to get home?'

'Well, you're coming back, aren't you?'

'Oh Tess,' he groaned, 'what's the point? You'll only be there for a few more days and then you'll be coming back for the funeral.'

'But you were coming back before, and we'd only have had a few more days then.'

There was a pause. I frowned.

'David?'

'Well . . .'

I stared at the receiver incredulously. 'You weren't intending to come back at all, were you?'

'Look, I'm so snowed under here you wouldn't believe it. Honestly, it would have been almost impossible to get away.'

'But not impossible to go shopping, eh? Mummy said you weren't even in court today!'

'Ah yes, well, today was – an exception. My case was taken out of the list. But as from tomorrow, God, I'm absolutely chock-a-block again.'

'David, I just don't believe this. You mean you're not coming back? How on earth are we supposed to get home?'

'Well, you were *supposed* to have an au pair but you seem to have given her away. Can't you ask Laura to drive you?'

'Laura!' I said hotly. 'Why the hell should she drive us? She'll want to go back with Edward!'

Laura popped her head round the drawing-room door on hearing her name. 'What's this? What will I be doing?'

'David wants you to drive us home so he doesn't have to come back. He's insane!'

'Oh yes, I'll do it,' she said eagerly. 'Anything rather than sit in a car with Enigmatic Ed for sixteen hours.' She grabbed the receiver. 'It's OK, David, you're off the hook. I'll drive them back with pleasure.'

'Laura!' I was appalled. 'Where is Edward? He'll hear!'

'No, he won't.' She handed me back the receiver. 'He's gone painting. Anyway, frankly my dear, I don't give a damn.' She sauntered back into the drawing room again.

'Well, there you are, darling, you have a driver,' drawled David's voice in my ear. 'Now don't rush back, I think it's as well the children stay up there as long as possible. It's baking hot in London at the moment. Now, any more problems? Anything else you'd like me to sort out long distance or d'you think you can cope now?'

I stared at the receiver in disbelief. Why was he being so weird? So . . . horrid?

'No,' I said coolly. 'No, that's fine, David. Everything is absolutely under control now. It's all just tickety-boo. You carry on window-shopping and filing your nails or whatever else it is you've been doing and don't you worry about us. This single-parent family is doing *just fine*!'

With that I slammed the receiver down and stalked back to the drawing room.

Laura raised her eyebrows. 'Problems?'

'The bastard!' I exploded. 'He's not coming back!'

'Well, you can hardly expect him to fly up here just to chauffeur you down again, can you?'

I stared at her. 'Whose side are you on?'

'No one's, but you can see his point, can't you?'

'No, I bloody can't,' I fumed, grabbing the newspaper and stomping upstairs. 'I can't see it at all!'

Chapter Twenty

Madelaine rang the following morning. The bush telegraph had reached Gilduncan and she wanted to offer her condolences. Laura took the call in the kitchen. She put her hand over the mouthpiece and turned to me as I fried bacon in my pyjamas at the stove.

'She wants to know if we'd like to go up for a swim,' she hissed.

'Jesus, no! Certainly not.'

'Shall I take the children?'

I swung around. 'No! Laura, for heaven's sake, I don't want the children up there.' Suddenly I felt panicky. I didn't want any of my family anywhere near that place.

'So what shall I say? It looks so rude, Tess –'

'Just say we're busy.'

She frowned and turned back to the telephone. 'Madelaine? Um, that would be lovely, but I'll come on my own if I may . . . Yes, look forward to it . . . OK, bye.'

She replaced the receiver and turned back to me, folding her arms. 'Just because you've fallen out with Patrick it doesn't mean we have to snub Madelaine again. It's not fair.'

'I think "fallen out" is putting it rather mildly when I've rejected his twelve-year love vigil, don't you?' I snapped. 'And I'm not snubbing Madelaine, I've written her a very fulsome thank-you letter, I just don't particularly want to see her son, that's all. But you go ahead, if you must.'

She grinned. 'I must. Think of me sipping my pre-lunch apéritif, won't you?' She pinched a piece of bacon from the pan and sauntered out of the room.

I threw the spatula in the sink. Oh terrific, I thought grimly. Just swan off up there when I've specifically asked you not to, and leave me here with your abandoned suitor and two quarrelsome children all day, why don't you? Thanks very much. God, my sister was such a bloody teenager sometimes, so *thoughtless*.

I picked up the plate of bacon and marched down the passageway into the breakfast room. Yes, we had five more days to get through on our own up here now, with no grandparents to amuse the children, no au pair, no father, and I couldn't even drive. What on earth was I going to do with them? I slammed the bacon down in front of Hugo and Clemmie who were even now fighting over a free gonk from the Frosties packet with Edward making a futile attempt to referee.

'Um, Hugo, how about letting Clemmie have a little go first and then you could – oh dear, now look, you've pulled its leg off. Don't you think –'

'PUT THAT DOWN THE PAIR OF YOU!' I bellowed.

They dropped it like a hot coal and Edward recoiled in fright.

'Now, eat up your bacon –' Edward instantly picked up his knife and fork in terror – 'and then for heaven's sake go out to play or something. Isn't that what children are supposed to do?'

'We don't want to. There's no one to play with now,' whined Clemmie. 'Can we go to the beach?'

'Don't be ridiculous, how on earth am I supposed to get you there? No, you can play in the garden.'

Edward wiped his mouth with his napkin and cleared his throat. 'Er, might I be of some assistance?' he ventured timidly.

Three pairs of eyes regarded him doubtfully.

'In what sense, Edward?' I enquired as politely as possible.

'I wondered if they might like to go bird-watching. Apparently, there are some capercaillie over at Beacon's Top. I thought it might be worth trying to spot them.'

There was an awed silence. I held my breath. He might just as well have suggested four hours' devout prayer in Invertarn Church.

Hugo's eyes were wide. 'Bird-watching! I've never done that – what d'you do?'

'Watch birds,' I muttered darkly, 'and keep very still,' I added with a smirk. I could see my lot lasting precisely five minutes, but if Edward was game, by God so was I.

I dropped the smirk and beamed widely. 'What a marvellous idea. That would be lovely, wouldn't it, children? Come along, eat up all of you and off you go!'

And so it was that Edward, in a small, but intensely practical way, finally came into his own. To my amazement, he didn't just set off blindly up a mountainside with two bored children at his heels as I would have done, he did it properly. First he took them into Invertarn to buy little rucksacks, a bird book, pencils and paper to draw what they saw, and even special whistles to call the birds.

Then he packed sandwiches in each dinky rucksack, found some old binoculars in a drawer, saw that the children had appropriate footwear and off they went. And not just once, but every day for four days. Yes, every morning after breakfast this ornithological trio would solemnly pack up their knapsacks, hold hands in a row, and more or less singing *The Happy Wanderer*, toddle off in search of lesser-spotted whatjamacalits, and every afternoon at about teatime they would return; happy, stimulated, and most important of all, exhausted, so that all I had to do was feed them, bath them, and pop them into bed. God, I could have kissed Edward, in fact I could have – no. Perhaps not.

'It's amazing,' I enthused to Laura as I came down from tucking the sleeping beauties into bed one night. 'I mean they really enjoy it, and what's more they enjoy *being* with him.'

'So he's a success with the under-fives,' she muttered from the depths of her newspaper. 'Terrific.'

'Oh, don't be such a bitch, Laura. He's really trying and the children are having a wonderful time, thanks to him.'

'Yes, well, he's a teacher, don't forget. It's the one thing he's supposed to be good at.' She folded her newspaper, threw it on the floor and stalked out of the room.

'Where are you going?' I called after her.

'Out!'

The front door slammed behind her and not for the first time I felt exasperated with my sister. I was well aware that a little irritation with a man could quickly flare into full-blown revulsion but it seemed to me she couldn't bear to be in Edward's company even for a moment. Not only did she make herself scarce during the day, 'when it isn't even as if he's *here*,' I reasoned, but she didn't come back until late in the evening either, by which time Edward had usually gone to bed.

'Where on earth do you go?' I demanded, as she finally put her head round the drawing-room door at half-past ten that night.

'Has he gone?' she whispered.

'Yes, he's gone. Where do you go?' I repeated. 'This is the third night in a row!'

'Oh,' she said airily, flopping down into the sofa, 'just around and about.'

I frowned down at her from the window seat where I'd been reading. Her cheeks were flushed and her eyes strangely bright, and if she'd been one of the children I probably would have taken her temperature.

'Yes, but where?'

She stared into space then turned dreamily. 'Hmmm? Oh, just down to the beach. I sit on the rocks or walk along the cliff tops. It's glorious in the evening, so quiet and peaceful, gives me a chance to think. And after all, we're not here for much longer, got to make the most of it.' She stretched her arms up above her head and yawned expansively. 'God, I'm tired though. Must be all that fresh air. I'm off to bed!' She jumped up with a sudden burst of alacrity.

I put down my book. 'Laura, I couldn't just talk to you for a sec, could I? It's just that I really need to –'

'Oh Tess, can't it wait till the morning? I'm absolutely bushed. Look, my eyes are closing as we speak.' She feigned sleep, staggering about a bit. 'I've really got to go up. G'night.'

''Night,' I muttered after her.

She went, and with a lump in my throat, I picked up my book and tried to read again, the same page I'd been trying to read for the last four days. I put it down. Why was I feeling like this? So depressed? I *never* felt depressed, damn it. Irritated, angry, stressed out, murderous even, but not depressed. Why then? I shook my head, banishing his face. His eyes. No. I would not think about him. I breathed deeply and got up, pacing around the dimly lit room. I paused at the window and looked out. In the night sky I saw him, serious, anguished, intense, down at the river.

'No, I will not *think* about him!' I repeated savagely, throwing my head back and scratching it energetically.

The stars winked back knowingly at me from the dark outside. I sighed. God, these last four days had been difficult to say the least. Thank heavens we were going home tomorrow. I leaned my hands on the windowsill and peered out, pressing my nose to the glass. Actually, it wasn't the days that had been so bad: I'd kept very busy, hobbled around doing quite a bit of gardening one way and another. Dad was too stingy to employ a gardener so I'd taken on the role and had managed to get rid of much of my frustration by uprooting weeds and digging over what must once have been flower beds.

No, it wasn't the days, I thought, limping slowly round the room; it was the nights. These endless quiet evenings when he would keep popping into my mind. And having no one to talk to about it didn't help . . . I felt a tear roll down my cheek. I brushed it away furiously. Why did I keep doing that? Bursting into tears for no reason . . . why?

Of course, I reasoned, stooping down to turn off a lamp, there was bound to be a certain amount of shock. Patrick's admission had been a complete bolt from the blue; it had taken me flying back with a whoosh. It was like being in a time warp, suddenly, there I was, all those years ago. I was eighteen again. Yes, the whole thing had been very unsettling, but – I bit my lip and straightened up – somehow, in my heart, I knew I was reacting too violently.

Perhaps you're just missing David, I told myself sternly as I bent down to pick a newspaper up off the floor. That's what it is: you're up here on your own with the children, you've got a seriously sprained ankle, there was all that business with Willie, all that guilt, your uncle's just died and your husband's not around – God, it's no wonder you're bursting into tears every five minutes. But somehow, this didn't quite ring true either. I turned off the final light switch at the door, paused for a moment, gazing back into the dark room, then went slowly upstairs to bed.

It was, therefore, with a huge sense of relief that we finally swept floors, stripped beds, packed cases, loaded up the cars and set off back to London the next day. Edward had decided to do the whole journey in one go so he left at the crack of dawn, thereby missing out on any embarrassing goodbyes, much to Laura's relief. We'd decided to break the journey and stay overnight somewhere around Yorkshire, we thought vaguely. I was actually quite looking forward to driving back with Laura. It wasn't often we had the chance to be on our own and I was keen to pour my heart out to her, get it all off my chest.

I turned Vivaldi down slightly as we swept along the lanes towards Belgadoon.

'Strange, seeing Patrick again, wasn't it?' I mused.

'Hmmm,' she agreed, keeping her eyes firmly on the road.

'Did I tell you what happened down at the river?'

'Briefly.'

I sighed. 'Funny. I still can't seem to get him out of my head.'

She frowned at me, then jerked her head in the direction of the back seat, at the children. I glanced around.

'Oh, it's OK, they're plugged into their stereos.'

'Yes, but even so.' She turned Vivaldi up again.

I glanced sideways at her. She was staring straight ahead, humming away to the music. Oh well, I thought, leaning back with a quiet sigh, maybe later. And at least she was getting me out of this place, putting the miles between us. I turned and gazed out of the window at the mountains, the lochs, the valleys, letting *The Four Seasons* drift over me.

On and on we drove; the children behaved, the traffic was light, Laura really put her foot down and we ate up the miles, the result being that we drove far too far and in true Fergusson fashion left it much too late to find a bed and breakfast, let alone a hotel. Nine-thirty saw us still frantically scouring the Yorkshire Dales when everything was either fully booked or shutting up for the night. Or so they said. I have to say, Laura's selection technique might well have put a few backs up. She would insist on cruising up to each prospective establishment in the BMW, purring down the electric window, and in a loud, expensive southern voice saying something like – 'Looks a bit shabby, the paint's coming off the walls. Still,' she'd sniff, 'there's not much else in this crummy old place, give it a go and don't forget to ask if the sheets are cotton or nylon.'

With a flushed face I'd dutifully hop out of the car – I'd dispensed with the crutches now but still did a certain amount of hopping – and convinced that every single curtain in the village was twitching with indignation, scurried dutifully up the garden path, while she sat in the car, drumming her fingers on the steering wheel, engine still running.

All the landladies looked exactly the same to me: floral housecoats, carpet slippers, corrugated iron curls, permanently folded arms and lips that had disappeared with years of pursing. Certainly the reaction I got on each doorstep was identical. They all stared at me as if I were barking mad.

'A room?' they'd repeat incredulously.

'No, two rooms actually.'

'Two rooms! What, for the night?'

'That would be helpful,' I murmured to this particular old bag who all but filled the doorway of her supposed guesthouse.

As if on cue the arms folded and the lips disappeared. She shook her corrugated curls firmly.

'Oh no, not two rooms, not for the night, any road.' For what then, I wondered? 'Try Tom Shilling's up the road, number thirty-two. It's not that clean mind, but beggars can't be choosers!'

And with that encouraging remark, she slammed the door in my face.

'Charmless old bitch,' I muttered as I hobbled down the path.

Laura stuck her head out. 'Well?' she demanded. 'What was she like?'

I nodded thoughtfully. 'Sweet. Very sweet. But unfortunately she's booked up. She said there was somewhere nice up the road though.'

I climbed back in, deliberately failing to inform her of the questionable hygiene standards at number 32, because at this stage, frankly, I was desperate. The children were over-tired, irritable and rapidly reaching fever pitch and I knew from experience that unless we found a room soon – any room, a cave would do – blood must surely spill.

Laura drove cautiously up to number 32 and pulled up outside. One of the bedroom windows was broken, there were at least four cats in the garden – OK yard – and an old lavatory was nestling lovingly up against the front door.

'Jesus,' she muttered, shifting into first gear again. 'Forget it.' But by this time I was already out of the car and halfway up the path.

'You must be joking,' she cried after me. 'I'm not staying there!'

'Let's just see, shall we?' I shouted back.

'Well, don't forget to ask about the sheets!'

I gave a confident backward wave as I galloped on, privately thinking – sheets? Blimey, dream on.

I rang the bell, literally a second before I spotted that the wire was hanging out of the wall, so I rapped instead on the distressed green door – and I don't mean that in a trendy paint effect sense. Hmmm, well this really was tourism at its most discerning, wasn't it? Off the beaten track and all that. Could be interesting.

Moments later the door swung back and I can't remember what struck me first, the fact that Tom Shilling was wearing a dress or the smell of dead cat that zoomed up my nostrils.

'Um – good evening!' I gasped, instinctively holding my breath. 'D'you have a couple of rooms for the night?' I tried hard not to stare at the thick hairy ankles that protruded from his pinny.

His moustache bristled. 'Plenty of rooms,' he barked, 'but I'd have to make up the beds, wouldn't I?'

'Do you have a problem with that?' I gasped obsequiously. Any sentence, however short, was a trial.

'No problem,' he growled menacingly, 'but I'd 'ave to ask me 'usband first!'

With this mind-boggling sentence still ringing in my ears I followed my host across the threshold and it was at this point – probably something to do with the sexless swing of the generous behind – that I realized my host was in fact my hostess, who just happened to have rather a lot of facial hair, a boozer's nose, rheumy eyes, thick ankles, bushy eyebrows and a baritone voice. I breathed a sigh of relief. I wasn't at all sure what Laura's views on cross-dressing landlords would be.

He – she, tapped on a closed door halfway down the corridor.

'Tom?' she growled. 'There's some folk here want to stay.'

There was a long, no doubt incredulous, pause.

'Stay?' came the gruff response eventually.

'Tha's right.'

Another pause.

'Wha' for?'

She shrugged. 'The night, most like.'

Another, much longer pause.

'Give 'em the rooms right at the top,' came the rather chilling response. I shivered.

She nodded curtly and turned to me. 'You can have the rooms right at the top. Want to see?'

'Please!' I said eagerly. I might be mad but I wasn't that mad and I didn't want to spend the rest of the summer de-fleaing my children or visiting them in hospital while they recovered from the first outbreak of typhoid England had seen for fifty years.

As I followed Mrs Shilling up the dark staircase she jerked her head backwards. ''E won't come out,' she hissed conspiratorially, 'on account of his halitosis!'

'Ah!' I responded sympathetically, although what difference it would make to this atmosphere I couldn't imagine.

It soon became clear that 'not that clean' had been the understatement of the century. Cat-litter trays decorated every landing together with tottering pagodas of old newspapers, saucers of rancid milk, bundles of blind kittens, piles of mangy old cat, in fact, every corner was a shrine to feline fecundity – what you could see of the corners, anyway. It was so impossibly dark I had to feel my way upstairs after her, a deliberate ploy, I suspected, to keep one from spotting the dirt.

Up and up we went, with me hugging the walls blindly as we passed landing after landing, until eventually we reached the top floor, where suddenly, something little short of a miracle began to happen. Perhaps it was some-thing to do with the altitude or just call it wishful thinking but it seemed to me the air was thinning appreciably. The smell didn't seem nearly so pervasive, or the cats so prolific – in fact they were positively extinct up here – and as I followed her down a corridor I distinctly saw a small shaft of light filtering bravely through a skylight.

I wanted to turn to her and shout joyfully – 'Oh, Mrs Shilling, I can breathe!' or, 'Oh, look – paintwork, and isn't that – yes it is, how charming – a window!'

I restrained myself however and limited myself to rather daringly lowering my hand from nose-clutching level to throat-clutching level, so that by the time she'd led me into two small adjoining rooms my hand was almost at my side and I was positively euphoric.

Although not spectacularly clean the rooms did appear to have at least seen a duster and a Hoover at some time in their lives, and what's more there was a window so that at least one could get a breath of fresh – oops! Perhaps not. As eagerly as I'd opened it I slammed it shut again as more cat pong zoomed up from the garden.

'Best to keep it shut, with kiddies,' remarked my land-lady darkly.

'Oh! Yes, of course,' I agreed.

I nervously felt my way around the room. The beds had indeed not been made up yet and one swift glance at the pink nylon eiderdowns told me all I needed to know about the sheets. Laura's rigorous terms could not be complied with, but by this time I'd spotted a shade on the light bulb, something approaching a curtain at a window, a washbasin – albeit cracked – and it was too late.

'I'll take it,' I beamed confidently.

'Both of them?' She eyed me suspiciously.

'Both of them.'

'That'll be seventeen pounds fifty upfront then.' She promptly held out her hand.

I rummaged dutifully in my handbag.

'Like cats, do you?' she asked suspiciously.

'Oh yes, very much,' I gushed, 'in fact I've got one – or two,' I added quickly, lest one should sound amateurish. 'I miss them terribly when I'm away, they sleep on my bed you see.'

Her huge eyebrows shot up. 'Tha's not a problem, my two tabbies will sleep with you.' She jerked her head back downstairs. 'Tom too, most like.'

I stared at her aghast. 'T-Tom?' What, the halitosis-ridden husband?

'There's no extra charge,' she said sharply. 'I'll go and get him. Smells a bit, but he's a good ratter.'

'Oh!' I breathed as it dawned. 'You have a cat called Tom!'

'Large black one on the landing.' She folded her arms. 'Why, who did you think I meant?'

'Oh, I – wasn't sure!'

She eyed me sharply. 'Not after me husband are you?' she demanded.

'No! No of course not.'

She glared at me for a moment, then threw back her head and cackled loudly. 'Well you're welcome to that old bugger! I haven't been near him for fifteen years on account of his gums, but if he's your cup of tea, you have him. He'll be tickled pink when I tell him.'

'Please don't!' I squeaked, putting a restraining hand on her arm. 'Really Mrs Shilling, it was just a silly misunderstanding.'

She cackled some more then patted my hand. 'Aye well, perhaps it's best I don't, any road. Old Tom 'asn't had a whiff of a woman for so long, who knows what it might do to his ticker, not to mention his vitals.'

'Yes, well let's not upset his . . . vitals, shall we?' I muttered, feeling rather faint at the thought.

She tapped her nose conspiratorially. 'Your secret's safe with me, chuck,' she said, and with that she pocketed my seventeen quid and went chuckling downstairs.

I breathed a sigh of relief then followed her down. I hastened out to report to Laura and the children in the car. Now, how to phrase this . . .

'Not bad,' I said solemnly, head on one side. I nodded thoughtfully. 'Not bad at all. Heaps of character, very olde worlde.'

'Oh Tess, you can't be serious!' Laura protested. 'I can tell just by *looking* at it it's the pits!'

'Now that's unfair,' I scolded. 'Appearances can be very deceptive and once you get upstairs it's really rather pleasant. Come on, I'll lead the way.' I hopped back up the path.

'You mean you've taken it?' Incredulous, she followed at a safe distance with two very doubtful children hanging on to each hand. 'Have you seen the rooms? What about the beds?'

'She hasn't made them up yet – a good sign, don't you think?' I smiled brightly. 'Must mean they're clean.'

'Was there ever any doubt?' She cried as we crossed the threshold, 'Jesus, what's that SMELL!'

'There's no smell,' said a voice out of the darkness making us jump out of our skins. 'We keep a very clean establishment here, very clean indeed and if you don't like it you can go elsewhere.'

'Ah, Mrs Shilling!' I exclaimed as her moustache caught the light. 'This is my sister and my two children. May we go to our rooms, please?'

'You can do as you damn well please,' she retorted, disappearing into the depths of the cat-ridden bowels. A door slammed. I groaned. And just as we'd got to the cosy, husband-sharing stage.

'So refreshing,' I whispered as we groped our way upstairs, 'that sort of northern directness, don't you think?'

'Bloody rude, you mean,' snorted Laura. 'Tess, you must be out of your mind. And what the frigging hell was that, a transvestite or something?'

'Don't be silly,' I chortled merrily, 'she's just a bit *au naturel*, probably forgot to put her make-up on this morning. It happens, you know. Now, here we are,' we finally felt our way upstairs, 'right at the top. Isn't this nice? Hugo and Clemmie, you two are in here – look, a connecting door – isn't this exciting? See, here are your beds . . .' I groped around blindly in the dark and finally found a couple of flat things in each corner, 'one . . . two . . . and Laura and I will be just through here. OK, darlings?'

Through the gloom, two pairs of huge blue eyes blinked at me in disbelief.

'Are we really going to stay here, Mummy?' whispered Clemmie.

'Of course, my love.' I clapped my hands joyfully. 'It'll be an adventure! Now, come on, buck up, into your pye-jams' — I *never* call them that — 'clean your teeth till they're clean and sparkling and then hop into beddy-byes. *Won't* Daddy be sorry he missed this.'

Dumb with disbelief they slowly obliged and when I'd finally got them into bed having, on Clemmie's orders, looked in every single drawer, cupboard and under the beds for bears, ghosts, ghoulies and from my point of view, dead cats, I shut the connecting door, and with a huge sigh of relief leaned heavily against it.

Gazing up at me with equally shocked, disbelieving eyes was Laura, perched very gingerly on the edge of a chair, sucking hard on a cigarette. She'd put a hanky on the chair before sitting down so that her navy-blue Nicole Farhi trousers did not actually have to come into contact with it, and it was this last, small detail that finally did for me. Hysteria began to well up in my throat.

'Oh God!' I gasped, going weak at the knees. 'Isn't it awful, Laura? Isn't it just *awful*!' I clutched my mouth with one hand and held on to the door-handle for support with the other.

'It's disgusting,' she said firmly, but I distinctly saw her mouth twitch. 'Quite disgusting.'

'Quite!' Hysteria was rising fast now. 'Quite the most revolting place I've ever seen!'

Laura was not my sister for nothing and in seconds we were clutching each other, crying with silent laughter, tears streaming down our cheeks, trying desperately not to wake the children.

'And what about that thing with the moustache!' she gasped. 'The one you said had probably forgotten her make-up!'

'More like her hormones!'

'Rather pleasant upstairs! Really rather pleasant, that's what you said, you lying cow!'

'Oh God, I feel sick,' I said weakly, clutching my throat and staggering to a chair. 'I don't know if it's the smell or because I've laughed too much!'

We finally fell into our pink nylon double bed at about ten-thirty, still giggling like schoolgirls.

'Where d'you think they sleep?' Laura whispered.

'With the cats, I expect. They're probably all tucked up in bundles of newspaper as we speak.'

She giggled. 'What d'you think Tom's like?'

'Ten to one he's ginger, but take it from me, he hasn't been neutered. His "vitals" are still intact, if a little rusty. Pussy Galore told me.'

'Oh yuk!'

'Still,' I mused quietly, 'awful though it is, I'd still rather be here than at Kilmarnoch. It went on for too long this year.'

'Oh no,' she said quietly. 'I could have stayed up there for ever.'

I turned my head towards her on my pillow. 'Don't be silly – you, in Scotland? You'd miss Sloane Street in seconds.'

'Oh, I don't know. I'm not so sure I haven't grown out of Sloane Street.'

'Well, you certainly haven't grown into a country bumpkin yet, so don't give me that.'

'I don't think you have to be a country bumpkin to live up there. Look at Madelaine.'

'Yes but she doesn't live there all the time.'

'Then perhaps that's the answer,' she murmured quietly. But I wasn't really listening.

'She seems to have mended her fences with Patrick, doesn't she,' I mused.

'Mmmmm . . .'

'Seemed pleased to have him back.'

She didn't answer.

I sighed. 'God, it was strange seeing him again after all this –'

'Oh, for heaven's sake Tess, stop banging on about it!' She sat bolt upright in bed.

I stared at her in the darkness. 'I'm not banging on, I'm just saying –'

'Yes, but you *keep* just saying. It's not fair to anyone, Tess – not fair to him, to David, to the children – anyone! You've made your decision so now for God's sake stick to it and let everyone else get on with their lives, OK?'

I sat up too. 'Hey, what's got into you? I mean, of course I'll stick to it, but it was after all a fairly momentous decision. I can surely discuss it, can't I?'

She turned on me, eyes blazing. 'Momentous, was it? Really? You mean there *really* was a chance you'd leave David for him? Sell the house, take the children away from their schools, make David an occasional father?'

'Oh Laura, of course I couldn't do that, but –'

'Well then, SHUT UP!' she exploded. 'Stop titillating yourself with the idea of him still being in love with you. Forget it. For ever!'

There was a silence. She lay down again in the bed and turned on her side, away from me.

I stared at her back.

'Why are you being like this?' I said after a while.

'Like what?'

'So . . . aggressive?'

She sighed. There was another long pause. 'Because I'm sick of you just thinking about yourself. There are other people's lives at stake here, Tess, people who depend on your decision. You've got to stop playing with them. You've hankered after this man for twelve years now and –'

'That's not true Laura, I –'

'Yes you have! And now you've finally been offered the chance to have him. Well fine. Have him. Or *don't* have him, but for pity's sake make a decision one way or another and *stick* to it. Don't spend the rest of your life dithering and hankering and wondering what might or might not have been! Let him be, let him live again, let *everyone* live again and –'

'*AAAAAAHH!*'

A piercing scream cut her off in mid-diatribe. The connecting door flew open and there stood Clemmie, white-faced in her nightie.

I leaped out of bed and ran to her. 'Clemmie! What's the matter, darling?'

'There's a man.' She pointed, quivering. 'Outside the window! It's Burglar Bill, I'm sure it is!' She clung to me, sobbing.

'Don't be ridiculous, of course it isn't. Let me see.'

I dashed through the connecting door across to her window with Laura close on my heels.

'I wouldn't be at all surprised in this house,' she said in an undertone as we rubbed the filthy windowpane with Clemmie hugging my knees.

I peered out. There was definitely something going on out there. I couldn't see anything, but there was a sort of banging, scraping noise coming from directly beneath us in the garden. I strained my eyes and made out a shadowy figure, with a spade . . .

'Oh, it's all right darling,' I said with relief. 'It's just Mrs Shilling digging the garden.'

'At this time of night?' Laura said, peering out.

'Well she's probably getting the potatoes in or something. Perhaps she couldn't sleep and thought she'd get on with it, you know how it is. Come on, Clemmie, back to bed.'

She clung to me. 'I want to sleep with you, Mummy,' she whimpered.

I sighed and turned to Laura. 'Do you mind?'

She shrugged. 'Why not, the more the merrier.'

The three of us trooped back to the double bed and Clemmie snuggled in between us. I'd left the connecting door open and we could still hear Mrs Shilling scraping away outside.

'Surely you don't dig potatoes at this time of year, do you?' whispered Laura.

'Oh, I don't know.' I was still thinking about what she'd said earlier. About me. Hankering, wondering, dithering. I sighed. 'Perhaps she's burying cats.'

There was a pause. Then Laura sat up. 'Or worse!'

I stared at her back for a second then joined her in the bolt upright position.

'You mean . . .'

'Why not? It's always the back garden, isn't it? And they look mad enough.' She put a hand on my arm. 'Perhaps she's getting the holes ready! *Four* holes!'

I shook her off. 'Oh, don't be ridiculous, Laura. Honestly, you're worse than the children!'

I lay down again. A second later I shot back up again.

'HUGO!' I roared at the top of my voice.

'What?' came a sleepy response.

'Get in here this instant,' I bellowed.

'Why?'

'Because we're all sleeping together tonight. Now don't argue, just get in here!'

Chapter Twenty-one

Needless to say we were up and out of that place by seven o'clock the next morning, having politely declined to breakfast on dirt and dead cat, thank you very much. We said our goodbyes and instead, took our custom to a little café just down the road.

We piled into the small, already packed café, giggling about our close shave with the spade-wielding Shillings and got the last, Formica-topped table in the corner. The place was warm and steamy and the clientele a mixture of truckers and locals; all male and all resolutely working-class. They gave us a cursory glance as we walked in, but then got on with the serious business of hoovering up the traditional start to an English day – eggs-bacon-sausage-beans-tomato and half a gallon of steaming hot tea.

I smiled smugly as the children looked around in wonder. Oh yes, I prided myself on showing them all sides of life. We didn't just go to the Early Learning Centre and the Science Museum, oh no. There was an awful lot to be learned from this salt-of-the-earth stuff, and far be it from me to have cosseted children.

I did think rather longingly of my usual yoghurt and muesli as I sat down to an artery-furring plateful, but gamely played along and even mopped my fried egg up with my Mother's Pride. I had a nasty feeling it was going to play havoc with my bowels later though. We stuck out like sore thumbs naturally, but since everyone was minding their own business and getting on with the important things in life like eating as much as possible, burping loudly and reading the *Sun* from cover to cover before shuffling off to the Gents with it, no one took much notice of us. That is, until to my horror, my son abruptly took it upon himself to tweak up the atmosphere.

Short of the mandatory tomato ketchup for his sausage, Hugo held up his hand and summoned the waitress.

'Hey, servant!' he cried, in an imperious voice.

A horrible hush fell over the buzzing café. My mouth dried, as all around us knives and forks were lowered and teeth ground to a halt. All eyes were suddenly trained on the southern, middle-class table in the corner. Horrified, I swung around to Hugo.

'What the hell d'you think you're playing at?' I cried loudly, in what I hoped was a suitably outraged tone.

'Well, that's what we call them at school,' he retorted.

'What,' I glanced around nervously, 'servants?' I hissed, appalled.

He shrugged. 'Something like that.'

Something like that. I thought quickly. 'Oh, servers! You call them servers, darling!'

'That's what I said, isn't it?'

'He means servers!' I cried triumphantly, turning to what was now a decidedly hostile-looking crowd.

The waitress in question had been joined behind the counter by what appeared to be a huge steroid-tripping chef. His enormous muscles were rippling through his white overalls and he folded his arms grimly. God, he even seemed to have biceps in his eyes. I smiled brightly.

'It's what he calls the dinner ladies,' I trilled, 'at school,' I added quickly, in case he thought I meant at home, back at the Grade II Jacobean manor or something.

Steroid chef came no closer but his well-upholstered arms stayed folded and a sharp black knife twinkled in his hand. He kept up his penetrating stare. A low and dubious murmur began to circulate around the room. I kept on nodding and smiling in what I hoped was a conciliatory manner but no one looked mollified enough to resume their bacon and egg. Clearly the thought going through most people's minds was – what better excuse for a revolution?

'Shit,' muttered Laura, echoing my thoughts. 'They're probably sharpening the guillotine in the kitchen even now. Come on, let's get out of here.'

She rummaged in her expensive Mulberry purse for a wodge of money, then ostentatiously waved a twenty-pound note in the air with a flourish. She shoved it under a saucer. The murmur stopped and a disbelieving silence descended. The tension, if possible, mounted.

'For God's sake, Laura, I've already paid,' I hissed.

'I know,' she muttered. 'That's a tip,' she said loudly, beaming around magnanimously, like some wealthy benefactress.

'Are you mad? They'll think we're bragging, or trying to buy our way out of here or something.'

'Well, we are, aren't we?'

The low murmur resumed. It gained momentum around the room and to my mind it was far more ominous and sinister than the silence.

Laura and I slowly got up from the table. I grasped the

children firmly by their shoulders and with a great deal of nodding, smiling and scraping back of chairs, reversed in the direction of the door, the street and hopefully, the free world.

'Delicious breakfast,' I chirped as we backed through the door. 'No offence meant!'

The door banged shut behind us. As we scuttled past the half-curtained window to the car, it seemed to me that most of the café surged across to the window to watch. My nervous fingers struggled with Clemmie's seatbelt. I glanced back and between the faces at the window saw the waitress in question saunter over to our table and pick up the twenty-pound note. She looked at it for a moment, then stuffed it down the front of her dress. Then she looked around at the assembled diners and smirked. A shout of raucous laughter rang out and moments later the café was fairly heaving with hilarity. The joke, it appeared, was well and truly on us.

Scarlet with shame and rage I snapped the children quickly into their seats, marched round to the passenger seat and slammed the door shut. As Laura started the car I shook my head wearily. I was quite sure the good people of Yorkshire were full of the milk of human kindness, but it didn't seem to be flowing in our direction today and I wasn't at all sure I would be returning to this part of the world in a hurry.

We drove off, the children, for once, shocked into silence. Laura was clearly as pissed off as I was.

'Bloody peasants,' she muttered at length.

I sighed, thinking it was just as well she hadn't expressed

that sentiment a few minutes earlier. I wondered if that was where Hugo was getting his arrogant ways.

I leaned my head back on its rest and shut my eyes. It was throbbing soundly now and I felt lousy. I'd been awake half the night listening on the one hand for sounds of knife-sharpening from the Shillings, and on the other hand going over and over in my mind what Laura had said. I snuck a sideways glance at her now as we drove along. What did she mean, let him live? Let everyone live? What difference did it make to her?

I brooded on it off and on for most of the journey, but lack of sleep had made my brain furry and it wasn't until we'd completed about 600 miles and were almost home, that a finger, rather like the one on the ceiling of the Sistine Chapel, suddenly appeared in my head and slowly slotted the piece of jigsaw into place. I turned and gazed at her as we drove over Putney Bridge. It was as if I were suddenly seeing her for the first time. My eyes widened with horror, my chest felt tight. She couldn't be . . . good heavens. In love with . . . Patrick? *Could she?*

I stared at her as she began to negotiate the network of roads that led up to the top of Putney Hill. Somewhere, deep down in my subconscious, I realized I'd known all along, suspected, but dismissed it out of hand, as something too painful to believe. But now it was as if I could no longer fail to see. I kept staring at her as she swung the wheel this way and that, thanking drivers for letting her through, smiling, her pink lips parting, white teeth gleaming, her bare arms slim and brown as they skilfully guided the wheel. So, had they . . . slept together? My tummy lurched. I gulped. In all probability, yes. And why not, I thought with a jolt. I hadn't wanted him, had I?

I turned away, unable to look at her any more. Of course, I thought feverishly, that's where she'd been going these past few days. Secretly, on her own, all day and then all evening. Ever since the day after Robert had died when she'd gone up to Gilduncan for a swim. That must have been when it all started, lying by the pool in her gold costume, Patrick stretched out beside her. I clenched my fists tightly on my lap. God, how stupid of me not to realize! Was this what she'd always wanted then? What she'd been looking for all this time, ever since she'd met him again at that wedding years ago, knowing she couldn't have him because in his heart he still belonged to me? But he didn't any more, did he? I'd rejected him categorically, and this time, he'd heard it from the horse's mouth. Not just from engagement notices and birth announcements in the newspaper, as he sat miles away in Italy wondering if I really wanted all that commitment or whether I'd been forced into it because I was pregnant; wondering if I was really happy, or if there was still a chance I might give it all up and come away with him. No, this time he knew for sure. It was well and truly over, and with that realization ringing loudly in his ears, he'd gone home to Gilduncan. A sad, depressed, lonely man.

But not for long, eh? Oh no, not for long, because the very next day – guess what? Behold! A vision had appeared to him by the pool! A vision with the face of an angel, wearing a gold swimsuit, sipping a Martini and jangling a Rolex watch, and she said, 'Fear not, Patrick old boy, for I bring you tidings of great joy. A younger, prettier, cleverer, more toned-up version of the thing you crave has been delivered to you this day, and is sitting beside you even now on your very own terrace. Not the next best thing, but a far, far better thing – if you think about it.'

I swallowed hard and gripped my hands together tightly. My God, the scales must have fallen from his eyes with a plonk, straight into the pool as he beheld this fair – *virgin* – beside him. I snarled and dug my nails into the palm of my hand. He must have thought – of course! Stone the bleeding crows – Laura! Because deep down in his subconscious, he'd probably known all along that he'd been waiting to be let off the hook by me so that he was free to take my younger sister. After all, hadn't he been watching her secretly, all these years? Hadn't he told me himself of his speculations on her virginity? Hadn't he been quietly monitoring her progress? Well you don't do that unless you're pretty damn interested, do you?

So . . . I breathed hard and dug my nails deeper. Had he initiated it, the seduction? Or had she? I recalled her flushed cheeks as she'd come in at night, her bright eyes, her secret smile, her exhaustion. And of course, I thought, breathing fast now, if he *was* right, and she'd never done it before, it must have been rather marvellous, mustn't it? That first time, and then the second time, and then the third when she was just getting into her stride, going berserk, thrashing around – *Breathe, Tess, breathe!* I commanded. God, I was in danger of passing out here. I sucked in hard through my nose and out through my mouth; in through the nose, out through the mouth . . . Don't think about them, I told myself, don't think about them writhing and twisting in barns, in beds, in haystacks, by the river, *in* the river, covered in water, in weed, in frogspawn, in God knows what – but it was no good. By the time Laura pulled up outside our house, my teeth were gritted, steam was pouring from my nostrils, I was making strange, incoherent, animal noises and I was just about ready to kill her.

Laura turned off the engine and looked at me. 'You all right?'

'Fine,' I whimpered shrilly. 'Just fine!'

She frowned. 'You don't look it.'

The children, desperate to get out, were clambering over our heads as Laura opened her door.

'All right, all right,' she laughed as Hugo climbed into her lap and raced up the garden path. She turned to me and grinned. 'Looks like they're glad to be back.'

I nodded, unable to speak.

'I'm just going to drop you off if you don't mind, I'm dying to get home now and have a bath. I'll bring your car back later, OK?'

She smiled, but as I stared back at her, her eyes sort of slithered past me. Oh yes, now I knew. Laura never avoided my eye; she never looked past me like that. She was getting out of the car now, reaching into the back for various dolls and jigsaws the children had left behind. I watched as if she were in a film.

'God, it looks like a kindergarten back here,' she laughed.

'Laura, can I ask you something?' I muttered, not moving from my seat.

She poked her head in. 'What? Aren't you getting out?'

'Can I just –'

'David, hi!' She swung around and waved as he came smiling down the path to meet us.

'Hello, you two horrors!' He swept the children up joyfully in his arms and gave Laura a big smacking kiss on the cheek.

'Laura, please,' I said desperately.

David stuck his head into the car. 'Hello, darling. Aren't you getting out? Can't be that disappointed to see me, surely? How was the drive?'

I slowly got out of the car. My legs seemed to be full of lead, my mouth full of acid.

'Oh not bad,' Laura answered for me as they unpacked the boot together. 'With the exception of a couple of serial killers and a lynch mob in a café in Buckden, not bad at all!' She chuckled merrily. 'But please take your family away, David. Lovely though they are I've had enough of family life for a few weeks. I can't wait to get back to my flat for a spot of solitary confinement.'

And to ring *him*, I bet, I thought viciously as she snapped the boot shut with a grin.

I watched as she laughed and chatted to David on the pavement. I imagined her talking to Patrick like that. Flicking back her silky blond hair with her tanned, jewelled fingers. An invisible hand took hold of my gut and twisted it hard. My upper lip curled unattractively. Oh no, I thought grimly, I'm afraid it's not that simple, Laura. You see, it doesn't matter that I don't want him any more, he's still my property – OK? You can't have him, *all right*! I tried the deep breathing again but it was no good, I was seething demonically now and although on one level I knew I was being selfish, irrational and a total dog in the manger, on another level I didn't give a stuff. I had to make it quite clear to her that he was mine. Just a word, a gesture, that would do the trick, she'd understand. Just like when we were young and she'd got a toy of mine. A quick swipe, a grab, that was all it took – hands off, tiddler, get one of your own.

She was hugging the children now, saying her good-byes, promising to come and see us soon. Now she was hugging David, planting a kiss on each cheek, laughing, and now finally, it was my turn.

'Bye, Tess,' she cried, hugging me round the shoulders.

I stood there like a lump of granite. She kissed my cheek. The Judas kiss, I thought bitterly, the betrayal.

'Laura, don't do this,' I muttered in her ear. 'Please don't do this, I can't bear it.'

She drew back and dropped her hands from my shoulders. She stared. 'Do what?'

I flushed scarlet. David was standing close by, watching, listening.

'This . . . thing,' I whispered. 'You know.'

Our eyes locked in combat. She knew. Hers turned to stone.

'One of these days, Tess,' she said in a quiet, level voice, 'you'll realize that being my older sister does not give you the right to tell me how to live my life.'

She turned, got into the car and slammed the door. The window was open and I bent down. Her face was very pale.

'Laura –'

'I'll do as I damn well please!' she said icily. Then she shunted into first gear and without looking back, sped off down the road.

David stared after her as the car shrieked around the corner at the end of the road.

'What the hell was that all about?'

'Nothing,' I said in a strangled voice. 'Nothing at all!'

I turned and barged past him, marching up the path to the front door. David scratched his head.

'Blimey, you sisters. You're either at each other's throats or you can't bear to be apart.'

He followed me to the door. 'So how was the journey?'

'Terrific,' I said, chucking my handbag down on the hall table. 'Just terrific, David, all five hundred and eighty-two miles of it.'

'Now look here, Tess,' he said irritably, 'there's no need to take your row with Laura out on me, is there?'

I rounded on him. 'Well, what do you *want* me to say? Actually it was a frigging long way, the children quarrelled non-stop, my foot was agony, my head ached and I would have been glad of your help? Is that what you want – the truth?'

He was dead right of course, I did need a vent for my anger. For my selfish, irrational, homicidal rage, and right this minute he would do very nicely thank you. Just stand right there, David, don't move an inch.

'Particularly,' I added venomously, 'since it appears you didn't have much work to do anyway.'

He stared at me. 'You really are a spoiled little girl, aren't you?' he said quietly. 'You really expected me just to drop everything and fly back to Scotland, with all the expense that that incurs, just to ferry you back again?'

'What I expect David,' I cried, 'is a little support. A little more loyalty, that's all. I expect that since I spend the

357

best part of the year looking after the children we might, just once a year, have a holiday when we *share* the responsibility, when we can be a family. What I don't expect is for you to bugger off back to London in order to do a spot of shopping, for God's sake! Had a nice quiet house all to yourself, did you? Saw a bit of the Test Match? Read a few good philosophy books? Snoozed in the garden with no children around to turn the hose on you or empty the sandpit on your head? Yes, well, actually *darling*, that's *my* idea of a holiday too, and I can't remember the last time I sodding well had one!'

I'd really lost it now. I was a loony woman, shaking, spitting, saying the very first thing that came into my head.

David regarded me coldly. 'You're a fine one to talk about loyalty, and as for the children, I thought you enjoyed looking after them. I didn't realize it was a chore. I thought that's why you didn't want to work.'

'Oh, don't be obtuse, David,' I yelled, 'we're not talking about me working here, we're talking about me having a flipping holiday! Yes, of course I like looking after them, I just don't want to do it to the exclusion of everything else, that's all. I wouldn't mind if there was just a little bit more to my life than these four walls and our two children. I wouldn't mind having a bit of life *outside* my bloody family, that's all. Is that too much to ask?'

He regarded me for a long moment. 'I don't know why you have to ask, Tess. *Alea jacta est.*'

He turned and walked towards the kitchen.

'And what's that supposed to mean?' I shrieked after him. 'Another one of your stupid smart-arse remarks that means *nothing*, David! Well, I'm sick of it, sick of your whole pompous attitude, OK!' I burst into tears and raced up the stairs.

'Nice to have you back, Tess,' he remarked before I slammed the bedroom door.

Sobbing with rage I looked around wildly for something to bash, to rip, or to maim. If I'd been a yob I probably would have rushed out and beaten up a few phone boxes, but being a middle-class Putney housewife, I seized my hairbrush and beat the living daylights out of my Laura Ashley pillow. I can see that a phone box might have been more satisfying. Finally, I threw myself onto the bed and sobbed into the duvet.

Great shoulder-shaking, self-pitying sobs. As I lay there, crying like an idiot, I gradually got it out of my system. I felt it drain away. All that venom, all that rage, all that ghastly, pent-up, horrible self-pity went pouring down into the designer sheets. At length I sat up, grabbed a tissue and blew my nose loudly.

Suddenly I was mortified. It came over me like a wave. Oh God, how *awful*! What a bitch I'd been. Poor, poor David, what on earth had he done to deserve such a tirade? It wasn't as if it was anything to do with him, was it? It was Laura, Laura and Patrick. I flopped on my back and stared up at the ceiling. Was that how they were to be referred to then, in future? Laura and Patrick, a couple? To be said in one breath like that? I swallowed hard. Yes, what if this affair went from strength to strength, what if they really fell in love – married even . . . I gasped, jerked upright and stuffed a tissue in my mouth. What if they came here together for dinner, for Christmas, for the children's parties, what if – oh Christ – *they had children of their own.*

I bit hard on the tissue then spat it out. I got up and walked to the window. I felt ill. Really ill and sick. I breathed deeply to calm myself, pressing my hot face against the cool glass. I gazed out at the long row of identical terraced houses below, all pressed up against each other with their identical London families inside. Suddenly it wasn't so reassuring, it was depressing. I felt hemmed in. I stared at the cars crammed bumper-to-bumper in the street, at the gardens, every square inch utilized. Then I thought of Laura and Patrick in Italy, in Scotland, with all that space, that love, that freedom. I turned my face and leaned my other cheek on the glass. And I'd always have them there before me, wouldn't I? As a shining example. Always be able to look at them, at their life and say – that could have been me.

Down below me the front door clicked. I looked out as David emerged from under the porch, a child swinging on each hand. They dragged him down the garden path and at the gate, turned right and trotted up the road. He was taking them to the park, no doubt. Off to the swings after their long sit in the car, then on to the corner shop for a lolly. I dredged a heavy sigh up from the soles of my feet. How like him to do that and what a cow I'd been to suggest he didn't. He did his share and more. I watched, wondering if he'd turn at the end of the road, look back at the house. I'd wave if he did, smile. I willed him to. He didn't.

I went back miserably to the bed and sat down again, tearing my tissue into shreds. More self-pitying tears were welling. God, this whole Patrick affair was conspiring to ruin everything. But I still couldn't bear it if it were true, I really couldn't. I bit my lip. Then I turned and stared at the telephone. Well, OK then, why not just ring Laura? Talk to her, reason with her, tell her it's simply too much for you to handle? Ask her to reassure you that it was just a holiday romance, nothing more than that? Yes, of course, I thought with a surge of relief, that was probably all it was. And here I was getting all het up about it! Ha! Silly me. Yes, and I could apologize too, I thought eagerly, for being so Draconian, so high-handed. We'd probably laugh, make up, everything would be fine again!

I quickly dialled her number. Engaged, damn. I drummed my fingers impatiently, then on a sudden impulse, rang Directory Enquiries and got Gilduncan's number. I rang that. Bloody engaged! I slammed the phone down in a fury.

'You bastards!' I shrieked into the empty house. 'You selfish, thoughtless, self-centred BASTARDS!'

Chapter Twenty-two

The following day was Robert's funeral. I limped, miserably, through the day, then at four o'clock went upstairs and dressed slowly, frowning critically in the mirror at my chosen outfit. Having never actually been to a funeral before, and not being a career girl with a limitless supply of little black suits to choose from, I'd had to improvise with an extremely limited wardrobe. If I'd been on speakers with Laura I could have borrowed something, but that was clearly out of the question. The only black skirts I possessed were a short cocktaily one, or a long maternity one. In the end I opted for the short one with a black shirt, black jacket and the tatty old shoes I'd been wearing all summer but which were supremely comfortable with my swollen foot. I was just looking doubtfully at my reflection when David came in.

'What d'you think?' I asked nervously, hoping he'd speak to me. 'Too tarty?'

He raised his eyebrows. 'Hoping to razz up the vicar?'

'Oh. Right,' I said sheepishly. 'OK, how about this then . . .' I swiftly changed into the maternity number.

'Now you could actually *be* the vicar,' he observed as he regarded my billowing black tent. 'The choice is vicar or tart, is it?'

'You could at least be constructive in your criticism,' I snapped, not one to stay sheepish for long.

'I'm not convinced you have to go for total blackout, that's all,' he said, changing from his cords into a dark suit. 'How about your green suit or that flowery Liberty skirt with your navy blazer?'

'David, it's a funeral not a hula-hula party! Now hurry up and stop titivating, we're going to be late.'

I flounced down the stairs in my vicar's kit, knowing full well that he was being reasonable again and I was being *un*reasonable again. Damn it, I fumed, why was it always *me* who was in the wrong? Why was it always *me* who was left feeling like a heel?

As I marched down the stairs into the hall I almost tripped over Tricia, a friend's nanny, who in the absence of Josie had come in to look after the children for the day. She was crouched over Clemmie who was lying doubled up on her side, clutching her stomach, moaning and writhing around in agony.

'What is it?' I yelped, running fast. 'What happened? What's wrong!'

'I don't know.' Tricia looked up anxiously. 'I just found her like this.'

'Did she fall? Has she eaten something? Clemmie, what's wrong?'

I crouched over her, pushing her hair back so I could see her face. It was twisted with pain. She whimpered.

'Oh God!' I gasped. My heart hammered, my mind raced – appendicitis, meningitis – but what were the signs, the symptoms? Hugo came sauntering out of the kitchen.

'Hugo,' I yelled, 'get Penelope Leach for me quick – on the dresser!'

'Who's she?' he asked, strolling on.

'It's a book,' I screamed, 'for Clemmie! She's in agony, now *run*!'

Hugo regarded his sister on the floor. 'Oh, it's OK,' he remarked nonchalantly. 'She's in labour.'

'*What!*' I leaped up in horror.

'Yes, she saw it on *Home and Away*. Sandra's having a baby at the moment.'

I stared down at Clemmie, writhing in agony on the floor. Then I lunged down and hoicked her up under her arms.

'GET UP AT ONCE!' I bellowed, pulling her to her feet.

'Oh my baby, my baby!' she moaned, clutching her tummy. She wilted in my arms and rolled her eyes dramatically. 'Gas,' she gasped. 'Give me gas, quickly!'

'Stop that at once!' I shook her.

'Jesus,' muttered David, passing briefly through the hall to the kitchen. 'Why on earth are they allowed to watch these things?'

'It's not a question of being allowed,' I retorted, 'but short of becoming the television police I can't stop them.'

'Could have been worse,' offered Tricia reasonably. 'She could have been *making* a baby. I'm pretty sure they do that on *Home and Away* too.'

'Thank you, Tricia,' I said weakly as I delivered Clemmie into her arms. 'That really strengthens my case.' I turned to my husband.

'Ready?' I demanded.

'Ready,' he snapped.

I drove fast and furiously to Hanover Square where the funeral was taking place. Fast, because we were late as usual, and furiously because it was symptomatic of my mood. As a result, I succeeding in riling quite a few of my fellow motorists, one of whom was so pissed off he deliberately followed me and carved me up in return at a roundabout.

'Right,' I snarled, in the grip of what I believe is now called road rage. 'We'll soon see about that, buster!'

I sped after the red car in question, eventually managing to carve him up and nearly causing an accident at the following roundabout.

'Tess,' began David, 'I really don't think –'

'Don't speak to me,' I hissed. 'Just don't speak, OK?'

He raised his eyebrows wearily. 'OK, OK.'

Moments later I was seething again. We were stuck, doing precisely two miles an hour down some Fulham back street, behind a lorry which was not only travelling at the speed of a snail but was slowly losing its load.

'Oh, for heaven's sake,' I muttered, beeping my horn loudly, 'he hasn't even noticed!'

The lorry didn't stop and cruised slowly on.

'Are you deaf as well as retarded?' I thumped my horn again. *Beep beep* BEEEEEEEEEP!

Finally the lorry stopped. I leaped out and ran up to his cab. The driver stuck his head out.

'What's your problem, lady?' he shouted.

'You're losing your load, you moron!'

He stared at me. 'I'm gritting the road.'

I gasped. 'Oh!' I flushed, turned and ran back to the car, red-faced. 'He's gritting the road,' I muttered to David.

He raised his eyebrows. 'Clearly.'

'Why didn't you tell me?'

'You told me not to speak.'

I uttered some obscenities under my breath and drove on. After a while though I felt myself begin to simmer down slightly and knowing the usual row about parking was due to start shortly, resolved to wind my neck in and let David do the talking. Annoyingly he guided me expertly round the back streets of Regent Street and we parked, with comparative ease, on a meter just behind Hanover Square.

As David and I walked to the church and joined the solemn family group assembled on the steps outside the main door, it occurred to me that at least our silence could be construed as a mark of respect rather than seething irritation with each other.

Daddy left the group and came to greet us, giving me a fleeting, economical peck on the cheek and David a quick handshake. He had his stony, far-be-it-from-me-to-show-any-emotion face on. I kissed him warmly then turned to Aunt Rachel.

'Rachel,' I whispered, taking her hand and kissing her. 'I'm so sorry . . .'

'Don't be,' she smiled, and pressed my hand with both of hers. 'It's what he wanted. It was time for him to go.'

I gazed up at her beautiful, composed face. Would I ever be like that, I wondered. Would I ever be anything like her?

I turned to Penny who was sobbing uncontrollably beside her, supported by Piers. Little Leonora was holding her hand tightly, looking baffled. I wondered at the suitability of bringing her but we all hugged each other, then I took Penny's other arm and we went into the church. As we all made our way down to the front pew I looked around for Laura. Late again as usual, I thought cattily, intent on making a dramatic entrance, no doubt. As we sat down, she hurried down the aisle. Sorry, no room, I thought childishly as I spread my handbag and service sheet along the pew, but David, who was on the end, smiled and beckoned her down. Laura slipped in beside him. She bent her head forward.

'Budge up!' she whispered.

I grudgingly moved an inch or two, then pretending I hadn't seen her lean across to kiss me, dropped to my knees and clasped my hands piously in prayer. Out of the corner of my eye I saw her look at David and raise her eyebrows. He sympathetically raised his in response.

Oh, so they think I'm behaving badly, do they? I thought savagely, well let them. Ask me if I care. They can go to hell, the lot of them! And with this truly Christian thought in mind, I bent my head in prayer.

The funeral was sad, but not tragic. Robert had been expected to die quite a lot sooner than he did and in fact there were some light and even humorous moments. Rachel's short address in particular was moving but also funny. As she recalled his rather unorthodox methods of teaching young children to fish by hanging sandwiches and even sausages on hooks, I laughed, remembering, and inadvertently caught Laura's eye. She smiled but I quickly turned away. Oh no, I thought, it's not going to be as easy as that.

I caught a glimpse of what she was wearing though, a sort of burgundy linen suit with a white body underneath. Well really. Did she honestly think that was appropriate?

Had she *no* idea? I pursed my lips and looked around at my fellow mourners. It was then that I realized, with a jolt, that it was I who was inappropriately dressed. Everyone else seemed to be in smart, but not particularly sombre clothes, and certainly there was nothing quite like the ankle-length Widow Twanky kit I was in. God, I looked like something out of a Catherine Cookson period drama! I hastily hoicked my skirt up a bit and undid the top button of my shirt.

It was when my father got up to speak though, that everyone reached for their hankies. It wasn't so much what he said, which was predictably religious and prosaic, but the way he said it. As he struggled to be so formal and correct, every now and then his bottom lip would quiver or his face would buckle, giving him away. He'd pause as he struggled to regain his composure. No one dared breathe, wondering if he was going to break down. His voice shook with emotion every time he mentioned Robert's name. I gripped Mummy's hand tightly as together we mopped up the tears we were crying for Daddy, as much as for Robert.

By the time we all stumbled out of that dark church into the low, early evening sunshine, I for one was emotionally exhausted and in desperate need of a drink. All that sorrow had made me thirsty and I could quite see why the Irish were so keen on a wake. The plan was, apparently, to go on to Dukes Hotel for an early supper, but for the moment, everyone seemed content to mill around on the steps outside, chatting and commiserating with Rachel and no one looked inclined to move on. I hovered near the back, watching. What was the protocol here, I wondered. Was it rather like a wedding where one didn't want to get to the reception before the bride? Should we wait for Rachel? If I'd been on speaking terms with David I could have suggested a quick dart to the pub before going on to the hotel, and likewise with Laura, but obviously both options were out of the question.

I looked around for them. David was talking to an elderly aunt of mine, and Laura to an old schoolfriend of Penny's. She looked distracted though, and once or twice I spotted her glancing at her watch. Another of Penny's friends interrupted their conversation and at that point, I saw Laura smile, murmur something apologetic, then with a brief glance around, turn and quickly slip away.

I watched, fascinated, as she sped down the steps at the side of the church. Where was she going, I wondered. Not for a solitary drink, surely? No, that was unlikely, but perhaps she'd decided to leave her car and walk to Dukes for some fresh air. Yes, this was far more like it and actually, just what I needed too. Suddenly I realized this was my one chance to talk to her. To catch her on her own, reason with her. It would be more or less impossible to talk later, surrounded by an army of relatives over supper. Yes, I'd do it now. I glanced across at David who was still deep in conversation. I waved, caught his eye and mouthed – *I'm going on*, OK? He frowned, but didn't mouth anything back, so I turned and slipped away with no further ado.

I hobbled determinedly after Laura, tracing her footsteps across the square. Yes, this was definitely the right thing to do. I'd nip this thing in the bud before it had a chance to blossom. The worst thing I could do would be to sit back and let the affair gain momentum, until it was too late to do anything about it. I quickened my pace as much as possible with my ankle, but as I did so, realized that I was losing my skirt. It was after all, a maternity skirt and the elastic had at one time catered for two and a half – all right, four stone of extra weight – and all this exertion was making it swivel down my hips, putting the hem somewhere around foot-level. As I hurried along I reached down to hoick it up but – too late – tripped over the hem and landed face down on the pavement with a resounding smack! Damn.

I picked myself up, shaken, distinctly embarrassed – this was after all practically Bond Street – but not badly hurt, so I hurried on. At least I did, until I felt something hot and runny trickle into my mouth. I put my hand up and looked at my fingers. Blood. Bother, a flipping nose-bleed. I stopped in my tracks and quickly rummaged in my bag, still peering around for Laura who'd just disap-peared round a corner. I found a tissue, ripped a piece off, rolled it into a ball and stuffed it up my nostril. There, that would have to do for the moment. I hurried on, looking around wildly – where the hell was she? I stopped still and gazed about. I was sure I'd seen her Manolo Blahnik heels trip this way, but now there was no sign of her. Blast. That little nasal interlude had cost me my prey. Where the devil had she got to?

I stood at the crossroads outside Fenwick's, looking around blindly. Had she gone up there, past Russell & Bromley, or over there towards Berkeley Square? I hesi-tated, then on a sudden impulse, plumped for a side street. There was a pub up this alleyway that we'd both been into once together. Perhaps she'd remembered it and slipped in for a quick one? I pushed open the frosted door. The gloom and the smoke hit me instantly. The bar was six deep with braying suits as surveyors, accountants and other West End businessmen thirstily sank their after-work pints. It looked like the relief of Mafeking. I let the door swing back. No, she wouldn't have gone in there, not on her own. Perhaps up here? I hastened up another side street, then another, then turned right, back onto Bond Street, at which point I realized, with a sinking heart, that I'd lost her.

I stopped running and clutched my side, panting hard. Damn and blast, where on earth was she? Oh well, I thought wearily, the only thing to do was to walk on to Dukes myself. You never know, I might be able to drag her into the Ladies and threaten to beat the living daylights out of her if she so much as laid a finger on him again. I shrugged. Something like that anyway. I limped on.

My foot was excruciatingly painful now after all that activity and I was really having to limp. Added to this, my skirt, if left unattended, wanted to hover down by my thighs hipster-style, so I had to clutch the waistband in a ball with one hand and hold the tissue to my nose with the other. I stopped for a second to renew the tissue and a beautifully coiffured girl dressed from head to toe in Chanel stared as she walked past. What's the matter, I thought savagely, haven't you ever seen a nosebleed before? On the other hand, I thought with a jolt as I caught sight of myself in a shop window, I did look rather a strange sight. A tall, dark woman in outsized widow's weeds with half a ton of soggy red tissue up her nose dragging a gammy leg. I grinned. Not exactly *à la mode*, shall we say?

I moved slowly through the rush-hour crowd, looking around at the mixture of glamorous businesswomen in Armani suits, secretaries clip-clopping to the Tube in too-high heels, pinstriped businessmen, striding out, brandishing the *Evening Standard*, younger men in pale grey suits with white nylon shirts. It was rather nice not to be rushing with them, just to be passing through. A spectator rather than a participant.

As I hopped slowly along I gazed in the shop windows. I lingered for a second outside one particularly daft establishment with a silver body suit in the window complete with conical Madonna-like boobs. Hmmm . . . just right for getting to grips with the dusting. I could just see David's face when he came in of an evening to be greeted by that little ensemble frying up his liver and bacon. I grinned and moved on, feeling way out of touch. I passed another shop-front, brightly lit and thronging with people. I slowed down for a moment and blinked. Very glamorous people actually, and it was clearly a party of some sort, a new shop-opening perhaps. I moved slowly by, staring at the groovy, minimalist crowd. Most people seemed to be in either black or white – a touch uninspired to my way of thinking, but then who was I to be sartorially critical? There were one or two touches of colour, a man with an outrageous floral shirt, a girl in a fuchsia pink skirt that just about covered her bottom, and a blonde girl in a – *burgundy linen suit*.

I stopped and stared. What on earth was Laura doing in there? Did she know these people, or had she just barged in for a glass of champagne, uninvited? It wouldn't be difficult, she certainly looked the part but – no, she was chatting, laughing with someone as if she'd known him all her life. He had his hand in the small of her back. His own back was towards me, but I'd know it anywhere. He turned to lift a couple of glasses of champagne from a waitress's tray and I saw his face. It was Patrick.

I watched, rooted to the pavement as they laughed and chatted together. Patrick handed her a drink, they clinked glasses, toasting each other over the rims, gazing into each other's eyes. He leaned forward and whispered something in her ear, Laura threw her blonde head back, laughing, then she leaned forward and rested her hand on his shoulder, drawing him closer towards her so she could whisper something back. He laughed, nodded, agreeing with her, but as he bent his head to sip his champagne, his eyes strayed towards the window. They met mine. He froze over his drink. We stared at each other. Suddenly I was galvanized. With my heart pounding and the blood rushing up to my face I pushed through the plate-glass door. I shoved my way roughly through the fashionable, tinkling throng and strode right over to them.

'So, Patrick,' I hissed, 'didn't waste much time getting over your broken heart, did you? Tell me, how do we compare in bed, as sisters I mean!'

Chapter Twenty-three

They stared at me in horror.

Patrick put his hand on my arm. 'Tess, slow down –'

'Don't you touch me!' I shook him off. 'How DARE you! How dare you even *look* at me after the lies you've told! Broken-hearted, eh? Waited for me for all these years, eh? Bullshit! You're an opportunist, Patrick, and you know it. You're a sad, despicable man, an aging, sex-crazed Lothario who's looking for some action, and when you couldn't get it with me you got it the very next day with my sister instead. That's about the size of it, isn't it!' My voice had risen; I was shaking with rage.

All around us conversation hushed and glasses stopped clinking. Elegantly coiffured heads turned and all eyes were on the madwoman in black. Laura took my elbow.

'Tess, you're making a fool of yourself,' she said in a low voice.

'Oh am I!' I spat, shaking her off. 'Then that's entirely appropriate, since I clearly *am* the fool here! Gosh, how you two must have laughed as you sneaked off to meet each other behind my back in Scotland! Oh yes, you must have thought it a huge joke. Well, it's not a joke, Laura, it's pitiful. Pathetic, deceitful and PITIFUL!' My voice, by now, had reached lunacy level and I was aware that I was very much the floorshow.

'Tess, for heaven's sake!' Laura coloured up and looked around nervously.

'For heaven's sake what!' I countered loudly, unstoppable now. 'For heaven's sake why shouldn't you sleep with him? Eh? Is that it?'

'Good God,' she muttered, mortified.

'No reason at all, Laura, none at all, except perhaps for a tiny matter of sisterly loyalty. Ring any bells, hmmm? A little matter of sibling consideration or is that too difficult a concept for you to get your selfish head around? Well is it?' I cried.

'I've never been so embarrassed in all my life.' Laura's face was flaming now. 'Not only are you totally and utterly wrong, but –'

'Wrong, am I?' I raised my eyebrows in mock surprise. 'Oh yes of course, it's time for the big denial, isn't it – time to wriggle out. I wondered when we'd get to that. Well, come on then.' I stood back and folded my arms, waiting. 'Come on, Laura, show me how you do it. I'm keen to learn,' I nodded encouragingly. 'Come on, don't be shy!'

A few people behind us began to titter. Laura seized my arm in a vice-like grip.

'Out!' she muttered furiously. 'Come on, out. I've had enough of this. Help me, Patrick.' She began to drag me towards the door. I struggled but Patrick took my other arm. Between the two of them I began to slide doorwards, my skirt slipping down at the same time. The murmuring mass parted to make way for us.

I looked around wildly as I slid along the polished floor and out of the corner of my eye glimpsed a waiter, mouth open, balancing a tray of champagne. With a superhuman effort I wrenched a hand free, seized a glass, and threw it in Laura's face.

'Argh!' she squeaked, dropping my arm.

A gasp of shock rose up. She stood there, horrified and dripping, her face, hair and immaculate suit soaked.

'Tess!' Patrick thundered. 'What on earth –'

'And you can have one too, you bastard!' I grabbed another one from the bemused waiter and chucked it over him.

Another horrified gasp went up from the crowd. Patrick stared at me through his soaking-wet hair. It was plastered to his face and dripping rather satisfyingly all over his elegant Armani suit. Behind me I was dimly aware of camera bulbs flashing, then a little cry rang out.

'Patreek! Patreek, what ees going on! Who ees thees crazy woman?'

A little moustachioed Frenchman, all dusty pink suit and gleaming Gucci shoes came bustling over.

'*Allez-vous en!* Out!' he cried, poking me in the shoulder with a sharp, manicured finger. '*C'est trop, alors!* Get out, madwoman, get out!'

There was only one glass of champagne left on the tray and it seemed a shame not to use it.

'And I don't know who you are, you mincing little poofter, but you can have one too,' I panted, aiming it at the immaculate pink concoction.

His suit went a satisfying shade of dark red, his moustache drooped, his jaw dropped and his little wet brown eyes blinked at me in horror.

This time a rather delighted gasp went up from the

crowd. I slammed the glass back down on the waiter's tray and with my head held high, limped, with as much dignity as I could muster, towards the door. The gaping throng parted nervously and everyone hung on like billyo to their glasses, just in case I should feel like lobbing some more around. Outside in the street I blundered into the traffic.

'That'll bloody teach them,' I muttered, dragging my leg across the road. All around me taxis honked furiously and fists waved. A car screeched to a halt inches from my feet.

'That'll wipe the smiles off their smug little faces, won't it?' I ranted on to one bemused taxi driver through his open window. 'They won't try that again in a hurry, will they?'

'I very much doubt it, luv,' he agreed, scratching his head.

Curious though, I thought limping on, because I'd never done anything like that in my life before, never made a huge scene in public, and it had proved not only satisfying, but quite easy. I must remember to do it more often. Behind me I became aware of running footsteps. I quickened my pace.

'Tess! Stop!' It was Patrick. He caught up with me, grabbed my arm and swung me around to face him.

'Get off me! Let me go!'

'Now just you LISTEN!' he thundered. 'For God's sake shut up AND LISTEN!'

'I don't want to listen,' I spat. 'I don't want to hear it!'

'You'll hear it whether you want to or not.' He dragged me forcibly to the side of the pavement where there were a few tables and chairs outside a café.

'Sit!' he ordered.

'No, I –'

'SIT!'

I sat. All around us cappuccino cups lowered, bacon sandwiches cooled and all chatter stopped, as once again, we became street theatre. The café clientele wasn't quite as elegant as it had been across the road, but it was just as interested and there's nothing élitist about my performances: I play to the cheap seats as well as to the boxes. The audience held their breath as the man in the wet Armani suit grasped the wrist of the lame woman in black. Holding on firmly to stop me escaping, Patrick sat down opposite me. He looked decidedly fierce. I mentally flexed my muscles. Not fierce enough to frighten *me* though.

'Laura and I are not having an affair, OK?'

His steely blue eyes bored into mine. Any coffee cups that hadn't already been lowered certainly were now. You could hear a napkin drop.

'There is nothing,' he said slowly, 'repeat, nothing, going on between us, have you got that? *Comprende?*' He thrust his finger to his temple and wiggled it around furiously.

'Oh yes, *comprende*, Patrick,' I sneered. 'That's why you were gazing so lovingly into each other's eyes just now, isn't it? That's why she kept sneaking off to meet you in Scotland, because you can't bear the sight of each other!'

'I was not gazing at her,' he said in a measured tone. 'I was merely looking at her, and she wasn't sneaking off to meet me in Scotland, she was sneaking off to meet someone else.'

'Oh sure,' I scoffed. 'Like who?'

'Like Willie.'

I stared at him. He rather tentatively relaxed his grip on my arm.

'Willie!' I gasped, staying still.

He nodded.

'Oh, don't be ridiculous!'

'What's ridiculous about it? Willie's a nice guy.'

'Yes, of course he is, but – but not for Laura,' I spluttered. 'He's not Laura's type at all!'

'And who is – Edward?'

'Well no, but –' I stared at him, flummoxed. My mind was spinning.

'So why not Willie? After all, countless other women have fallen for him. Look at Penny.'

'Yes, but that's sort of understandable,' I stammered, trying to digest this. 'You know what Penny's like, and he was just a bit of –'

'Rough?'

'Well –'

'A bit of rough on the side for married London women?'

I stared at him: he was serious. Good God, he was serious! It *had* been Willie . . . That's who Laura had been skulking off to meet, down at the river no doubt. Good heavens, I thought with a jolt, so we'd *all* got to grips with him – me, Penny and now Laura. What must he think of us? But *Laura*! I shook my head incredulously, trying to imagine the two of them together . . . and to my surprise, I found I could. Because when you think about it – why not? And who better, in a way? Particularly if it really was her first time and particularly if she really had been hung up about sex . . .

'Actually I reckon he was just the man for the job,' said Patrick with a grin. 'Just the man to break her in joyfully.'

'Oh Patrick, don't be so crude,' I snapped as he eerily echoed my thoughts.

'Who would you have preferred for her sexual debut, then? Some smooth bastard with a Porsche dragging her back from Draycotts to his pad behind Harrods, pinning her to his leather sleigh bed, peeling off his black Hom underpants?'

'No,' I said slowly, 'no, I wouldn't. It's just – so unexpected.'

I shook my head distractedly. Laura and Willie. So not Laura and Patrick. Suddenly I felt a rush of blood to my head. I almost gasped at its force and my hand inadvertently flew to my mouth. Oh – thank God! I stared at him across the table from me. He was still talking, laughing now, about Laura and Willie. I watched his lips move, studied his face as if in a dream.

'You see, rather amazingly, they conducted this little clandestine liaison at Willie's house,' he was saying. 'No fishing huts and gorse bushes for Laura, oh no, she must have put her foot down about that, but I must say it's totally unlike Willie to be so indiscreet. He just walked her straight in through the front door apparently. The whole village is literally buzzing with the gossip and Kirsten's absolutely furious! I'm surprised you didn't hear about it sooner, Tess. I teased Laura about it the moment she walked into the gallery. That's what we were laughing about back there. I told her she was known locally as "the scarlet fisherwoman". She said she –'

'Hang on,' I interrupted. 'Did you say – in the gallery?'

'Yes, where we were just now, over the road.' He jerked his head back. 'Champagne-slinging alley.'

My jaw began to drop. 'I didn't know it was a gallery,' I breathed. 'I thought it was a party for the opening of a shop or something, one of Laura's dos.'

He grinned. 'No, it was one of my "dos" actually. My exhibition. I told you about it at Gilduncan.' He smiled ruefully and ran his fingers through his hair. 'Yes, my first night too, quite a stir you caused pitching up like that and dousing the artist.'

My hand flew to my mouth. I gazed appalled at his drenched suit. 'Oh Patrick! Oh God I'm so sorry! Your exhibition!' I stared at him, horrified. 'But – I didn't see – where were the pictures?'

'On the walls, that does tend to be the accepted thing. You were probably too busy chucking Bollinger about to do any art appreciation though.'

'But the window,' I blustered. 'I didn't even notice –' I swung around and stared back.

'Yes, only a small picture I grant you, but then Pierre likes to go for the minimalist look to get people to walk in. He's not keen on window shoppers.'

'P-Pierre?'

He grinned. 'Pink suit, moustache, French accent? Sorry, correction, *wet* pink suit.'

I cringed. 'Oh my God! That was Pierre Boulavère?'

'The very same.'

'Oh Patrick,' I gasped, 'what can I say? Have I ruined everything for you?'

He laughed, shrugging. 'Who knows? Possibly, but on the other hand possibly not. In fact, you may even have increased my chances of success. You may not have noticed, but quite a lot of the press were there, flashing away at the *moment critique*. It's not often they get a photo opportunity like that and you gave them three decent cracks at the whip too. If they weren't poised and ready when you went for the third glass they've no right to call themselves photographers. I bet you anything that'll be the shot that makes it to the Arts pages of the *Guardian*. Most people have wanted to do that to Pierre for years, particularly journalists. Anyway,' he lit a cigarette and blew the smoke out with a smile, 'you know what they say – all publicity is good publicity!'

Still aghast at what I'd done, I leaned my elbows on the table and groaned, clutching my head. I couldn't remember what had made me . . . Yes I could! I looked up and frowned suspiciously. 'So why was Laura there then?'

He shrugged. 'She just walked past. On her way to Dukes Hotel, she said, after your uncle's funeral. Unlike you she spotted the words *Patrick Cameron – One-Man Show* at the top of the window. Popped in to wish me luck.'

'It was the way you were looking at her,' I murmured, feeling exhausted suddenly.

'Yes, one does tend to when one's talking to someone, don't you find? It's quite normal in polite society.'

Of course it was. But I'd been so eaten up with jealousy I'd imagined it was much more than old friends just having a laugh. I stared past him at the bustling crowds on the pavements. Patrick ordered us a couple of coffees. I was still staring into space when the waiter put the cappuccino down in front of me. My mind was taking a while to absorb all this. So . . . Laura and Patrick weren't together at all. I looked at him sitting opposite me, stirring his coffee. His still-damp hair was flopping into his eyes. He smiled up at the waiter as he left the bill. Suddenly a great black cloud seemed to lift up off my shoulders and a huge swell of relief flooded through me.

'Oh Patrick, I'm so relieved!' I blurted out, reaching across and grabbing his hand impulsively. 'I had visions, awful visions of you and Laura together, stupid, crazy thoughts – you know how your mind goes into overdrive. God, I had you practically engaged, married even! I imagined you coming to dinner together, kissing in the kitchen and then sort of breaking off when I came in, her jumping up off your lap, embarrassed in front of me, and then all of us sidling around each other, trying not to catch each other's eyes as we stacked the dishwasher, stupid childish things like that. God, I even had you coming for Christmas, sleeping together in the spare room, in the room next door to ours!'

He stared down at my hand on his. 'And that would have been so terrible?' he said quietly.

'Oh Patrick, horrendous,' I urged, squeezing his hand, still in the grip of my euphoric joy, 'don't you think?'

'I do, yes.'

'I mean, imagine,' I rushed on, 'you and her together, my *sister*! And me, always on the outside looking in – awful!'

'We'd certainly have seen a lot of each other, wouldn't we?' He was watching me very closely.

I laughed. 'Yes, but under what circumstances! It would have been ghastly! Always apart and never as we really want to –' I stopped abruptly, horrified.

'To what?' he said quickly, gripping my hand.

'To . . .' I stared down at our hands, together on the tablecloth and felt the blood rush to my face. Slowly I pulled mine away. I shook my head.

'Tess?' he urged.

'Nothing,' I mumbled. I bit my lip and reached down on the pavement for my handbag. 'Patrick, I must go,' I faltered. 'It's my uncle's funeral . . .'

I stood up without looking at him, but as I made to go he came round the table and took one of my hands.

'You were going to say never as we really want to be – together – weren't you?'

I stared at the pavement in silence.

'Weren't you, Tess?' he insisted.

I slid my eyes up to the red-checked tablecloth. The pattern seemed to blur in front of my eyes. Tears flooded into them. I looked up.

'Patrick, I don't know what to do!' I blurted out.

There was a long silence. His eyes were full of love. And hope.

'Well, that's something, I suppose,' he said quietly, after a while. 'A few days ago you knew exactly what you wanted to do and it didn't include me. Now you don't know.' He smiled. 'It's not much, but it's a start.'

I licked my lips. 'Look, you won't . . . pressurize me, in any way?'

He shook his head. 'No, I won't, but –' Suddenly he seized both my hands and shook them urgently. 'Tess, you've got to do the right thing this time! This is for ever, it's important, you know that, don't you?'

I nodded dumbly. The right thing. What was the right thing? And for whom? There was another long pause.

'I have to go now,' I whispered eventually.

'Yes, I know.'

Neither of us moved. We stared at each other and it seemed to me he could see right into my soul. Everything went very quiet, very still. I could feel the blood pumping in my veins, my ankle gave a quick, sympathetic throb and my tissue twitched violently in my nose. Oh God, it was still there! Mortified, I longed to take it out but – would that look like an invitation?

As it was he didn't need one. He rested his hand gently on my face, tilted my head towards him, leaned forward, and his lips brushed mine.

We stood back. I blinked. There was a brief silence, then suddenly, raucous cheering broke out. We looked around, startled. All the people at the clutch of tables on the pavement were smiling and clapping, nodding their heads delightedly. I suddenly remembered our rather dramatic arrival at the café and blushed. Patrick grinned.

'Looks like I've got one or two supporters anyway.'

I glanced over his shoulder. 'Uh-oh, and there's one of mine,' I muttered, 'and he's coming this way.'

Behind Patrick, Pierre Boulavère, now dressed in a pale blue suit, was hustling over. He hadn't seen us yet, but he was getting closer, peering around, clearly looking for his artist.

'I'd better go,' said Patrick quickly. He squeezed my hand, gave me a last hot stare that was enough to singe my eyeballs off, then pointed quickly at my nose.

'That's pretty, incidentally.'

He gave a wicked grin, then turned on his heel and went swiftly back towards Pierre and his gallery.

I blushed and delicately removed the tissue from my nose. Then I bent down and picked up my bag and aware that some people were still looking, swung it as nonchalantly as possible over my shoulder. As I moved through the tables I surreptitiously put my fingers to my lips. Still there. They hadn't frazzled off with the heat then. My mind was racing and I didn't feel entirely with it. I shook my head as if trying to clear it. He was so adamant, so sure of himself, so convinced. But then of course, he always had been. And I wasn't, and never had been. I felt my lips again. I didn't want to consider the implications of that kiss, of what it meant, not just now. I could do that later. Plenty of time for all that. Right now I just wanted to savour it.

I limped slowly along the pavement, passing in a daze through the crowds, when suddenly I was pulled up short. My arms were both seized from behind.

I gasped. 'What the –'

'You little tart,' hissed a voice in my ear. 'You disgusting, filthy little tart!'

I froze in horror, and then with great force, was abruptly swung around. I stared.

'Daddy!' I gasped.

Chapter Twenty-four

'Shame on you,' he said fiercely, shaking me. His hands gripped my upper arms tightly. His face was contorted with rage; he looked almost possessed.

'A married woman,' he spat, 'kissing and flirting with another man. You little hussy!' He kept on shaking me, it was as if he couldn't stop.

'Daddy please,' I gasped, my head wobbling violently on my shoulders. 'Just let me explain.'

'Explain?' The force of his final shake flung me backwards and a couple of gaping tourists dodged nervously out of the way as I hit a shop window like a splattered fly, arms outstretched.

My father towered over me. 'Go on then,' he said threateningly. 'By all means have a go. Explain why you were canoodling with that ne'er-do-well when you should have been at your uncle's funeral!' He was trembling with fury. 'My own beloved brother,' he quavered, 'and neither of my children, it seems, can be bothered to turn up and pay their last respects. So finally, when in dumb disbelief I go looking for them, I find that one of them has been waylaid at some party or other and is covered in champagne, and the other is kissing and canoodling with that *degenerate*, in the middle of the street. You, Tessa! A wife, a mother, a supposedly respectable woman, have you no shame!'

By now a small and very interested crowd had gathered

at a safe distance. I recognized a tourist from the café and saw her fish eagerly in her bag for her camera, keen, no doubt, to capture on celluloid this quaint English eccentric, the professional scene-maker.

'Daddy, please –'

'And what about David?' he thundered on. 'What about Hugo and Clementine, have you thought about them? Have you considered the implications of anything beyond your own deceitful behaviour?'

'Hang on, Dad, just wait a minute, can't you? I'm trying to explain, just let me –'

'Oh, I've despaired of you before,' he went on with a tremor in his voice. 'I've prayed for you long and hard, my girl, but all along I've known you were a bad lot. In my heart I've known how rotten your soul is!'

'Bloody hell,' I muttered, my legs giving way a bit under all this fire and brimstone.

'I've prayed to God for forgiveness for you but I've always known the futility of it because you can't help yourself, can you?' he droned on relentlessly. 'It's in your nature, this dirty, lustful craving for sex. You just can't do without it.'

'Stop!' I cried, putting my hands over my ears, trying to block out his words. I'd never heard him talk like this before.

'But it's true, isn't it,' he urged, pulling my hands away from my ears. 'That's why you don't want to hear it! You've always longed for that man, haven't you?' His face was inches from mine and he had my wrists firmly. '*Haven't you!*' he insisted, giving me a little shake, as if somehow he could rattle it out of me.

I stared at him, his face was trembling with fury, but he looked – afraid, somehow, too. I drew myself up. All of a sudden I felt very calm.

I nodded. 'Yes, it's true,' I said, looking him in the eye. 'I've always wanted Patrick.'

He stared at me and for a moment I thought he was going to hit me, but then abruptly, he let go of my wrists. His face crumpled, his shoulders sagged and for an awful moment I thought he might cry.

I stared at him. The fight had completely gone out of him. I straightened myself out and glanced around quickly. Our little audience was still with us and we were still in the middle of a busy West End street. This wasn't exactly the place for histrionics. I took him firmly by the arm.

'Come on,' I said decisively.

To my surprise he came like a lamb. He let himself be led very meekly through the murmuring, disappointed crowd and off down the road until I spotted what looked like a quietish side street with a pub in it; an empty bench stood outside. I hustled him down to it.

'Sit there,' I ordered.

He sat obediently and I went inside. The pub was practically empty and I was served immediately. I hurried back outside and handed him a glass of wine. When he drank it I noticed his hand was trembling but he sank half of it straight down in one go. I sat next to him and sipped mine, watching him. His face was very pale. He didn't look at me, just sat staring straight ahead. I dug deep for courage.

'This is all your fault, Daddy,' I said quietly. 'You realize that, don't you?'

He turned and looked at me, but it was as if he didn't quite recognize me. 'Hmm?'

'You should have let me go.'

He shook his head, puzzled. 'Go? Go where?' he muttered.

'To Italy, with Patrick. Years ago. You should have let me go.'

His face cleared. He shook his head and smiled, laughed almost. 'Oh no, Tess. No, no.'

'But don't you see?' I urged. 'If I'd gone I could have found out for myself! I could have found out if Patrick and I were any good together, whether it would have worked. For all I know it might have fizzled out after a few months, or even a few years, but at least we'd have known for sure. Instead of which we're still dithering around in the dark, wondering if it was to be or not to be, and all because you insisted on putting the lid on it. Well, you can't just put the lid on something like that, not if it's still alive, still burning. All you get is an explosion when the lid flies off, and that's what's happening now!'

It was my turn to tremble a little now. 'And I've tried, Daddy,' I whispered, 'I really have. When Patrick told me in Scotland that he still felt the same way about me, I told him it was hopeless, but it's one thing to say it and another to feel something completely different.' I stopped and tore my hair briefly. 'And – and the crazy thing is I'm not even sure I *do* want him, necessarily. What I'm saying is that I don't know – and that's *your* fault. Because you never gave us a chance to find out, we're all reaping what you sowed twelve years ago – me, Patrick, David – all of us!'

He raised his eyebrows. 'Ah, I see. So you think I should

390

have given you and Patrick a chance then, eh? Taken you to the airport, let your mother go with you as chaperone perhaps?'

'Yes! Yes I do!'

He smiled and shook his head. 'Oh no Tess, I couldn't do that.'

'But *why*? It wasn't as if we were under-age. God, I was eighteen, almost off to university – and let's face it, everyone shacks up with someone in their first term anyway, so what difference would it have made?'

He looked at me properly for the first time. 'A big difference, as it happens. You see, if you'd shacked up with someone at university I was pretty sure it wouldn't be your brother.'

For a moment I couldn't speak.

'My . . . brother?' I whispered eventually.

He didn't say anything. Just watched me. I shook my head incredulously.

'Oh no, no, that can't be . . .' I faltered. I searched his eyes. Oh God, it could be. *It was.*

'Madelaine?' I breathed incredulously.

He nodded. Suddenly his eyes wavered from mine and fled for the safety of the pavement. There was a terrible silence. Then: 'It was years ago,' he began softly, 'before your mother and I were married. Not before we were engaged, but before we were married. We were at Kilmarnoch with your grandparents. Madelaine was at Gilduncan. She was . . .' he sighed, shook his head slowly '. . . so beautiful you can't imagine, Tess – and so young. And he was – God, he was awful to her. Marcus, her husband.' He leaned back on the bench and gazed up at the sky, cradling his drink, remembering. 'He was away for most of that summer, on business or so he said – one never really knew with Marcus. So there she was, up there on her own, for weeks and weeks at a time in that big empty house. She'd just got married you see, a young bride, a young foreign bride and we felt so sorry for her; me, your mother, Rachel and Robert.' He paused, sipped his drink. 'We invited her for dinner once or twice and then it became a regular thing. She came a lot, most nights in fact. Your mother and she – they got on very well. They became great friends.' He paused. A muscle twitched in his face. 'Then one night, when everyone else had gone to bed, we stayed up, Madelaine and I, talking, by the fire. She told me about her marriage. About how cold it was, how empty. She said she knew she shouldn't have married him but now that she'd done it, she was afraid. Afraid to get out.' He narrowed his eyes, still staring at the sky. 'And then she cried,' he said softly. 'She cried and I held her, and she was so . . .' he shook his head, remembering '. . . so vulnerable. Lovable.' I watched in disbelief, as tears filled his eyes. Tears and something else, something so soft and so tender and so uncharacteristic, I almost didn't recognize it. 'And then later that night we went for a walk and – we made love.'

I stared. 'With Mummy back at Kilmarnoch?'

He nodded. 'My bride to be. In the room next to mine.' He looked down at his shoes. 'We met other nights too, Madelaine and I. All that summer, in fact.' He frowned. 'It was so strange, I just couldn't help myself you see, Tess. Just . . . couldn't . . . help myself. It was this dreadful craving I had – lust, I suppose.' He shot me a sudden look.

'And you have it too, I know you do. You see you're so *like* me,' he insisted. 'That's what frightens me.'

'And Mummy?' I whispered, ignoring this last observation. 'She never knew?'

He shook his head and sighed. 'No, she never knew. Still doesn't know. Marcus came back a few weeks later from abroad and Patrick was born in January.'

'Your son,' I breathed.

He nodded. 'My son. My only son.'

There was a silence. Tears welled in his eyes. He shook them away and with an effort, collected himself.

'But I had to hate him, you see. Had to hate Patrick. It was the only way for me to get over it. I couldn't stand by on the side-lines watching him grow up, knowing he was my boy, hankering after him. I washed my hands of him right there and then, called him "that little bastard" to myself. I refused to see him or have anything to do with him.'

'And Madelaine?'

'Madelaine too,' he said shortly. 'I knew it was madness. It was a madness that lasted a summer and that was it. After that I made sure we cut ourselves off from that family for good.'

'So . . . you didn't love her?'

'Good God no,' he said quickly. 'I didn't love her.' He gave a short, sharp laugh. 'How could I? Madelaine is everything I despise in a woman. She's flighty, insecure, flirtatious . . . No, she's not my sort of woman at all. She wouldn't have been remotely suitable.'

'Suitable? There's no agenda for falling in love, Dad.'

'Whereas your mother,' he went on as if I hadn't

393

spoken, 'was everything I was looking for in a wife. Steady, practical, down to earth, and from good, sensible stock.' He nodded firmly. 'Oh, I married the right woman, there's no doubt about that. But I –' He stopped.

'You wrecked your life in the process.'

He gazed down at the pavement and frowned. 'Yes, I did.'

'And mine too,' I said.

There was a long silence. It had been hot all day but there was a sudden chill in the air that hadn't been there before. I shivered. I couldn't think straight, couldn't even begin to get my head around this.

'Why didn't you tell me? I said eventually. 'When I was eighteen, when I'd just met him, that time on the beach? Why didn't you take me aside, and tell me gently? I'd have understood.'

He shook his head. 'Couldn't,' he muttered gruffly. 'Couldn't have you think ill of me, Tess, know me for the sham I was.'

'I'd have thought *more* of you,' I said fiercely, 'much more! It would have helped a great deal to know you were human!'

He bowed his head.

'And I could have accepted it then, too, in the beginning. I could have accepted that there was no way Patrick and I could ever see each other, no way we could ever fall in love. If you'd told me then I could have set my heart against him, maybe even loved him as a brother, been proud to have him as that, but now . . .'

'Tess, you must!' he cried, seizing my hand. 'You must!'

'But it's not so easy now!' I blurted, snatching my hand

394

back. 'And so what if he is my brother,' I cried hopelessly, 'so what? I don't want more children, so it doesn't matter!'

'No!' he cried, appalled. He seized my shoulders. 'No! It's a mortal sin, brother and sister!'

I knew he was right but I wanted to hurt him. 'But we already have,' I said coldly. 'Sinned.'

He shrank back. 'You can't have done – I was so careful!'

'Not careful enough, Daddy. Needs must, as you well know. Like you, that summer with Madelaine. Who knows, perhaps we all picked the same spot – down by the riverbank, eh? In the middle of the night?'

He stared at me aghast. The blood drained from his face. 'Oh God,' he breathed, 'thank heavens nothing came of it.'

'No, nothing came of it,' I said flatly, 'but you see, the deed has already been done. We wouldn't be breaking new ground.'

'Tess, promise me you won't do this, promise me! Don't you see that in God's eyes it's damnable?'

I stared at him. 'In God's eyes, Daddy, you've got an awful lot to answer for. I don't know how you have the nerve to –' But I couldn't go on. His head was already bowed in shame.

'Preach,' he finished for me. 'I know, Tess, believe me, I know. I've lived with it for thirty-four years now and there hasn't been a day when I haven't thought about it.'

We fell silent. There was so much I wanted to say, to reproach him for. I wanted to scream and yell, to pummel my fists on his chest, call him a hypocrite, a liar, a cheat, tell him I could see him for what he really was now. Not the strong, powerful figure occupying the high moral ground, that elevated position he'd always led me to believe I could never hope to reach even if I clawed my way up by my fingernails, but a weak, selfish, vain, flawed man. I wanted to tell him I knew all this, but more than anything I wanted to get away from him. I wanted to get away and think about where this left me.

Eventually I cleared my throat. 'Daddy, we must get back. Rachel will be wondering . . .'

He nodded. 'I know. You go on, Tess. Just give me five minutes to collect myself and I'll come on after.' He jerked his head. 'Go on.'

I gulped. After all this he was still telling me what to do! I wanted to shriek, 'No, damn it, you go on! What about *my* five minutes? What about *me* collecting myself?'

Out of habit, I put my glass down and got up. I started off down the street, doing as he'd asked.

'Tess!' he called after me suddenly. I turned. 'You won't say anything to your mother?' His eyes were pained, haunted.

Mummy. Oh God, Mummy. 'No,' I whispered.

'One more thing.' His face buckled. He fought with it. 'Will you forgive me?'

I looked back at him sitting there in his dark suit and dog collar, on a pub bench, looking so old suddenly, so lonely, so incongruous. He looked – pathetic. With difficulty, I nodded curtly. Still he held my gaze. It wasn't enough. He wanted a word. He wanted absolution. I took a deep breath.

'Yes,' I muttered.

Relief flooded his eyes. I turned and walked quickly on.

Chapter Twenty-five

Somehow, by putting one foot in front of the other and clicking onto automatic pilot, I made my way to Dukes. I limped slowly and methodically through the crowded streets; past Selfridges, through Berkeley Square, registering the shops, the parks, the statues, but not really seeing them, just dragging my foot and staring straight ahead. I felt numb with shock, but at the same time my mind was kaleidoscoping fragments of chaotic information around. I tried to assimilate them. Patrick was my brother. We shared a father. He was my father's son. Sister and brother. Brother and sister. Daddy and Madclaine.

I limped on and on and after a while, the numbness began to thaw; I started to get some feeling back in my mind. The shards of light stopped flitting around and settled down into some sort of cohesive order. Slowly, surely, I began to get the picture and as it came into focus I realized it wasn't very pretty. Rage began to well up from somewhere deep inside me. It started in the pit of my stomach and unfurled in waves, surging up through my throat until I felt I'd almost gag on it. *He'd done it again, hadn't he?* Once again my father had blocked me, stopped me in my tracks.

The first time, twelve years ago, he'd done it physically, by barring my way, refusing to let me leave the country – or even the house, for that matter – and now this time, when I was too old for such bullying tactics, he'd done it by presenting a stumbling block so awful and so insurmountable, that however much I'd insisted it would make no difference, I knew it would, despite my show of bravado. There was no earthly way Patrick and I could ever be together now, my father had seen to that. Once again he'd taken away my freedom of choice. Once again he'd steered the course of my life, taken the helm, put an end to everything, but in another way, he'd ensured that there was no end. He'd just made the waters even murkier, because he hadn't taken away our attraction for each other; he'd just highlighted it by its impossibility.

I'd want Patrick even more now I couldn't have him, wouldn't I, I thought bitterly. I'd probably dream about him all the time now, moon about the house in my nightie thinking about him, eat too much, take up smoking, die of chocolate, wonder what might have been, stare out of rain-streaked windows, pull myself together for just long enough to put a coat on over my pyjamas and take the children to school then sink back into wistful melancholia with a vengeance, surrounded by the washing-up, yesterday's papers, crawling through the days, resenting my life with David . . . Oh yes, I thought sourly, there was no hope for me now. I'd end my days a twisted, bickering, frustrated old hag with a poor, henpecked husband who could do no right. That was the fate that awaited me and David, my father had seen to that. He'd condemned us to an unhappy marriage. My father, the preacher man, and all because his inflated pride and vanity had meant more to him than my happiness. All because he couldn't bear me to think he was anything less than The Right Reverend Perfect. Well thank you so much, Daddy.

I limped grimly into the hotel. The doorman gave me a quizzical glance but I swept past him, on and up the stairs to the suite where our party was gathered.

As I hobbled into what was now quite a noisy and jolly throng – and certainly less than sober – I spotted David hovering near the doorway. He was waiting for me, looking around anxiously. My anger dissipated in a moment. I stopped for a second and looked at him without him seeing me. There he was, tall, elegant, poised, his chin raised as he peered around, with that kind intelligent face. My heart gave a sudden lurch. Poor, lovely David, my darling husband, who'd done nothing wrong apart from follow Patrick chronologically in my affections. Who'd loved me, given me children and was now caught up in this God-awful mess by dint of the fact that he'd met me second and not first.

'Tess!' His face cleared with relief as he saw me. He walked quickly over. 'Where on earth have you been? I've been worried sick.'

'Oh David, I'm sorry. I needed some air, went for a walk, but I ended up wandering around for a bit. Sorry.'

'But you've been ages, an hour at least, and you look terrible!'

'I know, I know. I – I think Robert's death affected me more than I imagined.' I cringed inwardly at my hypocrisy.

David took my arm and steered me towards the bar. 'Well come on, let's get you a drink, that's obviously what you need. You'll feel much better after a brandy. It doesn't do to dwell on these things for too long, you know. That's the whole point of a wake ... you get pissed and it takes your mind off all that death. And you're probably starving too, which doesn't help either. You can't grieve on an empty stomach.' He produced a plate of salmon and salad from behind a potted palm. 'Everyone fell on the food like gannets when they arrived but I managed to save you some. Here, tuck into this.'

Tears welled up in my eyes. Right, so let's get this straight, Tess. While you've been out hand-holding with another man, your hunter-gatherer here has been storing up food, squirrelling it away behind plants, lest his homemaker – sorry, home *breaker* – should be the teeniest bit hungry when she arrives. Lest she should have even the remotest of hunger pangs. I mentally flogged myself and took the plate.

'Thanks,' I whispered.

What I really wanted to say was, 'For God's sake don't be so frigging nice to me, David. Why on earth didn't you spike the cucumber with arsenic, garnish the lettuce with a nice touch of cyanide, finish off your cheating, conniving witch of a wife once and for all, eh?'

He peered at me under my fringe. 'Sure you're all right? You look decidedly clammy if you don't mind me saying so.'

I felt my forehead. It was damp. God, how disgusting. I nodded and forced a smile. 'Fine, fine honestly.'

Silently I bent my head and toyed with the salad. At least with a plate of food I didn't have to look at him. At length, he broke the silence.

'Look, Tess, I'm sorry,' he said briskly.

I looked up. 'What for?'

'For everything. But mainly for not coming to help you back from Scotland. Leaving you in the lurch like that, with your leg and the children. It was just – well, it was a rather difficult time for me . . .'

I smiled. God, that seemed so long ago now. 'It's OK, David. I was just being a selfish cow as usual.'

'It won't make any sense now,' he went on hesitantly, 'but maybe later on you'll understand. I needed that time to – well. There were lots of things I wanted to sort out. For myself. Alone.'

I frowned up at him, watching his mouth twisting and turning awkwardly. How strange, he looked almost shifty. David never looked shifty. And what on earth was he going on about? What things? Sort what out? I sighed. No, I had enough chaos on my plate without trying to take on any more. Whatever it was would have to wait. I put down my salad.

'David, you've got nothing to apologize for. It's me who's behaved abominably.' Tears of shame and self-pity filled my eyes. I kept my head low and reached for my wine glass.

'That's not strictly true,' he said quietly, 'but there's a limit to the extent I can . . .' He hesitated.

'The extent you can what?'

He shook his head. 'Nothing. I should have come and got you, that's all. Shouldn't have left you there alone.'

'David, stop banging on about it, will you? You were right not to! It's about time you stopped jumping at my commands, for heaven's sake. I'm just a spoiled, arrogant girl who expects you to leap through hoops at a moment's notice and quite frankly I don't know why you put up with me. Most husbands would have shot me through the mouth long ago. Honestly, sometimes I haven't the faintest idea why you don't just bugger off and leave me.'

He smiled. 'Sometimes I haven't the faintest idea either.'

There was a pause.

'So – would you?' I said suddenly, recklessly.

He looked at me carefully. 'What exactly are you asking me here, Tess?'

I was playing with fire and I knew it. All at once the room seemed very still. It was as if we were the only two people in it.

'I'm asking you if you'd ever leave me,' I said breathlessly, feeling my colour rise.

'What sort of a question is that?' he said quietly.

I stared at him. Wasn't he going to answer it then? Why the hell not? My heart stopped for a second. Then I mentally shook myself. Why not? Because you're in a room full of relatives at your uncle's funeral, you fool, that's why not. And because there's a time and a place for everything. I could still feel his eyes burning into me. As abruptly as the madness had taken me, it left me. I felt my damp forehead as if maybe that was to blame.

'Oh, God, I'm so sorry, David,' I gasped. 'I don't know what came over me just then. Actually I'm feeling decidedly dodgy right now – it's all this emotion I suppose, makes me hormonal. You know what I'm like at weddings, I can get through a dozen hankies in one sitting. Must be the same with funerals, I suppose, only worse. Forget I said anything, I'm – I'm raving at the moment.' I looked up with the brightest smile I could muster.

He stared back at me. His face seemed white, colourless. I glanced away. *Don't talk to him now*, a little voice in my head said. *Don't say any more, not in this state. You'll spill the Patrick beans, blurt it out, confess it, you know you're dying to unburden yourself. You're just ripe for a confession but once it's out you can never un-say it and my God you'll live to regret it* . . . And quite apart from anything else, I thought bitterly, there were precious few beans left to spill now, weren't there? My eyes, which had been preoccupied with my wine glass, took a quick flit to David's ashen face.

'Darling, I simply must go to the loo,' I muttered. 'I've got to do something about my face. I can feel how ugly I am without even consulting a mirror.'

He nodded and managed a thin smile beneath his pallor. 'You've looked better, I must say. Go on, I'll guard your food.'

'No, no, I don't want it really. You go and talk to everyone. I'll probably be a while.'

I turned and without looking back, elbowed my way through the throng in the direction of the Ladies.

Once inside I leaned heavily on the marble washstand and stared at my battered, tear-stained face in the overlit mirror. I looked about a hundred years old and felt it too. I delved in my bag and found a blunt eyeliner and attempted a shaky line. I tried some mascara too, but made such a hash of it I wiped it off and ended up with black eyes. I slapped some lipstick on instead. Then I stared at my clown's face with its swollen eyelids and red mouth. It seemed entirely appropriate somehow.

'What a mess,' I whispered. 'What a God . . . awful . . . mess.'

I could see by my reflection that such wanton self-pity had triggered the tear ducts again so I hurriedly stuffed the make-up back in my bag and tempting though it was to stay in the safety of the Ladies for the next hour or so, turned and went back outside.

The hum of social chatter swirled around me. I took a glass of champagne from a waitress's tray, and then on an impulse, another. It was an old trick of mine at gruesome parties, to wander around with two glasses, and if accosted by the bore of the century, say I was actually just on my way to deliver a drink. I looked around nervously. And let's face it, there were plenty of people I simply couldn't speak to here, ones I really had to avoid, like David, Laura, Mummy. I was circling around the edge of the crowd when suddenly, my elbow was seized in a pincer-like grip. An ancient cut-glass voice barked in my ear.

'Trying the old two-glasses-at-a-party trick eh? That doesn't fool me. I've been looking for you.'

I swung around and my heart sank. 'Aunt Elspeth!'

I leaned forward and kissed the paper-thin cheek that was presented to me. Oh hell. Blind, boozy, belligerent Great-Aunt Elspeth, just what I needed. As usual she reeked of stale Chanel and pink gin, was smothered in jewels and had the usual eccentric hat complete with ostrich feathers foaming out of the top like some kind of extravagant bantam cock. Still, I reasoned, at least she wasn't a member of my more immediate family and at least I wouldn't have to say anything to her. There was no such thing as a conversation with Elspeth: hers was the only voice that mattered so she simply held forth.

'How lovely to see you,' I lied.

Tall and thin she swooped down with her watery blue eyes and hawk-like nose.

'Don't lie, my dear, you know you avoid me like the plague, everyone does; but just think, it could have been worse. It could have been mad bad Uncle Arthur. At least I won't pinch your bottom. I might just pinch that extra drink, though. It's like the bloody Gobi desert in here.'

I grinned and passed it over to her. 'Be my guest.'

'But as it happens, my dear,' she took a huge slug of champagne and fixed me with her rheumy old eyes, 'I've got a bone to pick with you.'

I groaned silently and braced myself for a flurry of confusion. No one would ever be foolish enough to accuse Elspeth of being senile because in actual fact she was quite astonishingly on the ball. It was just that being half-blind, it was almost invariably the *wrong* ball. She tapped me with a heavily bejewelled hand.

'You must give up that dreadful job of yours. It'll be the ruin of you!'

I sighed. 'No, Elspeth, that's not me. That's —'

'Find yourself a nice young man. It's high time you were settling down and having babies, my dear. It's all very well swanning round in your designer suits fancying yourself as a captain of industry, but your biological clock is ticking away. You're running out of eggs, young lady!'

I groaned. 'Elspeth, it's Laura who's —'

'Yes I can see it's Laura. What d'you think I am, blind as well as old? Now look here, my girl, if you don't get yourself sorted out soon you're going to end up on the shelf like your poor Aunt Beatty and no amount of dusting off is ever going to get *her* down again!'

I cringed for poor Beatty, Elspeth's elder sister. I glanced around and – ah yes, as luck would have it she was standing right behind us. I tried to convey this to Elspeth with a series of extravagant head nods and winks, but to no avail.

'You know what happened to her, don't you?' she barked.

I saw Beatty's back stiffen. 'Elspeth, I really don't think –'

'She left it too late and then in desperation had a *disastrous* flirt with a married man. She threw herself at him, poor cow, absolutely *threw* herself; it was embarrassing to watch. Of course he swore blind he'd leave his wife for her but he never did. Pitiful it was – and in those days it wasn't even as if she had the satisfaction of a proper affair! Some decent hanky-panky! Oh no, it was all conducted in public, lots of feverish glances across a crowded room, sweaty palms, heaving bosoms – just one long, wretched, knee-trembling flirt, poor devil. Shall I tell you something,' she hissed loudly, putting her hand on my arm and glancing around furtively. I braced myself, knowing exactly what was coming. 'Poor old Beatty's never even had it up!'

Behind me I could almost hear Beatty's teeth grinding to dust. 'Elspeth, I know, you've told me before and –'

'Imagine,' said Elspeth loudly. 'Imagine going to your grave never knowing what it is to have a fuck!'

'Elspeth, please!' God, she was worse than ever. I took her arm and forcibly steered her to the side of the room where hopefully it was a little quieter and she could insult everyone to her heart's content. Unfortunately I inadvertently steered her into little Leonora who was kneeling up at a table drinking orange juice.

'Not that lack of sex will ever be your problem though, eh?' she observed loudly.

I cringed and tried to steer her away from Leonora's pricked-up ears, but the Perfect Child looked strangely delighted to see her great-great-aunt. She left her juice, climbed down from the table and followed us, attaching herself firmly to Elspeth's side. She gazed up at her intently.

'Eh? What? Quite the opposite I should imagine,' Elspeth roared on. 'You've probably been getting far too much and all from the wrong sorts of people! Who's this soppy teacher chappie I've been hearing about? Not a bloody Communist, is he?'

I sighed, recognizing my father's intervention. 'No, Elspeth, he's not, but –'

'What? Don't whisper, girl! They're all Lefty bastards now, aren't they? Or so your father tells me. Can't abide bloody Communists, they should all be taken out and shot through the testicles.' She frowned down for a moment at Leonora who was staring up at her now with quite disconcerting intensity.

'What are you staring at me for, child?' she barked.

'I want to see you drink like a fish.'

Elspeth blanched. 'Eh? What's that?'

'Well, Daddy said –'

'Leonora, run along, darling,' I said hastily. 'I think Mummy's looking for you.'

'But Aunt Tess, Daddy said she could! He did, he said she could dri –'

'Leonora, please!' I snapped desperately. I turned her around, pointed her in the direction of her mother and gave her a little shove. 'Now run along.' God, this wake was going from bad to worse. All the same, I made a mental note to tell Hugo his pupil was coming along rather nicely.

'Hrmph!' snorted Elspeth. 'That child's going to turn out just like her mother if she's not careful.'

'Yes, well, anyway, Elspeth, look,' I muttered, desperately inching away, 'it's been lovely to talk to you but I really ought to go and ring the babysitter. I said I'd check in about now and –'

'You'll do no such thing, young lady. I haven't finished with you yet. Now just hold your horses a moment while I tell you what you need.' She seized my wrist in her bony old hand. There was no escape. 'What you need is a nice solid barrister like your sister. Doesn't matter what he looks like, as long as he works hard and he's got a bit of money, then you just knuckle down and get breeding, all right?' She leaned forward with a conspiratorial hiss. 'But for heaven's sake don't let yourself go to pot afterwards like she has. I shouldn't think she even shaves her legs any more, let alone her armpits. Talk about getting your man and breathing a monumental sigh of relief! No, no, that's not the way at all. You can still wear your fancy frocks and carry on chasing Lefties – if you must – but at least you'll have got the staples under your belt.' She tapped my hand. 'Know what I mean? It's no good helping yourself to the little luxuries in life without having the staples first!'

I grinned in spite of myself. Old Elspeth had notched up precisely three staples in her time; three rich, solid, boring, unquestioning husbands, who'd sat by and watched as she'd steadily peppered her life with a string of caddish luxuries, most of whom had had yachts in the Bahamas, castles in the Black Forest and villas in the South of France.

'I blame the pill,' she declared hotly, 'and the so-called sexual revolution.'

I looked around desperately, wondering if anyone else would like to hear this as many times as I had.

'Liberation,' she scoffed. 'Liberation for whom? For men, that's who! Oh yes, they have a very cushy time of it now, don't they? They get a nice young gel to take to bed on a regular basis and all for the price of a bottle of Chablis and a *coq au vin*. What could be more liberating than that? Wouldn't have happened in my day. Oh no, in *my* day if some fellow wanted to get you between the sheets he had to marry you first, he couldn't just scatter his seed around like some sex-crazed tomcat! I mean, that's all very fine for him but where does it leave you?'

'Exactly,' I murmured distractedly.

Out of the corner of my eye I spotted Laura and David, huddled in a corner over by the fireplace, talking earnestly. In fact it was Laura who was doing all the talking. David was just listening intently, his head tilted to one side. I went cold. What was she telling him? That I was so obsessed with Patrick I'd marched into a gallery like a scorned, jilted lover, doused her in champagne and accused her of having an affair with him? My heart stopped for a moment. She wouldn't do that, would she?

'Up the creek without a bloody paddle, that's where! With no ring on your finger and not even a bun in the oven to force his hand!'

But – if she wasn't telling him that – what was it then? What was so riveting that it was being related in such hushed tones and listened to so avidly? I watched their faces, trying desperately to read her lips.

'I tell you, if I was a young gel these days I'd throw that wretched pill packet away and have him marching up the aisle beside me with a bump under my dress. The next time you're bedding down with your drippy little teacher fellow you bear that in mind, my dear. After all, it's not as if *he*'d take the wretched thing, is it – so why should you? Don't swallow it!'

I turned back to Elspeth and blinked. 'What?'

'I said the next time you're in bed with your teacher chappie – don't swallow it!'

I gazed at her incredulously. Good heavens. Elspeth really had gone from bad to worse; she shouldn't be allowed out.

'Spit it out!' she barked.

My mouth hung open. Luckily I was saved from spluttering a reply by a cool hand on my arm.

'Darling – a word.'

'Mummy!'

'Elspeth, I'm so sorry to barge in but could I drag Tess away for just a moment?'

'You're going as barmy as I am, Daphne. It's Laura, not Tess, but yes, have her, by all means. See if you can talk any sense into the gel. I certainly can't!'

'I'll do my best,' purred my mother. 'Oh, and incidentally, I think Beatty's looking for you.'

She pushed Elspeth in the direction of Beatty's bristling back and steered me the other way.

'She's got worse, Mummy,' I muttered as we moved off. 'Honestly, some of the things she says . . . she's unreal!'

'Ah well, that's the arrogance of old age for you, makes you feel you've lived so long you can say what you like. To tell you the truth, I'm beginning to feel a little like that myself these days.'

She smiled as she linked arms with me and led me over to a window seat overlooking the street. She sat down and patted the cushion next to her. I perched gingerly beside her. She frowned.

'Why so grim, darling?'

'Me?' I forced a smile. 'Oh, no reason. I'm fine really. Fine.'

I couldn't look at her. What a bastard my father was. What a complete and utter first-division shit. He didn't deserve someone like my mother.

'Really? You look a bit – distressed.'

I sighed. 'Oh I'm all right really, just a bit tired, I suppose. This wretched ankle doesn't help and – oh I don't know. Everything seems to be getting on top of me at the moment, conspiring against me . . .' I trailed off, looking out of the window at the traffic in the street below.

'Is it Patrick?'

I swung round abruptly. 'Wh-what d'you mean?'

'Come on, Tess,' she said quietly. 'You don't think I don't know, do you?'

I looked away. 'Does . . . everyone know?' I muttered.

'If you mean David, I don't think so, no. But I've always known.'

We were silent for a moment.

'To be honest, Mummy, I hadn't really realized myself,'

I said quietly. 'But now I can see that it's always been there, that sort of . . . dull ache. Sometimes it's hardly there at all. I can go for weeks, months, years even, without thinking about him, but then suddenly, like now, it just gets me in its grip and it's as if I can't breathe. Can't think rationally, it just – takes me over.' I caught my breath in a gasp.

God, it was a relief to talk about it, to tell someone. I looked down at my hands, twisted them together. But I mustn't talk too much, must I? I turned to her with a bright smile.

'But not any more. As from today that's all in the past. I intend to quit the habit; it's my New Year's resolution! No more pain, no more longing.'

She shook her head. 'I don't think so.'

'Oh yes, definitely. This holiday was the main culprit of course, seeing him again, bringing it all back, but I'm going to put it all behind me now. Get back to normal. You'll see.' I gave a brave little smile, but it shook a bit as she gazed into my eyes.

'I doubt it. It's not as simple as that, is it?'

'Oh, so what do you suggest then, Mummy,' I said, exasperated. 'An affair? The break-up of my marriage – something jolly like that?'

'No,' she said calmly, 'but one way or another this will wreck your marriage anyway and you know it. The rot's already set in as far as I can see, and whether you go with Patrick now or just hanker after him silently for the rest of your life it doesn't make much difference. You're not giving your all to David.'

I hung my head in silence. It was true. But since there

was no way I could be with Patrick anyway, what was the point of talking about it? But I couldn't tell her that.

Mummy put her hand on mine. 'Look, Tess,' she said gently, 'I just don't want you to be as trapped and frustrated as I've been, to think there's no way out. It's not true. You *do* have a duty to other people, of course you do, but your real duty is to yourself. Don't live the life of a martyr, it doesn't help anyone.'

'Like you have,' I said quietly.

'Like I have.'

There was a silence. I realized I'd always known that, just never acknowledged it. I looked at her.

'Do you wish you'd left Daddy then?'

She sighed and shook her head. 'Oh, it's too late now so what's the point in talking about it?' She lifted her chin and breathed deeply. Then she stared into the middle distance and nodded slowly. 'But yes, since you ask, there've been plenty of times when I thought if I didn't get out he'd drive me insane. Really insane.' She shrugged. 'But then, every time I was about to go I'd think of you and Laura. I thought you wouldn't survive the break-up, that you'd both be psychologically affected by it for the rest of your lives and that it would be all my fault. The usual thing.'

I nodded miserably. I couldn't even think about Hugo and Clemmie, just couldn't think.

'So, I just put up with him. Martyred myself to the cause, marriage and family life.' She shook her head. 'Not a very healthy situation, but inside I consoled myself with the thought that I might actually do it one day, when you were older. Get up and go, have a life of my own. I kidded myself I had a secret hidden agenda. That kept me going.' She smiled sadly. 'Too late now, of course.'

I bit my lip. 'Mummy – David and I, we're not like that, like you and Daddy. Not at all, in fact. We love each other very much. It's just –'

She patted my hand. 'I know. You just can't get rid of Patrick, can you?'

'No, I can't, but Mummy, it's no good!' I blurted out suddenly. 'There's no point in even thinking about it.'

'Because?'

'Because – nothing.' I stood up. God, shut *up*, Tess, just shut *up*. I smoothed my skirt down. 'Come on,' I said gruffly, 'let's go and get another drink. I reckon I could drink this bar dry today. In fact, I look upon it as a positive challenge.'

She put a hand on my arm. 'Because of something your father's just told you?'

I whipped around and stared back at her. Slowly I sat down beside her again.

'How did you know?' I whispered.

'Well, I knew he went looking for you and I guessed you'd be with Patrick. I assumed he'd find you together and have to tell you.'

'So you know – about Patrick?'

She smiled. 'I've known for years. Since it happened, in fact.'

I stared at her. 'Does he know that you know?'

'No, of course not.'

I blinked. 'How did you find out?'

'Oh, it wasn't difficult. It was quite obvious at the time that he was having an affair with Madelaine. I knew from the word go. I can remember the precise moment it started, in fact. She stayed late after supper one night at Kilmarnoch and they sat up talking together.' She smiled. 'After that it was just a joke. You know what your father's like, he's hopeless at subterfuge. He kept imagining he was sneaking noiselessly out of the house in the middle of the night, whereas in fact every floorboard was creaking violently and every door banging shut and he kept whispering "Bugger" under his breath as he stubbed his toes in the dark. It was enough to wake the dead. I had the room next to him and I used to get out of bed in my nightie and stand at the window, watching him disappearing down the drive to meet her.'

'And you didn't mind?' I said incredulously.

'Oh, I *minded* all right, I minded like anything, but what could I do? I was engaged to be married to him the following month and at the time assumed I was very much in love. You see, he was the only man I'd ever met really. I was very young, very confused and my parents were dead so I felt totally alone.' She shrugged. 'I thought – if I run out now, what will happen to me? Who will have me? I panicked, I suppose. I reckoned if I kept my head down and kept quiet, the affair would run its course and fizzle out, which of course it did.'

'Crumbs,' I breathed. 'I'm not sure I'd have been so stoical.'

'And neither should I have been, nor so forgiving, but when you're as young and naive as I was in those days . . .' She trailed off back into the past. Then with a start, collected herself and came back to the present. 'Anyway, Marcus returned from abroad and Madelaine went back to him. Your father and I got married and I thought I'd won. Thought I'd got what I wanted.'

'And you guessed that Patrick was their son?'

'Well, it wasn't hard. When we heard at a dinner party that Madelaine was expecting, your father went as white as a sheet, was nearly sick in his soup and had to leave the table. He came back ten minutes later visibly shaken, couldn't eat a thing and looking as if he'd seen a ghost. Then for the next six or seven months he practically fought the paper boy for *The Times* in the morning, propped it up behind his boiled egg and scanned the births avidly, frowning with concentration and imagining he was being *so* discreet.'

I smiled in spite of myself. I could just imagine it.

'When it was finally announced the paper shook in his hand like a jelly. He dropped it straight into his coffee and ran upstairs. I reached across the breakfast table, picked up the sodden paper and read about Patrick's birth. I mean, what does he think I am, brain dead or something?'

'And Madelaine? Does she know you know?'

'Oh yes,' she smiled. 'I mean, it's never been mentioned, but it's very much understood.' She looked at me. 'You know, between women. Something unspoken. There was a little friction at first, but there's no animosity now. Quite the reverse in fact. In a way I think we both feel rather bonded.' She stared out of the window. 'And of course, we've both been too unhappy in our marriages to get in a state about that sort of thing now. We both know why it happened.'

'You'd say that then, would you?'

'What?'

'That you've had an unhappy marriage?'

She took a deep breath. 'I'd say that I've had a desperately frustrating, unfulfilled –' she hesitated – 'unhappy marriage, yes.' She looked at me intently. 'And I don't want that for you, Tess, however high the price. Take it from me, it's not worth it.'

'But then – don't you see?' I said desperately, 'for God's sake, there's just no way! Patrick and I – we're brother and sister. It's impossible, Mummy!'

She looked at me squarely. 'Ah, but you're not, you see.'

I stared. 'But you just said –'

'I said Patrick was his son, but –' Suddenly she faltered. She glanced away, then down at her hands. She twirled her wedding ring. I stared at her in mounting horror.

'But I'm not his daughter?' I breathed incredulously. 'Mummy!' I seized her hand, shook it. 'Mummy! Is that what you're saying? *That I'm not his daughter?*'

She looked up. Her face was composed, but very pale under her make-up. Her lips, bloodless. 'Yes that's right. That's exactly what I'm saying,' she said. 'You're not his daughter, Tess.'

Chapter Twenty-six

I gazed at her, my throat, mouth and lips as dry as sand. 'So,' I breathed, 'who is my father then?'

She glanced at me quickly, then away. 'This is very hard for me, Tess.'

'Mummy!' I squeezed her hand hard. 'For heaven's sake just tell me! Is it someone I know?'

She nodded. 'Yes, it's someone you know.'

I gasped. 'Good God! Who?'

'Hamish McPherson.'

For a moment the name meant absolutely nothing to me. My mind raced feverishly around, winding forwards, backwards, searching desperately for a face, but coming up with nothing. I blinked. 'Hamish McPherson?'

'The old gillie. Willie's father.'

I stared at her incredulously. 'Hamish – from the river? You mean – no! I don't believe it!'

'You don't believe it's Hamish, or you don't believe I'd do such a thing?' She was watching me carefully now.

'Good God – both,' I spluttered, briefly tearing at my hair. 'I mean,' I stood and paced up and down by the window seat, backwards and forwards, turning small circles, 'well, I just can't believe it, that's all. Any of it!'

'Having decided to tell you, it's hardly something I'd lie about, is it?' she said calmly. 'Hamish *is* your father, darling.'

I stopped pacing, turned and stared at her. For several seconds I was bereft of speech. Then I sat down next to her again. I thought of Willie's father, the old gillie, a huge bear of a man with grey woolly hair, a beard, a deep Scottish brogue. A nice man, quiet, kindly, twinkly-eyed, helpful always, but – my father? I dug deep and found some kind of a voice. It didn't sound like mine at all.

'But how on earth did you and he – how did you ever come to . . . I mean, with someone like that?'

She smiled. 'How did I ever come to sleep with someone as old and raddled as that? You forget, my love, that I too am old and raddled now but in those days we were both young and Hamish was extremely attractive. He was terrifically,' she hesitated, 'well, virile, I suppose. He had this huge powerful frame and a shock of blond hair – looked rather like his son does now, in fact.'

'Of course,' I breathed. 'Willie.'

'Not unattractive in his way, wouldn't you say?'

I blushed and glanced away. 'Er – no. No, I suppose not.' God, to think I'd nearly slept with my *brother*.

'And certainly your sister seems to find him so. Not really your type, of course – too rustic, not urbane enough, but still, he has a certain rakish charm, as did Hamish. And Hamish was such a gentle man, so unlike your father. He was tender and kind and – yes, passionate. And let's face it,' she brushed some imaginary crumbs off her immaculate navy skirt, 'passion was very lacking in my life at the time.'

I looked at her in amazement as she sat, gloves clasped on her lap, Dickins & Jones hat on, talking matter-of-factly to me about virility and tenderness and passion as if for all the world she was discussing the price of spring greens. I blinked. My mother, Mum, who cooked and sewed and gardened – what on earth did she want with things like that, was the question that sprang shamefully to mind.

'So,' I struggled to make sense of this, 'so all of this happened the same summer that Daddy and Madelaine . . .'

'Oh dear me, no. No no, it was a few years after all that, three or four years, by which time I'd realized what a terrible mistake I'd made. That the man I'd married was not the man he'd purported to be. My fault too, of course,' she smiled. 'I hadn't read the small print properly, and I expected too much. Women always do though, don't they? It's only natural. We've all been spoonfed true romance from puberty and whether it's Mills and Boon or *Anna Karenina* one still comes to expect it as a matter of course. As a girl's divine right. So it comes as a bit of a shock to realize you're not necessarily going to get it. That this is as good as it gets. First you're angry, as I certainly was and there are rows, furious rows because you can't believe you've been so short-changed, but then a sort of post-purchase dissonance sets in. You're irritated, you'd like to take it back, get a refund, try something else, but at the end of the day it's just too much effort. So you live with it, let it grow on you, try to get used to it. And to some extent you do get used to it.' She looked over my shoulder, into the past, nodding slightly. Then her face hardened. 'But not that summer. No, no, that summer I hadn't got used to it at all. I was still at the good old angry stage. Gloomy resignation had not by any means set in and I was livid.'

She looked at me sharply. 'And fed up with being constantly blamed for not having produced any babies!'

I jumped. 'Wh-what?'

'Your father was desperate for children. In all honesty I think that's probably why he married me. He took one look at my childbearing hips and thought, She'll do. Then when I still hadn't conceived after four years he made up his mind it was all my fault. Penny had just been born and we were all up at Kilmarnoch with the baby. Your father was at his most – well, cruel, actually. That's the only word. He more or less pointed the finger in public, pondered aloud at dinner parties as to why it was that other women could have babies and I couldn't, wondered how the dickens he'd managed to marry a barren one, what on earth could be wrong with me.'

She swallowed hard and bit her lip. 'And of course, I naturally assumed it *was* my fault because I knew he'd fathered Patrick and he certainly thought it was my fault because he knew he'd fathered Patrick too.' She grinned. 'Sometimes I'd even deliberately irritate him, say something like – "But darling, how can you be so sure, it could be something to do with you, couldn't it? Couldn't you be firing blanks?" I'd watch him go absolutely puce in the face, clench his fists and almost implode as he struggled to resist the temptation to bellow – "No, you silly cow! It can't possibly be my fault because I already have a son!"' She laughed, but it tailed off into a sigh. 'Yes, that summer at Kilmarnoch. God, how I hated the place, year after year after bloody year!'

I blinked, shocked by her vehemence. 'But I thought you loved it there.'

She looked at me absently. 'Did you, darling? Yes, well, I suppose it wouldn't be quite true to say I loathe it now. I learned to tolerate it because you and Laura loved it so much but I'm afraid midges, driving rain and gutting fish on a riverbank is not actually my idea of a holiday. Give me India or Thailand any day.'

'Thailand!' I gasped. 'Have you ever been?'

'No.' She smiled. 'Probably never will now.'

I caught my breath, silenced. Not for the first time I realized there was much I didn't know about my mother. About how she'd subjugated herself for my father, for Laura and for me. But she hadn't had to do that for me, I thought fiercely, and I resented the fact that she had. God, if she'd so much as mentioned that she'd wanted to travel to any of those places I'd have been down at the travel agents buying her the tickets – God, I'd have gone with her! Then a seeping doubt crept into my mind. Or would I? Might I not have dismissed it as one of Mum's funny ideas and not have bothered? After all, she never made a fuss, did she? My chest felt tight suddenly. It hurt me terribly that I'd never properly got to know her, never bothered to find out what made her tick. My own mum.

'And of course,' she went on, 'being up there by the river always reminded me of your father's affair with Madelaine. Not that it hurt any more, quite the opposite in fact. It just rammed home to me how stupid I'd been not to take my chance when I'd had it. It was as if Fate had handed it to me right there on a plate, a month before I was due to be married and said: "Go on, Daphne, take it! Quick, run with it!" But I didn't. I fumbled it, dropped my chance . . . God, in my own quiet way I even *fought* for him.' She gave a hollow laugh. 'And for what?'

She looked beyond me, out of the window. Her eyes were far away. 'I used to go for walks that summer, solitary walks, down to the beach, along the cliffs, by the river, thinking, cursing myself for being such a fool. Telling myself I should get out now while I didn't have children. But I was still too scared. Scared of what everyone would think and say, scared of what would happen to me, but most of all – *scared of him*. I know it makes me sound like a complete wimp, Tess, but he was all I had, you see and he has – *had*,' she corrected herself, 'such a hold on me. Such power.' Her eyes swivelled back from the window and looked at me squarely. 'He's a bully, of course.'

I nodded. 'I know,' I whispered. Suddenly I had an awful thought. 'Not –'

'Oh no,' she said quickly. 'Not that. Just mentally.'

I nodded, relieved.

She grimaced. 'Just as bad in a way. The only thing is, you don't have the bruises to prove it.'

We were silent for a moment. I tried not to think about what she might have been through, how much I'd never known.

'Anyway,' she went on briskly, 'one day I was walking – and crying – by the river as usual and I bumped into Hamish.' She paused. 'No, that's not right, I didn't bump into him. I was sitting with my head on my knees, crying by the river when I suddenly realized he was there beside me. He didn't say anything, just stayed there while I sort of snivelled away next to him, trying to get control.'

I stared at her. 'Go on.'

423

She coloured slightly. 'Must I, darling? I mean it just sort of went from there. He comforted me, put his arm round me, I put my head on his shoulder, he stroked my hair as I remember and – well, that was that really.'

'You mean there? By the river?'

'Well, no, we went – somewhere.'

'To the hut?' I squeaked.

She looked at me quickly. 'Yes. How did you know?'

'Oh! I er – guessed, that's all.' My mind boggled. Talk about history repeating itself.

She looked at me sharply. 'You're shocked.'

'No! No, I'm not actually. Well, only in the sense that it's a surprise, so unexpected and you are after all my –'

'Mother.'

'Quite.'

We were silent for a moment, watching as the crowd milled around in front of us, ebbing and flowing, hats tilting this way and that, talking, drinking.

'If I told you that it was the happiest, most fulfilling time of my life would that make it any easier for you?' she said quietly.

I looked at her sharply. 'It's not a question of making it easier for me. If you must know, I'm glad. I'm glad you had that time, had some happiness.' I paused and bit my lip. 'Does Hamish know?'

'That you're his daughter?' She shook her head. 'No, I never told him. But he's always been there for me, Tess, he's always been my friend.'

I nodded, thinking back to all the times I'd seen them fishing the river together, year after year, quite often on their own, upstream, on distant pools, shoulder to shoulder. I'd never given it a second thought.

'He's a good man you know, you mustn't be ashamed.'

I shook my head. 'I'm not.'

I was surprised, in fact, how totally unashamed, unshocked and unfazed I was by all this. If someone had told me at sixteen that my father wasn't my father I probably would have gone into a flat spin, got into a terrible mess, experimented with all manner of dubious substances, stuffed things up my nose, into my arms, down my throat, gone in for therapy and counselling, felt it was a marvellous excuse to get thoroughly mixed up, and consequently come out at the end a totally screwed-up individual. But now, at the ripe old age of thirty with two children of my own and set against my own heavy domestic backdrop, it really didn't seem too cataclysmic in the scheme of things. I mean, so what? My father wasn't my father, but I was still the same person, wasn't I? Yes, OK, maybe later on I might feel slightly taken aback, a bit rocked by it all, I might even get out the old holiday snaps, search feverishly for one of Hamish by the riverbank, look for resemblances. Doubtless I'd feel some delayed shock, feel bewildered, uprooted, cry a bit, maybe I'd even persuade Mummy to tell Hamish who I was. And then perhaps I'd want to get to know him better. Go on my own to Scotland, spend some time with him. Or, then again, maybe I wouldn't. Maybe I'd want to keep it all safely locked away in the past, where it had been for the last thirty years. Maybe I'd still want Hamish to be the retired gillie from the river and me to be the vicar's daughter from Claygate. Right at this moment, I didn't know. Because right now all that came shining through, clear as a megawatt light bulb, was not the fact that the man I'd been calling Daddy for the past thirty years was not actually biologically related to me, or even that the old man by the river who helped me to wind in fish on a regular basis *was* my father . . . No, the one single, glorious light that lasered its way through this ghastly heap of old marriages, old affairs, old bitterness and old bones, was that Patrick was not in any way, shape or form my brother. We were not, by any stretch of the imagination, related.

I felt excitement bubbling up inside me, but tried to calm it down, quell it. I turned to my mother.

'So, Patrick and I –'

'Are free to do exactly as you please.' She looked at me sharply. 'Not that I would necessarily encourage it, but it is your choice, Tess. You see, I wouldn't condemn it either.' She struggled to get a balance. 'All I mean is, whatever you do, don't get to my age and look back regretfully. It's not worth it.'

I looked at her sitting there in her smart navy suit, her small pillbox hat with veil perched on her grey curls, her discreet diamond brooch placed just so on her lapel, the perfect vicar's wife. Who would ever guess a life of heartache, misery and savage regrets?

'No, I won't,' I said quietly.

I reached across and gave her hand a sudden squeeze. She squeezed mine back. Our eyes watered simultaneously. We sat there, side by side in the window seat and I realized that, apart from when I was a small child, this was the closest I'd ever got to my mother. It was a glorious, joyous moment. She felt it too, I know she did, and we sat there together, hands clasped, blinking back the tears, savouring it greedily.

Suddenly I knew that I wanted more of this. I wanted to feel this way with Patrick. I needed to see him now, to feel a similar sort of happiness, to get that rush of joy, to have just a few, wonderful, uncomplicated moments before things got oh so incredibly screwed up as they inevitably would. It was so long since I'd felt this happy and I wanted it to go on and on. I wanted to be selfish, to think about me. I could feel my heart beginning to pound. I stood up.

'Mummy, I think I'm going to slip away for a bit.'

She nodded, knowing exactly where I was going. She watched me.

I flicked my tongue nervously over my lips. 'Listen, you couldn't just tell David I felt a bit unwell, could you? Say I won't be long and – and that I'll make my own way home?'

She smiled. 'No, darling, I won't do that. You must make your own excuses.'

I flushed and looked at my feet, ashamed. 'OK, well I'll explain when I get home then,' I mumbled. It had begun already, hadn't it – the lying, the deceit; it was already getting underway. But I still wanted those moments, I thought desperately.

I bent down and kissed her cheek. 'Bye, Mummy.'

'Take care, Tess.'

'I will.'

I turned and disappeared into the crowd, giving her one last backward look as she sat watching me, framed by the window, hands clasped tightly in her lap. Then I slipped away.

Outside I flagged a taxi down.

'Where to, luv?'

I stared at the driver. Could I do this?

'Give us a clue, darlin'.'

'Cork Street, please,' I said decisively.

I jumped in. Yes, I could. I *could* do it, and I would. I sat in the back, my heart pounding with excitement. I wanted to run there, like I used to run on the beach when I was young, tearing along the London pavements, ducking and weaving through the crowds, but my ankle put paid to anything as impulsive and romantic as that so instead I leaned forward in my seat and urged my cab along.

'Come on, come on,' I muttered.

The driver's window shot back. 'Doing my best, luv, but these back streets are murder at this time of day. You'd be better off walking.'

We were stationary now. Would Patrick still be at the gallery? If not, where was he staying? Surely he wouldn't go straight back to Scotland? I looked around in desperation at the clogged streets. Damn it, I could hobble faster than this. I got out, pressed a fiver into the driver's hand and limped off like I'd never limped before. As I flashed past shop windows I caught sight of my reflection. It was still pretty strange sartorially speaking, but the odd thing was that my face had changed. It looked more alive, younger, more like – yes, more like Tessa Fergusson than Tessa Hamilton. Well there you are, I thought joyfully, sweeping my hair back off my forehead like I used to wear it when I was young. Perhaps I'd come back at last!

As I rounded the corner into Cork Street I literally bumped into a street-trader selling bright silk scarves.

'Ooops – sorry!'

I was about to move on, but a vivid length of fuchsia silk caught my eye and on an impulse, I bought it. It suited my mood. Grinning, I wound it around my neck and hurried off. I reached up and touched it as I neared the gallery. I'd remember this scarf, I thought. It would represent freedom, the first thing I bought after – after what, Tess? No decisions, remember, no plans, nothing remotely concrete.

I reached the gallery and stopped outside, peering through the window excitedly. It was dark, the lights had all been turned off except for a tiny lamp on the front desk and – oh God, it was empty. Everyone had gone. My heart stopped for a moment in panic, but then through the gloom at the back of the room, I spotted movement. Two men were talking, coming this way, and Patrick was definitely one of them. As they moved into the semi-light of the main front room I watched. Patrick's head was bowed; he was listening intently to the Frenchman. He stroked his chin thoughtfully, nodded, then threw his head back and flicked a piece of dark hair out of his eyes. I felt a sudden rush of – was it love? I didn't know, but whatever it was certainly had a proprietorial element to it. He could be mine again, I thought excitedly, if I wanted him. Here he was doing his own particular thing, painting his pictures, exhibiting them, seemingly on his own, except that with the wave of a wand I could be part of it, part of his life, if that's what I wanted. And the thing was that if I did, it would be *my* decision, *my* choice, no one else's and certainly not my father's.

So – how had he done, I wondered, at this, his first major exhibition? I glanced swiftly round the walls and for the first time saw the beautiful pictures which previously had been obscured by beautiful people. Landscapes and seascapes full of rich swirling colour abounded. As did the little red stickers. I puffed with pride. He'd done well.

Just then the Frenchman turned and gestured at a picture near the window and saw me standing there. His arm froze, high in the air in mid-gesticulation. His face darkened and he advanced towards me furiously.

'Pees off!' he shrieked, flicking me away with his hand like a fly. 'Go on, pees off, you mad crazy woman!'

I grinned and gave him a dinky little wave back. He looked around furiously, desperate no doubt for a large heavy object to hurl through the window at me. It was probably just as well Patrick wasn't a sculptor. In the end he settled for the telephone.

'I call the poleece!' he squeaked, brandishing the receiver.

Patrick glanced over at me and put a restraining hand on his arm. He had a quiet word with his hot-blooded friend who, looking only slightly mollified, did at least remove his hand from the telephone, only to clench it into a fist and shake it furiously at me instead. He then seized Patrick by the shoulders, kissed him passionately on both cheeks and then with a final throat-slitting gesture at me – a nice touch, I thought – turned and stalked back into the dark of his back room again.

Patrick smiled and came out to meet me.

'He'd like me dead,' I breathed in awe.

'Oh no, much worse. He'd like you strung up on his walls as a live exhibit for people to throw darts at.' He shut the gallery door behind him. 'So you're back.'

'I am. I came to tell you something.'

'You've made a decision already?'

'Nope, that's what I came to tell you. Come on.' I breezed off in front of him, my hurt ankle forgotten. He fell in step beside me and I turned and grinned up at him as we went. 'I'm not going to make a decision, Patrick, because you see I can't. And since I can't make it, I won't. So instead, I've got a new set of rules.'

Patrick raised his eyebrows. 'Go on.'

'First of all we make no plans. We have no heavyweight discussions and no demands are made by either party.'

He frowned. 'Ever? Isn't that slightly unrealistic?'

'It may be but I'm fed up with realism. I'm sick to the back teeth of it, if you must know. I'm fed up with all the soul-searching and agonizing it entails when all I really want to do is just *be* with you again, get to know you again, to talk, to laugh, to *enjoy* myself with you.'

His mouth twitched. 'I see. You're looking for undiluted frivolity, is that it?'

I laughed. 'Something like that. Something totally pleasurable, anyway. I'm fed up with being fed up. I want to laugh, for God's sake, not cry all the time!'

He shook his head, a wry grin on his face. 'No pleasure without pain, Tess.'

'That's as maybe but we can at least have the pleasure before we get to the pain, can't we? Not vice versa?' I glanced at my watch refusing to be deflated. 'And at the moment I've got precisely half an hour before I have to get back so let's make it snappy.'

He laughed. 'Right. So tell me, where exactly is this fun-packed half-hour to take place?'

431

'Oh, I don't know,' I said airily, enjoying myself already. 'Wherever you like, really. I had no fixed venue in mind but I suppose an attractive London park complete with bench and daisy-strewn grass would suit?'

'Fine. Limp on, Miss Macduff, I'm in your delightfully frivolous hands.'

Together we wandered towards Green Park. It was still warm and a mild evening breeze ruffled my hair. He didn't say anything as we walked but I was aware that he was looking at me.

'You look different,' he observed eventually.

'It's the scarf.' I put my hand up to my neck.

'No, more than that, something else. You look younger.'

I smiled. 'That's because I've changed my attitude. From now on, Patrick, I'm only allowing youthful thoughts to filter through my consciousness. I'm blocking out all the elderly, rational ones and going back to my instincts, which you've got to admit is much more fun. You see, the way I see it, there's no point in letting this situation get to us. We just have to let it run, because at the end of the day,' I threw up my hands, 'what will be will be, and any other timeworn clichés you care to mention.'

'You mean go with the flow? Play it by ear? Lap of the gods and all that?'

I laughed. 'Perfect.'

'*Que sera sera?*'

I grinned. 'Maybe just a bit *too* timeworn, and anyway, we had it earlier in English. Perhaps you missed it, but I think you're getting the idea. There's simply no point in torturing ourselves. We'll just throw ourselves into it with gusto and see what happens.'

'Gusto, eh? I like the sound of that.'

My heart was beating wildly now. I felt scared but very excited. We'd reached the park. The deckchairs had all been stacked away but we found a handy bench that still had a smattering of sunlight on it. As I sat down I could almost feel my eyes shining, every nerve tingling. Yes, this was great, this was a glorious feeling. For the first time in ages I felt really alive and it felt terrific. He sat down next to me.

'Is this OK? I mean I'm new to this game, Tess, all right if I sit next to you like this?'

'Perfect.'

'And pass the time of day?'

'Exactly.'

'And as long as there are no searching questions . . .'

'I'll tell you no despicable lies.'

'So we just – meet and chat?'

'Almost.' I looked up at him quickly.

He held my eyes. 'Ah. I wondered.'

I felt myself flushing. 'Crazy not to, don't you think? Especially since we're talking about instincts here. And anyway, if we don't, how on earth will we ever know?'

My heart pounded as I looked at him. I'd almost dared myself to say it, to be a brazen hussy, to be selfish, to seize my bit of life at whatever the cost. And I had, I'd done it.

He stared at me. 'So you won't come away with me but you'd like an affair, is that it?'

'That's it.'

For an awful moment I thought he was going to turn me down. Claim his love was too high, too moral, too pure, that he could only exist on a more elevated, exclusive plane, that it was all or nothing with him. Then I saw his mind begin to whir in a different direction. Because after all, an affair is only despicable if one is not involved.

'I'll stay here in London,' he said quietly, thinking as he spoke. 'If I can paint in Italy I can paint here. I'll rent a studio, with a couple of rooms, maybe even a balcony. In Chelsea perhaps, with a view of the river. For the moment though, we can go to a hotel. I'm booked in at Claridges. We can go there.'

I gulped. A flat in Chelsea. Claridges. Why did such smart locations suddenly sound so . . . tacky? Horrified, I felt my bravado slipping, my frivolity ebbing away and taking – oh my God – my libido with it! No, no, come back, I thought desperately. I can do this, I know I can, I can have an affair! I can go to a hotel, piece of cake, honestly, and anyway I have to because otherwise – otherwise how on earth will I ever know? How on earth will I ever get him out of my system?

'Patrick, let's not talk about that now,' I said quickly. 'That can all be worked out later, can't it? Can't we just – well, enjoy being here together, for a few more minutes? I have to get back soon.'

He smiled and slid his hand along the back of the bench and nodded. 'Sure.'

I stared out at the evening haze over Green Park, breathing heavily as his hand stroked my hair. So. An affair, eh, Tess? I shut my eyes trying to block out the word, trying not to let it spoil this moment. I felt his warm hand thread through my hair to the back of my neck, and after a while, it was all I could feel. The soft caressing, the exquisite lingerings. My body seemed to turn to liquid jelly. Bliss. I could hear myself breathing, in fact I was breathing so hard it was snorting out of my nostrils like a dragon. I seemed to have far too much air all of a sudden, but yes, this was definitely more like it. Let's have no more talk of hotels and flats, Patrick. Let's have no more planning, no more conniving, let's just encourage the passion to sneak up on us and sweep us off our feet, away and down into the abyss until we've fallen and it's much too late. Until it's not our fault. Let's take refuge in a grand passion, let's be overtaken by events, by the power of something much stronger than our intellects, so that in the end – oooh, yes, that's wonderful, keep on doing that, Patrick – so that in the end they can all just throw their hands up in despair and say, 'Well, the girl just simply . . . couldn't . . . help it . . .'

His hand slipped round from the back of my neck and turned my face towards his. One finger stroked my cheek. I gasped, whinnied almost – embarrassingly – all my senses sizzling with desire. He gazed down at me but still he didn't kiss me, he just looked, watched, drinking me in, and not just my face but all of me, my shoulders, my hands, my arms – up and down roved his eyes as if he wanted to roll back twelve years all in one glance. I tingled all over; it was as if his hands were caressing me. I began to tremble, my toes curled, my blood pumped. Come on, come ON, I urged, I can't take much more of this, when – suddenly, he froze. He frowned. Looked down at my feet. I blinked. What? Why had he suddenly got stuck down there? What was so compelling about my feet?

'Your shoes,' he muttered.

My shoes? God, what about them?

'What about them?' I breathed, still staring hard into his eyes, willing him to carry on. I was beginning to panic now. Come on, Patrick, get on with it! I've decided to do it now and it was no mean decision, I can tell you, so sodding well get on with it before I lose my nerve!

'I've seen them somewhere before.'

Realizing that the moment was totally blown, I joined him in the contemplation of my footwear. Oh yes, charming. My filthy old red loafers complete with a cut down one side to get my foot into. Not at all the thing for smart London streets or even a funeral for that matter, but quite simply the only shoes I could get my swollen foot into.

'Russell and Bromley,' I muttered into his ear, nibbling it briefly. 'Last year's sale, thirty-nine ninety-nine.' Now come on, Patrick, let's go!

'Yes, that's it. Down by the river.'

I stopped in mid-nibble. What on earth did he mean?

His face had become terribly pale. He took his hand off my neck. Drew it back along the bench. His eyes were still on the shoes.

'Yes, outside the hut, that night when I –' Suddenly he turned to me aghast, his eyes incredulous. 'It was you, wasn't it?'

I stared at him. My mouth was dropping open now of its own accord.

'It was you I saw through the window, thrashing around in Willie's hut that night. It was you, Tess, *wasn't it?*'

Chapter Twenty-seven

I stared at him, aghast. After a moment of sheer immobilized terror, my mind went into frantic overdrive. It scuttled around like a pin-ball machine, looking for a way out. Had I perhaps lent the shoes to someone, to Laura perhaps, or Penny? Could either of them have kicked them off with gay abandon outside the hut and then frolicked around in the nude inside it? Both would fit the Willie bill, but . . . No. *He knew it was me.* His blue, piercing eyes were the trap and I was the rat. All of a sudden I had a violent desire to be watching *The Antiques Roadshow* at 42, Pelham Road with a gin and tonic in one hand and a packet of Phineas Fogg's in the other.

'It's not what you think,' I whispered.

He gave a thin smile. 'I see. Not what I think, eh? What is it then, exactly?' His face had gone very pale under his tan.

'Well,' I struggled, 'Willie and I – it wasn't planned, it just sort of happened.' God, this was awful. 'I bumped into him down by the river one evening and we just sort of – slipped into it.' I winced – that sounded terrible! Far too explicit. I hastened on. 'But the thing is I changed my mind and we never – well, we never actually did it.'

'Like hell!' he scoffed.

'It's true, I swear it! We just larked around a bit, then fell asleep together.'

'Oh, sweet,' he sneered. 'A little slumber party after some energetic nude wrestling.'

'Look, I know it sounds unlikely, but it's the truth, I didn't –'

'Tess, I saw you! I was there, remember? I saw you with my own eyes! And whether you did the dirty deed or not, frankly, hardly matters, does it? You certainly weren't having a cosy cup of Ovaltine!'

'No,' I admitted, 'I wasn't, and I'm not proud of myself, it was a ghastly mistake, but – well, that's all it was, Patrick. A mistake, and to be honest, I don't even know why it happened. It just did!'

God, this was embarrassing.

Patrick's top lip curled in disgust. 'You fancied him.'

I shrugged uncertainly. 'Maybe it was just lust, but there was something else. Something . . .' I bit my lip. Suddenly it all flooded back – of course! I'd been crying – I'd been upset about Patrick.

'It was because of you, because you went off with Josie!'

'Ah, so it was my fault?' His mouth was set in a thin line now and a muscle was pumping away in his cheek.

'Well, indirectly, yes. I was jealous, and when Willie found me I was crying, and I suppose I just sort of – rebounded into his arms.'

He stared at me coldly. I licked my lips nervously.

'Look, Patrick, it was just sex, OK? And it's not as if we went the whole way. And anyway, there was nothing meaningful about it so what difference does it make?' I said this desperately, aware that I was trying to brazen it out in a laddish sort of way. It lasted about half a second before one lad shrivelled under the other lad's penetrating blue gaze.

I stared down at the grass feeling my face flame, fiddling with the fringe of the pink scarf in my lap. There was a terrible silence.

'Is this really you speaking, Tess?' he said at length, a slight tremor in his voice. 'Tessa Fergusson? Sweet, innocent Tess of one boyfriend and one husband? "Just sex"? Since when have you been so free with your sexual favours? So keen to resort to nothing meaningful?'

I stared at my shoes, those damn shoes.

'What are you, just another frustrated housewife who can't wait to get her leg over with the resident holiday stud because her husband's not paying her enough attention or something? That's why they all go to bed with Willie you know – *Willie*! Of all people, he's renowned for it – Jesus it's a local joke! How many London women will he get this summer . . . and now you,' he said bitterly. 'Another notch in his belt.'

'I've told you,' I muttered. 'I'm not another notch, and anyway I didn't go looking for sex, I was just upset and Willie just happened to be there. He comforted me, he –'

'Shagged you? Oh yes, I can see how that must have been very comforting, very comforting indeed,' he sneered.

I gazed down at my hands. How awful. We were rowing. He didn't believe me. I could feel him slipping away, distancing himself.

'Patrick, I'm sorry,' I pleaded. 'Can't you just forgive me? It happened, it was a mistake and I'm sorry, but what more can I say apart from apologize? I mean, these things happen. Look at you with your Italian harem, your Marias and your Lucianas!'

'These things happen to men and a certain type of woman,' he said coldly. 'Women who look for sexual release with any Tom, Dick or Harry. They do not happen to women like you, or so I thought. Clearly I was wrong. Tell me, how often have you felt this urge?' His face was very grim now.

I boggled. 'Never! Good heavens, never, I'm too flipping knackered most of the time. I've never slept with anyone other than you and David!'

'I said how often have you felt the urge, Tess, not how often have you done it,' he said harshly.

I looked at him over in the far corner of the bench. His black hair highlighted his white face and his eyes looked strangely pale. It was as if emotion was wiping away all the colour.

'I don't,' I whispered, 'feel the urge.' God, why was I whispering? And why on earth did this remind me of something?

'Don't lie,' he spat, his lip curling again. 'You feel it all the time, don't you? You lie in your marriage bed night after night dreaming about it, about doing it with other men – any man! You fantasize, don't you? Well, let me tell you something, Tess – that's tantamount to the real thing. You might just as well go out there and get your kit off and get on with it!'

I stared at him. He was right, of course – I'd done a terrible thing, a dreadful thing, but his reaction seemed over the top, somehow. Suddenly I realized who he reminded me of. Yes, it was my father. The hectoring tone of voice, the

440

stream of vile invective. I glanced back at him. Well – why not? said a little voice in my head. He is after all your father's son, isn't he? A wave of revulsion threatened to wash over me. I looked away, told myself not to be ridiculous. This was Patrick, my Patrick, and he was justifiably furious. God, any man would be in his position. I'd just let him simmer down a bit. I'd sit here quietly, wouldn't say anything for a minute. I avoided his eye and stared straight ahead.

Just in front of us two little girls were playing on the gravel path, picking up the stones in handfuls and throwing them into the air. A woman, not their mother, a nanny possibly, was admonishing them, telling them to stop, brushing the dirt off their hands. I was aware that Patrick was staring at me but I concentrated like mad on those girls, looking to see if their hands were clean, if their dresses were dirty.

'Just the two of us, Laura said,' he muttered quietly, breaking the silence. 'Just David and me. Bullshit.'

I swung round, frowned. 'Laura? What are you talking about? When did she say that?'

'And now I find that there have been others. Lots of others, no doubt. And that you're no different from Penny and all the other sexed-up little tarts who can't wait for their husbands to go to work so they can slip their knickers off and hop into bed with the first travelling salesman or plumber or window-cleaner who takes their fancy.'

'Penny's not like that,' I said, horrified. 'And neither am I!'

'You're all the same,' he muttered. 'Scum.'

I gasped. 'What?' I gazed at his profile, hard and uncompromising. Rather shakily I found my voice.

'So one little indiscretion changes everything, does it? Suddenly I'm a sex-crazed tart. From being the only woman you've ever wanted I've rather unexpectedly plunged into the abyss. I'm a scarlet woman, fit only for Hellfire, is that it?'

He didn't answer, just sat staring into space, eyes narrowed.

'Look at me, Patrick,' I quavered. 'I'm still the same person.'

'Except Willie's had you,' he said bitterly.

I gazed at him, then nodded slowly. 'Ah yes, that's what it's all about, isn't it? Who's had what, little boys with their toys. Willie's had this one so it's not so good any more. And of course,' I went on, my voice trembling, 'you've always had all the best toys, haven't you? Always had every woman you ever wanted. God, you've turned them away in droves – Penny, Josie, half the Italian female population, no doubt – they all fell for the handsome, scowling, poor little rich boy and you could take your pick, couldn't you? Except for me. I was the one that got away. You wanted me, not because I was the best, but because you couldn't *have* me!'

'I loved you, Tess,' he said grimly.

I noted the past tense, whether deliberate or not, with a sharp intake of breath.

'If you loved me,' I went on quietly, 'this wouldn't matter as much as it clearly does. But this isn't about love, is it? It's about obsession. And about winning. But now that the prize has been tampered with, now that it's soiled, it's not so covetable, is it? You've had a space in your trophy cabinet for twelve years. Now you discover that the cup is a little bit tarnished and it's not the same thing, is it?'

He didn't reply.

'That's not love, Patrick, that's a spoiled child completing his collection.'

I stood up shakily and wound my scarf around my neck. He looked up quickly.

'Where are you going?'

'Home.'

He stared at me, wondering if I was calling his bluff or if I meant it. I meant it. He licked his lips. There was a silence.

'Look, all right,' he faltered eventually. 'I'm sorry. Sit down and we'll talk this through sensibly. I probably did overreact, but you did rather spring this on me.'

'I didn't spring anything on you,' I said coolly. 'You spotted my shoes.'

'Yes, well, whatever. I'm sorry, OK? I was surprised, that's all. Shocked.' He flicked his dark hair back from his face. 'But I think I can overlook it.'

I stared down at him. 'Well, I can't.'

'What?'

'Overlook your reaction.'

'My reaction!' He laughed. 'For God's sake, my reaction was perfectly understandable under the circumstances! I'm a red-blooded heterosexual male and I'm in love with you so I'm bound to be as jealous as hell, aren't I? What did you expect me to do, pat you on the back and say – terrific! So Willie's slipped you a length! Good on yer girl, have another crack at him next year?'

'No, but I didn't expect a stream of misogynist abuse either.'

'Misogynist? Me? Oh, don't be ridiculous.'

'Oh yes, you are,' I said warmly. 'Thank God, though.'

'Thank God for what?'

'Thank God you saw my shoes, that we had this conversation, that it's not too late.'

Patrick was on his feet now; he grabbed my hands. I pulled away, but he lunged at me and caught the ends of my scarf, drawing me towards him.

'I'm sorry,' he said desperately. 'Don't go, I really am sorry. I just couldn't bear to think you were like all the rest, but you're not really, I know that.'

'All the rest?'

'Oh everyone,' he said impatiently, 'Penny, Luciana, Kirsten – God, my mother even!' He gave a short hysterical laugh.

'Your mother?' I stared at him.

He backtracked quickly. 'No. Nothing. Forget I said that, I'm just – well, I'm upset.'

His *mother*? I gazed at him. He knew. He knew about Madelaine, that she'd had an affair, and he'd known all along. He'd known when he was just a boy, when I didn't know. When it would have mixed me up too, made me a bit crazy. When he was so hurt and rebellious, so dark and brooding, staring out to sea, loathing his parents, he'd known! Known he wasn't his father's son. But had he known about Daddy? No, he can't have done. And I certainly wasn't going to tell him. Suddenly I felt terribly sorry for him. For the pain and hurt he must have been through. His father hating him because he knew he wasn't his son and Patrick hating the pair of them for making it so. I felt compassion for him but I didn't feel love.

He was still holding on tightly to my scarf. 'Patrick, please let me go.'

He stared at me, knowing I meant it, that I was really going. I saw him tighten his grip. I stepped back, but as I did so, could feel the scarf, which was wound twice round my neck, tighten.

'Let me go,' I said quietly.

He blinked. I saw him glance down at the scarf in his hands. Then he looked up at me. All of a sudden the park seemed very quiet, very still. It was getting late now. Most people had gone home. My heart began to hammer. I licked my lips.

'Patrick, let go of my scarf and we'll sit down again,' I whispered. 'I promise I won't go home yet. We'll just sit and talk, OK?'

I looked into his eyes. Suddenly I felt very scared. There was something I didn't recognize there. And then I realized there was an awful lot I didn't know about this man. This man I'd known for just a month, twelve years ago. I gulped, but only just: the scarf was quite tight. I swivelled my eyes right then left, wondering if anyone would hear if I screamed, wondering if I should yank the scarf from his hands and make a run for it. Suddenly he let go.

His hands fell to his sides and his head dropped in defeat. I stepped back hurriedly, unwinding the scarf from my neck in relief. He hadn't hurt me but it had been quite tight.

He sat down on the bench again, his back hunched. My

heart was pounding. I wanted to go, I badly wanted to go, but I made myself stay.

'Do you want to talk?' I whispered.

For a moment he didn't answer, then he looked up with a strange, unnatural smile.

'No, there'll be no more talk today, Tess. If it's all the same to you I'll resist the offer of therapy, the few minutes of park-bench counselling. You've already heard more about me in the last few minutes than I care to reveal. It wouldn't do for you to hear any more – you might get me locked up or at the very least committed to long stretches on the psychiatrist's couch.' He gave a twisted smile. 'Go on, be off with you. Go back to David and your children.'

I looked down at him sitting there, shoulders hunched, hands tightly clasped. His hair was really quite heavily flecked with grey from this angle; funny how I'd never noticed it before. Suddenly he looked smaller too; thinner, older and his fashionable Armani suit looked exactly what it was. Expensive packaging designed to make the older man look younger. I had a lump in my throat, a lump of sadness, but at the same time never had I wanted to be somewhere else so badly.

I looked around. The park was nearly deserted now. Unfriendly, alien territory. I felt an awful wave of horror. What was I *doing* here, anyway? Why wasn't I at home, putting the children to bed, reading them stories, cooking David's supper? My hand went to my mouth, I felt sickened by myself. I looked down at his shoes – trendy, black Italian loafers and thought of David's dark brown English brogues. I fiddled with the strap on my handbag, scuffed the dirt with my toe.

'Well, I will go then actually, if that's all right.'

He gave me a wounded smile. 'Of course it's all right. You're free to do exactly as you please, you know that.'

I nodded. 'Right. Goodbye then.'

There was a pause.

'Goodbye, Mrs Hamilton.'

Perhaps it was a last-ditch attempt. Perhaps he said it to conjure up visions of bourgeois respectability, a straitjacket I'd never break out of now, but if that was the case, it backfired. All it conjured up for me was home, glorious home, my children, my husband, my garden, my security, my nest, and my dazzling, mind-boggling stupidity at putting it all at risk. I turned on my heel and walked quickly out of the park.

I went as fast as I could, breathing deeply, filling my lungs with clean fresh air. As I went through the park gate I paused to let the two little girls and their nanny pass through ahead of me. They smiled up cheekily as they pushed on ahead, and I found myself almost reeling as I watched them go. I had to hang on to the railings for support for a second. I touched my forehead briefly with my hand. Was I mad? Insane? How could I have been such a fool? Risked it all, the children, the whole fabric of my life for a man who'd just parachuted back into my life after twelve years of absence? A man who, because I'd loved him then, I assumed I still loved now? I walked on in a daze. But then, I'd always worked on that assumption, hadn't I? In some kind of warped, crazy way I'd assumed that because no conclusion had ever been reached, we must still be in love, back there in that same position or thereabouts, simmering away gently on the back burner, ready to bubble up into a boiling passion at a moment's notice.

I shook my head. What a fool I'd been. It wasn't as if I'd really known him properly then and I certainly didn't know him now – and how can you love someone you don't know? And what about the bits I *did* know now – what about those bits that reminded me of – horrors – my father?

I clattered down the steps to Green Park Tube. No, no, come on, Tess, that's not altogether fair. You're just trying to make your father's cap fit Patrick, force the jigsaw into place, make the picture more grisly than it really is but – all the same, I pondered, biting my lip, it was odd, wasn't it, the way Patrick had that same desire to control as Daddy did? The way he'd held my scarf back then, for instance? I was quite sure now that he wouldn't have hurt me . . . but it was enough to frighten me, and he must have known I was scared. And that strange way he had of suddenly spitting venom – just like Daddy, as if it was all simmering away inside waiting to spew out at a moment's notice, and that awful, warped way of looking at women, madonnas or tarts, and the way he – Suddenly I stopped, shocked at myself.

Good heavens, Tess, steady on. I mean, half an hour ago you were ready to jump into bed with the man and now he's a bully, a tyrant and a misogynist? I walked slowly onto the platform. Wasn't *I* the one who was overreacting a teeny bit here? How come I didn't feel more of a wrench? A spot of – oh gosh I'll always have a soft spot for Patrick – wouldn't that be more normal? Yes, perhaps it would, but I didn't. All I thought was – thank God for a lucky escape.

I blinked in astonishment at this revelation and stepped onto a Tube bound for Earl's Court as if for all the world it were bound for Damascus. Yes, how odd – he almost *repulsed* me. I sank down in a seat and leaned my head back on the window. How extraordinary. He'd rattled my cage for twelve long years, but finally, and in a matter of minutes, the rattling had stopped. All was quiet. He'd gone for ever. Relief flooded through me, euphoria even, and it was so overpowering that I laughed out loud.

'Ha ha ha!'

I sat up and looked around with a grin. Yes, I was certainly getting some odd looks from my fellow commuters. The Indian lady opposite, swaddled in silks with her incongruous M&S cardigan over the top was staring at me in terror, her husband beside her was looking boot-faced in the opposite direction and the young girl next to him was peering nervously at me over the top of her *Woman's Own*, twiddling her long bleached hair. All of them were clearly wondering how long it would be until the train pulled into the next station and they could nip into the adjacent carriage. I wanted to lean forward, smile and say: 'It's OK, I'm not a nutter. I'm just wildly, ecstatically, deliriously happy! You see, I'm shot of him now and I can get on with my life!'

Yes, the best thing about all this, I acknowledged joyfully, was that I could get on with everything now, without the ghost of Patrick Cameron constantly hanging over me. Because however much I'd always denied his presence, I knew he'd always been there in the background of my mind, putting me off my stride, holding me back from doing the things I'd always intended to do. Like writing articles and children's books, the ones I'd had in my head since I was nineteen, the ones I'd always meant to write but had somehow felt were too wrapped up with my dreams of Patrick. Yes, subconsciously I'd shied away from all that. I'd had some misguided notion that writing in the spare room in Putney wouldn't be quite the same as writing on a sun-drenched terrace in Florence with my lover painting masterpieces in the studio beyond, that it would be a pale shadow of my creative life as I'd imagined it. But I knew now that that was crap. I'd put my life on hold for no good reason and now I wanted to get cracking.

The train rattled along the tracks and my mind rattled with it. I'd write while Hugo and Clemmie were at school. I'd clear out the spare room, make it into an office, and when they came home I'd spend more time with them. I didn't need an au pair! With two children at school it was crazy, I could do it all myself. I'd enjoy it, throw myself into it, take them round London on buses, go to museums, teach them to cook – all the things I'd meant to do with my children but somehow had never got round to. And I wanted to spend more time with David too. I didn't want us to flop exhausted in front of the telly every night with our M&S suppers on our laps, I wanted to eat in the kitchen, have candles even, make an effort, do a cookery course, test out the recipes on him and not sneer at all that but *enjoy* it. Enjoy all those things I'd secretly boycotted thinking they'd make me dull, suburban, a housewife, so very married.

I hastened up the steps at Putney Bridge. My ankle hurt like hell now. As I limped past a pub I spotted a bin outside and instinctively tore off the pink scarf and threw it in. I wouldn't be needing *that* any more, would I? As I rounded the corner into Pelham Road, I stopped for a moment gazing up at our house. There it was, slap bang in the middle on the left-hand side, pale yellow with a bright blue front door and a black wrought-iron balcony above. A huge, gnarled old wisteria snaked all over the front, and in the front garden a flurry of roses – my roses – pink, white and red, frothed over the small brick wall. God, it was pretty. And whenever people had told me so, I'd looked at them in surprise thinking – is it? Hmm, yes I suppose it is, but after all it's only a semi in a row of semis, it's no big deal. Suddenly, I could see that it was. It was a humungously big deal. It was *home*.

I walked on slowly, staring at it. There was still so much to do, of course. I'd always meant to paint the little railings on the wall outside, grow a clematis round the door, put pots of geraniums on the balcony. And inside, the drawing-room curtains were still minus a pelmet – they'd been like that for three years. Jane Churchill had a sale next week. I'd go, queue up if needs be and – oh, Clemmie's bedroom, I'd always meant to make her a quilt. I'd do that too now, collect scraps of fabric, enjoy doing it! Oh yes, I decided happily, I was going to crawl along in the slow, safe lane of domesticity from now on. I was going to throw off the horrors of that fast, dangerous, adulterous lane, the one I'd so nearly swerved into. I wanted to write, to bake, make marmalade, be on the school committee – I hesitated. No, not that. I couldn't *quite* bring myself to do that . . .

I hastened up the garden path and opened the front

door. David was sitting on the hall chair, telephone in hand. He quickly put it down when he saw me. He stood up. Flushed.

'Tess! Where the devil have you been?'

'David, I'm so sorry,' I gasped, falling against him and wrapping my arms round his waist. 'Please – don't ask me where I've been. I don't want you to ask me anything, I just want you to know that everything's all right now, everything's fine!'

I held on tight, burying my head in his soft, lambswool shoulder, breathing in his smell. Oh God, I was married to such a nice man – how come I'd never seen that before? It was as if I'd always had a smear over the lens, and the smear had been Patrick, always obscuring my view. But now I'd wiped him away; in ten, glorious minutes I'd wiped away twelve years of grime – but how awful that it had obscured the most important years of my life!

'Delighted to hear it, but where have you been?'

'Oh, just walking,' I said breathlessly. 'Sorry I deserted you at the funeral, I just needed to get away.' I glanced at the telephone. 'Who was that?'

'Oh, no one. Wrong number. Good God, look at your ankle, Tess – it's swollen up like an elephant's! Have you been limping round London on that? You are a fool. Come on, come and sit down.'

I grinned and let him support me down the hall to the kitchen.

'I know – a mad, stupid fool but I promise you, David, I intend to put all my foolish ways behind me now, once and for all.'

I lowered myself into a chair and looked around the

kitchen. Blue and yellow, very pretty. Good choice, Tess. How odd, it was as if I was seeing it for the first time. God, that doorframe could do with a lick of paint though, and look at the state of those windows . . .

'Tea?' David reached for the kettle.

'Please.' I sank back happily into the wheelback chair. Yes, please. Tea, comfort, home, you. I watched his back as he filled the kettle, reached up for the teapot on the top shelf. How like him just to make a pot of tea. Not a scene, not to give me the third degree, not insist on knowing exactly where I'd been, just a pot of tea. I felt a rush of love.

'David?'

'Hmm?' He was staring blankly into the caddy. 'Extraordinary isn't it, how no one can replace the tea-bags when they run out? Everyone's capable of taking tea-bags *out* but not of putting fresh ones *in*. Why not get a new packet out of the cupboard, I ask myself, or is that too much of a radical concept?'

I grinned. 'Beats me, darling.'

He was on his hands and knees now, rifling around in the store cupboard. He stood up. 'It's no good, the war of attrition is still raging in that larder. Everyone's waiting for someone else to buy the sodding things. It'll just have to be coffee.'

'Fine, fine, darling. Just *listen* a minute.'

'What?' He reached for the Nescafé.

'Forget the bloody coffee.' I limped over and put my arms round him. He turned. I smiled, reached up and stroked the back of his neck. 'Why don't we just go to bed?'

I stretched up on tiptoe and kissed his surprised mouth. 'Hmm? Does that sound like a good idea? Why don't we just go upstairs, take our clothes off and –'

'She's in my bed again!' bellowed an angry voice behind us.

We jumped. I turned around and saw Hugo standing in the passageway, indignant in his pyjamas.

'Get her out,' he ordered. 'Right now! She's brought all her stupid dolls in with her and that one with the hole in its bottom has peed on my pillow!'

We sighed and unclinched.

'I'll go,' said David. 'Come on, Hugo. Clemmie!' he yelled as he mounted the stairs. 'Get back to your own bed!'

Hugo followed grimly then stopped and turned back.

'Were you two kissing?'

'Trying to,' I agreed.

'Oh yuk.' He looked suitably disgusted and went on upstairs. Then he stopped again and popped his head through the banisters. 'Mummy?'

'What?'

'If you're going to do it, don't shut the door like last time, OK? It's not fair.'

'Jesus,' I muttered. 'Just go to bed please, Hugo. NOW!'

I walked wearily back into the kitchen as the telephone rang. I sank down into a chair and picked it up.

'Tess, we have to talk,' said a cold voice.

I sighed. Oh hell, Laura. What an awful lot of ruffled feathers there were around at the moment. Last time I'd seen her was when I'd doused her in the gallery. That would all have to be smoothed out, of course, but although

I was very much in a sorting-out mood, now was actually not the time.

'Definitely,' I agreed, 'and Laura, I'm so sorry about all that. There really is quite a simple explanation, but I'm a bit busy at the moment. Could we –'

'*I'm* busy too!' she retorted, clearly trying to out-busy me. 'I can't talk either. But I'll see you tomorrow, in my lunch-hour. Twelve-thirty in the Harvey Nichols restaurant, all right?'

'Fine,' I said meekly. I knew I had to be meek, oh God I'd have to crawl.

'See you there,' she said grimly, 'and don't be late.'

I put the phone down and scratched my arm. Oh well, I thought sheepishly, I deserved all I got from her, I supposed. I looked bleakly round the kitchen. Heavens this place was a mess. Look at all that crap on the dresser – unopened letters, school reports, free magazines, socks, mouldy apple cores, headless dolls, and the bin was positively overflowing with rubbish. Didn't anybody think to take it out? Did they think Mary Poppins would just sail in and do it? I rolled up my sleeves and got to work. By the time David came back down I had my head in the oven and was scrubbing away for England.

'Won't be long,' I called from inside my Mr Muscle cage. 'Someone's cooked God knows *what* in here and just let it drip everywhere!' As if that someone, of course, hadn't been me.

'I'll just catch the news then,' came the muffled response.

Half an hour later I emerged, covered in muck and stinking of detergent, but my God I was happy. I folded my arms triumphantly. Yes, I was cleaning up all right.

This was definitely the life. I grinned, threw the cloth in the sink and went into the sitting room, just as Trevor McDonald was shuffling his papers and bidding me a very good night over his spectacles. David was sprawled in the armchair in front of him, fast asleep. I smiled. Oh well, that was the end of my romantic evening; there'd be no waking him now. He wouldn't stir till he'd had at least two hours of comatose slumber, and then he'd stagger up to bed at about midnight. I removed his glasses, turned the television off and went upstairs to bed.

Chapter Twenty-eight

The following morning I had every intention of embarking on some serious domesticity. That is, until I opened my cookery book. Practically every recipe seemed to begin with something like: *If you don't have a smoke-house . . .* or *Take two pints of fresh venison stock . . .*

'Bugger off,' I muttered, slamming it shut with irritation. The doorbell rang.

'Yes, I'm coming!' I barked as the ringing persisted. 'Oh Josie, it's you.'

She fell through the front door and ultimately onto me. I staggered back as she hung on to my shoulders, gasping with relief and looking rather wild about the eyes.

'Tess! Oh God, it's wonderful to see you. I can't tell you what a terrible time I've had!'

She staggered past me into the kitchen and sank down on a chair, panting hard. Then she stood up again and instantly jettisoned rucksack, hold-all, carrier bags, and layer upon layer of sweat-shirts and jackets until she'd swiftly transformed the place into an Aussie youth hostel. I followed her through and found a chair amidst the sea of shell-suit paraphernalia. She sank down again and lit a shaky cigarette.

'Jesus Christ,' she gasped, 'your bloody cousin! She made me wash the kitchen floor twice a day, and not with a mop but on my hands and knees.' She sucked hard on a Marlboro Light, eyes wide with horror. 'She wouldn't let me smoke and I had to bloody well cook supper every night and even scrub their front step! That's positively Dickensian, isn't it? Jeeze, I thought she'd have me up the chimney next!'

I tutted and murmured something sympathetic, at the same time reflecting that actually, this was what all of us lily-livered employers would *like* these Aussie girls to do, but only Penny had the guts to do it. Front step, eh? Kitchen floor? Good on yer, Pen.

'*And* I had to clean the fridge out and wash the bath and *dry* it too, for heaven's sake – and dust all her poxy china ornaments and cut tomatoes into flipping water lilies *and* I had to look after Leonora all day long, too! That woman didn't lift a frigging finger!'

'Terrible,' I muttered, patting her hand.

'Talk about the white slave trade. If I'd had to stay there a moment longer I would have reported her to the Australian High Commission.'

She stubbed her cigarette out on one of my best saucers and flung her Doc Martened foot up on a chair. She gazed around appreciatively.

'God, it's nice to be back, Tess. Penny's place is so bloody antiseptic and perfect and up-yer-bum. This place is – well, it's lived in, isn't it? It's a real home.'

I looked around despondently, realizing that despite my efforts to the contrary there was already a tottering pile of washing up in the sink, a pile of children's pyjamas under the table, a runner bean in the milk jug and a Power Ranger face down in the butter. I rescued him and tossed him wearily in the sink, secretly yearning for a little more up-yer-bumness myself.

'All right if I catch Richard and Judy before I pick Clemmie up? I haven't seen it for a week, she wouldn't *let* me!' Josie informed me incredulously.

'Sure, sure,' I said weakly, watching her pert little Levi'd backside undulate casually into the playroom. 'But perhaps before it starts you could tidy the children's bedrooms? If you've got time, that is.' I scratched my neck hopefully.

She plucked an apple from the fruit bowl and consulted her watch. 'Nah. It's just about to start, but tell you what, if I get time I'll have a go later, OK?'

So saying, she sank into the sofa, swung her long denim legs up over the arm and sighed happily. Then she zapped on the telly with the remote control and sank her perfect white teeth into the apple. She smiled up at me.

'It's *so* nice to be back, Tess,' she informed me again warmly, as if perhaps I should be pleased and proud. Then she turned back to the television.

Oh is it, I thought grimly, folding my arms and watching from the doorway. A certain amount of steel was creeping into my soul. Yes, well enjoy it while you can, Josie, because nice though you are your days here are numbered. This house is poised for some radical changes and jettisoning the eldest of my three children is going to be one of them!

I stalked back into the kitchen and set about tidying up the mess, *her* mess, until my eye caught the clock. Half-past eleven! Jesus! I dropped the dustpan and brush in horror. I was still in my dressing gown, I hadn't had a bath yet and if I didn't get a move on I was going to be late for

Laura and our lunch-date. I flew upstairs in a panic, jumped into the shower, threw on the first thing that came to hand and blundered downstairs and out of the house.

Forty minutes later I burst through the swing doors into the terribly tasteful Fifth Floor Restaurant at Harvey Nichols, panting and cursing, looking like somebody's grandmother and at least ten minutes late.

'Sorry,' I gasped to my unamused sister who was perched neatly at a corner table.

Her white cotton shirt looked crisp and flawless, her hair was silky and unruffled and her distinctly tight lips were leaving only the faintest trace of lipstick on her low tar cigarette. A tiny blue suede bag was swinging delicately from a chain on the back of her chair. I blinked. Was that hers or her dolly's, I wondered?

As I sat down opposite her, I flung my own, huge leather sack onto the floor. Unfortunately I hadn't done the zip up and as it hit the metallic tiles, out popped quite a few things of an extremely intimate and feminine nature. They instantly rolled away in all directions, intent, it seemed, on having a good old roll around on this nice shiny surface. I dropped to my knees with a 'Bugger!' and grovelled around under occupied tables retrieving them, an appropriate menstrual blush enlivening my features.

'They do a discreet little travelling case for those,' Laura informed me patronizingly as I clumsily stuffed them back in my bag. 'I discovered it when I was about sixteen.'

'Yes I know, been meaning to get one,' I muttered, straightening up, still feeling distinctly self-conscious. I glanced across at her.

'Oh! Sorry, Laura, how are you?' I leaned forwards to

peck the soft, flawless cheek that I suddenly realized she'd been resolutely proffering since I arrived. And I thought she'd just got a cricked neck or something. Oh well, at least we were still on kissing terms.

'Very well, thank you,' she replied icily.

I flopped back into my chair again feeling decidedly hot and sweaty now. I billowed my shirt about to get some air in.

'Phew!' I gasped, looking around. Then I stopped and sank into my Perrier. No, it wasn't really a 'phew' sort of place, was it?

I peered over the rim of my glass. The clientele here was distinctly ladies wot lunched, not ladies wot sweated. There was also a fair smattering of smart young gels with their mummies, the former looking faintly bored but not *too* bored, since Mummy did after all control what went into those smart carrier bags plumped down beside the designer chairs, and one wouldn't want to get on the wrong side of her until a great deal more trendy gear had been safely stashed away. Instead, these expensive beauties were restricting themselves to gazing superciliously around, hoping perhaps to see a girl from the lower fourth whom they could studiously ignore and at the same time doing a lot of flicking back of long silky tresses. It occurred to me that Clemmie would be doing the 'flick' before she was much older; in fact I wondered nervously if I hadn't spotted an embryonic 'flick' just the other day.

'Warm radicchio and goat's cheese salad and then the polenta, please,' murmured Laura.

I looked up to see another potential flicker standing right beside me. Crikey, they all looked the same, didn't they, these well-bred girls – except that this one had a white apron on, a pad in her hand and pale blue china eyes that looked even less friendly than Laura's. She also had a distinct – 'I may have failed my A's at St Mary's Wantage but I'm only working at Harvey Nicks until Daddy sorts out something at Sotheby's' – look about her. She obviously found it difficult to talk as well as pass exams because she simply raised her eyebrows enquiringly at me. I gazed back at her, wondering if there was anything behind those blank eyes besides a pile of old *Tatler* magazines, an Ascot race card and a Henley Regatta Members' Enclosure badge.

'Shall I order for you?' asked Laura, as if I'd never been to a restaurant before.

I jumped. 'Oh! No thanks. I'll um, well, I'll have some wine for starters,' I blurted oafishly.

Laura smiled. 'A glass of Sancerre,' she murmured to her friend the waitress as if I'd just come over on the boat from Bog-Land.

Her friend the waitress smiled back and nodded, full of understanding.

I rallied quickly. 'No, not Sancerre, I'll have a half-bottle of house red actually and –' I ran my eye down the hyperbolic menu '– I'm not sure I'm in the mood for fashion-victim fodder today so could I have a cheese omelette and chips, please?'

Pale blue eyes blinked. 'Aim not actually sure if we –'

'You've got eggs in the kitchen, haven't you?' I enquired brightly. 'And surely some cheese and potatoes?'

'Oh, yah but –'

'Perfect.' I snapped the menu shut and handed it back

462

to her with a fixed smile that distinctly said, 'Don't get patronizing with *me*, Blue Eyes, or I'll order off the beaten track, all right?' She flushed and stalked back to the kitchen.

'You're not in a Little Chef now, you know,' said Laura frostily.

'More's the pity,' I said briskly, feeling braver by the minute. No, I would *not* be intimidated by a seventeen-year-old waitress, or by my little sister, come to that.

'So what's this all about then?' I demanded, folding my arms.

Laura stared at me incredulously. 'What's it all about! You've got a nerve. God, the last time I saw you, you threw wine in my face and accused me of having an affair with Patrick, you tell *me* what it's all about!'

She had a point. I caved in dramatically. 'Ah, yes, right. Sorry. I forgot about that.'

'Well, I haven't, so come on, what's going on? Are you having an affair with him or what?'

It was a relief to answer in the 'or what' category. 'No,' I said firmly. 'I'm not. It's fair to say I was considering it –'

'Panting for it.'

'But I've dismissed the whole idea out of hand. There is absolutely nothing going on between me and Patrick Cameron and there never will be now. The whole thing was preposterous in the first place and –' Suddenly I dropped the pompous tone and looked at her beseechingly. 'Look, Laura, I know I owe you an explanation but to be honest I haven't really got one. I'm off him, that's all, for various reasons but I don't want to talk about it right now. If I just said I was totally devoted to David and the children and I'll never look at another man as long as I live, would you let me off? Please?'

She stubbed her cigarette out and smiled snidely. 'I see. A born again married woman.'

I shrugged. 'If you like.'

'Ready to play Happy Families again.'

I looked at her sharply. 'There's no playing about it, we *are* a happy family – and anyway, what's it to you, Laura? Why does that get up your nose so much? Don't you like happy endings? Would you have preferred it if I'd disappeared over the horizon with Patrick?'

'No, but –'

'But what?'

'Well it all seems to revolve around you, doesn't it? Everything hangs on your decision, what *you* think, what *you* decide.'

I considered this. 'Yes, I suppose it does. Do you have a problem with that? As far as I can see, you call the shots in all your relationships. I don't suppose Edward wore the figurative trousers, did he?'

'Oh Edward,' she said dismissively.

'Or Phillip or Michael or any of the other poor pathetic lost souls you gave the kiss of life to and then tossed back into the pool again?' Suddenly I felt angry. Annoyed with her supercilious attitude. 'I suppose you've got the same treatment lined up for Willie, have you? Or does he get a reprieve because he had the balls to give you one?' I tossed this out wildly, like a yob lobbing a firework into a bonfire.

Laura flushed from her white shirt upwards, her neck and face suddenly blotched and mottled. I hadn't seen her do that since she was a child, when Daddy was horrid to her. My tummy churned. Oh God, how awful – what was I doing? Bullying my little sister because I'd been afraid of her judging me?

I leaned across quickly and seized her hand. 'Laura, I'm so sorry. I shouldn't have said that – I didn't even mean it!'

She searched my eyes, then nodded quickly, forgiving me, knowing I was sorry, knowing it was just my repulsive tongue getting out of hand as usual. I let go of her hand and cursed myself. We were silent for a bit.

After a while Laura swallowed. 'Did Patrick tell you about Willie, then?'

I nodded. 'Yes, but Laura, why didn't *you* tell me? You didn't have to sneak off every night at Kilmarnoch like that. You could have told me – I'd have understood.'

She shook her head. 'It was . . . special. I didn't want it spoiled.'

'And you thought I might do that?' My heart ached quietly.

'I thought you might have laughed. Or tried to put me off.'

I wondered, would I? Possibly, yes. It was all right for me, wasn't it, a quick fling with Willie, but for Laura?

I sighed. 'You may be right.' Then I grinned. 'I tell you what, if you're still keen on him next summer I promise not to say a word, OK?'

I stared down as an enormous cheese omelette suddenly appeared in front of me. Blue Eyes looked at me challengingly. I blinked at its proportions.

'Next summer? I'm going back on Thursday.'

I glanced up. 'What?'

'The day after tomorrow. I'm going back.' She took a sip of Perrier and calmly flicked back her hair.

'But can you do that? Will they give you the time off?'

She shrugged. 'Don't have to. I've resigned.'

'What!'

She popped a radicchio leaf into her mouth, 'Resigned this morning. Half an hour ago, in fact.' She chewed slowly, watching me.

I put my fork down. 'But Laura, what will you *do*? Your fabulous job – you loved it, it was your life!'

'Only because I didn't have any other life.'

'But – you were so good at it!'

She sighed. 'Because I had to be and because, to be honest, it was piss simple. You don't get it, do you, Tess? I'm in love with Willie.'

I gazed at her in amazement. 'Willie? Oh come on now, Laura. I know he's the first guy you've ever slept with and all that, and it *is* a bit emotional, but you're surely not suggesting . . .'

'I surely am. And I'm moving up to Scotland to be with him.'

I rocked back in my chair and stared at her aghast. A holiday romance yes, maybe even a bit on the side every other weekend, but to *live* with him?

'OK,' I said, as calmly as possible, 'OK, why not take a sabbatical? Take a month off, two even, try it out. Try living up there together –' try a cold winter, I thought privately – 'and if you don't like it, come back.'

She shook her head. 'Don't want to.'

'But –'

'Listen, Tess.' She leaned forward abruptly. 'I loathe my

466

job, OK? I loathe my designer flat, I loathe my life in London, I loathe a lot of the false, pretentious people I know and I loathe the poncy drinks-party lifestyle I lead, got it?'

'But then – why did you do it in the first place?' I said, flabbergasted.

There was a silence.

'Because you didn't.'

I stared at her. 'What?'

'Because it was something you hadn't done. You got the husband, the house, the children, I looked and couldn't find what you had so I did something completely different. I did the career bit instead, OK?'

I stared at her. I'd never known I'd had such an effect on her, that she should feel driven, by me, to such extremes. To compete. I'd never felt threatened by her lifestyle, so why had she felt threatened by mine? I struggled to understand.

'Was it – Daddy?'

She shrugged. 'Partly, I suppose. I suppose I wanted to shine in his eyes, succeed like he'd hoped you would after university. I think subconsciously, I decided to step into your shoes for him.' She looked up. 'But it was quite clear it was never quite the same. He was proud of me, but not enough. Not as much as if it had been you.'

'Laura, that's not true,' I whispered. But I knew it was.

'And the stupid thing is,' she laughed, 'I don't even really like him! Why should I care what he thinks? But I do.'

I nodded. 'I know.'

'It wasn't just Daddy, though. There was something

467

else – something I had to get away from. I wanted to hide myself in my work.'

'What?'

She hesitated, looked for a moment as if she might tell me, then shook her head.

'I'll tell you one day. Not now.'

I pushed the half-eaten omelette away miserably. Terrific. The second person in my family I'd failed. First Mummy and now Laura, and all the time, instead of trying to please my sister and my mother I'd been running round in circles trying to please the one person in the family who resolutely *refused* to be pleased, my father. And of course, that's what Mummy and Laura had been trying to do too, struggling to get some approval, some peace, some harmony, but there never would be peace and harmony in our family, would there, because none of us could ever match up to the one he'd lost. The one he'd always hankered for. The son. Patrick. I looked at her for a second.

'Laura, about Daddy.'

'Hmmm?' She was chasing a piece of goat's cheese round her plate, miles away.

I hesitated. 'There's – well, there's something fairly monumental I have to tell you about him.'

She looked up. 'What?'

'He's not, actually . . . my father.'

She stared at me blankly for a moment. 'What did you say?'

'I said he's not my father. You see, the thing is, Laura . . .'

'WHAT!' she shrieked, her fork clattering down onto her plate.

'Shhhh!' I put my hand on her arm and looked around

nervously. Several well-bred ears were pricking up like frisky ponies; the next thing we knew we'd be in *Jennifer's* blinking *Diary*. 'Mummy told me yesterday,' I whispered. 'You're his daughter, but I'm not. Mummy had an affair.'

She stared at me in disbelief. 'I don't believe you.'

'It's true,' I said patiently. 'I didn't know whether to tell you or not but then I thought I couldn't go on for the rest of my life with me knowing and you not, so I decided I would.'

'Christ – you're very cool about this aren't you, Tess? I mean how d'you *feel*? It's a bit bloody cataclysmic isn't it, that Dad isn't your – Jesus!'

'I know, I know, and I suppose I am being calm, but I think the reason is . . .' I struggled to rationalize it. 'Well – in the first place I have a family, my own family, so perhaps it's not as momentous as it would be,' I was going to say 'if I were you' but I hurried on, 'if I wasn't married, but also Laura,' I hesitated, 'rather like you, I've decided I don't actually *like* him very much.' I shrugged. 'To tell you the truth, that helps enormously.'

She was still staring at me aghast, mouth open, cigarette suspending a good two inches of ash. She flicked the ash off.

'All right,' she said steadily, although her fingers trembled, 'if he's not your father, who is then?'

I looked at her squarely. 'Brace yourself.'

'What? WHO?'

'Hamish.'

'Who's he?'

'Willie's father.'

She stared at me. 'Hamish?' she shrieked. '*Hamish*

469

McPherson! Oh, bugger off, Tess,' she scoffed. 'Mum and Hamish? It's outrageous!'

'Is it? Look at you and Willie.'

She started, flushed and looked down at her napkin. There was a silence.

'And you,' she said softly.

I looked at her sharply. 'He told you?'

She nodded.

I gulped. 'Laura, it was just a one-off, and we didn't go all the way. I bottled out –'

'I know,' she interrupted quickly. 'He told me. And anyway,' she went on, 'why should you have to explain? It was before I came along, wasn't it?' She gave a wry smile. 'Just.'

Our pale-eyed waitress came back to gather up our plates. Having been such a troublemaker I, of course, had only eaten a few mouthfuls. She looked at me accusingly as she cleared away. We were silent when she'd gone. Laura, I knew, was thinking about Daddy not being my father. I was thinking about her and Willie. Was she running away? Was this another violent manifestation of wanting to compete with me again? And was this decision just as alien and unnatural to her as having a career had been? What would they be like together, the sophisticate and the country boy, and what about his harem – would he still be running that?

'Laura,' I said gently, 'about Willie. There have been others, I think.'

She grinned. 'Others? Don't be ridiculous, Tess, there've been hordes! I know, he's told me all about them. Kirsten, a wide variety of Wee-Marys, all the London women on holiday, Penny too.'

She grinned at my expression. 'I know – even Penny. Can you imagine? All that pink angora flying around, pearls swinging, reinforced black bra sailing into the gorse bushes . . .'

'Shrieking and whooping – I shouldn't imagine she's a quiet lover, would you?'

'Oh no, and terribly athletic I should think, in a jolly hockey sticks sort of way. Nude leap-frog, perhaps –'

'Or fireman's lifts through the woods, that big white bottom wobbling around on Willie's shoulder –'

'Yes, thank you, Tess, that will do. I'd rather *not* imagine any more, if it's all the same to you.'

We giggled and she reached across and helped herself to a large slug of my wine.

'Want some?' I asked.

'Mmm, why not.'

I poured her a glass. We sat quietly for a while, supping away together, closer by miles suddenly. I put my glass down abruptly.

'But where on earth are you going to *live*, Laura, have you thought about that? Not in that boxy little bungalow, surely?'

I knew I sounded like a complete snob, but I just couldn't imagine Laura sitting in one of those G Plan armchairs with the antimacassar on the headrest warming her designer shoes in front of the two-bar electric fire.

'Oh no, Willie's already looking at places. He's seen a row of old cottages that need renovating – he thinks we could make them into one house. It's over near Kilmaglen, on the coast. We might take that on, do it up together.'

'But what with? I mean, how would you buy it?'

'Oh I'd sell the flat of course.'

I looked at her. Of course. That's how they'd finance it. I took a sip of wine. The nasty, rather cynical side of my nature said what a super wheeze for Willie then; lots of lovely money, big pad, no worries, but then happily, the slightly bigger, more generous side of me suddenly got a glimpse of Laura. Laura, halfway up a ladder in an old pair of jeans and a large checked shirt of Willie's, hair tied up any old how, pot of paint in her hand, spot of magnolia on her nose, laughing down at Willie as he held the ladder and I thought – so what? How on earth could I begrudge her that? Having fun, being in love, turning a wreck into something decent in much the same way that David and I had done. How could I begrudge her the freedom from her stifling, lonely, single-girl life? What did it matter whose money it was? Why shouldn't she have a stab at happiness with a man she loved, and what could be better, really, than that man was Willie and not some anally retentive merchant banker who insisted she polished the silver every week and entertained his boss every month and who brought out all her uptight neuroses – of which she had her share – instead of her carefree girlishness, of which, if the truth be known, she had a lot more . . . The trouble was that all that free spirit had been hidden away for so long I'd almost forgotten it was there. Forgotten that that was the real Laura. And why should she work for ever, either? Why should she sacrifice real life on the altar of a career?

Suddenly I felt a rush of love and warmth for her and a real sense of relief too. She was out, she'd made it across to the other side, and now she was running like blazes, she was free.

I leant across and seized her hand. 'You're right, you're absolutely right. Go for it, Laura! This is the best decision you've ever made in your life. Get up to Scotland, to Willie, buy your house on the coast, have four children, make jam, bake bread and don't let anyone tell you that you've opted out! There's more peace and sense and dignity in all of that than there is in a lifetime of client meetings and expense-account lunches and warm radicchio sodding salad and – oh, anything else in the world!'

Laura flushed with happiness, and not that nervous, mottled flush of a moment ago, just a lovely pink glow. Her eyes watered and a smile shot across her face.

'Do you really think so?' she said happily. 'Oh Tess, I'm so glad you agree. I was so afraid you'd censure me and – and –'

'Put you down?' I said miserably. I'd had no idea that with no great thought on my part I'd manipulated her life so abominably up to now. That she'd set such store by what I thought.

'Willie's going to try and start a salmon farm,' she went on eagerly. 'Well, we both are actually. We're going to work together, except when the babies come along, of course, then I'll want to be at home. I expect . . . although the farm will hopefully *be* at home so maybe I can do both!'

I let her gush on happily, all her plans pouring out at once now, as if someone had opened the flood-gates. I listened, nodding, smiling, so pleased for her. For her happiness.

All the same, I reflected, swirling my wine around in my glass, I couldn't help thinking that after the initial shock, this was much easier to be pleased about than any of the God-awful Trevors and Vincents and Edwards she'd paraded before me in the past. I mean, snobbish reservations aside, Willie was undoubtedly a nice bloke, which was more than could be said for the rest of the motley crew.

'And whatever snobbish reservations people may have about Willie . . .' I looked up quickly; how on earth had she known I'd been thinking about that? '. . . he must be infinitely preferable to any of my past beaux, don't you think?' I knew she was wondering about Daddy, about what he'd say.

'Absolutely,' I said warmly. 'I must say, I never quite knew what you were up to with all those wallys before him. No one did. Patrick had a hunch you were looking for something you couldn't have.'

She smiled and sipped her wine.

'That's why I thought it was Patrick,' I went on, 'because he was my ex-boyfriend and you couldn't have him because he was still in love with me and all that jazz. I thought perhaps you two had had a bit of a fling when he met you in London, years ago at that wedding.'

She laughed. 'God no, you must be joking! What – Patrick, with all his hang-ups about his parents and that weird obsession he had with you? No thanks. No, he just took me out to supper a couple of times when I was at a loose end, but all he wanted to do was talk about you. Honestly, Tess, I thought he was a bit unhinged. He even wanted to know how many men you'd been to bed with and was I absolutely sure it was only him and David and hadn't you perhaps bonked someone else at university and what did I think of your marriage, were you really

474

happy . . . all that sort of thing.' She shook her head. 'Weird. No, I had no desire to get entangled with the ultimate mixed-up bad boy like you did.'

'And me neither, any longer,' I said with feeling. I shivered. God, it was as if he'd been keeping an eye on me, all this time.

'All the same,' she went on, 'Patrick was right. I *was* looking for something I couldn't have, but it wasn't him.' She stubbed her cigarette out in the ashtray and looked me right in the eye.

'It was David.'

Chapter Twenty-nine

I felt my mouth drop open. For a moment I had neither air nor words to call on. Was this some kind of a joke? Was she, in a rather warped sort of way, having me on? I stared at her. Her eyes told me she wasn't.

'David?' I whispered incredulously.

'Yes,' she said calmly. 'Didn't you know?'

I could still hardly speak. 'No – no, I didn't. *David!*'

'Oh it's OK, I'm over it now, but it's taken nine years. Nine years to meet what I should have realized from the start was the antidote, his antithesis – Willie, and all this time I've been out there searching for a replica.' She laughed. 'I was looking for a clone you see, a thoughtful, brainy, fount-of-all-knowledge sort of chap – a polymath no less, but with that crucial, fatal ability to make me double up laughing at a moment's notice. A sublime combination, of course, but one that I'd never have found in a million years.'

I was transfixed by her mouth, by the extraordinary words it was forming. 'David! But when did you –'

'Fall in love with him?'

I nodded, mute.

'Oh, more or less the moment I saw him, as soon as you brought him home, in fact. I remember it distinctly. You were coming back from university with "some chap" and Mummy was in a bit of a flutter getting tea organized in the garden. It was July, very hot and we were all sitting around in deckchairs on the lawn when you breezed in with him, this tall blond boy in cricket whites with grass stains on his knees and that shock of hair that he pushed back impatiently when it got in his eyes. He shook hands with us all and then sat down next to me. Mummy passed round scones with jam and cream and he chatted a bit about this and that – ghastly cricket teas and philosophy and Rag Week – being funny and disparaging about it all – and he smiled quite a lot and made us laugh even more and I just wanted to kill you. I wanted to plunge the butter-knife through your heart right there and then.'

'But – you were only a child, fifteen . . .'

'Sixteen – and I knew what I wanted. Always had done. Knew I'd recognize the man I wanted to marry the moment I saw him. Imagine how I felt when you led him into the garden that day – and then decided to marry him yourself?' She laughed. 'And always, from your point of view, as someone who, in the absence of Patrick, would probably do!'

'Is that what you thought?' I gasped.

'It's what everyone thought. It's what you thought too, if you're honest. You *deigned* to marry him, to have his children, to share a home with him.'

'Stop it, Laura!' I felt panic-stricken.

'I'm sure you did actually deign to love him, but it was always a bit of a condescension on your part, wasn't it?' She played ruminatively with some crumbs on the table, smiling down at them. 'I, on the other hand, was absolutely gagging to love him and to be loved by him. And I used to think – what if you hadn't got pregnant? What if

477

you hadn't been stupid and naive enough to let that happen . . . might he not have loved me instead? Might you not have just been the catalyst, the middle man, bringing him home for *me* to love, delivering him to *me* in the garden that sunny afternoon before moving on to something else? Might not that have been the way it was destined to be? But no, you cocked up, didn't you. Forgot to take your Smarties and I had to content myself with being his sister-in-law.' She looked at me defiantly. 'But it didn't stop me living and dreaming that man every day for nine years. In my mind I ate with him, drank with him and slept with him too. And I can tell you all this now, Tess, because I don't any more.' She lit a surprisingly steady cigarette and blew a stream of smoke reflectively over my shoulder.

'Oh I think I'll always love him,' she admitted, 'but not with that same terrible passion. That gnawing, compulsive, debilitating passion that takes over your whole life, swallows you whole, colours everything you do, everyone you meet . . .' She tapped the ash off the end of her cigarette, and gazed over my shoulder into the distance.

'Is that why you never went to bed with anyone?' I breathed.

'Yes,' she laughed. 'Crazy, isn't it? I was saving myself for my sister's husband. I never admitted that, even to myself, but I think it's probably true.'

'Did David know?' I whispered. I could barely speak.

'Oh, I'm sure he did. David's not stupid, is he? But he was always very, very kind about it. I only once made a terrible fool of myself,' she gave a twisted smile, 'just after Hugo was born. I think I knew then that that really was the end, had to be. I got extremely drunk one night, lurched round to your house – you were still in hospital – and literally threw myself at him, flung myself on his neck, covered him in frantic kisses, then broke down hysterically.'

'Wh-what did he do?'

She grinned. 'Patted me on the back, took me out into the garden and gave me a large brandy. Then he sat and talked to me under the apple tree and the stars for about two hours. Not about us, him and me, about what I'd said and done, but just about me. About my life, where it was going, what I wanted to do. He tried to find a path for me, steer me onto it, a nice solid safe one far away from him. He's always done that for me, in his own quiet way.'

I nodded. 'Yes, yes he would. He's a – lovely man.' My heart ached for him suddenly.

'The best,' she corrected. She grinned. 'Bar Willie, of course.'

I breathed deeply, struggling to comprehend. 'He – never said.'

'Well, he wouldn't, would he? Being David. Lesser men would have loved it of course, bragged about it – "Oh, your sister's got the hots for me" and all that sort of stuff – but not David.'

I gulped and looked down at my napkin. I'd've liked to have torn it into tiny shreds right there and then; only the fact that it was pure Irish linen stopped me. We were both silent for a moment.

Laura broke the silence. 'Quite a lot to take on board in one lunch-hour isn't it?' she said quietly.

I nodded dumbly. I badly wanted to see him. To get home. To claim him, to *re*claim him. The idea of someone else wanting him was so terrifying it made my chest tighten, made breathing difficult.

'And you so nearly left him, didn't you?' she mused. 'I got so excited, thought that maybe there was a chance, that I could really have him after all these years. Given time, of course. We would have left a respectable gap, given you and Patrick a chance to go off to Italy, live together for a while, maybe even have a child. Then that would have been my moment, you see. I could have stepped quietly out from the shadows and picked up the pieces. It would have been the best thing for everyone under the circumstances. Aunty Laura.'

My hand shot to my mouth. I stared at her, horrified. 'No, Laura, don't!' I felt sick.

'Pipe dreams,' she said briskly, waving away my alarm. 'Don't worry, Tess, it would never have happened. I'm quite sure David would have found the idea as repellent as you do. I don't kid myself that he even remotely fancied me, but while we're here spilling the beans you may as well have the whole rotten canful. You may as well know what was going on in my crazy mixed-up head.'

'Is there any more?' I gasped. 'Only if there is, I shall have to order the other half of this bottle. Two glasses isn't going to be enough to sustain me!'

She hesitated for a moment, then shook her head. 'No. No, that's all.' She reached for her glass and took a quick sip of water. Too quick.

'What?' I pounced. 'What? Come on, out with it, Laura. Is there a love child lurking about somewhere, or did you drug him, drag him back to your flat and bonk him senseless? Come on, I want the works.'

Her eyes flitted over me momentarily, then slithered over to the door. 'No, it's nothing like that.' She paused, shook her head. 'In fact, it's probably nothing at all.'

'WHAT!' I shrieked, seizing her wrist. 'I want the nothing at all, if you don't mind. I want the whole sodding lot!'

'OK, OK, stop shouting,' she muttered, looking around nervously, 'but listen, this is pure conjecture, OK?' She licked her lips. I waited, tortured beyond belief. 'I – just wonder if David . . . well, if you haven't taken your eye off the ball for too long. If you haven't left rejecting Patrick in favour of David too late.' She fidgeted miserably in her chair.

'What d'you mean?' I breathed.

'Well while you've been busy sorting out your own life, it wouldn't be unreasonable to assume he's been doing the same, would it?'

'You mean he's having an affair,' I whispered. I felt faint. Could feel the life blood slipping away from me, draining out of my face.

'I don't know, for sure. It's just – well, when I got back to London, Janie – you know, the girl I work with – said: "Oh, I saw your gorgeous brother-in-law the other day, having lunch."'

'Where?'

'In Bibendum.'

'Bibendum! Oh don't be ridiculous,' I scoffed. 'David wouldn't be seen dead forking out for a trendy place like that.'

'With a blonde. Very young.'

My heart stopped. Then it raced on again. I shook my head. 'Rubbish! No, that's absurd, Laura. That's not

David's style at all. If you'd told me he'd been spotted lurking round the fossils in the British Museum with a blue-stockinged, middle-aged brunette I might have believed it, but a blonde in Bibendum – no.' I shook my head firmly. 'She must have been mistaken.'

'She wasn't,' said Laura quietly. 'She knows David quite well and anyway I phoned and checked. He booked the table in his own name.'

'You – checked?'

'Yes, well I've known his movements for the past nine years now; it's a difficult habit to break.' She had the grace to blush.

I stared at her, two fierce emotions battling for supremacy in my breast. One, that unbeknown to me, my sister should have had such an obsession with my husband for so long and the other, that now someone else had one too. It was as if Laura had passed over the baton – here, take it Blondie, it's your turn now. Pick it up and run with it, he's all yours. I struggled to keep calm but I wanted to stand up and shriek: 'Hands *off*! Just bugger *off* will you, you greedy grasping bastards. He's *my* husband, all right? Get one of your own!' I touched my forehead with a shaky hand. It was damp with sweat; I felt awful.

Laura leaned across the table. 'Tess,' she said gently, 'I'm telling you all this in the hope that maybe you can do something about it. That it's not too late. I don't want you to go on blithely taking him for granted only to discover he's . . . well.'

'Leaving me for someone else,' I whispered. 'Yes, thank you Laura, I'm indebted to you. Grateful to be so – informed.'

I reached down for my sack on the floor and pulled it onto my lap. I found my purse and with a shaking hand managed to open the clasp. I pulled out a twenty-pound note and pushed it across the table to her. She pushed it back.

'Don't be silly,' she murmured, 'I'll get this. Listen, Tess, have another drink, a soft one perhaps. I'm not sure you should go back on your own yet.'

I shook my head. 'Got to. Got to get away. Have a think.' I could speak only in clipped little staccato sentences now. I had to control my mouth or God knows what would come out of it – sobs, curses, wails, invective and serpents too, no doubt. I could feel them writhing around inside me, twisting my gut, stealing my breath, looking for a way out. I stumbled to my feet.

'Tess, just let me pay this then I'll come with you, walk you to the Tube at least.' She looked at me anxiously, then around the restaurant, searching desperately for our waitress, waving the bill in the air.

'No, really, I'll be fine. Rather be alone. Bye.' I bent down to kiss her.

'I shouldn't have told you,' she whispered.

I managed a brave smile. 'Best thing you ever did. Brought me to my senses. Thank you.' I meant it.

I turned and made my way through the sea of sleek heads in their black velvet hairbands, noticing with a stab that most of them seemed to be blonde. I lurched through the swing doors. The first of a series of escalators snaked down in front of me and since the ability to put one foot in front of the other seemed to have temporarily deserted me, this was convenient. I stepped on and waited, wide-eyed and frozen like the mannequins I was slowly gliding past, stepping off one escalator and picking up another until ultimately I was safely delivered to the ground floor and Perfumery.

As I moved blindly through the counters I caught a faint whiff of Diorissimo, the pong of my choice when I'm in the mood and the one David always buys me for Christmas when he's stumped for ideas. I wondered what *her* choice was, whoever she was, this blonde, this lunchtime and probably night-time companion of my husband's. My husband's mistress. Suddenly I had to stop and clutch a make-up counter. Several exorbitantly priced lipsticks wobbled precariously in their display stand. I stood there, head bent, taking deep breaths, looking at the sparkling floor beneath me. For an awful moment I thought it was accelerating up to meet me, but in the nick of time I gritted my teeth, and thought hard about the ERM and John Major's Social Charter and the way he now wears nice stripy cotton shirts instead of grey Bri-nylon ones and the mixed blessing that must be for Norma, a pleasure to look at but a pain in the arse to iron – and gradually, such dull contemplation sobered me up and the wooziness left me. I slowly raised my head. No, I determined, I would not faint in the Perfume department of Harvey Nichols. I looked up and saw the heavily made-up girl behind the L'Oréal counter peering anxiously at me.

'Are you all right, madam?' she asked, blinking through her blonde fringe which hung rather seductively in her eyes. Blonde again. Everyone seemed to be blonde these days.

'Yes, yes I'm fine,' I said. 'Just a bit hot, that's all.'

I stared at her. Is it you? Are you the one, you bitch, you vixen, you cold-blooded husband-snatcher? Are you the one intent on breaking up my world?

'Only Madam looks a little pale . . .'

I managed a wobbly smile, thinking: yes, well, you'd look a little pale under the circumstances.

'No, I'm fine,' I nodded, baring my teeth and preparing to move on, but as I did, I caught a glimpse of someone in the huge mirror behind her. I stopped. How odd: she looked just like me but older, thinner and much more lined. I stared. It was me, of course, but how strange that I hadn't noticed how truly terrible I was looking. Why hadn't I noticed that? I reached up and stroked my face absently with my fingertips. Dry, middle-aged skin, whereas hers was no doubt young, soft and peachy.

'Perhaps Madam would like a make-over? There's no obligation and you could sit down for a moment – take the weight off your feet?'

She was talking to me as if I was an old dear, and yet I could only be – what – ten years older than her . . . I stared. What on earth did they say to one another, I wondered. What did David find to say that would interest someone like this? 'Read any good Kafka recently?' 'Nah, but I bought a brilliant new nail-varnish in Top Shop yesterday, whaddya think?' Or was there no need to speak; did they let their bodies do the talking? Was all communication on a far more primeval, carnal plain? Oh God, that floor was definitely coming this way again, and even Norma doing the ironing was going to have a job to stop it. I clung on to the counter with both hands, my knuckles white.

485

'Madam?'

I took the chair quickly. 'Go on then, a make-over,' I whispered.

My word was her command. In a second my little blonde friend had whipped a sheet around my neck and swung into action, organizing herself with brushes and palettes, bottles and potions, for all the world like a surgeon marshalling his instruments.

'Now,' she murmured, swiftly wiping a piece of damp cotton wool over my face, deftly removing all traces of make-up, dirt and tears. 'Did Madam have any particular image in mind?'

'Yes, Madam had the image of a nineteen-year-old blonde in mind. Take twelve years off me and I'll do the rest at home with a bottle of peroxide,' I snarled.

The girl started, then gave a nervous laugh. 'Well, of course, I'll do what I can, but Madam must appreciate that although she has quite marvellous bone structure there's no guarantee I can –'

'Make a silk purse out of a sow's ear? Sorry,' I muttered quickly. 'Bad day. Just do whatever you can.'

'Party make-up perhaps,' she suggested.

'Oh yes,' I said ironically. 'Make it nice and jolly.'

I sat mesmerized as her slim white fingers swept over my face, oiling, massaging, colouring. Slim, white, ringless hands, girlish hands with soft, pink fingertips, expertly soothing and stroking and painting. I imagined similar hands on David, young and soft caressing his shoulders, massaging his back, running down his spine, gently turning him over, stroking his tummy, his –

'That's enough!' I cried suddenly.

I jumped up and tore the sheet from around my neck. The girl dropped her make-up brush in alarm and took a step back.

What was I *doing* here, for heaven's sake? My husband was having an affair and I was calmly getting a make-over in Harvey Nichols?

'So sorry,' I gasped, 'but I'm afraid I must be going. Supposed to be somewhere else you see, just remembered. I'll pay you, of course . . .'

'There's no charge, madam, but I've only done one eye. You can't go yet. At least let me —'

'Sorry, I have to go.'

I turned and hurried away, catching as I did a last glimpse of myself in the mirror. As she'd so rightly said, one eye was garishly made up, complete with glittering gold shadow, whilst the other one next to it looked naked, small and frightened.

I stumbled down Sloane Street and round the square, narrowly missing a bus, and then plunged into the dark abyss of the Tube station. As I reached the platform the train was just disappearing into the tunnel, leaving me alone for a moment, staring blankly down a dark hole. But this was lunch-time and within seconds the platform had filled up again as people poured down the escalators like rats down a drain. I stood and gazed unseeing as they surged around me; shoppers, tourists, office-workers in their lunch-hours, businessmen, executive women, two young men in pale grey suits surreptitiously munching sandwiches beside me, the unmistakable whiff of prawn mayonnaise on wholemeal wafting over, and next to them, an older man in expensive grey flannel, chatting to a young girl. His secretary? Perhaps. I stared. Or perhaps not.

He was tall, mid-forties with thinning grey hair but an attractive, slightly arrogant face and he was smiling down at his young companion who was small and fluffy, bright eyes in a sharp little face, thin painted lips and a too-short skirt. She was recounting something eagerly and he was listening with a superior smile, indulging her pea brain because of her splendid performance between the sheets no doubt. When she'd finished he gave what must have been a mocking response because she pouted indignantly and elbowed him in the ribs. He rocked back on his heels and roared with laughter, she pouted some more and he put his arm round her shoulders, giving her an affection-ate little squeeze. I marched up to them.

'And does your wife know about this?' I hissed.

The train rattled noisily into the station. The pair looked at me blankly as I pushed furiously past them and waited for the doors to open. When they did it was a case of squeezing more minced human into the layers of lasagne, but I managed it somehow and as the doors closed behind me, I realized my lecherous friends had managed it too. We stood eyeball to eyeball.

'My wife died last year and my daughter periodically accompanies me to lunch,' he informed me icily.

As I opened my mouth to scoff I realised that not only were the two pairs of hazel eyes glaring at me identical, but that the slightly hooked Roman noses were too. There was no dodging the genes here.

'Ah,' I conceded weakly.

No more was said, but I had to stand chest to chest with them all the way to Earl's Court, at which point the daughter stepped off, leaving her father behind. She pecked him on the cheek and muttered something scathing about a 'stupid, barking, insulting old woman'.

The doors closed and I watched her go, frowning slightly. Old – me? Did she mean *me*? Suddenly it tore at me like barbed wire on skin. I felt tears of anguish well up into my eyes, filling my nose. I gulped them down. Old! Was that what I was, then? An older woman, being traded in for a younger model; was that tired old cliché to be my fate? Was I to be left on my own, an aging, single mother struggling to bring up her children, eking out the maintenance, hanging on to dear, middle-class life by her fingertips while her attractive, greying-round-the-temples, barrister husband strutted off into the sunset to set up home with his new model?

Don't be ridiculous, I thought. You're overreacting. David has been seen having lunch, that's all, and already you've got him marching into the divorce courts. Now *buck up*! There could be some perfectly innocent explanation. I mean, perhaps she was just a friend? And maybe I could meet her? Yes, perhaps we could be civilized about this. Maybe she'd like to come to dinner and perhaps I could . . . my insides curdled, my fists clenched – '*kill her!*' I gasped.

It was loud enough to make the people standing around me flinch away in alarm and the man I'd already accused of rampant incest blinked nervously. I quickly improvised a song on a theme.

'Killer que-en, yes, she's a killer – que-e-en . . .'

I could tell that Grey Suit wasn't convinced. He looked from one garish, glittering eye to one naked, mad-as-hell eye and came to a reasonable conclusion. He tucked his newspaper firmly under his arm, put his head down and pushed determinedly through the scrum for the sanity of the other end of the carriage.

A half-suppressed guffaw snorted out from behind me. I glanced around to see three or four teenage boys in semi-school uniform, ties askew, blazers frayed, shoes scuffed, oozing with testosterone, giggling into their hands.

'Keep takin' the pills,' one of them blurted out, which sent the others into paroxysms of hilarity.

I ignored them, and then also studiously ignored the fact that they were clearly daring each other to prod me in the back. Gently at first – followed by a muffled guffaw, then a bit harder – followed by louder guffaws.

Mercifully I didn't have to bear this oafish behaviour for too long as moments later the train pulled into Putney Bridge station. I stepped thankfully onto the platform and as I did so, my full cotton skirt floated gently to the ground leaving me standing on the platform in my pop socks and knickers.

'What the –'

Horrified, I snatched the skirt back up and swung around just in time to see the Tube doors close. The boys were choking with laughter, clutching their stomachs, gasping for air, sick with glee.

'You bastards!' I roared as the train chugged out of the station.

Helpless with laughter they hung on to each other, waving and whistling as the train drew away.

'Those bastards undid my skirt!' I spat to no one in particular. Several passers-by gave me an amused look, but an equally wide berth. Tears were pricking my eyelids as I zipped my skirt up at the back again and trudged on up the station steps. I shook my head bitterly. God it was unreal, wasn't it? I mean, those yobbos were some poor mothers' adored sons, fruit of their wombs. Imagine how I'd feel if Hugo behaved like that in a few years' time! I blinked, realizing with a shock of dismay that I could well imagine Hugo doing it *now* let alone in a few years' time.

And if he was like that now, I thought miserably, what would he be like without a father? And Clemmie too, my crazy, lovable wild child who could draw like a dream, sing like a lark but still ate with her fingers, slept with a toy gun under her pillow, stripped naked to go to the loo – something I could foresee becoming a problem at the job interview stage – and had waited three and a half years before she'd even bothered to talk? How would she fare without her beloved Daddy, without his pragmatic, calming influence?

Or maybe David would fight for custody, I thought with a sudden lurch of horror. Maybe he'd tell the court I was an unfit mother and that I once gave them Hula Hoops for breakfast, encouraged them to cheat at Patience, turned their muddy trousers inside out, failed to buy sugar-free Ribena, smacked in Sainsbury's, shrieked in Tesco's, bit in Waitrose, frisbeed Jaffa Cakes straight from the packet at teatime by way of a cake – yes – maybe they'd *all* go off and leave me and I'd be left alone, a bitter, twisted old woman with only her gin bottles and memories for company.

And maybe the children would want to go? Maybe Clemmie would take one look at Blondie's collection of pink cuddly toys sitting on the love-nest windowsill and bond instantly. Maybe Hugo would be lured by the promise of Blondie's younger brother having a season ticket at QPR, or maybe ... On and on scurried my poor overworked brain, dreaming up ever more lurid, mind-boggling nightmares as I made my way home, and all the time I knew I was egging myself on to be more outrageous, more melodramatic, because in my heart I knew things really couldn't be as bad as all that, and that if I let myself think the absolute worst, things could only be better, couldn't they?

Or could they? As I rounded the corner into our road I stopped dead in my tracks. I stared. There was my house, number 42, tasteful, wisteria-clad and just as I'd left it, except that right outside a black taxi was waiting. It was throbbing away ominously and pointing in the opposite direction. Standing on the pavement, leaning in through the open cab door and talking to a passenger in the back seat, was David. I quickly stepped back into a hedge to watch. He was wearing his suit, but minus his jacket, in shirt-sleeves and braces. I peered out from behind the privet, my heart hammering. I couldn't see who was in the back of the taxi, but I could just make out a vague outline. David was laughing, chatting, leaning on the taxi roof. Suddenly, he leaned in and ... kissed whoever it was who was sitting in the back. My tummy gave a lurch. I watched as he straightened up, smiled broadly and seemed about to shut the door when suddenly he clearly remembered something because his finger shot up in a little start of alarm. He turned, dashed up the path to the house, disappeared inside and reappeared a moment later carrying a large suitcase. I blinked. It was our suitcase. He lugged it down the garden path then threw it into the back of the taxi, laughing. He leaned in again for another kiss – reckless now – then slammed the door shut. As the taxi drew away and purred down the road he stood watching, waving, smiling fondly as it disappeared around the corner. He stayed there for a moment or two, gazing reflectively after it, then turned and went back into the house. The front door closed behind him.

My knees buckled and I sat down on the small wall under the hedge. I knew, of course I knew. There was no real mental exertion needed here. The cab had contained the mistress, the suitcase had contained David's clothes, the destination of the cab had been the love-nest and the object of the exercise had been to pick up David's wardrobe. He'd known that I'd be out of the house having lunch with Laura and that the children were out having a picnic with Josie. The coast had been crystal clear and they'd no doubt even found time to have a quick one on the bed – our bed – before he'd popped her and the case in the taxi bound for Maida Vale, or Ladbroke Grove or wherever it was that clandestine relationships were conducted these days. Thus far was perfectly plain, except for one tiny point. That case had been far too big to contain simply a spare pair of underpants and a clean shirt to pop into the extra-marital wardrobe. No, that case had been stuffed to bursting with clothes. He was leaving me. There was no doubt about that. Leaving me for whoever had been in the back of that taxi.

Suddenly I felt very calm, very cold and very still. A profound sense of fatalism rose up from my soul. There was nothing I could do about it. Nothing at all. Suddenly David's words came back to me. *Alea jacta est.* Of course. *The die is cast.* There was no going back. That must have been what he meant. I sat on the wall feeling not quite real somehow, as if this wasn't happening to me at all but to someone else and I was just an innocent bystander watching the scene being played to its conclusion. I gazed at the blue front door, waiting for it to open, waiting for David to reappear, as I knew he would.

And there he was, coming out with his suit jacket on now and a bundle of briefs under his arm, tied up with the distinctive pink ribbon. He shut the door behind him, locked it, pocketed the key, walked briskly down the path and turned right, in the direction of the station and ultimately, me.

At first he didn't see me, shielded as I was by the weeping ash and the overgrown hedge, but then, just as he was nearly past, he did.

'Tess!' He started, colouring up. 'How long have you been there?'

'Long enough.'

He frowned, but the guilt shone through. 'For what?'

'To see you with your mistress,' I hissed.

As I said it, all calm collected fatalism left me. In an instant I turned into the wronged, vengeful, tie-snipping wife and out poured the pure, smoking-white anger of rejection.

'Long enough to see you snogging and canoodling in the middle of the street, long enough to see the happily married, devoted father of two tickle some peroxide tart's tonsils!' I ranted. 'Long enough to catch sight of that bitch, that viper, that under-age blonde strumpet who you had the nerve to bring to *my* house . . .' My voice was rising hysterically now and behind me, I was aware of curtains twitching. 'And have sex with her in *my* bed, on *my* sheets, before packing her off in a taxi to your sordid little den of sin where no doubt at lunch-time tomorrow you'll be nipping round to SHAG HER SENSELESS!'

I bellowed this into his face, causing him to blink and step backwards into the road. He narrowly missed a car. Behind me an assortment of china dogs rattled violently on the windowsill as a curtain was hastily dropped in alarm.

'Tess, what are you talking about?'

'Oh, don't give me that wide-eyed incredulity crap!' I roared. 'I saw her with my own eyes! Who was it then, David, eh? If you're so screamingly, mind-bogglingly clever you tell me who that scheming little slut in the back of that taxi was! Who was that piece of filth!'

'That piece of filth was your mother.'

'What?'

'Your mother.'

Chapter Thirty

My mind battled, my head roared. I shook it, bewildered. Surely he wasn't having an affair with . . . my mother?

David watched the battle of the brain cells, saw the mystification in my eyes and sighed.

'No, you idiot, of course I'm not having an affair with your mother.' He took my arm, turned me around gently and led me back in the direction of the house.

'You know, Tess, I don't think you're very well. Did you know for instance that you've been out this morning with only half a face? You've got one gold eye and one . . .'

I shook his hand off my arm and pulled away angrily. 'Oh don't you try to distract me, David. Don't you try to fob me off with your smart-arse ways. My mother, indeed! You must think I was born yesterday! Who was in that bloody cab?'

'I've told you,' he said patiently. 'It was your mother. She stopped off at the house to say goodbye to you but you weren't there so I said goodbye instead.'

We were outside the front door now. I gazed up at him, stupefied. He opened it and pushed me gently inside. As he shut the door behind us I could have sworn I saw a hundred net curtains drop disappointedly back into place. I followed David numbly down the hall to the kitchen.

'Goodbye?' I repeated stupidly, lowering my bottom onto a chair at the kitchen table. I stared blankly as he opened the fridge and took out a bottle of wine. 'Why, where's she going?'

'She's leaving your father.'

'No!'

'Only for a couple of months to begin with. She says she'll reassess the situation after that.' He smiled as he wound in the corkscrew. 'What she actually said was she's taking a long sabbatical with a view to possibly renewing her contract at the end of it, but only on her terms.' He laughed. 'Not bad, eh? Not an all-out desertion but pretty monumental nonetheless – particularly for your mother. It'll certainly make your old man sit up a bit anyway.' He pulled the cork.

'But where's she going?'

'India.'

'India!'

'Yes, on a trekking and painting course with similar like-minded souls. Who knows, she might even find someone so likeminded she leaves your father altogether. Drink?' He sat down opposite me and pushed a glass over the table.

'Please.'

He poured us both a glass. 'She stayed with Rachel after the funeral, you see, never went back to Kent with your father. She said if she'd gone home she'd never have done it, wouldn't have had the guts to walk away.' He cradled his glass. 'I can see that actually, being in London probably felt as if she was halfway there. Anyway, she'd noticed this painting holiday in the back of *The Times* a few weeks ago, apparently. Got all the jabs done in secret and then chickened out. She rang yesterday on the off-chance and amazingly they'd had a last-minute cancellation. So she borrowed some clothes from Rachel, bought a few more and now she's on her way to Delhi. Piece of luck, eh?'

'Delhi? Jesus! Daddy will freak!'

David shrugged. 'Of course he will, and it serves him right. She should have done it years ago, we all know that. No point in living a lie, is there? No point in living with someone you don't love or who doesn't love you, is there, Tess?'

He regarded me coolly over the rim of his glass and my heart just about stopped beating.

'David,' I began awkwardly, gripping the stem of my glass for courage. 'What were you doing here this lunchtime?'

'Collecting a brief,' he said calmly. 'I forgot to take it into Chambers this morning and I've got a conference with the client at four. I popped back here to get it and ran into your mother pushing a note through the letter box to let you know the score. She'd been shopping and had everything stuffed into plastic bags so I lent her our case.'

'Really?'

'Really.' He held my eyes. There was a silence.

'And David,' I plunged on again, taking a quick slurp of wine, 'Laura said that – well, Janie said actually, the girl she works with – that she saw you quite recently, having lunch, in Bibendum.'

He nodded. 'Yes, I saw Janie.'

'You were with a girl,' I breathed. 'A blonde.'

'Quite so.'

'Who – was that?'

'That was Lucy.'

In my mouth my wine suddenly turned to rat poison, to lighter fuel, to Domestos, to cat's piss. I spat it violently across the table.

'Lucy?' I roared. God, even the name was enough to make my insides knot, it was so deliciously juicy and luscious and suggestive and skittish and rampant and roly-poly in the hayish – Lucy!

'My new clerk.'

My heart stopped – then lurched on again dementedly. 'Your new clerk is . . . female?'

'Do you have a problem with that?'

I blinked. 'N-no. No, not at all! But you took her to . . . Bibendum?'

He smiled. 'Yes, I believe that's the name of the hugely expensive joint we were lunching in. It belongs to that Conran chappie who's always banging on about American Express on the telly. Bit of a flagship for him apparently, but it was news to me.' He grinned. 'I was stitched up, you see. Lucy arrived on her first day at work and as usual no one had bothered to organize anything by way of a "hello" so a few of us who weren't in court thought we ought to show willing and take her out to lunch. Simon suggested this place I'd never even heard of and got me to book a table. He then discovered he was in court and couldn't come, and then Ben and Dick discovered *they* conveniently couldn't come either so it was left to old muggins here to escort her. I did vaguely ask if they thought this place was quite the ticket but they assured me, with much guffawing and back-slapping, that it was just my cup of tea, terrifically cheap and cheerful, lots of nursery puddings, Spotted Dick, Jam Roly Poly and all that sort of thing, I'd *love* it.'

I smiled in spite of myself. I could just imagine the worldly Dick and Ben chortling with glee as they sent a bemused David off on his way to bankruptcy.

'I realized I'd been had the moment I glanced at the prices on the menu, but I squared my shoulders and thought, Right, you bastards, in for a penny in for a quarter of a million – and ordered whatever I felt like, urging Lucy to do the same. Between us we got through foie gras, duck, snails, grouse and got quietly plastered on a couple of bottles of very passable Burgundy. We stayed there for most of the afternoon and very pleasant it was too. Lucy's extremely good company and very easy on the eye and the whole thing was very convivial. When I finally mortgaged our way out of there at four o'clock and went back to Chambers, I told the grinning bastards that they were absolutely right; it had indeed been just my cup of tea and I was indebted to them to adding it to my list of eateries and wasn't it marvellous, incidentally, that Lucy had managed to swing it on Chambers's expenses. Mind you,' he added ruefully, taking a sip of wine, 'it might explain why the work appears to have dried up recently. Lucy obviously thinks she doesn't need to send any briefs winging my way as I've clearly got private means. Either that or she thinks I'm trying to get into her knickers and isn't amused.'

I swallowed and searched for my voice which I hadn't used for a while. 'So – you're not having an affair?'

'With Lucy?' He laughed. 'No.'

'With anyone?'

He regarded me thoughtfully. 'No, not with anyone, Tess.'

I stared at him for a moment, then threw my head back exultantly and gave a great gasp of joy.

'Oh!' I pulled my hairband out and shook my curls all over the place. 'Oh God, David, I'm so relieved! I can't tell you how worried I've been!' I slapped my hands down delightedly on the table, could almost feel my eyes dancing for joy.

'You see, Laura thought . . . well, we *both* thought actually, that – oh God, David, you've no *idea*!' I seized his hand. 'For the past couple of hours I've had you shacked up with some bimbo in a basement flat in Bayswater. I've had you squeezing into black 501s, spinning groovy discs and rolling joints on beanbags, I've had you rumpy-pumpying on a futon with your nubile little strumpet like some born again teenager – God, I think I even had you on the floor in Stringfellows, smoking pot, getting down, chilling out . . . I can't tell you how berserk my imagination was going!'

David raised an eyebrow. 'Clearly,' he said drily.

'And as for me, oh God, there was no hope for me.' I shook my head emphatically. 'No no, I was dead meat. I was the deserted, passed-over droopy-boobed baby machine. I was last year's model, placenta brain, good for nothing except slouching round the kitchen in my cheesy old dressing gown and socks, Rice Krispies in my pubic hairs, J-cloth in my hand mopping bottoms, floors, puke and noses . . .' I got up and grabbed a dishcloth from the sink and slouched around like The Thing From The Swamp to demonstrate. 'Oh yes,' I laughed joyfully, chucking the cloth back in the sink and flopping down into my chair. 'I was ancient history!'

'Really.'

'Yes, really! Honestly, David, you've no idea the hell I've been through.'

'My heart bleeds.'

'You've no idea how arse-about-tit I'd got it all. When I saw you putting that suitcase in that taxi and lunging in for a kiss, I thought, Uh-oh, that's it, Tess.' I garrotted my neck with my finger. 'It's curtains for you, old girl. It's happy single-parent families from now on, I'm afraid. It's gritting your teeth as the paternal car rolls up outside the house, forcing a smile as you wave the children off for some quality time with Daddy, biting your nails and hitting the sherry while they're dragged round the zoo and stuffed with Big Macs and milkshakes and all the time wondering if *she*'s there with them, watching them come back laden down with guilt presents, catching sight of *her* in the car, holding on to the smile and the composure just long enough to shut the door then grilling them rigid – wanting to know and not wanting to know – knocking seven bells out of them if they so much as admitted she was, "OK, I suppose", hitting the sherry again, crying myself to sleep . . . Oh God, David, I can't *tell* you how awful I thought it was going to be!'

'And it's not?'

'What?'

'It's not going to be like that?'

'Well, of course it's not,' I laughed. 'Why should it be if you're not –' I froze suddenly, glass poised at my lips. I lowered it. 'What d'you mean, David? Why should it be?'

He didn't say anything, just looked at me. I felt scared. 'Why should it be like that?' I whispered again.

'You tell me,' he said quietly. 'The way I see it, you've still got things pretty much arse-about-tit here. Shouldn't *I* be the one asking *you* the questions? Shouldn't I be asking you if *you*'re having an affair?'

'Oh,' I breathed, as the dawn came up. 'Oh, I see . . . you mean Patrick. Oh no, don't be silly, I –'

'Silly?' His voice broke in harshly, making me jump. 'Silly? Is that what I'm being? Oh well, excuse me!'

He stood up and faced me furiously. His fists were clenched, his face pale, mask-like. It didn't look like David at all.

'Nine years, Tess,' he said in a shaky voice. 'Nine years I've lived in that little turd's shadow, with him peering over my shoulder, lurking behind us all the way, watching our every move, lingering around like some bloody spy in a belted overcoat, quietly smoking in darkened doorways, waiting for you.'

I stared at him aghast. 'B-but he's never been here. He's always been in Italy. How can you –'

'He's always been *there* though, hasn't he?' He leaned over and jabbed me hard in the chest. His eyes were like two pieces of flint. 'He could have been in fucking Timbuktu and it wouldn't have made any difference. He's always been there in your heart, hasn't he, Tess? Oh, not your whole heart, I grant you; you very graciously shifted him over and made room for two when I arrived and I like

503

to kid myself that over the years I've managed to all but push him out, but not quite. You've always let him cling to the edge by the fingertips, haven't you, and let me tell you, that's been bloody hard to hack at times.'

I opened my mouth to deny it, then I saw his face daring me to do so. I hung my head in shame.

'I suppose I have rather carried a torch for him . . .'

'Torch,' he scoffed. 'A frigging *bon*fire, more like!'

'But not any more,' I looked up quickly. 'Really, not any more.'

David smiled and shook his head.

'It's true,' I said urgently, grabbing his hand. 'I swear to God, David. It's over, it's –'

'It's more alive than it's ever been,' he said drily, pulling his hand away roughly. He turned his back on me, staring out of the window. At length he spoke.

'Tess, I want you to go away for a while.'

I stared at his back. 'What?'

'I want you to go back to Italy with him.' He jerked his head in the direction of the door. 'Go on,' he said quietly, 'sod off.'

My mouth fell open. 'But David, why?'

'Because I'm tired of playing second fiddle, that's why. I'm tired of filling someone else's flashy Italian shoes with my rather mediocre grey woollen socks. I'm tired of trying to make you happy when all the time there's someone a mere plane flight away who could make you happier still.' He swung around to face me. 'You see, for some time, Tess, I've been wondering how I could throw the pair of you together. I even had a half-baked notion about taking a family holiday in Florence this summer, dragging the children round the Uffizi, taking in the Duomo and then accidentally on purpose running into Him.' He smiled. 'Imagine my delight when I discovered I didn't have to go to all that trouble. Imagine how thrilled I was when I heard his father had died and he'd be within spitting distance of us in Scotland. Imagine my glee as I watched you pant after him the moment we got there, tart yourself up for him, tear out at midnight to meet him in darkened fields and get lost in the process whilst I bust a gut looking for you, and then, throw into the equation the terrifically handy fact that you oh so conveniently fell off your bike and muscled into his spare room at Gilduncan . . . I'm sure you can imagine, Tess, that my rapture was complete. Oh, it was perfect. All I had to do was invent some spurious excuse to leave the stage, return to London and let you get on with it.'

'You mean you had no work to do here?' I whispered.

'Of course not. Most of the courts are shut in August and I'd finished all my paperwork. No, I just mooched about a bit, watched the cricket, picked my nose, went to the pub and went quietly out of my mind.'

'So that's why you kept insisting I stayed there, at Gilduncan. You wanted me to have an affair with him. Go away with him.'

'I think you're finally getting the picture.'

'But – Jesus, David – supposing it had worked out? Supposing I had gone off with him, and taken the children. Talk about playing Russian roulette with your family!'

He eyed me coldly. 'That was a risk I'd finally decided to take. This wasn't a sudden whim, Tess, this wasn't a spur-of-the-moment decision. This was something I'd considered for a very long time.'

I gulped. 'Was it that obvious then, my – you know . . .'

'Obsession with him? No, not all the time, but it had a way of rearing its ugly head every now and then. You'd go all quiet and moody and wilt a bit over the scrambled-egg pan, mutter on about the drudgery of being a common-or-garden Putney housewife, referring particularly, I'm sure, to the monotony of being married to a boring middle-class barrister, but being j-u-st about polite enough to refrain from mentioning that. But you didn't have to, Tess. I knew your heart wasn't in it. You may have looked like you were burning the bacon with one hand, ironing a vest with the other, kicking the door shut on the oven chips and shaking your head at the Jehovah Witness through the window, but I knew in reality you were on some balmy Italian balcony somewhere. I knew you were shooting Lover Boy hot looks over the gin and tonics, I knew you were furiously tearing your clothes off, thrashing around on wet canvases and making a terrible mess in the bougainvillaea.'

I looked at my hands and shook my head. 'Stupid,' I muttered, 'naive.'

'Really?' He raised his eyebrows. 'How d'you know until you've tried it? Until you've tried living with a spoiled, sullen brat of a man who's never had anything in life except his own way? A man who has a totally warped view of humanity and more particularly women? How d'you know until you've tried living in a country where you can't speak the language and where, believe it or not, people *still* do the washing up and iron shirts and take children to school and go to the supermarket. Go on, Tess, off you trot. Get down to the travel agent and book a flight. I'll man the fort – try it for a bit.'

'I don't need to,' I whispered, 'I already know, and I'm over him, really I am. You must believe me, David!'

He looked at me squarely. 'Only yesterday I spoke to you at Robert's funeral. You certainly weren't over him then. I believe you even raised the subject of divorce – does that ring any bells? Tell me, what's happened in the space of twenty-four hours that's so radically changed your mind?' He leaned back on the sink and folded his arms. 'Talk me through it, Tess, I'm all ears.'

'Well,' I faltered, 'after the funeral – I went to see him.'

'Ah yes. That must have been when you said you needed a walk. A little air.'

I nodded. 'Yes, that's right.' I swallowed hard, my brain spinning. I knew I had to tell him everything now, however implausible it sounded. A lot depended on this. I spread my hands on the table as if I were laying out my cards and tried to think clearly. 'At that time,' I said slowly, feeling my way, 'I really believe I was planning to have an affair with him.' I looked up.

'Yesterday,' he said with difficulty. 'Only yesterday.'

I nodded. 'Yes, that's right, but then something happened. Something . . .' I struggled to explain – think, Tess, think and *talk*, damn you, *tell* him. 'I saw something in him, in Patrick, that I'd never seen before. A totally unexpected, weird side of him.' I shook my head. 'It was as if I was looking back into his past, into his soul really. I could see how unloved he'd been, what an appalling upbringing he'd had and how badly that had affected him. *Twisted* him.

I realized how he'd tried to hide all that before and why he was so obsessed by me. It wasn't love at all; it was more of a – crusade. I felt sorry for him but at the same time I found him creepy, odd. I tried to go, to leave him. We fought and he –'

'Your first quarrel,' he smiled. 'How very touching.'

'No, no, it was more than that. I – well, I felt completely repulsed by him, David. I couldn't bear the idea of him touching me.'

David raised his eyebrows sarcastically. 'How extraordinary! And yet only moments before you'd felt he was sexual temptation itself! But then – what, the scales literally fell from your eyes and you thought, Phew, that was a close shave. Quick, back to good old David. Back to good old doormat features. Back to Old Faithful.'

I looked at him squarely. 'If you like, except that when it looked like Old Faithful had got tired of hanging around for Old Faithless and moved on to New Model, I thought . . .'

'Yes?'

'I thought my world was coming to an end.' Tears filled my eyes.

There was a silence. David turned and stared out of the kitchen window. It had started to rain now and drops were coming in through the open window into the sink. He didn't close it, just watched them drip onto the windowsill, into the stainless steel sink, down the plug-hole.

'I don't know,' he said wearily. 'I just don't know.'

I looked at his straight back, at his square shoulders, his hands thrust deep in his pockets and suddenly I knew I had to fight for this one. I had to fight for my marriage.

I stood up behind him. 'Look, David,' I began in a low voice, 'just because I didn't do this thing properly, the way you'd planned it, just because I didn't clear my wardrobe, take the children and come back six months later saying, "Take me back, it was all a ghastly mistake," you're disappointed, aren't you? Just because my eyes were opened in an instant it's not enough, is it? You wanted me to go away, get it all out of my system, but don't you see,' I urged, 'I don't need to! In the same way that all I needed was a glimpse of you packing your bags into a taxi to bring me to my senses all I needed was that short sharp glimpse of Patrick! And I saw so *much* in that short time. I saw it all. It doesn't take twelve years to undo twelve years; nothing is relative in this game, there *are* no rules and it *can* all fall apart in a moment – you drop a stitch and the whole thing unravels – I'm rid of him, David! I swear to God I'm shot of him for ever and I can't tell you how liberating that feels. It's as if I've finally exorcized him, he's really gone!'

In the silence I could hear the clock ticking, could almost hear my toes creaking in my shoes. Then I saw his head shake.

'I just want you to be sure,' he said softly. '*Really* sure.'

'I *am* sure.'

I flew to him and hung on tight, arms wound round his waist from behind. I rested my head on his back, shut my eyes and prayed to God, Buddha, Allah, anyone, and slowly, very slowly, he turned around. His arms closed about me. I looked up at him. Tears were taking their chance now and fleeing down my cheeks.

'I love you, David,' I gasped. 'I've been a bloody idiot, I know I have, but I do love you. I've always loved you, don't ever think I haven't, that I've been living a lie all these years because that's just not true!'

I saw him blink hard and swallow.

'But it will be so much better now,' I whispered, 'now that we've got rid of him, now that he's not around us any more.'

He stared down at me.

'Please believe me, darling. I know I'm full of shit and clichés and I can't think of any other ways of saying this but I love you so much and please don't make me go away, please! I'd be lost without you!'

He gazed down at me for a moment, then his head bent slowly towards me. Before his lips touched mine, however, he stopped. Frowned.

'You know, the funny thing is, Tess, I never had the faintest idea what you saw in him. He reminded me of your bloody father.'

I gasped, but it was lost as finally his lips met mine.

Later that evening, as soon as we'd read to the children and tucked them into bed, we crept quietly along to our room and made love. Afterwards, as I lay in his arms contemplating his familiar, rock-like chest, David squinted sideways at me.

'Did you sleep with the bastard?' he growled.

'No!' God it was a relief to be able to say that. 'No, of course I didn't!'

David regarded me thoughtfully for a moment then shut his eyes. 'Hmmm. Just checking.'

I snuggled down again relieved. It occurred to me to wonder though, as I chewed my bottom lip reflectively, if I shouldn't perhaps admit to Willie? I mean, since we were coming clean and being all frank and fearless about everything? On the other hand, men were a bit funny about that sort of thing, weren't they? A touch sensitive about who their wives cavorted naked with. I swallowed hard and decided that on balance I might keep that one to myself. There was no point in rocking the old marital boat just when we'd got it nice and steady again. Instead I curled up in his armpit, feeling warm and tired and happy and heavy with sleep but not quite wanting to give in to it just yet. I wanted to savour this feeling for a bit longer. I gazed through the open window at the gathering gloom in the street outside. Yes, I just wanted to lie here and thank my lucky stars.

I sighed happily and after a while, heard regular deep breathing from the hump beside me. I propped myself up on one elbow and looked down at his sleeping form. I smiled, watching the way his mouth quivered slightly as he breathed out, the way his hair was just slightly receding at the sides and becoming flecked with grey and the way the laughter-lines round his eyes were fanning out, almost to his temples now.

'Stop it.' David opened one eye sharply.

'Stop what?'

'Stop looking at me like that.'

'Like what?'

'In that soppy, doting sort of way people reserve for their ancient golden retrievers.'

'I was not!'

'Yes, you were. I can tell. You were looking at me like a favourite old Leonard Cohen record or one of Clemmie's baby shoes and anyway, I was busy. You disturbed me.'

'Busy doing what?'

'Busy undoing Lucy's bra strap and letting her splendid, full young breasts fall into my outstretched hands.'

'David!'

'What?'

'That's outrageous!'

'Is it?' He paused. 'You're right, I should have kissed her first. The trouble with dreams though is that you don't always remember the formalities, you just bowl on in there and – ow! Oi, that was my ear you bashed then – Jesus, what is this – a fist-fight? I'll give you a fist-fight, I'll –'

'Oh great! Can we join in?'

David and I froze in mid-tussle as two small heads popped up from under the bed.

We stared at them.

'How long have you been there?' I breathed.

'Well, we missed the beginning but crawled in about halfway through, I think,' said Hugo. 'Clemmie got a bit bored but I thought it was great! Daddy, can you just tell me something though? You know when you bit Mummy's ear and she called you Stonky and you called her Tiger and then you sat on her and kind of –'

'OUT!' roared David, leaping up stark naked and chasing them from the room. 'OUT! GET BACK TO YOUR ROOMS BEFORE I LOSE MY TEMPER! I'M GOING TO COUNT TO THREE. ONE, TWO . . .'

Catching up with Catherine

We donned our wellies and trudged
through the mud to meet Catherine
for a catch-up on writing, reading,
and life in the country . . .

Catching up with
Catherine

How and where do you write?

In the garden in the summer, and on a sofa by the fire
in the winter, literally with the nearest pen,
which as a result often runs out.

Any tips for alleviating writer's block?

I'd probably go for a long walk with the dogs but also
never call it writer's block. It's just a day to do
something else; tomorrow will be different.
With luck and everything crossed, the muse
might perch on one's shoulder again.

You live in the countryside in a village not too dissimilar from those you write about. How does country life in your books compare to real life?

There are some remarkable similarities, but obviously
names have been changed to protect the innocent . . .

What do you like to do when you're not writing?

I ride my horses and, recently, wander round poultry
farms. I'm trying to decide which ducks to get for
my new pond: Indian Runners are terribly comical,
Aylesburys would be more geographically
appropriate, yet I'm strangely drawn to good
old Mallards, too. Decisions . . .

If you had to live the life within a classic novel and star as a literary heroine, who would you be and why?

Possibly Jane Austen's Emma Woodhouse,
who lived something of a charmed life,
even if she didn't realize until
it was almost too late.

What's your favourite place to escape to?

Over the hills and far away. The valley behind my house is actually not very far at all and the Downs start there so it's very peaceful. Devon is, of course, heaven, but a little further.

What's the best way to survive a day in the British countryside?

In an ideal world I probably wouldn't take my own very badly behaved dogs; I would take someone else's – that way I wouldn't be chasing them all day shrieking unattractively.

Catherine's top tips
for the perfect countryside break

The same rules apply for children as for dogs (see before), depending on age and reliability of your children – husbands, too.

Never picnic (as in the romantic ideal of rug, hamper, chicken drumsticks à la Delia). Pubs tend to be far more successful, although I am nostalgically drawn to beach picnics. Sand in sandwiches is surely part of any child's education and there's nothing funnier than the man of the family getting to grips with a windbreak in a force-eight gale. Particularly if his own childhood holidays were spent in Tuscany.

Don't be deceived by the English countryside. It looks pretty but can turn on you in an instant.

Leave the horses to the professionals – that doesn't include me. A horse that decides to nap (go home) in the middle of a village which also happens to be something of a tourist magnet is embarrassing for all concerned, particularly the red-faced, middle-aged woman on top.

Again on the subject of horses, 'not a novice ride' means bucks like fury, while 'a fun ride' means carts you into the next county. Male horse-dealers are fond of both expressions, but never forget they are stronger than we are. The men and the horses.

When you answer the door in your coat in winter to a surprised friend who asks if you're just going out, don't be afraid to let them stay an hour or two until they put their coats on too.

If invited to a dinner party in London in January, don't forget there will be women in little dresses who have proper central heating. In the car en route, turn the heater up full blast and try to shed at least three of your layers. Don't forget the Ugg boots. If you stay in the vest and the cashmere roll-neck, you will be in a critical state by pudding, particularly if you're approaching fifty.

If anyone offers you the use of a flat in town in winter, bite their hand off.

Catherine's top ten countryside reads:

The Pursuit of Love
Nancy Mitford

Untold Stories
Alan Bennett

The Irish R. M.
Somerville and Ross

High Fidelity
Nick Hornby

Persuasion
Jane Austen

Pomp and Circumstance
Noël Coward

84 Charing Cross Road
Helene Hanff

The Woman in White
Wilkie Collins

Franny and Zooey
J. D. Salinger

Atonement
Ian McEwan

'Supremely readable, witty and moving.
I adored this' *Daily Mail*

'If I'm being totally honest I had fantasized about Phil dying.'

When Poppy Shilling's bike-besotted, Lycra-clad husband is killed
in a freak accident, she can't help feeling a guilty sense of relief.
For at long last she's released from a controlling and loveless marriage.

Throwing herself wholeheartedly into village life, she's determined
to start over. And sure enough, everyone from Luke the sexy
church-organist to Bob the resident oddball, is taking note.
Yet the one man Poppy can't take her eyes off seems tantalizingly
out of reach – why won't he let go of his glamorous ex-wife?

But just as she's ready to dip her toes in the water, the discovery
of a dark secret about her late husband shatters Poppy's confidence.
Does she really have the courage to risk her heart again?
Because Poppy wants a lot more than just a rural affair . . .

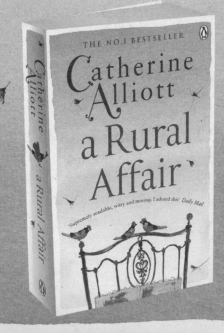

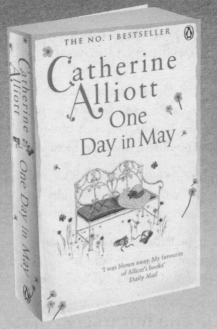

Catherine
Alliott
One
Day in May

'I was blown away. My favourite
of Alliott's books'
Daily Mail

May is the month for falling in love . . .

Hattie Carrington's first love was as unusual as it was out of reach –
Dominic Forbes was a married MP, and she was his assistant.
She has never told anyone about it. And never really got over it.

But years later with a flourishing antiques business
and enjoying a fling with a sexy, younger man, she thinks her
past is finally well and truly behind her.

Until work takes her to Little Crandon, home of Dominic's widow
and his gorgeous younger brother, Hal. There, Hattie's world is turned
upside down. She learns that if she's to truly fall in love again she
needs to stop hiding from the truth. Can she ever admit what
really happened back then?

And, if so, is she ready
for the consequences?

'A fun, fast-paced page-turner' *OK!*

**Evie Hamilton has a secret —
one she doesn't even know about. Yet . . .**

Evie's an Oxfordshire wife and mum whose biggest worry in life is
whether or not she can fit in a manicure on her way to fetch her
daughter from clarinet lessons. But she's blissfully unaware that her
charmed and happy life is about to be turned upside down.

For one sunny morning a letter lands on Evie's immaculate doormat.
It's a bombshell, knocking her carefully arranged world
completely askew and threatening to sabotage all she holds dear.

What will be left and what will change for ever?
Is Evie strong enough to fight for what she loves?
Can her entire world really be as fragile as her best china?

**'We defy you not to get caught up in
Alliott's life-changing tale'** *Heat*

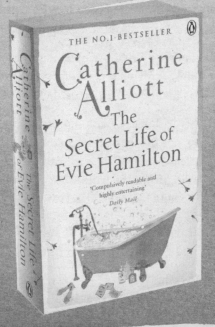

'Another gem from the pen of Ms Alliott' *Closer*

There isn't room in a marriage for three . . .

Painter Imogen is happily married to Alex, and together they have a son. But when their finances hit rock bottom, they're forced to accept Eleanor Latimer's offer of a rent-free cottage on her large country estate. If it was anyone else, Imogen would be beaming with gratitude. Unfortunately, Eleanor just happens to be Alex's beautiful, rich and flirtatious ex.

From the moment she steps inside Shepherd's Cottage, Imogen's life is in chaos. In between coping with rude locals, murderous chickens, a maddening (if handsome) headmaster, mountains of manure and visits from the infuriating vet, she has to face Eleanor, now a fixture at Alex's side.

Is Imogen losing Alex? Will her precious family be torn apart? And whose fault is it really – Eleanor's, Alex's or Imogen's?

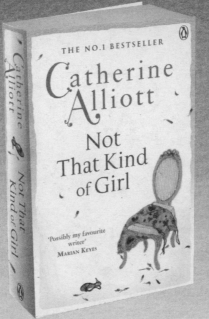

THE NO.1 BESTSELLER

Catherine Alliott

Not That Kind of Girl

'Possibly my favourite writer'
MARIAN KEYES

A girl can get into all kinds of trouble just by going back to work . . .

Henrietta Tate gave up everything for her husband Marcus and their kids. But now that the children are away at school and she's rattling around their large country house all day she's feeling more than a little lost.

So when a friend puts her in touch with Laurie, a historian in need of a PA, Henrietta heads for London. Quickly, she throws herself into the job. Marcus is – of course – jealous of her spending so much time with her charming new boss. And soon enough her absence causes cracks in their marriage that just can't be papered over.

Then Rupert, a very old flame, reappears and Henrietta suddenly finds herself torn between three men. How did this happen? She's not that kind of girl . . . is she?

'Compulsively readable' *Daily Mail*

**Annie O'Harran is getting married . . .
all over again.**

A divorced, single mum, Annie is about to tie the knot with David.
But there's a long summer to get through first. A summer where
she's retreating to a lonely house in Cornwall, where she's going to
finish her book, spend time with her teenage daughter Flora and
make any last-minute wedding plans.

She should be so lucky.

For almost as soon as Annie arrives her competitive sister and her wild
brood fetch up. Meanwhile Annie's louche ex-husband and his latest
squeeze are holidaying nearby and insist on dropping in. Plus there's the
surprise American houseguest who can't help sharing his heartbreak.

Suddenly Annie's big day seems a long, long way off –
and if she's not careful it might never happen . . .

'Alliott at her best' *Daily Telegraph*

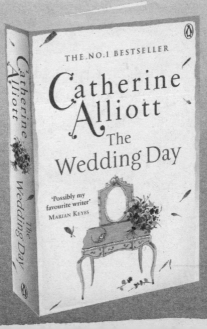

'What could be nicer than living in the country?'

Lucy Fellowes is in a bind. She's a widow living in a pokey London flat with two small boys and an erratic income. But, when her mother-in-law offers her a converted barn on the family's estate, she knows it's a brilliant opportunity for her and the kids.

But there's a problem.

The estate is a shrine to Lucy's dead husband, Ned. The whole family has been unable to get over his death. If she's honest, the whole family is far from normal. And if Lucy is to accept this offer she'll be putting herself completely in their incapable hands.

Which leads to Lucy's other problem. Charlie – the only man since Ned who she's had any feelings for – lives nearby. The problem? He's already married . . .

'Hilarious and full of surprises' *Daily Telegraph*

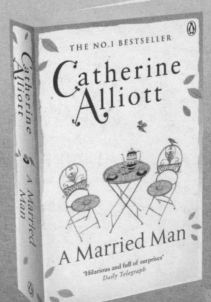

THE NO.1 BESTSELLER

Catherine Alliott

A Married Man

'Hilarious and full of surprises'
Daily Telegraph

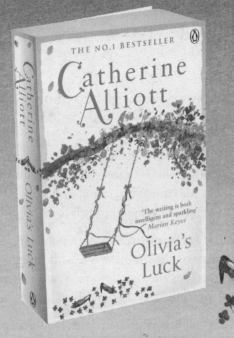

THE NO.1 BESTSELLER

CATHERINE ALLIOTT

'The writing is both intelligent and sparkling'
Marian Keyes

Olivia's Luck

'I don't care what colour you paint
the sodding hall. I'm leaving.'

When her husband Johnny suddenly walks out on ten years of marriage,
their ten-year-old daughter and the crumbling house they're up to their
eyeballs renovating, Olivia is, at first, totally devastated. How could he?
How could she not have noticed his unhappiness?

But she's not one to weep for long.

Not when she's got three builders camped in her back garden,
a neighbour with a never-ending supply of cast-off men she thinks
Olivia would be drawn to and a daughter with her own firm
views on . . . well, just about everything.

Will Johnny ever come back?
And if he doesn't, will Olivia's luck
ever change for the better?

'The writing is both intelligent and sparkling'
Marian Keyes

'Alliott's joie de vivre is irresistible' *Daily Mail*

'Tell me, Alice,
how does a girl go about
getting a divorce these days?'

Three years ago Rosie walked blindly into marriage with Harry.
They have precisely nothing in common except perhaps their little boy, Ivo.
Not that Harry pays him much attention, preferring to spend his time
with his braying upper-class friends.

But the night that Harry drunkenly does something unspeakable,
Rosie decides he's got to go. In between fantasizing how she might
bump him off, she takes the much more practical step of divorcing
this blight on her and Ivo's lives.

However, when reality catches up with her darkest fantasies,
Rosie realizes, at long last, that it is time she took charge of her life.
There'll be no more regrets – and time, perhaps, for a little love.

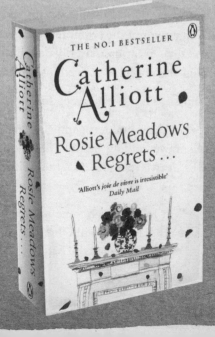

**Every girl's got one – that old boyfriend
they never quite fell out of love with . . .**

Tessa Hamilton's thirty, with a lovely husband and home, two adorable
kids, and not a care in the world. Sure her husband ogles the nanny more
than she should allow. And keeping up with the Joneses is a full-time
occupation. But she's settled and happy. No seven-year itch for Tessa.

Except at the back of her mind is Patrick Cameron. Gorgeous, moody,
rebellious, he's the boy she met when she was seventeen. The boy her
vicar-father told her she couldn't see and who left to go to Italy to paint.
The boy she's not heard from in twelve long years.

And now he's back.

Questioning every choice, every decision she's made since Patrick left,
Tessa is about to risk her family and everything she has become to find
out whether she did the right thing first time round . . .

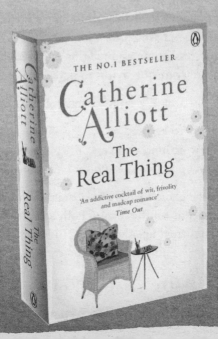

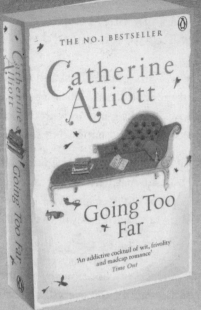

THE NO.1 BESTSELLER

Catherine
Alliott

Going Too
Far

'An addictive cocktail of wit, frivolity
and madcap romance'
Time Out

'You've gone all fat and complacent
because you've got your man, haven't you?'

Polly Penhalligan is outraged at the suggestion that, since getting married
to Nick and settling into their beautiful manor farmhouse in Cornwall,
she has let herself go. But watching a lot of telly, gorging on biscuits, not
getting dressed until lunchtime and waiting for pregnancy to strike are not
the signs of someone living an active and fulfilled life.

So Polly does something rash.

She allows her home to be used as a location for a TV advert. Having a
glamorous film crew around will certainly put a bomb under the idyllic,
rural life. Only perhaps she should have consulted Nick first.

Because before the cameras have even started to roll – and complete
chaos descends on the farm – Polly's marriage has been
turned upside down. This time she
really has gone too far . . .

'An addictive cocktail of wit, frivolity
and madcap romance' *Time Out*

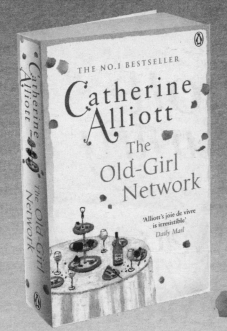

Finding true love's a piece of cake – as long as you're looking for someone else's true love . . .

Polly McLaren is young, scatty and impossibly romantic. She works for an arrogant and demanding boss, and has a gorgeous-if-never-there-when-you-need-him boyfriend. But, the day a handsome stranger recognizes her old school scarf, her life is knocked completely off kilter.

Adam is American, new to the country and begs Polly's help in finding his missing fiancé. Over dinner at the Savoy she agrees – the girls of St Gertrude's look out for one another. However, the old-girl network turns out to be a spider's web of complications and deceit in which everyone and everything Polly cares about is soon hopelessly entangled.

The course of true love never did run smooth.
But no one said anything about ruining your life over it.
And it's not even Polly's true love . . .

'Possibly my favourite writer' Marian Keyes

WIN wonderful *WELLIES*

by *joules*

WE'RE GIVING AWAY

10 PAIRS of JOULES WELLIES
MADE TO MAKE A SPLASH WHATEVER THE WEATHER!

To be in with a chance of winning this welly good prize visit www.catherinealliott.com/winwellies

Joules are also giving readers **15% OFF** *plus* **FREE P&P.**
Simply visit www.joules.com and enter offer code **WELLY12** at the checkout.

Competition closing date **31ST AUGUST 2012**
For full terms and conditions and details of how to enter visit www.catherinealliott.com/winwellies